Maiden Hills

N.L. Estrada

388 4170

Copyright © 3P Publishing
First published in 2020 in the UK

3P Publishing
C E C, London Road
Corby
NN17 5EU
A catalogue number for this book is available from the British Library

ISBN: 978-1-911559-97-9

Cover design: Marie-Louise O'Neil

Acknowledgements

A special thank you to my sister Sonia for her encouragement and feedback throughout this entire process, and to my "team" Charlie, Eladio, Amanda, Melissa, Jess, Monica, Jessica, and Eric, for their valuable input and support, and lastly, to my parents Sylvia and Eladio for their love and encouragement.

Thank you to my developmental editor, Kristen Hamilton, and to Andy, Caroline, and the entire staff at 3P Publishing.

And finally, thank you God! For with God, nothing shall be impossible.

Chapter 1

Princess Juliana ran through the great hall, footsteps echoing off the high ceiling of the massive stone castle. She sped, her heart pumping, pulling up her dress as she climbed each step of the long, winding staircase. When Juliana arrived at the doorway of the great chamber, she stopped, placed her hand over her mouth, and gasped at the sight of the thin woman collapsed on the bed. Queen Lucinda was the most elegant queen Yorkford had ever seen, with a rosy complexion and a spirited laugh. But on this day in the king and queen's chamber of the royal castle, Lucinda lay, face pale and sunken as she gazed at her twelve-year-old daughter through glassy eyes.

How could this be? Juliana struggled to grasp the sudden turn her mother's health had taken. Just two days ago, Queen Lucinda had hosted a gallant affair before five hundred guests in the great room of the castle, celebrating her husband King Matthew's thirty-fifth birthday. She captured stares of admiration when she entered the room draped in a luxurious silk lavender gown with sparkling crystals, and a gold crown with glistening diamonds atop her long auburn curls. But now she lay in her bed, struggling to breathe.

Juliana's hazel green eyes filled with tears as she walked toward her. She sat on a wooden chair next to her mother's canopied bed and picked up her limp hand, alarmed at the thinness. "Mother, speak to me."

Lucinda took a deep breath. "I don't have much time, dear daughter," she whispered, her voice hoarse.

1

"Mother, I wish you would not speak in such a manner. You can't leave me." A lump swelled in Juliana's throat. As the only child of Queen Lucinda and King Matthew, Juliana's life revolved around her parents.

Lucinda's eyes darted the darkened room. They were alone in the great chamber. Heavy royal-blue drapes covered the window as the trickling of a gentle fire emitted a soft glow. "Juliana, please listen. I… I must tell you about… our people."

Juliana tilted her head, brows furrowed. "Our people?"

"It's a secret I had to keep for sixteen years. Your grandparents were not my natural parents. They took me in when I was twelve years old after my parents… died in an attack. Your father never knew." Lucinda coughed.

Juliana reached for the metal water pitcher and cup on a table next to Lucinda's bed. "Here, Mother, drink this."

Lucinda lifted herself gingerly and, with trembling hands, took a sip of water and handed the cup to Juliana. She lay back and gazed at her daughter. "Our people were massacred."

"What?" The cup slipped through Juliana's hands, soaking her blue linen dress. As she patted her dress with a kerchief, she stared at her mother with wide eyes. "Mother, what are you saying?"

Lucinda reached for Juliana's hand and squeezed it. "We come from a long line of magical people… from a town called Maiden Hills."

"Magical people?"

"We received a gift of supernatural powers. No one outside of our town knew until one of our own betrayed us."

"Mother, what kind of powers? Who betrayed you?"

"Please go to my bureau... bring my jewelry box."

Juliana stared at her mother, frozen, trying to unscramble her mother's words, hoping they would make sense, but they hadn't. Time was waning. She hurried to the large oak bureau, and with both hands, lifted the bulky gold box and placed it on the table next to her mother's bed.

"Search for a small black bag."

Juliana lifted the lid and gazed at shimmering family heirlooms of necklaces, pendants, and rings. She stirred the jewels and found buried among them a small black cloth bag. Juliana gave the bag to her mother. "Is this the one?"

"It is." With clumsy fingers, Lucinda opened the bag and took out a golden locket with a black center and three overlapping gold circles. She unlatched the pendant and removed two small oval-shaped gemstones, one black with golden tones, and the other one green with black waves.

"These are our enchanted gemstones, given to me by my mother, Lady Victoria." A tear came down Lucinda's face. She dabbed her eye and continued. "We must activate them... to harness the magic within." She took a deep breath. "They are very powerful."

Juliana took the stones, held them in her hand, and examined them. They were smooth and cool, the size of her thumbnail. They radiated a faint, pulsating light. "How do they work?"

"The black and gold stone gives us the ability to move objects anywhere within our sight without touching them, we move them with our minds." She paused and gave a weak smile. "The green stone allows us to communicate with animals, and they will help us if we ask them. You need not fear them, for even the most ferocious animal will be at your command."

"So, if I wear the locket with the stones, I can do magic?" Juliana could not believe what she was asking.

"No… you must activate them. There are spells to recite."

Spells? Juliana wondered if she should encourage her mother to continue with the story. That's all it was—a story—*right?* It sounded much like a tale her mother often told her when she was a child before bedtime, but those days were long gone. *Is she telling a story now, or is she telling the truth?* It seemed absurd, but Juliana could see that behind her mother's almost lifeless eyes, she believed what she was saying. "What are the spells?"

Lucinda struggled to get the words out. "They're in the book… you must find it."

Juliana lifted her eyebrows. "A… a book of spells?"

"It's called *The Book of Secrets*. It contains the spells to activate the stones."

"Mother, where is this book?"

"I hid it in the castle, below… in the dungeon. A loose block on the wall. I hid the book behind it… about my eye level." She paused again, building up the resolve to continue. "I carved a small 'x' on the block, in the corner. Find it, Juliana, read it, and guard it. Let no one see it."

4

"Of course, Mother." Juliana held on to her mother's hand as a tear trickled down her cheek. *Why is she telling me this? Is this the last conversation I will have with my mother?* "Please try to rest. Speak no more," her voice cracked. "I wish for you to get well." Juliana's insides trembled as she had never seen her mother so frail and ill. At twenty-eight years old, Lucinda was a tower of strength for her family, but with a sweet gentleness that everyone adored. Juliana did not want to believe her mother was slipping away from her.

"I must tell you everything. There is also a third stone, a deep-red gemstone, the rarest of all." Lucinda went on, "Once you activate it, you can create an impenetrable shield that will… protect those around you." Lucinda sighed. "My father, Lord Gavin, had the stone, but he was attacked and… killed." Tears filled her eyes.

"What happened?"

"My mother had a bad feeling that something was to happen at my brother Josef's wedding and told me to go to Cedarville. On my way there… I saw my father on his horse." She took a breath. "I was about to call out his name when two knights from Yorkford came out from behind the trees and… stabbed him in the back. I hid in a small cave."

Juliana silenced her gasp.

Lucinda shut her eyes, and tears slid down the side of her face. She took a shallow breath and continued. "After they left, I ran toward my father, and… he was dead. The locket with the gemstones he wore around his neck was gone."

Juliana took her kerchief and blotted her mother's tears.

"I could not make out the killer's face, but he rode a black horse with white stripes on its hind legs."

"What did you do after that?"

"I kept running toward Cedarville, and when I looked back, the town was in flames." The tears continued to flow. "I'm sorry, dear… this is very difficult."

Juliana stroked her mother's hair, her forehead burning from the fever. "It's all right, Mother." Juliana took her kerchief and poured water onto it. She squeezed the excess and placed it on her mother's forehead.

"I took a carriage ride to Westmore and went to the castle to seek asylum, and that's where I met Duchess Agnes. She kindly took me in and told everyone I was her daughter." Smiling weakly, she added, "I later met your father, and we fell in love."

Juliana took her mother's hand. "You said the knights that killed your father were from Yorkford. Did Father order the attack?"

Lucinda shook her head. "No, your father told me that a knight from his army wanted to prove his prowess and took it upon himself to… massacre the people."

Juliana sat back. "Forgive me, Mother, but this is an unbelievable story."

"Alas, it is true, Juliana."

"Mother, people who practice magic get sentenced to death. This can't be who you are."

"It's who *we* are." Her eyes widened. "But our powers are not evil. People wanted to kill us because they feared us. We were bestowed with magical powers to protect the kingdom from evil forces. The massacre was a prophecy that came true. There is another prophecy in *The Book of Secrets* you must know. There is danger ahead." Lucinda's breath was quick and shallow.

"Mother, please save your strength."

Queen Lucinda clutched her daughter's hand. "Please, dear daughter, let no one see you with the stones. Find the book… recite the spells… and you will have magical powers. You must be prepared for what is to come. You must help save our people." She stared into her daughter's eyes and in a whisper, said, "Juliana, please give me your word you will do this."

"Mother, I…"

"Please!" Lucinda tightened her hold on Juliana's hand.

The anguish on her mother's face ripped through Juliana's heart. She squeezed the tears from her eyes and fought to release the words, "Of course, Mother," her lips trembled, "you have my word."

"Find Simon… do not lose that fighter spirit in you." Lucinda closed her eyes and took a breath.

"Who's Simon?" The queen lay motionless, the faint hissing of her breathing stopped. "Mother? Mother?" Dread, cold and dark, crept into Juliana's heart. She placed her head on her mother's chest and sobbed.

***

Hundreds of people from all over Yorkford and neighboring villages came to pay their final respects at the wake of Queen Lucinda Allington. Juliana thanked them and politely smiled as she sat in front of the closed casket adorned with fresh flowers, most of them lilies, her mother's favorite.

She wanted to be strong, but inside, her heart ached. The Allingtons were known for their strength. Ten generations of Allingtons ruled the Kingdom of Yorkford, and they kept their heads held high, no matter what happened, and a lot happened. They suffered many tragedies, but through it all, they never shed a tear in public. It was those early deaths that made Juliana an only child and left King Matthew without a male heir. Lucinda lost two young boys in two years due to illnesses. Juliana was just a child, but she remembered the dignified way her parents handled the deaths.

Juliana turned to her father seated next to her and gave him a faint smile. He smiled back—eyes dry but red. He put his arm around her, and she found comfort on his shoulder. He, too, needed comforting, for Matthew loved his wife dearly.

Lucinda's words echoed in Juliana's mind, *"Give me your word you will do this."* Her hand curled into a fist. How could her mother make her promise to do something she had no intention of doing? What was she to do, search for a book in the dungeon that was not there? The dungeon was a cold and scary place, not fitting for a princess. Besides, magic was illegal and a product of evil forces. If true, she wanted no part of it. But was it true? Her mother conveyed too many details to result from delirium.

Juliana closed her eyes and shook her head. *No, it wasn't true!* Her mother had suffered damage to her brain caused by the infection, and her mind concocted a fanciful story—that was it! *It's best not to mention this to anyone. It's best not to think about it,* she told herself. No one would know her mother had gone mad on her final day as she succumbed to her illness.

Bishop Dalton spoke a few words to her father, King Matthew, then stood in front of Juliana with knees bent to meet her eyes. "My child," he said, "take comfort in knowing that your mother is with the Lord in the Afterlife, for she was a fine lady."

Juliana sniffed. "I wish to be with her."

"The Lord calls us when our mission in this life is complete. Follow the righteous path as your mother did, and when it is time, you shall see her again. Do not stray, for the price of immorality and wickedness is worse than death."

Juliana nodded. "I understand." The bishop was right—her mother was righteous. She didn't come from a town of magical people. She would not think of it. Juliana resolved to put the last conversation with her mother out of her mind and follow the right path, for she would not allow anything to stand in the way of seeing her mother again.

"God be with you, child." The bishop kissed her forehead and left to comfort another mourner.

After the wake, Juliana ascended the stairs to the second floor and turned toward her bedchamber. She put her hand on her chest and felt the bump of the locket underneath her dress. She held back tears, envisioning her mother's face during her final moments. Juliana breathed deeply, then removed the gold chain from around her neck, opened the locket, and stared at the pulsating stones. *They are curious, but they're not magical,* she thought. She closed the pendant and inserted it in the small black bag. Juliana reached for the bottom

9

drawer of her wardrobe and buried the black bag among her old clothes. There they remained.

That is, until six years later when she discovered her mother spoke the truth, and the danger her mother warned her about was real, and it began to unfold.

Chapter 2

Juliana waited at the private entrance to the jousting field as the crowd of prominent guests gathered in the early afternoon for the tournament. The game launched the celebration in honor of Juliana's eighteenth birthday, bringing forth the eligible princes from all the kingdoms throughout the continent of Sparia. Royalty and nobility from Yorkford and neighboring towns and villages took their seats, with banners in hand, ready to root for their favorite knights.

"Are you ready?"

Juliana turned to see her father, King Matthew, smiling with glistening eyes. He was a handsome king, proper and distinguished. His brown hair had turned gray, which paired nicely with his well-groomed gray beard and mustache, and along with the lines on his face, gave him an air of profound wisdom. He raised his elbow, and she hooked her arm in his as they began the walk into the stands.

They arrived at the royal box under the tent, greeted by the widow Princess Katherine Clere from Yorkford and her twenty-two-year-old son Prince Edmund Wadham, son of the late Prince James Wadham from Westmore. Prince Edmund bowed before King Matthew and gallantly took Juliana's hand and kissed it as his deep-set smoky gray eyes penetrated hers. *Edmund is undoubtedly the most handsome of all the princes*, Juliana mused, admiring his raven black hair and firm chin. Growing up in the castle, she had limited interactions with him as he

11

was much older, and a bit pompous, she thought, but this day she saw him in a different light. The sudden enthusiastic roar of the crowd broke the stare, and they took their seats.

As the crowd settled, the announcer presented the jousters. King Matthew leaned over to Juliana and whispered, "You look breathtaking, my dear."

Juliana smiled. She wore a tight-fitting jade green silk gown with gold trim over her slim figure and with a velvet emerald green cloak draped over her shoulders. "Thank you, Father." She waved her feather fan as she stared ahead at the field.

"I'm proud of how you have grown into such a fine lady with decorum and poise after behaving like a spoiled princess in your youth."

Juliana chuckled. "Forgive me, Father, for I was a naughty child." She adored her father, and she rued having caused him much angst growing up. But following her mother's death, she had resolved to change her mischievous ways and sought to care for him and behave in a dignified manner. It saddened her that he never remarried, but it just made her more protective of him. Their eyes turned to the field in front of them as the mounted challengers took their places to fervent applause.

"I hope you enjoy your birthday celebration," her father continued. "All eyes will be on you, as many men will seek your attention."

"Is this your way of finding a husband for me?" She gazed at the knights in armor with their lances aimed at their opponent.

"You are long overdue. I need an heir for my throne."

"But Father, you need me to care for you."

"Someday, you will be the queen of Yorkford, and you will care for an entire kingdom. You must protect what I have fought all these many years to build."

"I'm not as strong as you." She gazed at her father. "You are a brilliant and powerful leader."

He turned to Juliana. "You are my daughter, and you have inside the strength that I have that makes me who I am, and someday you may be tested, and you will need to draw from that strength. Stand firm and yield to no one—you are an Allington!"

The trumpet sounded, and Juliana turned her attention to the tournament as she allowed her father's words to echo inside her. She didn't know what he meant, for as a princess, everyone took care of her. She didn't have to be strong, and as the queen, she would rely on her husband's strength. Fortunately, her father was strong and healthy, and it would be many years before she wore the queen's crown.

The presenter announced the next jouster. The crowd cheered as a knight from The Magnificent Seven came onto the field. This group represented seven young undefeated jousting knights from Yorkford. They were the talk of the town, and marrying one of them would be a prize for any young lady as it would guarantee them a life among the noble class.

The most skillful of The Magnificent Seven Knights was Jack Mauntell, Juliana's best friend, and the adopted son of Princess Katherine and the late Prince Marcus Allington, King Matthew's brother. Prince Marcus was Princess Katherine's second husband after Edmund's father, Prince James, died in battle. Marcus and

13

Katherine took Jack in, a precocious child, when he was six years old. They brought up Jack as royalty, and he learned to become a remarkable swordsman at a young age. Along with Edmund, he had gone into battles for King Matthew and conquered many lands that became part of Matthew's vast empire. Matthew knighted Jack six months ago, making him the youngest man ever knighted at eighteen years old.

Juliana watched the crowd. The ladies adored Jack, and although they swooned over him—with warm sky blue eyes, soft ash blond hair, and a clean-shaven face that gave him an adoring boyish look—Jack seemed uninterested in courting any of them, choosing instead to devote his life to becoming an elite fighter.

The crowd's anticipation heightened, and they continued to cheer and wave their banners in the colors of Yorkford—purple and red. Jack, dressed in full armor, stopped his steed before the royal box and, with a gloved hand, lifted his visor. He bowed to the king, smiled at Juliana, then turned to wave to the crowd. They roared.

Jack turned his horse and positioned himself at one end of the field opposite his opponent, separated by a wooden barrier. He lowered his visor. Juliana sat, watching, biting her lip. *Careful, Jack.*

At the trumpet blast, the announcer waved a flag signaling the match to begin, and both knights, with their lances aimed, spurred their horses and raced toward each other. The thumping of the horses' hooves echoed the thumping in Juliana's heart as she held her breath. Jack lowered his lance, and before Juliana could blink, he smashed it into the knight's left shoulder, knocking him from his horse. Juliana exhaled, releasing the grip on her dress. She was no stranger to the gore and death that could result from jousting matches, and although Jack was exceptional, she could not stop her nerves from trembling. The game continued throughout the afternoon with heart-stopping moments, and after unseating his opponents, Jack won the tournament.

After the joust, the crowd headed to the great hall for a night of feasting and dancing. Behind the curtain, Juliana stood. She had changed into a stunning golden silk brocade gown with lace trim and white sleeves. Around her neck, she sparkled with an exquisite diamond necklace and matching earrings. A glistening gold and diamond tiara adorned her hair as the long auburn locks cascaded to her waist. She waited, her nerves in a mild frenzy. *This shall be a night to remember.*

Juliana peeked through the curtain and watched as the steward stood in the center of the grand hall and faced the audience. He held up his hand and cleared his throat. "All rise." The murmuring dwindled, the people rose, and all eyes were on him. In a booming voice, he announced, "Your Majesty, kings and queens, lords and ladies, I present to you, Her Royal Highness, Princess Juliana Allington."

The guards pulled the curtain, and applause filled the room. Feeling everyone's eyes upon her, Juliana beamed with a radiance that matched her shimmering jewels. King Matthew strode toward his daughter, kissed her cheek, and escorted her onto the platform dais to her princess throne made of polished gold and scarlet velvet cushions.

Juliana sat with a glass of burgundy wine in hand and admired the magnificent great room. It was the grandest place in all the castle, with large chandeliers hanging from the high ceiling holding dozens of candles in sparkling crystals, and on the wall, richly colored tapestries depicting the history of Yorkford and all its conquests. Portraits of ten generations of the royal family of Allington hung alongside the pictorial drapes. It was a history she was proud of.

As the guests feasted, the soft melody from the minstrels settled them, and the boisterous roar lulled into dignified conversations and subtle laughter. From her royal seat, Juliana caught Prince Edmund staring at her. She met his eyes, then looked away. Juliana was inexperienced in matters of the heart. After her mother died, taking care of the castle and her father was her primary concern, and the thought of marriage was far from her mind, but now it was looming, and it created a fluttery feeling in her stomach. She sipped her wine, and it calmed her nerves.

When the band began to play, Edmund approached. "May I have this dance?"

Juliana blushed. She should be used to the routine, but something about Edmund caused her insides to quiver. She smiled and accepted, hiding her nervousness.

The evening continued with other suitors asking for a dance, including Prince Carsen from Etheland, a rival kingdom, but Edmund continued to vie for her attention. It was apparent he fancied her, and when he wasn't dancing with her, he remained nearby, keeping a close watch on her.

On their fourth dance, Edmund eyed Juliana and said, "It should come as no surprise that I am very much captivated by you. You have grown into the most beautiful woman I have ever seen."

She smiled. "Thank you, Your Highness, you flatter me."

"I remember you as a young child. A bit mischievous and stubborn." He grinned.

Juliana smiled as her face flushed. "Alas, that was me; however, I have matured." She paused, taking note of his imposing physique. She paused to normalize her breathing. "I must say, you are quite a dancer."

"Does it please you, Your Highness?" He gazed into her eyes, penetrating her as if he had a view into the depths of her soul. She found it hard to look away.

"It does."

The dance ended, and Juliana came to rest on the dais, enjoying the warmth of the burgundy wine as it trickled down her throat. Still reeling from her dance with Edmund and the accompanying frazzled nerves, she shook her head as hopeful dance partners approached, preferring to sit and observe. She had a wide view of the great hall where five hundred guests had gathered to celebrate her birthday. The women were dressed in their most luxurious gowns adorned with exquisite jewelry, and the men wore their finest linen and hats.

Juliana waved her feather fan, cooling herself as she watched the dancers swaying with elegance to the music in the middle of the great room. Servants paraded in and out of the room bringing in platters filled with meat, potatoes, bread, and jugs of wine while removing waste left behind. The more wine was served, the louder and boisterous the guests had become. She found the scene amusing.

"Juliana."

She turned and saw her uncle Richard Maddeson, duke of Westmore, standing next to her. He was a jolly man with a kind, round face, and eyes that sparkled when he smiled. He was never without a glass of wine.

"Uncle Richard, it's good to see you." Juliana beamed at seeing her favorite uncle.

He kissed her on the cheek. "You look lovely, my dear. I am having the best time. My brother-in-law sure knows how to spend his wealth."

"It's always a good time when the wine flows freely." She grinned.

Duke Richard let out a hearty belly laugh. "Truly, it is!" He stared at Juliana. "I can't get over how much you look like your mother. The resemblance is striking. Fortunately, you did not inherit your father's looks," he said playfully.

"Uncle Richard, my father is very handsome!" She smiled, aware of her uncle's teasing.

He chuckled. "I'm sure he is. Well, I must refill my glass. Enjoy yourself, dear."

"I shall." Juliana watched her uncle leave, then directed her gaze back to the dance floor. As she sipped her wine, her eyes focused on a couple whose graceful dance synchronized in perfect rhythm to the music. She turned her attention to the handsome young man twirling his partner and smiled to herself—it was Jack.

Jack Mauntell had been her best friend since they were six years old. He was kind and fiercely loyal to her, and when Juliana in her youth had gotten herself into mischief, Jack would rise to defend her. Juliana recalled when she was eight years old and when no one was watching, she poured salt into the wine jug at supper and ruined the wine. Her parents admonished her, but an eight-year-old Jack had said to them, "You can't blame her for wanting to improve the taste of the wine. It is rather bland, and the cooks always say salt improves the taste of everything." Juliana smiled at the memory. Everyone knew she was guilty of wreaking havoc in the castle, and they appreciated the lengths young Jack took to prevent her from getting into trouble—and so did she.

Applause filled the room as the men bowed to their partner, and the women curtsied. Jack glanced up at the dais and caught Juliana's eye. He smiled at Juliana, excused himself from his partner, and climbed up the steps.

"You are truly a vision," he said, a broad smile on his face.

Juliana blushed. "Thank you kindly, Jack, or should I say, Sir Jack. You were magnificent in the tournament earlier."

"Thank you, Your Highness." He bowed in mock deference. "I wish to have the next dance with you, but it seems my brother Edmund wants you all to himself." He lifted one eyebrow, contemplating his options as he referred to his adoptive brother. "It would certainly anger him to see you dancing with me." He grinned.

Juliana's mood soured. Edmund was born of royalty and privilege, the only son of Prince James Wadham and Princess Katherine. But after Prince James died twenty-two years ago, Princess Katherine married Juliana's uncle, Prince Marcus, and with the marriage came Jack, their adopted son of unknown lineage. Edmund was ten and Jack six, and Edmund should have embraced Jack as his younger brother, but it was not so. "Edmund has always resented you."

Jack scoffed. "He saw me as an intrusion in his life. Marcus favored me, and it irritated him. He did not like Marcus very much, but I admired him. Marcus was a good father. He taught me to be chivalrous and emphasized honor and loyalty above all. It was different for Edmund. He was—" He paused, searching for the right word, "—ambitious."

Juliana recalled her father, King Matthew, took a liking to Prince Edmund and gave him the guidance and support he didn't receive from his stepfather, Marcus. Matthew taught him to be a powerful leader so that someday he could rule a kingdom. He and Jack never developed a brotherly bond. In truth, they were rivals. "You two are vastly different."

"Truly." Jack sulked for a moment, then softened. "Now, about this dance, do you think Edmund will allow other men to have a dance with you?"

Juliana's face brightened. "I *have* danced with other men," she stated as a matter of fact.

"A few, but mostly with him."

"Have you been spying on me, Jack?"

"You know I'm always looking after you, Juliana."

Another song came on, and Edmund appeared in front of Juliana, ignoring Jack's presence. "Your Highness, may I have this dance?"

Not one to cower from his older brother, Jack brazenly interjected. "She has this dance with me."

Edmund's face turned into a scowl. "Very well, I shall have the next one." He stalked away with his head held high.

Juliana and Jack shared smiles. Jack put his hand out. "Your Highness?" Juliana took his hand, rose from her seat, and followed him onto the dance floor.

***

A fortnight passed since the ball, and King Matthew sat in his library, mulling over a financial report from Cedarville, a small territory owned by his Kingdom of Yorkford. Sir Leopold walked in, a balding, mustached, middle-aged man with a fierce look.

Matthew gave him a wide smile. "Ah, Sir Leopold, my most trusted knight!"

"You wished to see me, Your Majesty?"

"Please sit." Matthew sat back, his hands in a steeple. "We must move forward with acquiring Westmore. We should have done it years ago when Prince James married Princess Katherine."

"Prince James' death thwarted our plans," Leopold said. "His father, King Thomas, has been difficult to deal with ever since."

"He certainly has been. However, it was rather unfortunate what happened to Prince James. I was very fond of him as I know you were."

Leopold nodded. "I was."

Matthew continued, "But the time has come to bring in another prince from Westmore to join the royal family of Yorkford and this time form a permanent union."

Leopold raised an eyebrow. "Prince Edmund?"

Matthew nodded with a gleam in his eye. "Yes, Prince Edmund."

"How will you deal with his grandfather King Thomas? He will not give up the throne easily."

"Leave that to me." Matthew leaned back, staring at the map on the wall depicting the vast empire under his rule and below to the southeast, the coveted Kingdom of Westmore. His eyes shifted to his suit of armor standing tall in the corner with his sword and shield engraved with his coat of arms—two crowned lions opposing each other, ready for battle.

"You know, Leopold, that was the same suit I wore when I fought in battles for my father, King Reginald. When he died twenty-three years ago, I became the youngest king ever at eighteen years old. I conquered many lands to make Yorkford the dominant kingdom it is this day, increasing it three times from when my father was king. I swore I would protect his land and his legacy—and I have."

"Which is why you are the most feared of all the kings in Sparia."

"You can't rule if no one fears you, and you can't ignore an act of disloyalty. There needs to be retribution, or people will see you as weak. That is death for a king."

"You certainly are feared, Your Majesty. Mercy is not something you give much weight to." Leopold paused. "Why did you wish to see me?"

Matthew turned his attention to the parchment on his desk, reporting on the finances of his southernmost territory. "I have a task for you." He slid the parchment toward Leopold. "Lord Godfrey is the baron of Cedarville." Matthew pointed to a piece of land below the forest. "My keeper of books informed me that he has been stealing from me by paying me less than my rightful share of the earnings. I want you to get rid of him, but be discreet."

Leopold stared at the parchment. "As you command, Your Majesty, but who shall take his place?"

Matthew strolled over to his chess table, picked up a pawn, and moved it two spaces forward. "I have someone in mind, but you must make him believe it was his idea."

***

One month later, the frosty winter air thawed, and the freshness of spring draped over the kingdom. Juliana sat alongside the flower beds and joined the gardeners as they planted seeds in the castle's rose garden to begin preparations for the annual Festival of Flowers held in June. It was her favorite festival, and she took it upon herself to make sure the details and the scheduled events proceeded without a flaw.

Juliana glanced over her shoulder as King Matthew's maidservant Ella approached her. Ella, a portly woman, had been the king's faithful servant for twenty-four years since he was a young prince.

"Pardon me, Your Highness, His Majesty would like to see you in the great hall."

Juliana walked into the room, surprised to see her father and Prince Edmund sitting by the hearth in an intimate conversation. Prince Edmund would typically split his time between Westmore and Yorkford, but lately, he had been spending more time in Yorkford. She stood, waiting, neither of them taking note of her presence in the room. She cleared her throat. "Did you call for me, Father?"

They halted their conversation and turned toward Juliana. Matthew approached her with a wide grin. "Juliana, this is a spectacular day for us. Yorkford and

Westmore have formed a permanent alliance. We shall join the two kingdoms and retain the name of Yorkford. Edmund's grandfather King Thomas has abdicated his throne in Westmore and turned it over to me."

"Father, that is splendid news... but I am puzzled, why would King Thomas renounce his throne?"

"We reached an accord. For King Thomas to give up his kingdom, we agreed that Prince Edmund would marry you. Edmund would have been the ruler of Westmore, but as your husband, he shall be the ruler of the combined kingdoms." Matthew beamed at his master plan.

"I see." She suppressed a look of surprise. Although she suspected her father would choose Prince Edmund for her husband, she did not expect it on this day. She recalled when she was eleven years old, and Edmund fifteen, Edmund had gained favor with her father when she, Edmund, and Jack were walking too close to the moat, and Juliana slipped and fell, then Jack fell in. Edmund dove in to save Juliana, then rushed in to save Jack. News spread in the town, and everyone touted Prince Edmund as a hero.

Matthew said, "The wedding will take place in one month, but do not fret, Ella will make all the arrangements."

So soon? Juliana forced a smile. "As you wish, Father."

Edmund walked up to Juliana. "I am pleased to marry the most beautiful woman in the kingdom." He took her hand and kissed it.

The jittery feeling in her stomach returned. "You are most kind, Your Highness." *What do I feel for him? Is it an attraction, or is it something else?* Edmund was charming, yet

24

she sensed arrogance in him and strong ambition—traits helpful in conquering nations but would fall short for a loving husband. It saddened her, but she had to think about the good of the kingdom. Alliances by marriage were expected of royal families and often not based on loving feelings. Nonetheless, it was what her father wanted, and he knew what was best for her.

"I shall make you very happy, Juliana." Edmund stared deep into her eyes.

"We shall all be delighted!" her father exclaimed. "Edmund will make a fine king someday." He looked at Edmund and clapped a hand on his shoulder. "Your father, Prince James, would have been proud." He lifted his glass filled with red wine. "A toast, but first, I have news of my own I would like to share." He turned to his daughter.

Juliana raised her eyebrows. *More news? I have not digested this one yet.*

"Juliana, you know it has been lonely for me ever since your mother died, but I found a lovely lady who has captured my heart, and I intend to marry." He glowed, and Juliana had not seen him this happy in a long time. "Her name is Lady Rose."

"Why, Father, that is wonderful news. Lady Rose is indeed lovely. I am happy for you." Juliana embraced her father.

Matthew raised his glass. "To marriage!"

They all raised their glasses and cheered, "To marriage!"

As Juliana put her glass on the table, Edmund took her hand. "Would you care to take a walk with me in the garden?"

She smiled. "I would."

He lifted his elbow, and she put her hand in the crook of his arm as they walked toward the garden. They passed the gardeners feverishly at work, shoveling, planting, and preparing the flower beds. Edmund stopped when they arrived at a private area surrounded by bright green foliage and away from the busyness of the workers.

He turned toward her. "I realize the betrothal came as a surprise to you, but I hope you're not disappointed."

"I must admit I was a bit surprised, but no, not disappointed."

"We do not know each other well, for I spend most of my time in Westmore and traveling to other lands, but in time we shall learn more about each other, such as, what we like, what we dislike and what is expected in the marriage."

"I know what is expected of me. I have been the lady of the castle for many years since my mother died."

Edmund's expression turned serious. "It shall be different once you have a husband. I expect loyalty to me above everyone else."

Juliana recalled how her mother had always put her father's needs and desires above all else, including her own. It was a role she had accepted with unwavering devotion. She looked up at Edmund. "And you shall have it."

Edmund smiled, satisfied at her response. He brushed Juliana's hair away from her face, stroking her with a light touch, then leaned down and kissed her lips. This was the first time a man's lips touched hers, and it sent tingles throughout her body. She had dedicated her time to castle duties and had given little thought to anything else, let alone a man, and now she would have a husband to tend to. *I hope I can make him happy,* she said to herself. *I hope I can be a good wife.*

***

Juliana gazed at her reflection in the mirror while her maidservant Liza brushed her hair. Myriad thoughts traveled through her mind as the news of her betrothal to Prince Edmund continued to spread throughout the kingdom. Several days passed since the official announcement, and Juliana had not yet settled into the fact that she will wed Edmund in less than a month.

"Your Highness, the news of your betrothal to Prince Edmund is splendid."

"Yes, it is Liza." Juliana mustered a smile.

"The entire kingdom is celebrating, not just the wedding to be, but the two kingdoms of Yorkford and Westmore coming together."

"These are prosperous times for Yorkford," said Juliana.

"Indeed! Everyone from the lowliest peasant to the highest noble is celebrating our good fortune. King Matthew is a fine king."

"My father is very powerful... and clever."

"No one dares challenge him. We live in peace thanks to him," said Liza.

"We have a strong army with the fiercest knights of any kingdom," she said with head held high, then it dropped as she reflected on her own words. *Knights.* Her eyes widened. *Jack! Oh, my goodness! Does Jack know?*

Juliana walked down the stairs and was thrilled to find Jack in the great hall looking up at the wall, staring at the tapestries. He gazed with fondness at the scenes illustrating the battles he fought alongside King Matthew, his adopted father Prince Marcus, and the brave men from his elite cavalry—The Magnificent Seven Knights.

"Jack!" she called out in delight, rushing to meet him.

With his concentration broken, he turned toward her.

"It's lovely to see you. Where have you been?" Juliana's exuberance faded as the look on Jack's face did not share the same enthusiasm to see her.

"I have been traveling for tournaments, but I also thought it wise to keep my distance from you. I heard the news about the betrothal to Edmund, and it would not be proper for us to continue our friendship."

She scoffed at his absurdity. "That's rubbish, Jack. We can continue to be friends."

"If I were Edmund, it would not please me to see another man near my future wife. Besides, you know he does not like me much."

"Jack, I wish not to lose your friendship. I will not allow that to happen." A lump filled her throat as his words settled in. "You... you are my best friend, always have been."

"I'm sorry, Juliana, but I'm here to meet with Uncle Matthew and request permission to move south to Cedarville."

"But... that's hours away. When shall I see you?"

"That is the intent—you shall not see me. You will have a new life, and I can't be a part of it."

Ella approached. "Sir Jack, King Matthew will see you now."

Jack held Juliana's gaze, then turned and walked toward the king's library.

"Jack, wait," she called out to him, but he did not stop. "Come back here! I demand it!"

Tears welled up in Juliana's eyes. *It can't be. How could he walk out on me?* She sat on the nearest chair, feeling faint, confused. It was all so sudden. He was there for her when she needed him. She grew up lonely in the castle without brothers or sisters, and Jack was her only friend, but the idea of losing him made her realize... she swallowed. *Is he more than just a friend?* She fought back the tears, dabbed the corner of her eyes, and picked up her head. She couldn't entertain having feelings for Jack. The arrangements were made to marry Edmund. She was a princess destined to marry a prince, and since Jack was adopted, he was not a true prince. She would learn to love Edmund. Juliana played back Jack's words and knew he was right. It would not be proper for a married woman of her social standing to have a male friend. She would accept losing Jack, no matter how difficult. As hard as she tried to convince herself that it was the right thing, the thought of him leaving Yorkford devastated her.

***

Matthew quickly folded the map of Cedarville, tucked the parchment inside a book, and placed it on the shelf behind him. There was a knock on the door. "Come in, Jack."

Jack entered the king's library, and Matthew motioned him to sit across from his desk. "Jack, what can I do for you?"

"Uncle Matthew, I'm sure you're aware that Lord Godfrey of Cedarville was killed by one of his own men. He mistreated his people and was not well-liked."

"I am aware. My keeper of books studied his records and discovered he was not paying me the correct amount for what the village was earning. He not only cheated his people, but he cheated me. He kept it for himself."

"It has been five weeks, and Cedarville has been without a baron," Jack took a deep breath. "I wish for you to grant me that land."

Matthew raised his eyes, impressed with Jack's bold confidence. "Jack, for your past service and loyalty, you rightfully deserve your own land, but are you most certain you want Cedarville? I can grant you more fruitful land."

"I have visited Cedarville and examined the soil, and it is rich. The villagers shall cultivate the land and make it profitable for you."

Matthew squinted. "It's a huge task. Do you think you can handle it?"

"I do."

Matthew walked over to the wall and searched for a scroll. He found the one he was searching for and pulled it out of the opening. "Lord Godfrey's castle has a staff of twelve and a small army of one hundred knights and fighters. The castle was neglected, and some parts of it must be rebuilt. You must train additional knights to strengthen your army and hire villagers to rebuild and repair the castle."

"I will. I would also like to request complete autonomy over how I run my village. With your permission, I wish to grant land to the villagers who are loyal and hardworking and pay them what I believe to be their fair share in wages. But rest assured, I shall pay you the correct amount in taxes and rents."

Matthew studied Jack. "Very well, Jack, I trust your allegiance is with me. I shall grant you complete autonomy, but beware, to the south of Cedarville is Etheland. You are to protect Cedarville from King Carlton. No doubt, he would have seized the land if he thought it was valuable. If he sees that Cedarville is prospering, he may try to invade it. Make sure you guard it well once it prospers."

"I shall."

Matthew pulled out a scroll from an opening behind him, wrote a few words, then handed it to Jack. "Please sign the accord, and Cedarville is yours."

Jack studied the parchment, dipped a quill pen in ink, and signed his name. Matthew then signed it, and with a glob of hot golden wax, imprinted his seal on the document.

"When do you wish to leave?"

Jack rose from his seat with a determined stance. "After supper."

Matthew put his hand on Jack's shoulder. "All right. I wish you well, son. God be with you."

As Jack exited, Sir Leopold walked in, giving Jack a sideways glance. With Jack out of sight, he turned to Matthew. "Is he moving to Cedarville?"

Matthew's smile grew sinister. "He is. The plan unfolded as expected. I must keep him far away from Juliana."

Chapter 3

Jack draped his black velvet cloak over his fine linen blue tunic and wool tights and fastened it at the neck. He mounted Dex, a dark brown muscular destrier, as he began his journey to Cedarville, a trek that would take him south of Yorkford through the dense forest in a little over three hours. "It's just you and me, Dex," he said, stroking his horse's mane.

He looked back with melancholy at the place he called home for eighteen years, the first six years in a small village of Yorkford with his natural parents and siblings, then twelve years in the castle with his adoptive family. Time was stealing the memories of his first family although certain triggers would bring up bits and pieces of his former life. The scent of lavender flowers and roses in the garden brought back images of his mother dusting the wooden furniture and humming. Lavender and roses were her favorite flowers, and she kept them in vases filled with water throughout their small cottage. They didn't have much, but his mother made sure their surroundings were as pleasant as possible.

The air in the forest whistled, swaying the broadleaf trees, generating a spirited rustling. Black clouds hovered above, threatening heavy rain. If the weather turned, Jack had shelter in the forest where he would stay until it subsided. Since he was a squire, he had maintained a small cottage where he trained his falcons to hunt, practiced his archery, and spent a few hours away from castle life. He relished being outdoors surrounded by nature and clean air, a stark contrast from the mustiness of the fortress.

Jack made a left turn once he crossed the wooden bridge over the creek that divided the north and south of the kingdom and arrived at Cedarville. He passed through the village square, the central point of Cedarville, and the most active part of the town, but at this late hour, it was barren. He kept riding until he found himself in a wooded area. He scanned his surroundings. "I don't see the castle," he muttered to himself. Nighttime fell, and he kept riding, searching for a road. He was too far into the woods, nothing around him but thick trees and scattered wooden cabins. "Well, Dex, my friend, I think we're lost."

Sporadic drops of water turned into a steady stream of rain. The wind picked up, producing a soft howl, and delivering a piercing cold. Jack lifted his hood over his head and tightened the cloak around his neck. He feared a tempest underway. *It might be best to seek shelter until the storm subsides,* he told himself.

He passed several cottages in the woods but decided against knocking on a stranger's door late at night during inclement weather. He hoped to find an abandoned cabin so as not to frighten anyone. After all, the concept of being a lone male arriving on someone's doorstep in the middle of the night in a storm could be a deadly one.

Jack kept moving and found an abandoned shed filled with empty wine barrels and scattered straw. "Perfect," he breathed, his voice lost to the wind. He and Dex would stay inside until the weather improved to resume his search for the baron's castle. He shut the door and pushed the straw to a pile. Happy with his handiwork, he lay on it and closed his eyes.

A wind gust blew the door wide open, banging it against the wall. Jack jumped, laying a hand to his weapon. *It's just the wind.*

Jack rose to his feet and strode toward the door. Lightning illuminated the area for a moment, long enough for Jack to see a pair of yellow eyes staring at him. He froze. It was a wolf, gaunt and salivating as he eyed Jack. Tightening his grip, Jack raised his sword. Behind the first wolf, another appeared, snarling, baring its teeth.

From the darkness, both animals leaped onto Jack. He swung his sword, and one of them yelped, but the other remained on him, relentless. Fangs pierced his leg, tearing through the wool stocking. Jack cried out and swung his weapon, white dots flashing before his eyes. His leg throbbed as the warm gush of blood trickled down.

The wolf growled. Jack braced for another attack. He feared his end was near, when at that moment, the wolves backed away, turned toward the door, and scurried into the woods.

Jack panted, taking deep breaths. Something must have scared off the wolves, but what? He feared the wolves sensed a larger animal approaching—a bear, perhaps? He had to get out of there, but he had to stop the bleeding dripping from his leg.

Leaves rustled by the door. Was it the wind or a larger animal? He drew his sword, and with enormous effort, stood, hobbling. Sparks in the sky gave light to the darkness, and a shadow appeared holding an oil lamp.

Jack exhaled. He squinted to sharpen his vision, and a tall, middle-aged man came into focus. Blood soaked

Jack's leg as chills swept through his body, and white dots re-appeared. He could no longer hold himself up, and he swayed to one side, but before he reached the ground, a pair of arms grabbed him. The man put Jack's arm around him and propped him up.

"Come with me," he said. "That leg must be tended to." He and Jack trudged through the wind and rain and arrived at the man's cottage, a short distance from the shed.

With chills running through his body, Jack was relieved to be in a warm cottage. He hopped on one leg as the man led him into a back room and made him lie on his back on a table covered with a coarse wool blanket. Jack grimaced as excruciating pain traveled through his leg. Multiple bottles cluttered a bedside table filled with powders and liquids of varied colors, and alongside were several bowls with herbs.

"Do not worry, I am a doctor," the man said. "My name is Robert. I shall close the wound and give you something to prevent an infection."

Robert tore the wool legging on Jack's lower right leg and exposed the animal bite. He put pressure on the wound to stop the bleeding, then examined it, cleaned it, and applied herbs to the area. Jack bit his lip and cringed, never having experienced such intense pain. Robert bandaged his leg, then prepared a mix of powder and herbs and poured it into a cup of wine. "Here, drink this. It will prevent an infection and ease the pain."

Jack strained to sit up and drank the concoction, contorting his face after swallowing. "Thank you, Doctor."

With his vision clearing, Jack eyed Robert. He was a handsome man, Jack guessed, about forty, with dark brown hair mixed with gray and gray hair on the temples. The lines etched on his face revealed sadness and regret that stripped away his youth. His deep-set smoky gray eyes reflected pain but a kind heart.

He gave Jack a warm smile. "You are welcome. Are you hungry?"

He nodded. "I am, but I wish not to impose."

"It's no imposition." Robert left the room and returned with a bowl of tomato soup, a leg of chicken, and a piece of dark bread on a tray.

Robert sat on a stool beside the bed as Jack ate. "What's your name?"

"Jack." He dipped the bread in the soup and took a few bites of the chicken.

"What were you doing out here in the storm?"

"I lost my way. It began to rain, so I looked for shelter. I must have dozed off moments before the wolves came." After a few minutes, Jack left an empty bowl and a dry chicken bone. He wiped his mouth and hands with a linen cloth.

"Food has been scarce around here, for the people as well as the animals." Robert stared at Jack. "That's a fine horse you have. I know you're not from around here. Where are you from?"

"Yorkford."

"That's a long way to get lost. Are you running from something or somebody?"

"Why do you ask?"

"You have the sword and clothes of a knight, emblazoned with a crest. Knights do not leave their towns unless they are running from something."

Jack did not wish to reveal his desire to escape from his old life in Yorkford—which included Juliana. "I am the new baron of this village."

Robert raised his eyebrows. "You are quite young to be a baron, but I hope you are better than the last one."

"I intend to be."

Robert rose from his seat and gathered the medicine and unused bandages. "You should stay the night so you can heal. The rain is still coming down heavy, and you lost a lot of blood. You need to replenish it."

"Thank you, Doctor. I am most grateful." Jack glanced at the oval-shaped golden locket around Robert's neck. Three small gold circles overlapped in the locket's black center as gold decorated the outer rim. It was an unusual locket.

***

After two days, Jack regained the use of his leg, and the wound was on its way to healing. Robert bade him farewell, and Jack mounted his horse and rode into town in search of the baron's castle.

When he arrived, he saw the castle in significant disrepair and in need of considerable renovations. In the weeks ahead, he gathered the villagers and paid them a generous wage to restore the castle. The townspeople delighted in Jack, and the mood in the entire village changed. A once dreary and gloomy place was now filled with liveliness and good cheer. Lord Godfrey had no interest in developing the town of Cedarville. Jack, however, saw the enormous potential and envisioned creating a thriving village. This effort also distracted him from thoughts of Juliana.

His days as a lord consisted of long hours and numerous tasks. After a particularly arduous day, Jack wanted to try the pottage stew in the local alehouse. Sitting at a table, as he alternated between eating and drinking beer, Jack overheard a group of patrons behind him talking about an upcoming anniversary.

"It's hard to believe that it has been twenty-two years since the massacre at Maiden Hills," said a patron.

"I remember that day well."

"What happened?" asked the young patron.

"Maiden Hills was home to people with magical powers called Majians. They were a peaceful group of people, but the Kingdom of Yorkford viewed them as a threat and sent their knights to attack them and burn their village."

"They had magical powers?"

"They did!"

"Were there any survivors?"

"Some adults survived, but many children were rescued. It is believed they came to Cedarville and live among us."

Jack listened while he ate and drank. The story about the magical people was interesting, but most villagers enjoy telling folktales for entertainment. He recalled as a young lad sitting outside in the evening around an open fire and hearing similar stories from his neighbors. The stories had frightened him, but his mother had assured him they were fables. He motioned the servant for another pint of beer while the patrons continued their tale.

"Isn't the practice of magic seen as evil?"

"It is, but these were good people. They harmed no one. They used their powers to defend themselves."

"What were their magical abilities?"

"They moved objects with their minds and communicated with animals, but they had to wear a locket with enchanted stones, which gave them their powers."

Jack froze with the mug to his lips. *Robert wears a locket around his neck!* If his locket had stones with supernatural powers enabling him to communicate with animals, that would explain why two hungry wolves retreated without an apparent cause. He shook his head. His imagination had taken control of his good sense. The practice of magic was forbidden, but he did not believe people could actually perform magic. It was just not possible.

He swallowed the rest of his beer.

The next day, Jack visited Doctor Robert and sat on the table while Robert examined his leg and found that it had healed with minimal scarring. To show his appreciation, Jack invited Robert to the local alehouse for a beer and meal. Robert accepted, saying that he often drank beer and wine. "It's a way to numb the pain," he would tell Jack. Jack never pressed him to explain the pain he suffered from. He didn't want to seem intrusive.

"I heard a story about a massacre that occurred twenty-two years ago in what used to be Maiden Hills," Jack said over the rim of his mug. "Are you familiar with it?"

Robert hesitated. "I am." He gulped his beer.

"It's just a myth, is it not?"

Robert shook his head. "It's not a myth. There *was* a massacre."

"But the story about the magical people can't be true. Magical people do not exist." Jack expected Robert to agree with him. His eyes flicked to the locket partially hidden under his tunic. "They do not exist, is that not true?"

Robert lifted his eyebrows. "Perhaps they exist."

Jack leaned in closer. "Robert, are you one of the survivors? Do you have magical powers?" As he blurted out those words, he wanted to take them back, realizing they sounded absurd, but then Robert didn't answer and just stared at his beer.

Robert raised his eyes and looked at Jack. "Why do you ask?"

"You wear a locket around your neck, and the wolves could have killed me, but they didn't—they ran away for no reason, then you showed up."

Robert picked up the beer mug and put it to his lips.

"If you are, you can trust me," Jack said. "No harm will come to you."

Jack noted his hesitancy. As a knight from Yorkford, the people responsible for the massacre, if true, Robert would find it difficult to trust him. He stared at Robert with his eyes shifted down. The longer that Robert hesitated, the more Jack was convinced of the story's accuracy, and that Robert was one of the survivors.

"You sent those wolves away, did you not?" Jack pressed.

Robert studied Jack for a moment, then put down his beer. "I did, I sent the wolves away… with magic. Your suspicions are correct—I have supernatural powers."

40

Jack's eyes widened. "So, it's true!"

"I escaped the massacre twenty-two years ago. Most everyone died. There are a few survivors in Cedarville, but they keep to themselves. I hold on to my gemstones for protection, but mostly it serves as a reminder of who I am and what I lost that terrible night."

Jack understood why Robert drank often. "What happened?"

"Prince James of Westmore tricked a young woman named Beth into trusting him, and he betrayed her. The Kingdom of Yorkford ordered the attack and sent their knights to slaughter the people on the Majian Mountain." Robert motioned the servant for another pint of beer.

"I am a knight from Yorkford. I hope you do not mistrust me because of it."

Robert said with a half-smile, "I don't blame you, Jack. You were not yet born." He grew serious. "But you are the lord of Cedarville and can arrest me as the use of magic is forbidden."

Jack shook his head. "You have done nothing wrong."

Robert gave Jack a grateful smile. "Thank you."

"I heard the story of Prince James Wadham when I was a child, he was legendary," Jack said. "He died in battle twenty-two years ago. Was there a battle in Maiden Hills? Is that where he died?"

"There was no battle, only a massacre. But that's not how Prince James died. One of our people killed him for his betrayal."

Jack's beer mug slammed the table. He stared at Robert wide-eyed. "He was murdered?"

"He was."

Jack thought of Edmund, the only son of Prince James, who believed his father had died honorably in a battle. If he discovered the truth of how his father died, it would shatter the image he had of him. Edmund would be enraged. Jack knew his adoptive brother well. He would seek revenge, and it would consume him until he succeeded. Jack gulped the rest of his beer.

***

Juliana stared at her reflection, not recognizing the face in front of her, coated with heavy tinted creams used to vanish the slightest imperfections. Four servants fussed over her, making sure her dress, hair, and face were impeccable for this day. The seamstress worked for weeks on a cream and lavender silk gown similar to the one her mother had worn on her wedding day. *I wish Mother were here.* She dabbed the corner of her eye, careful not to ruin her maidservant's artwork.

"Your Highness, I must re-touch your make-up!" blurted Liza.

"It's fine, Liza. My face feels stiff enough."

Juliana walked toward the window, inhaling the morning spring air. She closed her eyes as she basked in the sun's heat. A mass of people had gathered below across the castle's drawbridge, waiting to catch a glimpse of her. The kingdom bustled with activity, as this was the day the townspeople eagerly anticipated. The wedding brought villagers and neighboring townspeople to Yorkford, as well as an army of guardsmen to keep the crowd under control. The servants meticulously planned and prepared for many weeks, and the day had finally arrived.

King Matthew's face glowed when Juliana came down the stairs. Her eyes moistened. It meant so much to see her father happy.

"You have never looked more beautiful," he said as he kissed her cheek.

Juliana smiled. "Thank you, Father." Her eyes searched the room. "Where is Prince Edmund?"

"He should be at the church, waiting for you." Matthew draped the veil over Juliana's face, straightened her diamond tiara, then lifted his elbow. Juliana wrapped her arm around his.

They climbed into a gold-trimmed white carriage led by six majestic white horses and soon were on their way. The carriage whisked passed the crowd and cheers erupted. Matthew held on to Juliana's shaking hands. The warmth of his large hands over her dainty ones calmed her, and she sighed, releasing the anxiety. Minutes later, they arrived. The knights and warhorses stood sentry in full armor at the entrance of the church.

Juliana stood before Bishop Dalton as he officiated the wedding ceremony. She glanced at Edmund to her right, and the fluttering in her stomach returned. Although she accepted her life would change, and Edmund would dictate those changes, it was, however, a troubling thought. She was headstrong with a mind of her own, but now she would measure her words and adhere to the role of a loyal and demure wife.

No one muttered a sound in the grand cathedral as the bride and groom recited their vows, and Edmund placed a ring on Juliana's finger. Edmund leaned down, and his lips met hers. The guests applauded. It was done.

As Juliana and Edmund exited the church, the townspeople shoved one another to catch sight of the royal couple, only to be held back by the guards. Among the commotion, Juliana's eyes darted the noblemen standing along the route, hoping to see Jack's face, but he was not there. Although she wasn't surprised, it disheartened her. She thought much about Jack, more than any respectable woman about to be married should. But she could not brush her feelings aside. Jack was dear to her, and he left a void in her heart. But on this day, she had to keep a smile on her face and wave to the crowd. It was her wedding day, and she had to appear as the blissful bride.

Juliana and Edmund arrived and stood at the entrance of the crowded banquet hall, her arm inside his. The guests rose from their seats and applauded. Juliana's silk lavender gown sparkled with hundreds of crystals sewn in, and Edmund was princely in his red and gold velvet doublet with a white pleated collar over a scarlet velvet cape.

Edmund escorted his new bride to the dais where they sat in their large royal canopied chairs, and as soon as they sat, the servants brought them the finest imported red wine. Juliana scanned the great room—*is he here?* But Jack was not among the nobles.

Rows of long, white linen-covered tables adorned with fresh orchids filled the great hall of the castle. The guests took their seats, and the servants placed large platters of meats, cheese, and bread as well as jugs of wine and assorted desserts on the table in front of them. It was the largest feast the kingdom had ever seen. Musicians began to play music, and everyone awaited the moment the bride and groom would have their first dance.

Edmund held his wife's hand, and they strode to the center of the floor and danced to applause and cheers. Edmund fixed his eyes on his young bride and smiled. Juliana smiled back, although something wasn't right. She should be happy. Edmund was a dream come true for any woman, for he was a strong and handsome prince, but something was missing.

King Matthew approached the couple, looking handsome and regal with his gold crown and wearing a gray velvet outfit and cape to match. Edmund stepped to the side, and Matthew held his daughter's hand. Juliana smiled as she and her father swayed to the music.

"You remind me of your mother," Matthew said. "She looked as lovely as you when I married her."

Juliana gazed up at him. "You were in love with her, were you not?"

"I was."

"She was fortunate to marry the man she loved."

Her father's eyes shifted. "You may not be in love with Edmund, but your feelings will change, and he will see in you what I see, and he will come to love you too."

Juliana's throat swelled, and her eyes watered as she and her father exchanged smiles. He was the perfect man, the most caring and honest person in the world. *I hope that someday I can say the same thing about my husband.* But the only other man with a kind heart like her father was Jack.

The wedding celebration continued throughout the late hours, and Juliana looked forward to getting a good night's sleep. However, she realized it would be the first time she would sleep next to a man—a terrifying and exciting thought. From this moment on, she would be his wife and expected to comply with her husband's wishes, whether or not she agreed with him.

Liza arrived to escort Juliana to her bedchamber and prepare her for the consummation of her marriage to Edmund. Inside the chamber, Liza and two maidservants, helped Juliana change into a nightdress, brushed her hair, and sprinkled rosewater on the bedsheet. Juliana perched on the edge of the bed, waiting for her husband.

"Are you all right, Your Highness?" asked Liza.

"I'm a little nervous," Juliana admitted.

Liza poured wine into a glass. "Here, drink this. It will help you relax."

She sipped the wine, and it soothed the fluttery feeling in her stomach. She didn't know what to expect. No one had spoken to her about physical intimacy. It was a conversation most young girls had with their mothers when their bodies changed, but Juliana never had that conversation. Her eyes grew misty. At a time like this, she missed her mother more than she could bear.

The warning knock on the door startled her. Edmund walked in and asked the maidservants to leave, then locked the door. Juliana's nerves were alight, for she was alone with a man in her bedchamber for the first time in her life.

Edmund sat on the bed beside Juliana. "I told your father we wished for a private bedding ceremony."

Juliana let out a sigh of relief. "Thank you." She gave him a half-smile. "Some of our traditions are just… odd, to say the least."

"I agree." He looked at her. "Are you nervous?"

"I am, but the wine helps to calm me."

"Please know that I will be as gentle as I can be." He reached for her hand. "I wish not to hurt you."

"I am most grateful."

"I shall wait for you to be ready."

Juliana took another sip of wine and set the glass on the table next to the bed. *Well, this is it. It's time that I became a woman.* She turned to look at Edmund. "I am ready."

Edmund tilted his head and pressed his lips against hers. Juliana's tensed muscles relaxed as Edmund slithered his arms around her waist. Warmth spread throughout her body, and she gave in to the moment. She put her arms around Edmund's neck and leaned back with him.

Oh, Jack!

***

"Princess Juliana, Princess Juliana, come quick."

A month passed since the wedding when, from Juliana's great chamber, she heard Ella call out below in a panic. Juliana rushed down the stairs. "Ella, what's the matter?"

"It's your father. He's not waking up."

"What? Where is he?"

"He's in the great hall by the central hearth."

Juliana rushed to the hearth, her heart pounding violently. When she arrived, her breath caught in her throat to see her father slumped over a chair, a broken vase shattered on the floor, water spilled with many-hued roses, and a wineglass rested in his hand as red wine dripped on the floor.

"Father!" Juliana pulled him up, grunting with the effort. "Father, speak to me, open your eyes." She patted his face vigorously, but there was no life in him. She looked at the wineglass. "Was he poisoned?"

She tried again to revive him, not wanting to accept he was gone, but he remained still and not breathing. She gave him a vigorous shake. "Father, wake up, wake up." Juliana stared at him. He was pale and motionless. *I've lost him!* "Nooo!" she wailed as she draped herself over his body and sobbed.

"Oh, no, it can't be." Ella's trembling hands covered her face as tears flowed. "How did this happen?"

Juliana lifted herself from her father and pulled the servant toward her. "Ella, what happened?"

"He had just come from the garden," she said, sniffling. "H-he picked flowers for Lady Rose."

"Did you see anyone come into the room?"

"The usual servants roamed the castle. I saw no one unfamiliar."

"It could have been someone familiar, someone in the castle. Think, Ella, who could have done it?"

Ella shook her head, distraught. "I don't know, Your Highness. Oh, it's terrible."

"Ella, go find my husband. Now!"

She ran out, shaking and sobbing.

Juliana stared at her father's lifeless body, tears streaming down her face. "Father, not you too. Why did you leave me?" She lay on his chest with her arms around him and wept.

48

***

Word spread quickly of the sudden demise of King Matthew. At the castle, noblemen and noblewomen from Yorkford and neighboring kingdoms as well as members of the clergy, and distinguished villagers came to pay their final respects. Juliana and Edmund sat in their royal chairs, greeting the mourners in the great hall and receiving their condolences. Bishop Dalton held Lady Rose's hand on the other side of the room. She sat expressionless, trying to put a strong façade, but the swell in her eyes bared her pain, for the next day would have been her wedding to King Matthew.

Juliana glanced over at Edmund, his face stoic. Was he sad at losing King Matthew or happy that he was now king of Yorkford? Edmund craved ambition and loved power. This is what he desired—to rule a vast kingdom. Did he have something to do with her father's death? Was he capable of murdering the man who treated him like a son? Juliana watched her husband. *How can I suspect him? He's my husband!* Still, she could not help but think the worst. She would find out what happened to her father, she resolved. Doctor Parker would examine her father's body and discover the cause of death.

Liza came to her with a glass of wine. "I thought you might want this, Your Majesty."

Juliana raised the glass to her lips, but before she tasted it, a guard stopped her.

"Apologies, Your Majesty, but the wine must be tested." The guard turned to Liza. "You must test the wine before Her Majesty drinks it."

Liza's face turned pale. She lifted the wineglass to her lips as she had done many times for Juliana. With trembling hands, she took a sip. The guard waited a few minutes, then took the glass from Liza, put the glass to his nose, and inhaled it. Satisfied the wine was not tainted, he handed it to Juliana. A relieved Juliana took a sip of the wine and allowed the warmth to flow down her throat. The tension in her body subsided.

Jack came to mind. It troubled her that he had not come for the wake. Her father was his adoptive uncle, who adored him like a son. Perhaps he did not wish to see her again, why is why he moved quite a distance from her. *But I thought he would be here... for Father... for me!* When her mother died, he had requested permission to leave his knight training for a few days to be with her, and he was a source of great comfort. Times were different, for she had a husband and should draw strength from him, but sadly, it was not so. Apart from sleeping in the same chamber, Juliana and Edmund spent little time together.

"Long live King Edmund! Long live Queen Juliana!"

The chants from the townspeople across the moat were surreal, echoing through a hollow tube, like a horrible dream. She stared ahead in a silent state of shock, never imagining the day would come when she would lose her beloved father and become the queen of Yorkford, at least not this soon and under such tragic circumstances. But she was an Allington, and Allingtons were no strangers to tragedies. It was a sad legacy. Suddenly, a coldness ran up her body. Her breathing became quick and shallow. She was suffocating, trapped—the large room was getting smaller.

She put the glass down and turned to Edmund. "I need air." He nodded, granting her permission to leave.

She rushed through the openings in the crowd. Voices called for her, but she kept going, hastening her pace. She feared she would faint. Finally, outside in the courtyard, she took a deep breath and put her hand on a pillar to steady herself. She exhaled and found the strength to continue.

Juliana took the path to the garden, the only place where she could find solace and comfort. Guards were everywhere, watching the guests to ensure the safety of the king and queen. Juliana avoided eye contact. She slipped past the guards and found a bench in the middle of the garden surrounded by flowering bushes, where she sat, put her hands to her face, and cried.

She sensed someone sitting next to her. "I know you came here to be alone," a familiar voice said.

She lifted her head, her face soaked in tears.

"But I thought you might need a friend."

She sobbed and leaned on him as he put his arm around her. "I'm so glad you're here, Jack." Tears streamed down her face, and he held her tight.

***

The day drained her energy, and Juliana looked forward to being away from the crowd and in the comfort of her bedchamber.

As Juliana brushed her hair, she studied Edmund putting away his outfit. She hoped she would grow to love him, but his cold and disconnected ways made it impossible for her to feel anything of romance for him.

"What do you think happened?" she asked.

"I beg your pardon?"

"Do you think someone killed my father?" She swallowed dryly. She hated saying it out loud.

He shrugged his shoulders and shook his head. "I do not know the fate that has befallen your father."

She narrowed her eyes, annoyed at his indifference. "Does it not worry you that a murderer has gone free?"

He looked at her. "What should worry you more is that if he was killed, the killer could be inside the castle."

"You believe it came from inside?"

"This castle is a fortress. It's difficult for an outsider to come in unnoticed. If someone murdered your father, the killer is lurking somewhere inside the castle."

Juliana's face turned ashen. "What a frightening thought! What do we do?"

Edmund paused, turned to meet Juliana's eyes, then shook his head. "I cannot say." He looked away and continued putting away his outfit.

For a moment, Juliana saw something she had not seen before. She didn't see a confident, self-assured man with an over-inflated ego and high ambition, a man who had all the answers and could be questioned by no one. Instead, she saw a man with a bit of insecurity, with a vulnerability that managed to sneak out. She saw a man suddenly thrust into ruling the largest and most formidable empire in the continent and perhaps not ready for it. Was she wrong about him?

Chapter 4

Juliana snipped the withered flowers and plucked the weeds surrounding the rose bushes, careful to avoid the thorns. Being outdoors and inhaling the fresh air brought a welcome change from sitting in her chamber, numb from the pain of losing her beloved father. She hoped tending to the garden would distract her from thinking of him and coping with the overwhelming sadness, but the repetitive motion of snipping and pruning left her mind to wander, and it drifted to images of the man who had been her protector and her hero, suddenly taken from her. Juliana held back tears, wanting to be strong like he had taught her, but she struggled with it. Edmund was settling into his new role as king and wasn't much help to her during her grief. She was alone in her mourning. When her mother died, she had her father to lean on, but now he was gone, and she had no one.

She caught sight of the bench where she sat during her father's wake with Jack's arm around her. That moment lasted a few minutes, but the tender feelings remained within her. After two months since Jack had moved away, seeing him again brought raw emotions to the surface, emotions she had not dealt with and didn't know how to manage. She missed him more than she ever imagined. Being with Jack filled an empty part of her, and for a brief time, she was whole, and she held on to it until it was time to say goodbye, and then the emptiness returned.

I am so alone. Edmund was growing more distant toward her, and now with the pressures of ruling a kingdom upon him, she saw no sign of things improving.

They spoke little since King Matthew's death a week prior. Each day she spent married to Edmund felt more wrong than the last. He had not been demonstrative toward her since they married, but what little attention he showed her in the past was now nonexistent.

Immersed in her self-pity, she snapped out of it when Sir Mark approached her. She sprang up, blinked away tears, and swallowed the lump in her throat.

"Sir Mark!" she said, smiling, although it pained her. Sir Mark was Jack's closest friend. They trained together when they were squires and became knighted on the same day. Along with five other men, they were part of The Magnificent Seven Knights, the elite group of fighters who captivated audiences in tournaments.

"Are you all right, Your Majesty?" Mark asked with a look of concern.

She sniffed. "I'm fine. How are you this day?" Mark was a handsome man, twenty years old with dark brown hair, a well-groomed beard and mustache, and chocolate brown eyes. *He's so much like Jack,* she thought, *of his manners and chivalry.*

"I am well." He looked around. "The garden looks lovely. It's just about ready for the festival."

"It is." She smiled as she admired her work. "Sir Mark," she paused, "have you spoken to Lord Jack?"

"I saw him at the wake, Your Majesty, but we did not have much time to talk. He had to hurry back. I went to Cedarville a month ago to offer my assistance. He completed his castle the way he likes with a comfortable great room, a new stable, and a secret passageway. Jack is a fanatic about those secret passageways." He grinned.

"He's helping the villagers grow their own food and raise livestock."

Juliana's heart gave a squeeze. "I am pleased he's doing well. I was happy to see him at my father's wake, even for a moment."

"He would not have missed being there. He is very fond of you."

Juliana smiled as she held back tears.

"If there is anything that I can do for you, Your Majesty, please call on me. I am at your service."

"Thank you, Sir Mark, you are most kind."

Mark walked out of the garden, and Juliana returned to tending to the flowers. Minutes later, Doctor Parker approached her. "Your Majesty, the steward told me you would be here. I would like to discuss the results of the tests we performed on your father."

Juliana's muscles tensed, not prepared for what he had come to tell her. She removed her gloves and placed them on a bench. "What did you discover, Doctor?" She took a seat to get off her shaky legs.

"It should relieve you to know we found no evidence that someone murdered your father. It was most likely that his heart failed and caused his death. The small amount of wine left in the glass was free of poison."

A sense of relief came over her. She reflected for a moment. "Father died two days before his wedding to Lady Rose. Do you suppose that had something to do with it?"

"It's possible. The anticipation may have been too much for him and could have caused his heart to fail. I have informed King Edmund of my conclusion. If there is nothing else, Your Majesty, I shall be on my way."

Juliana nodded. *So, Father wasn't murdered… why did I believe Edmund might have had something to do with his death?* For a moment, she thought him capable of such an act. *Who is this man I married?*

Her eyes caught the maidservant Ella guiding Princess Katherine, Edmund's mother and Jack's adoptive mother, through the rose bushes, holding her arm for support. Katherine's legs had been losing strength over the past several years due to a horse-riding accident. Juliana rushed toward her. "Princess Katherine, please sit here." Juliana walked with her to the bench and helped lower her until she sat comfortably.

"I shall return with the wine, Your Highness," said Ella.

Katherine studied Juliana. "Sit with me, dear." She tapped the seat next to her. "I saw you with Doctor Parker. What did he say?"

"He said Father's heart most likely failed, and it caused his death."

"You must feel comforted to know no one took his life."

"I do." Juliana lowered her eyes.

"How are you holding up?"

She shook her head. "Not well. I miss him terribly. I weep all the time, I can't eat, I'm sick in my stomach… I… I can't shake this off."

She held Juliana's hand. "It's understandable. He was important to you." She studied Juliana. "Are you certain there is not something else?"

Jack came to mind, but Juliana could not reveal her feelings for Jack to Edmund's mother. She shrugged. "What else could it be?"

"Never mind dear, it will get easier with time." Princess Katherine patted her hand.

"I know." Juliana swallowed. "It was difficult when I lost my mother, and even though the pain is still there, I'm able to handle it better."

Katherine stared at Juliana. "You remind me of your mother in so many ways. You look very much like her."

Juliana smiled at the invaluable compliment. "I miss her every day."

Ella returned with a jug and two glasses. She poured the wine into a glass and handed it to Princess Katherine, then turned to Juliana. "Would you care for a glass of wine, Your Majesty?"

"No, Ella. I'm going for a ride. I won't be long." Juliana excused herself and headed toward the stable to fetch her palfrey.

***

Edmund gazed at the portrait of King Matthew above the central hearth in the great hall. The artist had captured the late king's striking gaze when in deep deliberation, plotting his next conquest. Matthew was like a father to him, and now he was gone, just like James.

On the opposite end of the great room hung the portrait of Prince James, his natural father. Not a Prince of Yorkford, but a great ally to Matthew, and he had wanted to honor him with a portrait in his castle. Edmund stared at his father's eyes. They had a softer look than Matthew's, although still commanding. A sense of pride filled him as he continued to gaze at the image of his late father. Prince James was the son of King

Thomas Wadham of Westmore and destined to become king until his life ended twenty-two years ago.

Edmund moved to the table and poured himself a glass of wine, recalling the story they told him of his father. Prince James was an excellent commander and a fine swordsman but lost his footing in a battle—a simple mistake that cost him his life. Edmund never knew his father, for he died when he was not yet a year old. Stories abounded of the great Prince James, and Edmund dreamed of being just like him, a fearless warrior, and he fashioned his life to make it happen. Now, as the king, Edmund wanted to be a great ruler and be the king his father never had the chance to be. "I shall make you proud, Father," he said aloud as his eyes met James' staring back at him.

He walked out of the great room and into the garden where his mother sat alone, wine in hand, staring into the distance, many miles away. He cocked his head. "Mother?"

His voice startled Katherine and brought her back to the present. She looked up at him and mustered a smile. "I did not see you there."

Edmund sat next to her. "What were you thinking of?"

"I was thinking of your father." She sighed. "It has been twenty-two years since I lost him and for a moment... I felt as if he was here with me. I recalled sitting with him in this garden. Even though it was long ago, it seemed as if it just happened."

"I was thinking of him, too. I was admiring his portrait."

She smiled. "He looks handsome in that portrait. I remember the day he posed for it." Tears spilled from her eyes, and in a hurry, she wiped them. "I loved James very much, but it saddens me that I could not be a good wife to him. He deserved better."

"You were not at fault, Mother. You had an accident." Edmund gripped her hand. He loved his mother, as any man would, and she was the only person he showed a softer side to, not visible to anyone else, including Juliana.

"I remember it well. It was not long after the wedding." Tears filled her eyes. "I was thrown from my horse and stumbled into a ditch. The bone in my leg broke, and it caused me to limp and unable to walk with grace." She wiped her eyes, her face pained. "I lost my unborn child. The doctor informed us that it was not likely I could carry a child to term. James was despondent for several months at the possibility of not producing an heir. But then you came along." She managed a smile. "You were our miracle child." She paused, gazing into the distance. "Still, I can't help thinking, if I had been a good wife, James would not have gone looking for someone else, and he might be alive this day."

Edmund raised an eyebrow. "What do you mean?"

Katherine pressed her lips together. "Oh, dear, I never told you." She took a breath. "But your father had an affair twenty-two years ago. It devastated me, but I accepted that he needed to be with someone who made him happy."

"How did you know he had an affair?" Edmund was aware that men, especially noblemen in arranged marriages, took women outside of marriage, but they did it with discretion to not shame the wife.

"I had him followed. I wanted to know who she was, what she looked like, and where she lived. Her name was Beth, and she lived with her mother Helena, a seamstress, in Maiden Hills, south of Westmore. She was young and beautiful with long dark hair. Jealousy consumed me, but I did not show it. I suffered in silence."

Nauseating anger swept through Edmund, unable to control the trembling in his hands.

"I'm sorry to tell you this." Katherine retreated, noticing her son's reaction. "Do not blame your father, for he was a good man."

"I wish you had not suffered," Edmund ground out.

"I later forgave him. I then married Marcus, and he treated me well."

Edmund rolled his eyes and frowned.

"I know you did not care for Marcus," said Katherine. "God rest his soul."

"We did not have close relations. He favored Jack."

"Jack suffered a traumatic experience at a tender age, and Marcus knew he required special attention."

A conversation about Jack or Marcus was not what Edmund desired. He turned his attention to his mother's earlier words. "Why did you say, Father might be alive this day if he had not had an affair? Everyone told me he died in battle."

Katherine clasped her hands and placed them over her lips. "Edmund, please forgive me for not being truthful. We did not mean to lie to you, for we wished to protect you, but you should know the truth… James did not die in battle."

Edmund wrinkled his brow. "What are you saying?" He fixed his eyes on her, waiting for her to continue, to make sense of her utterance.

Katherine struggled to get the words out. "One of her kin… killed him."

"He was *murdered?*" Edmund's eyes narrowed, and his heart began to race. He clenched his teeth. "Tell me what happened."

Katherine was shaking. "Sir Leopold witnessed it. He went after him but lost him."

Edmund bolted from his seat. "I must go, Mother." He turned, and she grabbed his arm.

"Edmund, wait."

"Mother, please, it is not my will to continue this conversation." He cupped his mother's hand and freed his arm from her grip. He stormed into the great hall and summoned his steward, Samuel.

"Aye, Your Majesty." Samuel stood in front of Edmund, a tall, thin man in his fifties who had served three successive kings in the castle.

"Fetch Sir Leopold," Edmund commanded. "Now!"

"Right away, Your Majesty."

This can't be true! Edmund's heartbeat thumped forcibly in his chest as he paced the room in a frenzy.

A few minutes later, Sir Leopold walked into the hall. He was Prince James' confidant and, together with James, fought to protect the kingdoms of Yorkford and Westmore. After Prince James' death, Leopold looked after Edmund. "You called for me, Your Majesty?"

"Tell me what happened twenty-two years ago and tell it true!" His eyes bulged.

Leopold tilted his head. "I beg your pardon?"

Edmund drew closer to Leopold and stared into his eyes as he pronounced every word deliberately. "Tell me everything leading up to my father's murder."

Leopold's mustache twitched. "How did you come to know?"

"My mother told me, and she told me about an affair he had that caused it. Now I demand that you tell me everything. Leave nothing out."

Edmund had a temper that Leopold often had to quell. "May we sit, Your Majesty?"

Edmund's nerves were alight. He sat, reluctantly, legs fidgeting. He pointed to the chair opposite him. "Sit."

"Thank you." Leopold took a deep breath and clasped his hands. "Twenty-two years ago, your father met a woman named Beth from Maiden Hills, just outside of Cedarville. It no longer exists because we burned the town. He found out this woman he befriended—" Leopold cringed as he said, "—this woman practiced black magic, as did most of the townspeople. I was with him when a man from their village threatened your father in an alehouse."

Edmund furrowed his brow. "Black magic?"

Leopold nodded. "Yes, Your Majesty. King Matthew ordered us to kill them all as a punishment for their heresy, but James did not wish to do it. I believe he was in love with the young woman. I had to carry it out, but I feared he would try to warn her and the others, so I instructed the army to attack earlier than planned."

Leopold continued. "After the attack, one of her kin snuck inside the castle, found James, and… strangled him. I recognized him as the same man who had threatened James at the alehouse." Leopold wiped his brow and exhaled. "After he killed James, he took off on his horse, and we pursued him. When we entered the dark forest, wolves appeared and attacked my steed. I'm sure he used black magic to summon the wolves since one of their powers was having wild animals attack people." He lowered his gaze. "I lost sight of him, and I had no choice but to retreat."

Edmund thought this story was absurd, but Leopold, a man of sound mind and great nobleness, would not pass off a ridiculous story as true unless he was confident of its validity. "I trust what you tell me is true, Sir Leopold."

"I swear to it, Your Majesty."

"Are any of those people still living? Did anyone else survive the attack?"

"There could be survivors who live in Cedarville. I instructed my men to go there after James' death to find the killer and other sorcerers but found no one." He paused and looked at Edmund. "Your Majesty, I believe some are still alive. There are rumors that Beth's mother Helena still lives, although Beth died in the attack."

"Is there a way to recognize them?" Edmund asked, rage growing within the depths of his soul.

"They wear a locket around their neck with stones that give them supernatural abilities. The man who threatened James had such a locket."

Edmund bolted from his seat. "The murderer— would you recognize him if you saw him?"

"If he still lives, I would. He had a severe burn mark on the side of his head and lost his right ear."

"Find these people and find the one who killed my father. They will all answer to his murder and their crimes of heresy. Twenty-two years may have passed, but my vengeance is new. Bring them to me to face their punishment. I shall finish what King Matthew started."

"Aye, Your Majesty." Leopold bowed and left the room.

Edmund tried to wrap his head around what he just learned. Before this day, everything made sense. He was the son of one of the greatest warriors who had ever lived, who died with honor. This day he discovered his father was murdered in his home by a man who practiced black magic. *If any of them live*, he vowed, *they will all pay with their lives.*

Edmund called Samuel and asked him to send Sir Quinn to the great hall. A few minutes later, Sir Quinn entered. He was one of King Edmund's elite knights who earned a seat at his table. Quinn, a fierce fighter of medium build with dark hair to his shoulder, displayed a deep scar on the right side of his face that he proudly earned fighting in the Battle of Somerville—one of Edmund's greatest conquests.

Quinn stood before Edmund. "You wished to see me, Your Majesty?"

"Go to Cedarville and find people who practice magic," Edmund ordered.

"Magic? Did I hear you correctly, Your Majesty?"

"I learned one of them killed my father. If he lives, I must find him. He's missing his right ear. Arrest anyone you find with this ability. They're all guilty of heresy. One of them may lead me to my father's killer."

"How can I identify them?"

"They wear a locket around their necks. You are to leave now. Make haste."

"Aye, Your Majesty." Quinn bowed and left the great room.

Edmund paced the room, his hands clenched, contemplating his next step. He found it difficult to remain still. Many years had gone by, and everyone had kept this horrible secret from him—his mother, Sir Leopold, and even King Matthew! He had to know more. He stopped, remembering his father's private chamber that remained unoccupied since his death.

He opened the door to a single large room with a bed, a cold fireplace, and minimal furnishings. The maidservant kept it tidy by dusting it daily and removing the cobwebs. Edmund approached the tall cedar chest, opened each drawer, and found clothes and undergarments that belonged to James. He walked over to the wardrobe, pulled the doors open, and found cloaks, outfits, and hats. There were boxes stored underneath the clothes. He opened them and saw memorabilia from battles fought: maps, knives, spurs. Rummaging through his father's personal things, gave Edmund an intimate feel for the man who was a legend to him. A sense of melancholy came over him. He drew a breath and continued searching. He didn't know what he was looking for but hoped to find something that would reveal who James was and give him a glimpse of the life he lived. *What secrets did Prince James Wadham keep?* he mused.

He shut the wardrobe door and scanned the room. His eyes came upon a table next to the bed where he saw a book and a small fairy statue. He glanced at the title. With curious eyes, he picked up *The Book of Secrets,* a black leather tome with gold lettering and three gold circles linked. Edmund skimmed through the book and, to his surprise, found the story about the people of Maiden Hills. His eyes widened. *It's interesting that I should find this here.*

Edmund took the book to his library, sat down at his desk, and began to read. There were stories of the magical people called Majians and how they came to be, and a young maiden named Majia, who appeared before them. There were spells to activate the enchanted gemstones, which gave them power, and instructions on healing with special herbs. *This is dripping with black magic.* His hands shook at the vile contained in these pages, but if it would help him in finding these people and destroying them, he had to continue. When he flipped to the final section called *Prophecies*, the blood left his body as he read the passage:

Two decades and two years following the massacre, more violence will occur, but a new leader and protector will emerge, and the Majian people will regain their power. The Majian people will triumph over their enemies and overthrow the king.

He closed the book. It had been twenty-two years since the attack. If the prophecy were true, the magical people who survived the massacre would organize and threaten his kingdom. King Matthew was right to attack, but his error was in allowing some of them to escape. *If these people still exist, I shall order an attack, but this time there shall be no survivors!*

Chapter 5

Somerville, a territory of the Kingdom of Yorkford, was located two hours northwest of Cedarville and was famous for housing the most extensive library in the region where books of records were maintained. When Jack entered, he saw several workers behind a large desk tending to patrons. He scanned the room. Volumes of books lay stacked on tables down several aisles. *Where do I start?* A young man with long white hair, stood behind the desk. Jack approached him. He thought it odd, for he had never seen white hair on a young man.

"Pardon me," he said.

"How may I assist you, my lord?" The man had a gentle smile and bright violet eyes.

"I seek information on an incident that occurred twenty-two years ago. Might you have information from that time?"

"Yes, my lord. Follow me, please."

The young man led Jack to an area with rows of long tables and large dusty books resting on them. "These are our books of records and contain descriptions of notable events by year. Is there a specific event you are interested in?"

"I am interested in the massacre that occurred in Maiden Hills twenty-two years ago."

"I know where you may find it." He walked to the far end of a wooden table and examined the titles until he found what he was looking for. He pulled out a large book, took a few steps to an empty table, and placed it down with a loud *thump*. Flipping through the pages, he stopped and pointed. "It's here." He tapped on the page. "Not much information."

Jack scanned the page. The brief paragraph described a battle with the Kingdom of Yorkford against the residents of Maiden Hills for the unlawful practice of black magic. The people of Maiden Hills, called Majians, were arrested, charged, tried by the Church of Yorkford, and found guilty of heresy. *Something's not right,* Jack thought. *From what I heard, it was not a battle, and no one ever mentioned a trial.*

He read aloud. "The village was destroyed to ensure the safety of the monarchy and eradicate all persons with the ability to practice magic. Two hundred people were killed during the battle, and there were no survivors." Baffled, he closed the book. "I had hoped for more answers than questions." Jack smiled at the young man. "Thank you for your assistance." He turned to leave.

"My lord," the young man called out. Jack stopped and turned. "If you wish to understand what happened in Maiden Hills, you may be interested to know what happened in Cromer."

Jack raised an eyebrow. "What happened there?"

"Over one hundred and thirty years ago, sorcerous people lived in a small village of Somerville called Cromer. These people practiced evil magic by casting spells and commanding people to obey them and harm others. The Cromers had the ability to turn themselves into animals, and they worshipped an evil spirit who gave them their powers. The Church of Somerville condemned the practice and called them heretics. The Cromers were charged with breaking the law, and they were brought to trial and found guilty. Their punishment was death by fire. Upon hearing of this, the kingdoms of Yorkford and Westmore put a law in place that forbade the practice of black magic, and anyone found practicing such sorcery would be guilty of heresy and be put to death."

"I heard a similar story about the Cromers when I was a child. I did not believe it to be true."

"Truly, it was. When the Majians from Maiden Hills were discovered using magic, the king of Yorkford suspected they were just like the Cromers and ordered his army to attack their village and burn their homes."

"He was justified by law," Jack said. "Or so he reasoned."

The young man nodded. "Yes, my lord."

"But Maiden Hills was not part of Yorkford."

"The crime of the people from Maiden Hills was against a member of Westmore's royal family," said the young man.

"Prince James?" Jack asked, brows furrowed.

The man nodded. "Yorkford was an ally of Westmore, and they came to his defense."

"I see." Jack looked at the man and smiled. "Thank you. You have been most helpful." Jack walked away but then reflected on something the man had said—*What was the crime committed against Prince James?*

He turned to ask the man, but he was gone. His eyes swept the area, but there was no sight of him. *There was no way he could have walked past me*, he wondered, scratching his head.

A middle-aged woman with gray hair sat at the large table in the library's foyer.

"Madam, I wish to speak to the young man who assisted me a short time ago," Jack said. "He was young with long white hair."

"Forgive me, my lord, alas, no one employed here matches that description. We are all of advanced age."

Jack was bewildered. *Where did he come from?* He scanned the room as he walked out, hoping to spot the mysterious young man.

Jack rode to his castle and searched his library for the Kingdom of Yorkford Book of Law. He opened it and flipped through the pages until he found the section *Acts of Heresy*:

The following are considered acts against the Kingdom of Yorkford, and offenders must stand trial and, if found guilty, punished by execution.

Jack slid his finger down the middle of the page, then turned the page. He continued scanning the headings until he found the section called *Magic*. He read the law:

The practice of magic performed is forbidden in all its forms when done for evil purposes or with evil spirits. This is commonly referred to as black magic. Especially prohibited are fortune-telling, sorcery, omens, witchcraft, casting spells, mediums, psychics, or calling forth spirits of the dead. Any person using supernatural powers to threaten the existence of the clergy or monarchy or any of its members is black magic, and offenders will be put to death by sword or fire.

He closed the book. *Was Prince James threatened?*

***

Later that afternoon, Jack met Robert at the local tavern. They sat at the counter where the barkeep dispensed two pints of beer and placed it in front of them. Boisterous talking and laughter filled the crowded pub. Through the uproar, several women on the opposite end with broad smiles managed to catch Jack's attention. He smiled and lifted his mug.

"The women love you here," Robert said.

Jack chuckled. "This was a common scene when traveling for jousting tournaments. They just want a smile."

"I think they want more than a smile." Robert grinned. "Was there someone special back home?"

Juliana came to mind, the only woman who had his heart. "There was one."

"There's always one." Robert gulped his beer.

"Robert, I consulted the Book of Law. Your magic is not considered illegal unless it is for evil purposes or threatens the clergy or monarchy. They put the law in place after what happened in Cromer."

"Our powers are not evil." Robert paused for a drink. "We were given the gift to protect the kingdom *against* evil—against the Cromers should they rise again."

"Rise again? Are there survivors?"

Robert nodded. "I believe there are survivors."

Jack furrowed his brow. "Are you implying there could be a magical war?"

"It's quite possible."

Jack swallowed a mouthful of beer and wiped his mouth with the back of his hand. "If anyone else had told me that, I would have thought they had gone mad."

Not wanting to consider the possibility of evil beings rising, he turned his attention to Robert's treatment and the miraculous healing. "Robert, the herbs you used to heal me, were they magical?"

"They were. Conventional medicine is limited. You most likely would have died from the infection."

Jack let out a huge breath, then guzzled the rest of the beer. He motioned the barkeep for another pint. "I am grateful you found me."

"So am I."

Jack remembered the words of the mysterious young man in the library. "Robert, do you know if Prince James was threatened?"

"Lord Jack!"

Before Robert could answer, Sir Quinn shouted from the other side of the bar and strolled toward Jack, red-faced with beer spilling from his mug as he shouldered his way through the thick crowd.

"Surprised to see you, Lord Jack." He clapped Jack's shoulder with a gloved hand.

"Sir Quinn, no one is more surprised than me to see you here. What business brings you to Cedarville?"

"I wanted to check out the village. Beer is good, but not much more to it," he sneered.

"I disagree. It's a fine place," Jack said.

"Why are you here, Lord Jack? This is a wretched town. You're one of The Magnificent Knights, raised as a prince. You should have much better land than this." Quinn's words slurred.

"I like this one just fine."

"You're wasting your time. There's nothing here, just a bunch of peasants."

Robert swallowed his beer and glared at Quinn. "If you don't like it, you can leave." His voice cut through the chatter in the tavern, halting conversations. All eyes were on Robert, Jack, and Quinn.

Quinn staggered around Jack to get to Robert. Jack stood, blocking his path. "Back off, Quinn—you're drunk."

Quinn put his hand on his dagger. "I want this man to tell me again to leave."

Robert gulped his beer, slammed down the mug, then turned toward Quinn and said with a firm tone. "Leave!"

Quinn pulled the knife from its sheath and lunged toward Robert. In an instant, the blade bolted out of Quinn's hand and struck the wall across the bar. There were stunned looks among the patrons.

With wide eyes, Quinn stared at his empty hand, then at the knife far ahead buried in the wood. He drew his sword, but before he could point it at Robert, the sword left his hand and floated above Quinn.

Jack stared open-mouthed at the floating sword.

Sir Quinn jumped up, reaching for his weapon, but each time the sword floated higher. The patrons roared with laughter. Then Quinn floated up into the air, arms flailing, terror in his eyes. Gasps filled the tavern.

Quinn's face turned ashen. "Put me down, put me down!"

Jack cringed. He turned to Robert and gave him a grave look.

Quinn fell to the ground with a *thump*. He scrambled to his feet and slurred, "It's the killer! It's Prince James' killer!" He glanced around with bulging eyes, then darted out of the tavern, stumbling, shoving patrons along the way.

Jack was sure of what Quinn muttered under his breath—*Edmund knows the truth about his father!* He grabbed Quinn's sword floating downward, then rushed across the tavern, removing the dagger buried in the wall.

Robert caught up to him. "I'm sorry, Jack, but he brought it upon himself."

"You are not to blame, for you had to defend yourself, but we have a new king—King Edmund— Prince James' son. King Edmund knows a Majian murdered his father. He will hear about this."

***

It had been a fortnight since Edmund sent Quinn to look for magical people in Cedarville with no word, and his patience was thinning. He anxiously paced through the castle halls, snapping at everyone who crossed his path, barking orders, and locking himself in his solar. Edmund asked not to be disturbed and delegated his steward, Samuel, to handle most of his affairs. He grumbled throughout the castle, "Has anyone seen Sir Quinn or Sir Leopold?" Frightened heads shook. The anticipation gnawed at him.

At suppertime, Edmund and Juliana sat at the large oak table, chewing their meat and washing it down with wine, repeating the process without a glance or a word toward each other.

"Pass the salt," said Juliana. Edmund took the tin shaker and slammed it on the table.

"You seem distressed. Is something amiss?" she asked.

"Leading a kingdom this vast is not easy, Juliana. I have a lot on my mind." He washed down the venison with a gulp of wine.

"Is there something I should know? It's my kingdom too."

"No." He was curt.

She let out a heavy sigh. "Fine." They continued their meal in silence.

Early the next morning, sitting behind his desk, Edmund dipped his quill in ink and signed his name on a parchment. It was tedious work he could not delegate to Samuel, for he had to approve all new laws. He placed his seal on a glob of wax on the parchment and transferred it to a wooden box. He picked up the next document but was distracted when Sir Quinn entered the library disheveled and red-faced, apparently recovering from a night of excessive drinking.

Edmund rolled his eyes and shook his head. He was well aware that Quinn enjoyed drinking and regularly frequented taverns, but the drinking often got him into trouble as the alcohol made him argumentative and careless with his words.

Quinn stood tall. "Forgive my intrusion, Your Majesty. May I speak?"

Edmund returned his attention to the document. "I sent you on an important assignment, Quinn, not to indulge in your vices."

"But, Your Majesty, if I may, I have important information for you."

He stopped writing and picked up his eyes. "What do you have?"

"A man used magic on me in a tavern last night in Cedarville."

Edmund put the quill in the holder and stared at Quinn. "Are you certain of what you saw?"

"I am."

"Were you drunk?"

"I may have had too much to drink, but I am certain of what I saw, Your Majesty."

Edmund fell back in his chair and crossed his arms. "Did anyone else see?"

"Yes, Your Majesty, the tavern was full of patrons. I did not wish to believe it, but he disarmed me without touching me or my weapons, and then I was floating in the air. I thought I would die. Everyone in the tavern laughed."

Edmund leaned forward. "Did you get his name?"

"Apologies, Your Majesty, I was terrified and failed to obtain his name."

"Did he wear a locket around his neck?"

"He did. When I was floating in the air, I saw it. Also, you will find it interesting to know that Lord Jack was with him."

Edmund furrowed his brow. "Jack Mauntell? I forgot about him." Edmund recalled King Matthew had granted Jack lordship over Cedarville when he was betrothed to Juliana. Matthew was clever, and Edmund reasoned he planned it to ensure Jack would not interfere in Edmund or Juliana's life. "Is he associating with those people?" Edmund did not need another reason to dislike Jack.

"Lord Jack and the man appeared friendly. Your Majesty, the man at the tavern was about forty. Do you suppose he was the one that killed your father?"

"It's possible." He leaned forward. "Leopold can identify him. I sent him there to find my father's killer. Was he missing an ear?"

"I could not tell. His hair covered his ears, and it was dark in the tavern."

At that moment, Sir Leopold rushed in the library, panting. "Pardon me, Your Majesty." He stopped to catch his breath and was about to speak when he eyed Quinn. He held back his words and straightened his posture.

"You may speak freely, Sir Leopold. Did you find my father's murderer?"

"No, Your Majesty, but there is gossip in Cedarville that last night a man in a tavern used magic on a visitor who was causing trouble."

"That was me, Sir Leopold. I was the visitor causing trouble." Quinn's prideful face turned red with embarrassment.

Edmund clenched his fist, anxious to have a lead on the evil sorcerers responsible for his father's death. "Sir Leopold, go to Cedarville and tell the townspeople to surrender the man that used sorcery on Sir Quinn. The practice is forbidden, and the man must stand trial. They must do this by midday tomorrow, or there will be consequences. Take a few men with you, including Quinn. He might recognize the man from among the people."

"Your Majesty, should we inform Lord Jack?" asked Leopold.

"He will hear the decree, and as the lord of Cedarville, he will know what he must do." Edmund was eager to test Jack's allegiance.

"Aye, Your Majesty." Both men bowed and left the room.

***

Jack rode his destrier, Dex, through the packed village and arrived at the tavern for his noon beer. He dismounted, and a young squire pulled Dex by his reins and led him to the stables behind the inn. Midday saw the town of Cedarville bustling with villagers packing into the local alehouses and taverns for food and drinks, and others entering the merchants' stores for needed supplies. Horses pulled carriages on the paved road, and drivers assisted the women and the old from the shaky transport to the steady ground. The townspeople sat in the village square on benches soaking in the warm sun, enjoying the balmy breeze, eating, drinking, and playing games. Boisterous conversation and laughter filled the square, as was a typical afternoon in the village.

Jack sat at the counter inside the crowded pub across from the village square, swallowing his beer as patrons shouted out orders to the barkeep. Jeb, the tavern owner, worked feverishly on the other side of the counter, removing used mugs and placing them in wooden bins to send to the washroom.

"Are you ready for another pint, Lord Jack?" Jeb asked, wiping his brow.

"I shall be ready in a minute." Jack smiled and gulped the rest of the beer.

Jeb acted as the town's official spokesman, and Jack relied on him for reports on the activities of the village. The people trusted Jeb, and he was often present at town meetings to speak on their behalf. Jeb poured beer into a mug and placed it before Jack.

"This is the best beer in the kingdom," Jeb said with a proud smile. He was twenty-eight years old with auburn hair, hazel green eyes, and a smile that reminded Jack of Juliana, but then many things reminded Jack of Juliana.

Three months passed since he moved to Cedarville, and Juliana remained imprinted on his mind. Seeing her at King Matthew's wake three weeks ago brought back deep feelings, and he yearned to be with her, to tell her how he felt about her, but it was not to be. He had received word of the royal wedding from the townspeople who traveled to Yorkford to witness the historic event. Jack had decided not to attend. Although he would have had a seat at the dais among the nobility, he could not bear to see Juliana as Edmund's bride. It was a life he had left behind and would not turn back.

A young maiden sat next to Jack, smiling and twirling her blond curls. Her light blue dress revealed an ample bosom and a tiny waist. "I just love what you're doing to this town, Lord Jack." Her green eyes captivated him. "People are so much happier."

"I'm happy I'm able to make a difference," Jack said above the roar of the tavern.

"Pardon?" She leaned forward within inches of Jack. He breathed in and enjoyed taking in the scent of her rose perfume. For a moment, he welcomed the closeness. Jack had never courted a woman—his heart belonged to only one. But now, with Juliana out of his life, he had considered it from time to time.

Jack's attention turned toward the front of the tavern when a lad forcefully pushed the door open and darted his eyes until he spotted Jack. He hurried toward him, panting. "Lord Jack, there's a group of knights from Yorkford in the village square."

Jack, bewildered, walked out of the tavern, an uneasy sensation forming in the pit of his stomach, and to his surprise, saw Sir Leopold, Sir Quinn, and five other knights on horseback. After the incident in the tavern last night with Robert and Quinn, the visit was not unexpected.

The outdoor crowd activity dwindled until all was silent. This was an unusual sight in Cedarville, as they had never seen the king's men in their small village.

Jack stood by the door of the tavern with arms crossed and eyes fixed on Leopold. Jeb stood beside him.

Leopold spoke to the crowd. "May I have your attention, my good people of Cedarville?" They all turned to look at him, and some edged closer to get a better view. "We are here at the request of your king, His Majesty, King Edmund of Yorkford." Whispers and mutterings grew within the crowd. "It has come to his attention that among you is a man who practices sorcery. The king has requested that the town of Cedarville deliver this man at once to stand trial for heresy." Audible gasps erupted. "You have until midday tomorrow to comply with this request. If the town does not surrender this man, there will be consequences. That is all."

Jack's eyes locked with Leopold's for a moment before Leopold turned his horse and led the men out of Cedarville.

There were murmurs among the villagers.

Someone shouted out, "It's the doctor."

"We should turn him over to the king," said a villager.

"No, we should refuse. The doctor has done nothing wrong."

"You heard him—magic is against the law. It's heresy."

"What he did was not heresy. He was defending himself."

The crowd was getting into a heated debate, with each side clinging to their own verdict.

"No one is turning anyone over to the king." The crowd hushed. Jack spoke loud and with unwavering resolve. "We must protect our people. Doctor Robert is a fine man."

"But there will be consequences!" someone shouted.

"We must obey the king," someone else said. "He has authority over us. We must obey the laws of the kingdom."

"The knights will attack and kill us all."

"Then we shall defend ourselves. I will not have the people of Cedarville turn against each other," Jack said. "We must do what is right and protect the innocent."

Jeb spoke up. "Remember, Doctor Robert has helped every one of you. If not for him, most of you would be dead. I'm with Lord Jack. We must stick together. Who's with us?"

There were cheers, some more emphatic than others, but the unconvinced faces thought it best not to go against the crowd.

Jeb turned to Jack and leaned closer. "Lord Jack, can you appeal to King Edmund?"

Jack shook his head. "It will amount to nothing, for I know him well. There's a long history between us."

"What about Her Majesty, the queen?" Jeb asked. "I hear she's compassionate. She may be able to speak on our behalf."

Jack thought of Juliana, and his heart ached. He sighed. "There's a long history there too." He turned to Jeb. "We're on our own."

***

"Edmund, the rugs in the great hall are dingy, and I wish to replace them in time for the Festival of Flowers. We need to brighten up the room and replace the old drapes as well." Juliana lifted the chicken leg and took a bite.

Edmund stared into the distance, chewing his meal and washing it down with red wine. He heard his wife's chattering, but the words were indistinct, for his mind was elsewhere.

"Edmund, are you listening?"

He came back to the present. "Do whatever you wish." He rose from his seat, wiped his mouth, and threw the napkin on the plate, leaving Juliana by herself in the dining room.

It was midday, the appointed hour. Edmund entered the library and shut the door. Leopold and Quinn quickly rose from their chairs. "Has Cedarville surrendered the man?"

"Alas, Your Majesty, they have not," said Leopold.

Edmund's face reddened. "They have made a grave mistake, and we have no choice but to attack. They will learn to obey my orders."

"But Lord Jack is there," Quinn said. "Shall we speak to him?"

"He heard the decree and chose to disobey. He betrayed us."

"How many men shall we send?" asked Leopold.

"Gather an army of fifty men. They have one hundred fighters, but they'll be caught unaware. Do some damage and make it swift. That will send a message to the villagers and Lord Jack. Order them once more to turn over the man, or we shall return, but next time the consequences will be severe."

"When shall we attack Your Majesty?" Leopold asked.

"Suppertime."

They heard a sound, and all heads turned toward the door. Edmund rushed and pulled open the door. He scanned the hall but saw no one. "Search the area. I believe someone may have spied on us."

Chapter 6

On the way to the courtyard, Juliana grumbled, furious at Edmund for leaving her alone in the dining room. *Why must I put up with this behavior?* She fretted. *I am trying to be a good wife, but he makes it impossible!* Juliana passed Edmund's library, where the voices of Edmund and his knights muffled behind the closed door. This was common since he often met with them to plan and strategize, but she halted when they mentioned Jack's name. She pressed her ear to the door, and her body turned cold when Edmund gave the order to attack Jack's village at suppertime.

From inside the library, footsteps stomped toward her. Juliana quickly hid behind a dark alcove as Edmund's men walked by. She held her breath.

"I see no one," Leopold said.

She didn't know the reason for it, but it didn't matter, she had to warn Jack. Juliana leaned forward, glanced in both directions—the men were not in sight. She rushed up the castle stairs, lifting her beige silk dress, and arrived at the great chamber.

Liza's arms held a large basket with laundered clothes when she caught sight of Juliana hastening. "Is everything all right, Your Majesty?"

"All is well, Liza. If anyone asks for me, tell them I went for a ride." She reached in her wardrobe for her emerald green cloak, draped it over her shoulders, and ran down the stairs.

Juliana passed the bailey and turned toward the stable to retrieve her horse, Millie, a graceful white palfrey. She had never been to Cedarville but knew the path was south through the dark forest. A queasiness entered her stomach, for she had never taken a long trip by herself without a guard and never through the frightful forest. She mounted her horse and quickly left the castle grounds.

The ample trees in the dark forest blotted out the warmth of the late afternoon sunlight, and Juliana's fingers and face grew numb as she hastened her pace. It would be near suppertime by the time she arrived in Cedarville. The thought of seeing Jack was exhilarating, eclipsing the fear of riding by herself, and she rode faster. Three hours later, she crossed a small bridge and entered the village. The castle was not in sight. Her heartbeat quickened as she darted her eyes, looking for signs pointing toward the castle. She turned and soon reached an area where merchants were closing the doors of their small wooden shops, and townspeople headed home to prepare their supper meals.

She stopped a young woman carrying a basket of bread. "Pardon me, young maiden, might you know the location of the baron's castle?"

"My lady, you must turn back and make a left. It's behind the large trees."

Juliana followed the woman's directions, and when she passed the trees, the manor came into view. She sighed, relieved, and rode faster.

Once she reached the entrance, Juliana came down from her horse and ran toward the door.

A young maidservant greeted her. "May I help you, my lady?"

Juliana removed her hood. "I am Queen Juliana of Yorkford. Please inform Lord Jack I wish to speak to him and make haste. It is of grave importance."

"Your Majesty, forgive me for not recognizing you." The maidservant curtsied. "Please come in. Welcome to Lord Jack's castle. My name is Audrey. I shall fetch Lord Jack for you at once."

Audrey led Juliana into the great room, and Juliana sat on a soft red velvet couch. She rubbed her cold, trembling hands, blistered from the horse's reins. Her nerves were jittery. She took in a long breath, trying to control her anxiety. A few minutes later, a surprised Jack approached her. Juliana stood up and smiled at seeing Jack, then her smile faded and turned to worry.

"Juliana, what brings you here? Is something amiss?"

Juliana took a deep breath. "I have come to warn you, for Edmund ordered his men to attack Cedarville at suppertime. You must be ready."

"Are you certain?"

"I am. I overheard him speaking with his knights in the library. Do you know what this is about?"

Jack nodded. "I do. I will alert my knights and the villagers. We shall be ready for them."

Jack grabbed his sword and his cloak. Juliana remained still. "Juliana, but I must leave to warn the others. Please return to Yorkford."

"I suppose I should." Juliana's legs did not move. She missed Jack, and he was right there in front of her. She wanted to stay with him longer.

Jack approached her. "Juliana, you must leave in haste, for if Edmund's men find you here, they will tell Edmund, and he will know it was you who warned me."

"But Jack, I—"

Jack put his finger on her lips. He stared into her eyes. "I shall be fine. I know what I must do. Please go."

Juliana watched as Jack hurried toward the courtyard leading to the stable. She hated to admit it, but he was right. She had to return to the castle. Edmund was her husband, and she betrayed him by alerting Jack of the attack. But she could not sit by and do nothing. Jack was important to her.

She rode Millie through the forest, tightening her cloak. The galloping of her horse and the howling of wolves were the only sound until the faint thunder of horses' hooves emerged in the distance. Night fell, and the full moon illuminated the dark forest enough for her to see a small mounted army heading her way.

It's Edmund's men! I can't let them see me. Juliana feared it would be impossible to avoid them, for they would see Millie's white coat glowing against the brilliance of the full moon. She remembered Jack had a cottage in the forest that he used for hunting and falconry. He had taken her there a few years ago to teach her to shoot an arrow. The memory lived vividly in her mind, and she hadn't realized back then how special those moments were. But now, she had to act without hesitation. *I hope I remember how to get to the cottage.*

Juliana pressed her heels into the horse's side, urging her forward. Chancing a glance behind her, Juliana gasped. The soldiers were gaining on her. Millie dashed through the forest, but Jack's cottage was not in sight.

Juliana stopped and quickly darted her eyes. A fork in the path lay ahead of her. She reacted, jerking her reins to the left. Suddenly, arrows flew toward her. *They're shooting at me!* The fear engulfed her, and she spurred Millie ahead.

Millie pivoted, avoiding a low-hanging branch. Juliana lost her grip, fell from the horse, and landed her head on a tree stump.

Darkness.

***

Edmund sat by the central hearth, contemplating the attack on the small village of Cedarville. His expertise in battle wasn't necessary, but Edmund enjoyed combat. He had fought in battles ever since he was a young lad and developed a hunger for it. He recalled charging toward his adversaries, blood pumping at high speed throughout his body, steel in his hand, slicing, and jabbing everyone in his path. It made him feel alive.

He swallowed his wine when, from the corner of his eye, he spotted Sir Paul, a young knight with blond hair, carrying Juliana. He bolted from his seat, alarmed. "What happened?"

"She fell from her horse and lost consciousness."

"Lay her on the couch." Edmund placed his hand on the back of her head and found a lump the size of a small child's fist. He put his hand on her chest as it expanded with each breath. "Where did you find her?"

"She was in the dark forest, Your Majesty. We spotted her north of the Cedarville Bridge. She may have gone for a ride and lost her way. Shall I carry her to the great chamber?"

"No, leave her here. You are to go to Cedarville and join the others in the attack."

"Aye, Your Majesty." Paul bowed and departed.

Edmund stared at his wife, motionless on the couch. She had guards with her whenever she went for a ride, but she never rode through the dark forest, preferring the hills and valleys of the north.

There's only one reason she would go to the dark forest unaccompanied, Edmund realized—*to see Jack*. He recalled following Juliana at King Matthew's wake and seeing her sitting in the garden next to Jack with his arm around her. She and Jack were close, and he suspected they had an attraction for each other.

He called Samuel. "Fetch the dungeon guard."

A few minutes later, the dungeon guard appeared before Edmund. He was a big man with a black beard, mustache, and black hair, most of it concealed by a hood that covered his head, neck, and shoulders. "You called for me, Your Majesty?"

"Throw her in a cell." He directed the man's eyes toward Juliana lying on the couch. "But be discreet. No one is to know she is there." *That will teach her a lesson*, he told himself.

"Forgive me, Your Majesty, but you wish for me to lock the queen in a dungeon cell?"

"That was my command!"

The guard faltered. "As you wish, Your Majesty." The large man picked up Juliana and draped her over his shoulder. He carried her two levels below through the narrow winding stairs toward the dungeon.

***

Jack stood with his men by the bridge, some with swords and shields, and others with bows and arrows, waiting for Edmund's men. Soon the thumping of hooves shook the ground, and a small army charged toward them.

Jack's knights were ready with their weapons raised. "Hold, and wait for my command," said Jack. He turned to Robert and nodded.

Yorkford's knights reached the creek, and to their astonishment, dozens of alligators crawled from below the muddy brook, blocking the bridge, and snapping their jaws. The horses stopped straightaway, lifting their front legs, neighing, avoiding the alligator's powerful chops.

Jack smiled.

"Loose the arrows!" commanded Sir Leopold.

The men hurled their arrows toward the alligators, but as the arrows flew toward them, more alligators appeared from beneath the water.

"The bridge is impassable!" a Yorkford knight yelled.

"Loose!" came the order from Lord Jack.

The arrows flew toward Edmund's army. The men lifted their shields, then shot back, but the horses, surrounded by the alligators, staggered, preventing the men from hitting their target.

The soldiers in Edmund's army cried out as the alligators continued to crawl out of the creek. Horses reared up, their panicked neighing ringing out, ditching the riders. The men ran after their horses, and Edmund's men could do nothing but retreat.

Jack raised his fist in victory. His fighters cheered.

**

Juliana opened her eyes. She blinked, bringing her surroundings into focus. Light shone in through the window above her head from the bright full moon in view. She could make out a room made of cold gray stones, a small window with black metal bars, and to her left a locked, barred gate. *Where am I?*

Her head throbbed, assaulting her between the temples. She touched the back of her head and winced when a lump as big as her hand caused immeasurable pain. Her beige silk dress was soiled and torn. She wrapped her emerald green cloak around her, grimacing from the aches in her body as she rose to her feet.

Footsteps in the distance reverberated, echoing louder as they approached. When they stopped, a large hooded man with a black beard and round belly stood at the gate. The candlelight illuminated his scarred, weathered face. He inserted an iron key in the lock, swung the gate open, and placed a metal tray on the cement floor.

"I have come with supper," he said, his voice deep.

The light from the candle brightened the room, and Juliana gasped! *This is a dungeon cell!* She looked up at the large bearded man as she rubbed the back of her head, wincing. "Why am I here?"

"I was ordered to bring you here." He stared at Juliana, and his voice softened. "Are you all right, Your Majesty?"

"Your Majesty?" Juliana tilted her head. "Why did you call me Your Majesty?"

"Why, you're the queen, of course!"

She blinked. "I'm the queen? No, my mother's the queen." She tried to make sense of the situation, but it was no use. "My head hurts, and I am struggling to think. What happened?"

"You were unconscious."

"But why was I brought here?"

92

"Alas, I do not know." He walked toward the gate, closed it, and turned the key. "Forgive me, Your Majesty."

Juliana ran toward the gate and watched the candlelight fade. Her hands slowly slid down the bars.

She sat on the cold stone floor and reached for the metal tray. A leg of chicken, vegetable soup, and bread, were a welcome sight, grumblings stirred in her stomach. She took a piece of bread and dipped it in the broth, and the warmth of the soaked bread trickled down her throat. Her arms and legs had scattered dark blue spots and bloodied scrapes that had dried. *What happened to me?* The lump on her head produced unbearable pain, and tears filled her eyes.

The brilliant full moon had moved out of view and left her in darkness. She gazed up, and only the brightest stars peered through the hazy sky. Chills permeated throughout her body, and she rubbed her arms underneath her green velvet cloak. She could do nothing but pace.

She turned her head at the faint echo of footsteps. She listened intently as they approached. Heavy boots pounded the ground, forceful and commanding, unlike the bearded man's steps.

The gate opened, and a different man appeared—a younger man, dressed like a nobleman with fine clothing, raven black hair, and a clean-shaven face. From the light of the oil lamp, Juliana noticed his stern expression. Her nerves shook as he approached her.

He glared at her and held the oil lamp a few inches from her face. "What were you doing in the forest?"

"Forest?" Juliana tried to think, but her mind was devoid of thoughts or images. "I hurt my head and remember nothing."

His hand whipped across her face. "Liar! You were warning your lover."

The impact of the back of his hand burned her face and sent her to the concrete floor. The pounding from her head and the sting on her cheek disoriented Juliana, and she lay still, waiting for the room to stop moving.

He placed the oil lamp on the floor, hoisted her up, and pulled her toward him. His massive hands dug into her thin arms. She squirmed, trying to free herself from his grasp.

"You betrayed me!" he bellowed.

"I don't know what you speak of," Juliana said. "I demand you unhand me!"

He gripped her arms tighter and shook her. "Look at me!"

Juliana stared into the eyes of the stranger in front of her. "Who are you? What do you want with me? I demand you take me to my father!"

He narrowed his eyes and squeezed her harder. "You don't know me?"

She grimaced. "No, and I am not keen on being hit or manhandled."

He stared at her with piercing gray eyes. Juliana saw a familiarity, but her brain was not connecting the face to a memory.

She struggled to free herself from his grasp. "Let me go. You are hurting me."

He continued to stare at her. "What would you gain by denying you know me?" He released her, and she stumbled onto the floor. "You will remain here until your memory returns."

He picked up the oil lamp and stomped out of the cell. He banged the gate shut, turned the key, and the light dimmed.

Juliana rubbed her arms where his fingers had dug into her and paced the length of the small cell. She wished to be free, and she needed answers. Her memory failed her, but she knew she didn't belong there. *My name is Juliana, and I am a princess. I live in a castle with my father, King Matthew, and my mother, Queen Lucinda. God, that's all I know. What happened to me? Why can't I remember?*

A short time later, surrounded by darkness, a soft click by the gate roused her. Juliana remained still, trying to identify the sound, then it quieted. She suspected it was a rodent scurrying for food, but then the soft screech of metal on metal and the moan of a gate hinge caused her heart to palpitate.

"Is someone there?" she called out, her voice quivering. She backed away and leaned against the wall.

Faint steps crept toward her. Her heart thumped violently, about to burst. Just then, a hand covered her mouth. Her eyes opened wide, and she let out a muffled gasp.

"Do not be afraid. I will get you out of here," a voice whispered. "Do not scream."

She nodded her head at the shadowy figure next to her. He released his hand from her mouth.

She whispered. "Who are you?"

"Jack."

"I knew a young boy named Jack. I'm sorry, but my head hurt, and I have no memory. Are you a friend?"

"I am. Don't worry, you can trust me."

Something about his voice was reassuring. "All... all right."

"Please follow me. We must be quiet. There could be people lurking."

Jack halted suddenly at the sound of faint footsteps and stretched his arm, gently pushing Juliana against the wall. They remained frozen until the stomping faded.

Jack, peering cautiously, picked up the candle by the gate, dropped the key, and grabbed her hand. He led her through the dungeon halls then through a hidden door leading to a narrow and wet passage. The candlelight illuminated a few feet, just enough to see their path and avoid stepping on rodents and other dungeon dwellers.

Trailing behind him, Juliana stared at Jack. He was a handsome young man, strong and lean. There was something familiar about him, but she struggled to recognize the face. The Jack she remembered was a child, not a man.

"You seem to know your way around here," she said. "Do you live here?"

"I lived here until a few months ago. My friend and I played in the dungeon when we were children. We discovered the secret passageway." He smiled.

"The other man, does he know the secret passageway?"

"What man?"

"A tall man came to see me. He was terrible and mean. I fear of what he will do if he finds us."

"Edmund." He seemed sure of it. "I believe he is not aware of the secret path. He never played with us when we were children. He was older and proper and not much fun to be around." Jack grinned.

"How long have we been friends?"

Jack glanced at her. "Since we were six years old."

This had to be her young friend Jack. Had she forgotten all her years? Had they simply vanished from her memory? "I wish I could remember." She thought about the man named Edmund. "Why did Edmund lock me in the cell? Who is he? The name sounds familiar."

Jack turned to look at her. "He's the king, Juliana—he's your husband."

"M-my husband?" She wrinkled her brow. "But I am not married." She shook her head. "Nothing makes sense. Where are my parents?"

"Juliana, try to relax. Once your memory returns, which I hope it will soon, everything will make sense... at least, most of it."

After some time, Juliana sensed a change in the air, and the mustiness was fading. Jack held her hand as he led her up muddy steps, and soon her damp shoes pressed onto prickly grass. She inhaled, grateful for the clean air. Large trees loomed over the dark wooded area, and near the opening of the passageway, a brown steed stood tall. Juliana turned to see the flickering lights of the castle a safe distance away.

"Do you have the strength to climb on the horse?" Jack asked.

"I think I do." She put her left foot in the stirrup, and holding on to the reins, she lifted her right leg but could not swing it over the horse.

"Allow me to help you." Jack lifted Juliana with care until she was seated on the horse. He climbed on behind her, pulled the reins, and kicked his horse into motion.

They rode for several miles through the dark forest with the light of the full moon filtering through the tree branches and brightening their path. They arrived at a small cottage in the middle of the woods, a long way from the castle, the howling of the wolves echoing for miles. Jack dismounted and helped Juliana down from the horse and led her inside the cottage where a fire burned. He tossed wood into the fireplace as Juliana sat in front of it, cupping her hands and blowing warm air, thawing her fingers. She eyed the room, simply furnished with a couch, a table, two chairs, and a bed in an alcove. In a corner, leaning against the wall, were bows, arrows, and hunting knives.

"Is this your home?"

"It's my second home. I live in the next town, but I come here a few times a week to hunt and train my falcons."

Juliana winced, and touched her head. "Why can't I remember?"

"Permit me to inspect the bruise." He examined the back of her head, and she grimaced when he touched it. "My apologies for causing pain. I am no doctor, but the swelling may be affecting the part of your brain that remembers. Once the swelling goes down, your memory shall return. Allow it some time to heal, but in the meantime, you can stay here and rest. You are safe here."

"Thank you, Jack." She smiled.

Jack rose from his seat. "I have something that belongs to you. Can you come outside?" Juliana nodded, and Jack led her to the other side of the cottage, where a white palfrey stood tall. "Do you recognize her?"

"She's beautiful." Juliana stroked her mane. "Is she mine?"

"She is, her name is Millie. I found her here last night. She must have come here after they captured you, which is why I suspected you might be in trouble."

"I am happy she is well." Juliana smiled, then she felt the warmth leave her face, and her legs became unsteady. They buckled. Jack grabbed her before she hit the ground.

"Come, I shall take you inside so you can lie down."

He swooped her up and carried her petite figure into the cottage. She wrapped her arms around his neck and stared deep into his eyes, seeing a familiarity in the blue gaze she had seen many times before, but now a thick fog covered those memories.

Jack lay Juliana on a bed made of straw wrapped in linen and covered her with a warm wool blanket. The pounding in her head continued as her eyelids came down. Jumbled images in a nonsensical pattern crowded her mind. Pictures floated until they came together, forming recognizable faces. Her mother appeared, Lucinda, a lovely woman with dark auburn hair just like hers, but her face was pale, and her eyes drooped. She saw her mother lying on a bed in a darkened room with dark-blue drapes.

"We come from a long line of magical people... These are our magical stones... You need to find the book... It's called The Book of Secrets... I hid it in the castle, below, in the dungeon... I saw white stripes on his black horse's hind legs... He killed my father.... It was a prophecy that came true... You must help save

our people... Find Simon... Learn the spells... Give me your word you will do this."

Juliana abruptly opened her eyes and stared at the ceiling. She had pushed the story her mother had told her six years ago deep into the back of her mind, but now the memories returned, vividly recalling every detail. The bruise in her head scattered her memory, but the first thoughts of her mother were of a woman Juliana did not recognize. Had she gone mad with talks of magic spells and prophecies, or was it true? She shook her head, and it throbbed. It was absurd. There was no such thing as magic. People who claimed to practice it were sentenced to death.

Juliana slept a few more hours and woke up to a soft breeze coming through the window and the patter of light rain falling on swaying leaves. She touched the back of her head and noticed the lump had receded, although still tender. Her eyes searched the room and stopped when she spotted Jack sleeping on a couch by the fireplace. Her memories were coming back to her. She smiled to herself. *If you only knew how much I missed you, Jack.*

She and Jack were inseparable growing up in the castle. He had gone away for two years to train to become a knight, and she remembered how tortuous those years were without him. She never told him how much he meant to her and how alone she felt without him.

My parents are gone, and I have a husband who ignores me—a sad reality for Juliana as the regained memories washed over her. Juliana played the role of a wife and queen of Yorkford well, but she often thought of Jack. The rebellious nature she exhibited in childhood would threaten to resurface, and the idea of escaping the confines of the castle to see Jack ran through her mind, but she restrained herself. That changed last night when she overheard Edmund talking to Sir Leopold and Sir Quinn about attacking Cedarville. She had to warn Jack, even if it meant betraying her husband.

Juliana went back to staring at the ceiling. Her memory was returning, but she had so many questions. Why did Edmund attack Cedarville, what happened during the attack, and worst of all, what was he going to do to her once he found out she escaped from the dungeon?

Chapter 7

Jack rose with the sun and glanced over at Juliana asleep in the alcove. *How is it that you're back in my life?* He shook his head. He gathered his bow and arrows, slung the quiver over his back, and stepped out as the fresh, crisp air stroked his face. He inhaled the scent of luscious pine trees circling the cottage that had become his escape from the pressures of training. Knight training was arduous, and only the most skillful squires would become knights, but he had to balance himself from the rigor and discipline, and the forest was the place to unwind in total solitude.

He strolled over to the mews and signaled the falcons to hunt while he searched for wood. He gathered grains, fed the horses, and gave them drinking water from a barrel he used to collect rainwater. Fortunately, it rained while they slept.

With bow and arrow in hand, Jack stood still, staring at a deer grazing a few yards away. He nocked the arrow, careful not to make a sound, aimed, and when the deer was directly in his view, he released. Jack watched as the deer darted out. He let out a sigh and drew a second arrow from his quiver, as he sighted another deer foraging. He aimed, remained steady, then loosed his arrow, again missing his mark. His concentration was not at its optimum and thought it best to forego hunting and tend to Juliana. *I can't believe she's back in my life*, he continued to muse. He had moved to Cedarville to begin a new life and forget about her, only to have her back clouding his concentration… and stirring old feelings.

Jack suspected discord in Juliana's marriage to Edmund, but he could not get involved. Still, freeing her from the dungeon where Edmund had imprisoned her implicated him, and he was all too aware of the consequences, not to mention going against Edmund's men at the creek last night. He pushed down thoughts of what might lie in his future. But as much as he wanted to keep his distance from Juliana and not continue to provoke Edmund, he could not leave her in a dangerous situation.

The falcons returned with a small rabbit and a duck, and Jack gave the falcons a treat. He placed the warm carcasses in a canvas sack and carried the bag and wood inside the cottage.

***

Juliana sat on the bed, inspecting the wounds on her legs and rubbing the sore spots, thinking back at the sequence of events that led her inside Jack's sanctuary—it's what he had called it, and now it was hers. Although she felt safe at the moment, she would have to return to the castle, face Edmund, and accept the consequences of her actions. It was a sobering thought.

Her eyes looked up when the door swung open. Jack walked in, dropped a sack, and removed his quiver. He tossed wood in the fireplace and glanced in her direction. He did a double-take then strode toward her.

"Good morning. How are you feeling?" Jack leaned against the wall of the alcove, arms folded, aiming to maintain a respectable distance.

Juliana smiled. "Much better." She touched the back of her head. "Swelling's gone down."

"Did your memory return?"

She sighed. "I remember everything. How did you know where to find me?"

"The dungeon guard told me. After the attack, I wanted to make sure you were all right, so I rode through the forest and found Millie by my cottage. I then rode to Yorkford and snuck inside the castle through the tunnel. When I reached the dungeon, the guard asked me if I was looking for you, I said I was. He then told me where you were and that the key was on the ground by the gate. He also told me you remembered nothing."

Juliana tilted her head. "Why would he go against the king?"

"I don't know why, but I'm happy he did."

"Nonetheless, he did it at his peril." Juliana pondered for a moment. "Jack, what happened during the attack?"

"Edmund's men retreated."

"Why?"

"Alligators in the creek blocked the bridge and attacked Edmund's army."

"Alligators? There were no alligators when I crossed the creek yesterday. How did they get there?"

Jack shrugged, avoiding eye contact.

"Jack, if Edmund knew there were alligators in the creek, he would not send his men. He would not willingly put his men in danger."

"He must have made a mistake."

"Edmund does not make mistakes." She stared at Jack and saw through his evasiveness. "What is it you're not telling me?"

He lowered his eyes, avoiding her stare.

"Jack, why did Edmund attack Cedarville?"

Jack took a deep breath and pulled a chair and placed it next to the bed. "May I sit?"

Juliana gave a nod. "Please."

He sat down as he searched for words. He met Juliana's eyes. "Edmund was punishing us for not surrendering a magical person."

Juliana's eyes narrowed. "What?"

"You will find this hard to believe, but they live in Cedarville. I befriended a man named Robert, who has supernatural powers, and I saw him use it. When I told him about the impending attack, he summoned the alligators from the Etheland River to the creek." Jack looked at Juliana. "It sounds absurd, but it's true."

Juliana recalled her mother's words six years ago. She could hear her saying that they came from a long line of magical people. Thoughts of her conversation with her mother on her deathbed no longer sounded like the distorted imaginings of a sick woman. Had her mother told her the truth? "I must speak with him."

Jack's brow furrowed. "Why?"

Juliana hesitated. "Before my mother died, she told me a bizarre story that she came from a town of magical people, and there was a massacre that killed them all."

"But she was the daughter of the duke and duchess of Westmore."

"She told me they were not her natural parents. They adopted her after she escaped the massacre. It has been six years, and I told no one because I did not believe it. I thought her illness impaired her grasp on reality."

Jack cocked his head and looked at her with skeptical eyes.

"Jack," Juliana continued, "what if she spoke the truth? What if I come from a family of magical people? I shudder to think it is so, but if it is, I must know who I am and where I come from."

"Juliana, forgive me for doubting, but did she offer proof?"

"She gave me a gold locket with two gemstones in it and told me to find the book with spells to activate the stones so I can do magic. It sounded like madness at the time, but..." she paused, thinking. "But now it seems possible. She spoke with sincerity."

Juliana held Jack's gaze, confusion on his face. "Jack, how did you cross paths with this man?"

Jack described his harrowing encounter with the wolves and Robert's admission that he commanded the wolves to leave using his ability to communicate with animals.

Juliana recalled her reaction to her mother's story. "She spoke the truth, and I thought she had gone mad. I feel awful."

"Juliana, the reason why Edmund attacked Cedarville, is because he's after the magical people. He seeks to kill them."

"Jack, it's against the law to practice magic."

"Yes, but there's more. A man from Maiden Hills murdered his father, Prince James, twenty-two years ago. He seeks revenge."

"Did Prince James not die in battle?"

"He did not. They hid the truth from Edmund, so he would believe his father died with honor. Though he does not remember his father, he idolizes him. Prince James was a warrior, unlike Marcus, who was too polite

106

for Edmund. I don't know how he found out, but I am sure he did. He sent a spy into Cedarville."

"How do you know?"

Jack recounted the scene that took place when Sir Quinn attacked Robert at the tavern. "Sir Quinn had no business in Cedarville. He came to spy on us. Quinn muttered, 'it's Prince James' killer,' under his breath when he witnessed Robert's magic. Edmund knows magical people exist and where they live, and he knows one of them killed his father. He's vindictive and will stop at nothing until they're all dead."

"Jack, if Edmund wants them dead, they will not be able to escape, and you have put yourself in danger for helping them."

"Juliana, just like you came to warn me about Edmund, I *had* to help them. Sometimes we must do what is right, even though there are consequences."

Juliana sighed, her face falling into her hands. "This is madness." She picked up her head. "I must speak with this man before Edmund gets to him. He may confirm my mother's story and have information about my family. Can you please take me to him?"

Jack nodded. "Let's go."

The route to Cedarville was southwest from Jack's cabin and across the creek. As they neared the usually clear, shallow stream, its rocky bottom was no longer visible, and the water appeared muddier. "The water level seems higher," Juliana said.

"The creek rises when it rains. Fortunately, it had not rained much. During a torrential downpour, the water submerges the bridge, making it impassable."

"How do you leave Cedarville when that happens?"

"We don't. We must wait for the water to recede."

As they crossed the bridge, Juliana slowed her palfrey. "Jack, are… are the alligators still in the creek?"

Jack smiled. "It's all right. Robert commanded them to remain underwater and not attack anyone unless he orders them to."

Juliana swept her eyes back and forth across the brook as she closely trailed Jack. She held her breath and trotted over the creaky wooden bridge with trembling nerves. She exhaled when they reached the other side. Juliana followed Jack as he turned left toward the central part of the town, a direct route to Robert's cottage in the woods.

Jack came to a halt. "Juliana, wait, we can't go farther. I see Edmund's men up ahead in the square. He must have found out you're not in the dungeon and sent men looking for you."

"What shall we do?"

"Let's go to my castle. It's on the other side of the road. Hopefully, the guards are not waiting there for us. It's not easy to find."

When they arrived, Jack said, "I will hide Millie. If they see her, they will know you're here. Wait inside, and I shall return shortly." Jack opened the door, and Juliana walked in.

Inside the great hall, Juliana marveled at the castle's portraits, draperies, and furnishings. The baron's manor was a smaller replica of the royal castle of Yorkford with a great room, a courtyard, garden, and kitchen. A large fireplace with a grand hearth sat in the center of the room with a smaller fireplace on the far end. The room had an area to receive guests decorated with two red velvet couches, two matching chairs, and a wooden table to rest drinks. Above the fireplace, two swords crossed over a shield with Jack's coat of arms—the crowned lions of the Allington family. Jack kept his natural father's name of Mauntell, but when Prince Marcus Allington adopted him, he embraced their insignia. On the other side of the hall, long, wooden banquet tables rested against the wall, and on a platform dais, a table for the lord of the manor to sit with his most distinguished guests was prominently displayed.

Jack returned a few minutes later, handed the sack with the carcasses to his servant Audrey, then joined Juliana in the great room.

"I like what you did here," Juliana said.

"This was an old castle built many years ago. The workers repaired the parts that were crumbling, and they added extra rooms."

Juliana gazed at Jack. "Do you miss Yorkford?"

"I do, but I have grown fond of this town. The people are hard-working, and I pay them well. They are very grateful."

"I'm happy it's going well for you." Juliana forced a smile. She didn't want to show her discontent at Jack for leaving her, but in her heart, she wished to tell him to leave Cedarville and return to Yorkford, and everything would be just like it used to be. She pined, for those days were gone.

"Juliana." Jack held her hand and guided her to the velvet couch. He sat next to her. "I am concerned that Edmund is mistreating you."

She laid her hand on her cheek and remembered the burn from his hand. "It was just this one time. Since he has become king, he has been indifferent toward me and often rude, but he has not mistreated me, at least not until last night. I don't know what is happening with him since he does not share his troubles. Although it is clear now, it could have something to do with what he discovered about his father."

"He's a complicated man. He does not reveal much."

"My father saw something in him. He adored him. I'm sure he expected I would be in good hands, especially after Edmund rescued us when we fell in the moat when we were children—do you remember that?"

Jack twisted his mouth. "I do."

The loud banging on the door shook them. Jack and Juliana looked at each other. Juliana's heart raced. "Could it be Edmund's men coming for me?"

"Audrey," Jack called out.

Audrey entered with wide eyes, shaken by the incessant hammering. "Aye, my lord?"

Jack grabbed Juliana's hand and pulled her out of the room as he spoke to his servant. "Before you open the door, allow me a few minutes then stall before fetching me." He hastened his pace. "Come on, Juliana." They ran down the stairs leading to the dungeon. The banging resumed, echoing throughout the large hall.

Juliana held Jack's hand as he led her through a dark, narrow passageway then pushed open a door concealed within the walls. He turned to Juliana, "Stay here until it is safe to come out. You can hear sounds coming from the great hall from in here." He lifted a candle from the wall and handed it to Juliana, then closed the door.

Juliana's eyes scanned the second cell she occupied in less than two days. *Not again!* The room had no windows, but a door that matched the walls on the outside to blend in. No one would suspect there was a door leading into a room. This was not the life she was accustomed to, for as the queen of her kingdom, she had luxuries and servants, and she had freedom, but all that changed in so little time.

She pressed her ear to the door and heard footsteps above.

"What can I do for you, sir?" she heard Jack say.

"King Edmund wishes to speak to Queen Juliana. Do you know her whereabouts?"

"She's not here."

Jack did not lie, Juliana reasoned. She was in the dungeon, not in the great hall where they were standing. Jack was mindful to adhere to his code of chivalry, which required he speaks the truth at all times.

"We are to inspect the castle." The sound of heavy boots stomped above and around her. Her heart pounded as she stood motionless, her back against the wall.

"Queen Juliana is not here," she heard a knight say.

"You are to come with us, Lord Jack. King Edmund has summoned you."

"Very well, lead the way."

Juliana waited until all was quiet, then slowly pushed the door open and climbed the stairs. Servants greeted her as they tended to their duties. She sauntered toward the hearth, sat on the couch, and waited.

***

Edmund paced in the library, furious that Juliana escaped from her cell. Only one person could have freed her—Jack! He summoned the dungeon guard, and he was missing too. He did not believe the dungeon guard had released her, but he was delinquent in his duties. If the guard were involved in the plot to free Juliana, Edmund would have him executed.

Edmund suspected his wife had betrayed him by alerting Jack of his attack on Cedarville. She may have spied on him when he gave Sir Leopold the order. That's why she was in the dark forest, and that's why Cedarville fought back. They were ready. He believed she was having an affair with Jack, for which they would both pay dearly.

Most disturbing to him, though, was that he had proof magical people lived in Cedarville. The alligators showing up were no coincidence. He remembered from *The Book of Secrets* that one of their powers enabled them to talk to animals. The south river between Cedarville and Etheland was home to alligators, and Edmund was certain they summoned the alligators to the creek to fend off his army. The words of the prophecy haunted him, … *and they will overthrow the king.* He would not let that happen.

Edmund sat in his chair and pondered the turn his life had taken a fortnight ago when he discovered the truth of his father, James, the man he never met, and the people from Maiden Hills. What was it about the woman Beth that made James go against his principles? James, a legendary warrior, fought and won many battles for Westmore. He never conceded from an attack, and he never allowed his emotions to cloud his judgment. Edmund did not blame his father for the affair—he blamed him for falling in love with her.

"Samuel," Edmund called.

112

Samuel appeared at his door. "How may I serve you, Your Majesty?"

"Fetch Sir Paul." Edmund required the services of one of his more stable and trusted knights, for Sir Quinn had failed in his mission.

A few minutes later, Sir Paul arrived and stood before Edmund. Sir Paul, at twenty-two years old with blond hair to his shoulders, was devoted to King Edmund. He took quick action in bringing an unconscious Queen Juliana to the castle when she fell from her horse. This action did not go unnoticed by Edmund. Like all of Edmund's knights, Sir Paul desired to become an elite fighter and have a seat at the king's table like Sir Leopold and Sir Quinn.

"Sir Paul, you are to go to Cedarville," Edmund commanded. "Find an old seamstress named Helena who lived in Maiden Hills, and try to find her kin. If you locate any of them, bring them to me. Also, an incident occurred with Sir Quinn the other night in a tavern where a man used sorcery on him. There were witnesses. Find out who he is."

Sir Paul faltered, bewildered. "Did I hear you correctly, Your Majesty? A man used sorcery on Sir Quinn?"

"That is correct. The woman Helena also has sorcerous powers that she gets from a locket she wears with enchanted gemstones. It sounds unbelievable, but it's true. If you find either of them, arrest them and bring them to me."

"Aye, Your Majesty." Sir Paul bowed and left the room.

Edmund strode into the grand hall and sat by the fireplace, a glass of wine in hand. He came upon James' portrait and stared at it. His eyes tightened. *I will avenge your death, Father, this I vow!* As he sipped his drink, two knights entered the room accompanied by his adoptive brother, Jack. Heat flushed through his body.

"Your Majesty, we have brought Lord Jack as you requested," said a knight.

Edmund rose from his seat and rested the wineglass on the table. He turned to face Jack. The two men exchanged glares. "Leave us," said Edmund.

Jack watched the knights leave before speaking. "What can I do for you, Edmund?" Jack stood boldly before him.

"It's customary to bow before your king and address him as Your Majesty."

"Very well." Jack bowed. "Why do you wish to see me—Your Majesty?"

Edmund eyed Jack, sensing derision from him. His blood boiled, but he remained composed. "Your village disobeyed my command. Was it your call to refuse my order?"

"I will not deliver an innocent man for execution."

"There were witnesses who saw him use magic. It's forbidden in this kingdom."

"The use of *black* magic is forbidden. That's not what he did. He defended himself against Sir Quinn, who lunged at him with his dagger."

"With good reason, I am sure." Edmund glared at him, then strode to the table and poured himself another glass of wine. "Tell me, Jack, are these your new friends?"

"They're fine people."

"Jack, as the baron of Cedarville, it is your duty to enforce the law. Instead, you broke it, you went against your kingdom, and you're allowing lawbreakers to live free."

"Are you to imprison me?"

"I could, but not this day. I do not wish to distress my mother. She raised you like a son." Edmund approached Jack. "But, mark me well, if you betray me once more, I shall have your head."

Both men glared at each other.

"Am I free to leave?" Jack asked.

Edmund swallowed the wine and put the glass down. "One other thing, where's my wife?"

"Don't you keep an eye on your possessions?"

"We both know Juliana does what she wants, for she is her father's daughter. She has gone missing, and I suspect you are hiding her."

Jack shook his head. "I can't help you, Edmund."

Edmund studied Jack for a minute, then asked, "Tell me, Jack, are you in love with my wife?"

Jack's reply was solid. "We are friends, nothing more."

"But you were jealous of me when we were betrothed, which is why you moved to Cedarville. You could not bear to be in the same town as me knowing I was to marry the woman you love." He came within a few inches of Jack. "How does it feel knowing we share a bed?"

"What I *feel* is pity for her."

Edmund's face reddened. "Choose your words carefully, Jack."

115

"Edmund, I have known you for twelve years. You seek dominance and control. You married her for the throne, and you got what you wanted. Isn't that what King Matthew taught you, to go after what you want regardless of the consequences or the desires of others? Isn't that the code you live by?"

"It works for me."

"I was taught a different way. I was taught to respect women and be honest and courteous. That works for me."

"Yet, you're not the king, are you?" He taunted, a smug look on his face.

"You would not be king if Uncle Matthew had not died. Perhaps you killed him so you could take his throne." Jack struck back, baiting.

Edmund's face reddened. "I did not kill Matthew. He died of natural causes."

"How fortunate for you that he died so you could be king. Better hope no one desires the throne as much as you do, lest it happens to you. These are perilous times, Edmund."

"I have had enough of your words." Edmund drew his weapon and pointed it at Jack. "Take out your sword. Everyone says you're the best fighter in the kingdom. Let's see how good you really are."

Jack did not hesitate and slid the steel from its sheath. "Just like old times."

They clashed their swords, metal against metal, in a rhythm they had come to know. They fought each other often enough to anticipate the other's moves. Edmund aimed for the side, and Jack blocked it. Jack went for the center, Edmund dodged, and pointed the blade at Jack.

116

Edmund's animosity toward Jack intensified. There was a long history between them. He'd often engaged in sword fights with Jack to prove he was a better fighter than him. Unfortunately, for Edmund, this was how Jack became the most skillful of all the fighters.

The clashing of swords continued with each man unrelenting. Edmund clenched his teeth at the frustration of not being able to outmaneuver his opponent. Jack was agile and clever. The fighting grew in intensity.

A quick move by Jack and he brushed Edmund's side, ripping his tunic. Edmund countered and pricked Jack's arm.

"Stop," Princess Katherine pleaded as Ella escorted her into the great room.

"Oh, Lord Jack, you are bleeding." Ella lowered Katherine to her seat.

Jack glanced at his arm, a stream of blood dripping onto the rug. "It's all right, Ella, it's not deep," he said panting. He put his sword back in its sheath.

"I shall get a bandage and clean you up." Ella rushed out of the room.

"Jack, it's good to see you," Katherine said. She held out her arms from her seat, and they embraced.

"Mother, I have missed you. How are you?"

"I am well, but as you can see, I have trouble walking on my own."

"I have a friend who is a great doctor. I shall have him examine you," Jack said.

Edmund let out a sigh of frustration, as he had not planned for a family reunion. "Mother has a fine doctor."

117

"Why were you two fighting?" Katherine's eyes darted between the two men.

Ella returned with the bandage, cleaned Jack's wound, and wrapped his arm.

"I have to show Jack who's the king. He forgets."

Jack leveled his gaze at Edmund. "Fortunately, I have you to remind me."

Katherine did not appear convinced. "What's really going on?"

"It's nothing that should worry you, Mother." Edmund gave Jack a loathing look. "It's time you left, Jack."

Jack turned to his mother. "I must leave, but I shall return another day and visit with you." He kissed her on the cheek.

She clutched his hand. "I would like that, son."

Edmund met Jack's eyes, and they locked in a glare. Jack turned and hurried out.

***

Hours later, Jack arrived at the castle to find Juliana asleep on the velvet couch in front of the hearth covered in a wool blanket.

"She waited for hours until she tired," Audrey said as she wiped her hands on her apron. "I threw more wood in the fire and laid a blanket on her so she would be comfortable."

"Thank you for caring for her," Jack said.

"May I get you anything, my lord?"

"A cup of beer would serve me well."

"Right away, my lord." Audrey headed for the kitchen.

Jack stared at Juliana, sleeping as if she had no worries. He had never seen her more beautiful with her long dark auburn hair draped in front of her, flawless skin glistening with pink hues, and the reddest lips he had ever seen. Edmund was right—Jack loved Juliana, and he had loved her ever since he had first laid eyes on her. He recalled when he first arrived at the castle, watching six-year-old Juliana run from the maidservant and climb onto her father's lap after being caught causing mischief. Jack smiled at the memory. He watched her grow from a little girl to a beautiful lady, and each day the love he had for her grew, but she would never know how he felt about her. He had to be content just being there as a friend when she needed him.

He walked over to a chair across from the couch. His eyes gazed upon her. No other women he had known compared to her. He loved the way she smiled, and the way she laughed, and most of all, her strength. Many women were meek and defenseless, but she was different. She could stand up to anybody, even Edmund.

Audrey walked in with a mug of beer, and a grateful Jack swallowed it, relieving the tension that had swelled from his meeting with Edmund.

Juliana opened her eyes, blinking, then they widened. "Jack!" She pulled the blanket away from her and rushed to embrace him. "I was worried."

"I'm fine." He smiled, enjoying the closeness and taking in her scent.

"What did he say to you?" She glanced at his arm. "And what happened to your arm?" Juliana realized she was on his lap. Red-faced, she slid to the space next to him.

"It's nothing but a surface wound," Jack said. "Edmund's not pleased with me. We said some words, he got angry, and he challenged me to a sparring match. I ripped his tunic, and he repaid me by stabbing my arm."

"Oh, Jack, I am so sorry for I have put you in danger."

"No need to apologize, Juliana, I have put myself in danger. Besides, I never back down from a good fight." He grinned.

"You're a good man, Jack." She paused. "I could not get Robert out of my mind. I must speak with him. Can you please summon him?"

"We shall go to him. Edmund's men will seize him at my door."

"How will we get to him? They'll see me if we walk out."

"We shall leave from the rear of the castle. There's a hidden door leading to a tunnel that takes us to a small cottage away from the castle. It's where I left Millie and Dex. Just outside of the cottage is a trail to the woods where Robert lives, and the guards will not see us."

Chapter 8

A narrow river separated the village of Cedarville from the Kingdom of Etheland. As Juliana and Jack rode alongside the waterway, she recalled visiting King Carlton Goldwell, the ruler of Etheland, with her father a few months ago. Carlton, a ruler in many respects like her father, had amassed a large army, and just like the late King Matthew, had an eye out for new territory to expand his kingdom. King Carlton had set his sights on Yorkford, and the whispers across the land was that Carlton had prior discussions with King Matthew to persuade him to choose his son, Prince Carsen, to wed Juliana. However, Matthew's plan was to take over smaller territories to enlarge his kingdom, and Westmore fit right into his plan, thus choosing Prince Edmund. Etheland was a mighty kingdom in its own right, and a union between Juliana and Carsen would have had both kings battling for control of the other.

Juliana rode close behind Jack, heading west toward a wooded area, an active abode for deer, rabbits, and foxes. Large hawks flew overhead, outstretched wings gliding across the cobalt blue sky, their screeching echoing throughout the forest. Juliana raised her eyes as the hair on her arms lifted. "Are you sure this is safe?"

Jack smiled. "Don't worry. This is the long route to the wooded area of Cedarville."

"And you are certain there are no guards here?"

"I am certain. They would not come back here. It is too far out. We must avoid the main village and the castle grounds."

Jack reined to a halt in front of a large cottage made of sturdy red-cedar wood and dismounted. He helped Juliana down from her horse and pointed to a small shed. "That's where the wolves attacked me."

Juliana shuddered to think she had almost lost Jack. She scanned the area, and as far as her eyes took her, thick trees towered above her, and dense foliage covered the grounds with few dwellings in view. "This is a remote area, Jack. No one would have known you were here. You would have died."

"Fortunately, Robert arrived when he did."

Juliana and Jack walked to the door, and Jack pressed his knuckles on the wood. No answer. He tried again. After a few minutes, they heard movement inside. They looked at each other, and soon the door swung open. A disheveled and unshaven Robert appeared before them.

"Pardon the intrusion Robert, is this not a good time?" asked Jack.

"It's fine. I could not sleep and was up all night, so I lay down for a midday nap. What time of day is it?"

"It's suppertime," Jack said.

"I must have fallen into a deep sleep." He ran his fingers through his hair. "Forgive my appearance. Please, come inside."

Robert held the door open, and Juliana and Jack entered. Juliana sensed Robert's eyes on her as she walked past him. Once inside the cottage, Juliana removed the emerald green hood covering, and Robert stared wide-eyed at her.

"Forgive me for staring," Robert said, "but you remind me of someone from long ago."

"Robert, this is Her Majesty, Queen Juliana of Yorkford. Your Majesty, this is Doctor Robert Latham."

"Your Majesty," Robert said, bowing his head, "it's an honor to have you in my home." He glanced at Jack, then back at Juliana, confused. "To what do I owe your visit?"

Juliana caught sight of the locket around Robert's neck. She recognized it as the same locket her mother had given her six years ago. A chill ran up her spine. She smiled at Robert, knowing this man had a connection to her mother, and it was a thrilling feeling. "Who do I remind you of?"

"You remind me of a young girl from long ago. The resemblance is striking."

"What was her name?"

"Her name was Lucinda."

Her eyes lit up, and her throat swelled. "That was my mother," her lips quivered. "You knew my mother?"

"I did." Robert glanced at Jack, surprised at the revelation. "She was a young girl, the daughter of our baron, Lord Gavin Archer, and his wife, Lady Victoria."

"They were my grandparents, but alas, I never knew of them." Sorrow swept through her, realizing that a part of her family was unknown to her, and they lived a life she could only imagine. For the first time, she felt incomplete and needed to put the pieces together.

"This is unbelievable. I did not know what happened to Lucinda. I recall we had a queen named Lucinda, but I never saw her, and I would not have imagined she was the young girl from our village. I'm happy she survived, and she has a daughter. Does she have more children?"

"No, just me." Juliana's face saddened. "I had two younger brothers, but they died long ago." She sighed. "My mother is also gone. An infection took her six years ago."

"I am sorry for your loss, Your Majesty."

"Robert, I must know about my family. On her deathbed, my mother gave me a locket—just like the one you're wearing—with two stones. She told me that I come from a magical family. Is it true?"

"It is true, Your Majesty. You are magical, a descendent of the Majian people. Any offspring of a Majian inherits the same ability to tap into the power of the enchanted gemstones, even if only one parent is Majian."

She wrinkled her brows. "Majian?"

"Our name comes from the Majian Mountain that borders to the west of what was once our village of Maiden Hills."

She turned to Jack, then back at Robert. "Robert, the practice of magic is illegal. People who practice it are to be executed."

"Your Majesty," Jack said, obliged to addressing her by her proper title in the company of others. "The practice of *black* magic is illegal. Robert's magic and that of your family is not black magic."

Robert added, "Our powers do not come from an evil source and are not used to harm anyone, except in defending ourselves."

"How did we get this power?" Juliana asked.

"Please have a seat." In front of the fireplace was a small table, a bench, and two chairs where they sat. Robert placed a jug of wine and three glasses on the table. He sat on the bench and poured the wine into the glasses and handed one to Juliana, another to Jack, and he took the third.

Juliana and Jack sipped their wine as Robert spoke. "Over one hundred and twenty years ago, three noblemen were bestowed with magical gifts for their courage by a maiden spirit named Majia who appeared before them. Everyone from Maiden Hills is a descendant of one of the three noblemen. The land where the maiden appeared was granted to the noblemen, and for four generations, our people lived in peace... until everything changed twenty-two years ago."

"What happened?" Juliana asked.

Robert took a deep breath. "Prince James of Westmore befriended a young woman named Beth. He found out about our magical powers, and Yorkford sent inspectors to our village, looking to arrest anyone wearing a locket with the enchanted stones. Lord Gavin, your grandfather, collected the lockets to safeguard them until the inspection was over. I never gave up my stones, and since I lived in the wooded area, I avoided the inspection. The guards from Yorkford came to the village, inspected the people, and searched their homes. When they left, everyone thought it was over. The day Lord Gavin's son Josef was to wed, we all gathered on top of the sacred Majian Mountain for the nuptials. We waited for Lord Gavin to return with the stones, but he never did. Instead, the knights from Yorkford came."

Robert gulped his wine and paused. "They slaughtered everyone. Only a few of us had our gemstones, so we fought back and escaped, but most everyone died." Robert swallowed the rest of his wine.

Juliana's insides churned learning of the violence her kingdom had perpetrated on innocent people. She recalled her mother had assured her that her father had nothing to do with the massacre, but rather a rogue knight was responsible for the bloodshed. "Robert, why did the people surrender their stones? They could have used them to protect themselves."

"No one expected a massacre. We thought that after the inspection they would leave. It was important to keep the secret of our magic."

"What happened after the massacre?" Jack asked.

"The king's men burned the homes and killed everyone in the town." Robert lifted the jug and poured wine into his glass. "Those of us who escaped the massacre up on the mountain rushed inside homes, searching for people trapped in their burning cottages. We found many children whose parents left them with their young caretakers while they attended the wedding. We put them in carriages, and my father and uncle rode them into Cedarville. We found families to adopt the children. One of them was Lucinda's six-year-old brother Jeb."

Juliana's eyes widened. "My mother's younger brother survived! Does he still live?"

"Yes, Your Majesty. He's the owner of the tavern in Cedarville in the village square."

Juliana's face brightened to learn she had a blood relative still living, but then her smile faded. "My mother told me they had killed her father on the way to the mountain."

Robert nodded. "We later found Lord Gavin's body in the grassland bordering Maiden Hills and Cedarville.

His locket was gone, and the box with the villagers' stones was missing. To this day, we have not found the box. We suspected Prince James killed Lord Gavin and took the stones."

"My mother saw it happen," Juliana said. "She told me two men attacked her father. One of them rode a black horse with white lines on its hind legs."

Jack's eyes widened. "I remember who had such a horse. It was the knight who trained me—Sir Leopold. As his squire, I took care of his horses, and I recall one horse in particular because of the unusual white markings on his hind legs. It died many years ago, but I have never forgotten it."

Robert seemed bemused. "Are you saying Prince James did not kill Lord Gavin, that it was someone else?"

"It appears that it was Sir Leopold accompanied by his squire. He was one of King Matthew's most trusted knights—the same knight that came to the village square the other day," Jack said. "Robert, do you know who killed Prince James?"

Robert drew a deep breath and pressed his lips. "I do."

"Can you tell us?" Juliana asked.

Robert's eyes shifted down. Juliana sensed Robert did not want to divulge the name of the person who killed Prince James, for murdering a prince was a serious crime. They could get around the law that forbade the use of magic, but the capital crime of murdering a prince carried the penalty of execution.

"Robert," Juliana said, leaning forward, "I know what Prince James did was wrong, and it caused the deaths of hundreds of innocent people. I would be betraying the law of my land, but I will not divulge his murderer's name and bring him to justice. You have my word. It is more important that I know the truth of what happened."

After a long pause, Robert said, "While we were rescuing children, I realized that I had to get to my son before the king's men discovered the cottages in the woods. I had a baby with Beth, the woman Prince James befriended and betrayed." Robert choked up, then continued. "Beth's brother, Simon, and I rode to Beth's cottage, but it was too late. When we arrived, the cottage was in flames."

"What happened to Beth?" Juliana asked.

"Beth died on the mountain." Robert took a deep breath and finished his second glass of wine.

"I'm sorry, Robert," said Juliana.

"Simon was enraged that his sister and her baby were killed. He rode to the castle to look for Prince James to kill him."

Robert filled his wineglass again. "It's difficult to speak of what happened. It continues to haunt me every day."

No one uttered a word for a few minutes. Robert finished his drink and stared at the empty glass. Juliana sensed the pain emanating from him as he relived the tragedy he had endured long ago, and even though she was not yet born, she felt responsible for the actions taken by her kingdom that caused the deaths of many people who did not deserve it.

Jack broke the silence. "What happened to Simon?"

"The side of his head was burned badly trying to rescue the children, and he lost an ear. After he recovered, he left Cedarville, but he comes around often to visit his mother, Helena, and his daughter, Alice, who both live near the village square. He does not tell us where he lives since he must stay in hiding, for even after twenty-two years, there's a price on his head."

Juliana furrowed her brows, recalling her mother's final words. "Before my mother died, she said. 'find Simon.' Why would she want me to find him?"

"Your mother would have known him from our village. I don't know why she would mention him."

"Perhaps his mother, Helena, would know. I wish to speak to her," Juliana said.

Robert gave her a faint smile. "I'm sure she would like to speak with you too, Your Majesty."

"It will be difficult to get through to the village square. That's where the guards are stationed," Jack said.

Robert wrinkled his brows. "Guards?"

"King Edmund sent guards from Yorkford to look for you and Her Majesty."

"How are we to get past the guards, Lord Jack?" Juliana asked.

Jack glanced at Robert. "We shall find a way. Let's go."

***

Robert led Juliana and Jack toward the village square, taking the direct route from the wooded area. The bustling of villagers in the streets and the church bell ringing was a clear sign they were near the hub of the village of Cedarville, where merchants' shops for shoes, bread, meats, and candles lined up in a row. Alongside

129

the shops was a residential area with small wooden cabins.

Robert glimpsed at Juliana atop her white palfrey. She lifted her hood, concealing her face. He realized there were not many people of noble blood who would choose to live in Cedarville, and a woman as elegant and finely dressed as Juliana would attract attention.

Before they reached the main village, Robert reined his steed. "We should leave our horses here."

They dismounted and crept slowly, hiding behind the trees.

Jack took several steps closer. "I see the guards. Stay here in the shadows behind us, Your Majesty, Robert and I will move closer."

Robert and Jack took a few more stealthy steps, observing the activity in the center of the village. Townspeople crowded the benches and sat around open fires as they drank and chatted. Opposite the village square were the merchant stores and homes. It was the most active part of the village with a constant stream of horses and carriages moving along the paved road. Two Yorkford guards on horseback studied the faces of the people passing by.

Robert whispered, "That's where Helena lives." He pointed to a cottage near the village square. "Right where those guards are."

"Can you distract them?"

Robert nodded. "I can try."

The fire burned in the village square, warming the cool evening air as men drank their beer and ale and filled the area with raucous laughter. Robert focused his eyes ahead. A rock flew toward a man laughing, and it struck his head. The man turned around. "Hey, who hit me with a rock?" He blamed the man behind him. "Was it you?" He drew back his fist and punched the man in his face with a resounding *thwack*.

Bleeding from the nose, his opponent narrowed his eyes. He threw a quick jab, and the first partygoer fell to the ground.

Another man was hit with a rock and then another, and they each blamed the man behind them, and punches flew. A brawl broke out with more men joining the fight. Patrons from the tavern across the square jumped in, eager for excitement and the release of pent-up energy.

The two guardsmen rode toward the melee. "Order! Order! In the name of the king!"

Robert waited for the guards to leave their post, then motioned Juliana to follow them.

When they arrived, Robert tapped on Helena's door and waited for it to open. He looked back at the guards distracted with the brawl. He found it strange that Helena had not come to the door. After a few minutes, Robert turned the knob and pushed the door open. He slipped in and motioned Jack and Juliana to follow.

When they entered Helena's cottage, it had been ransacked.

Chapter 9

Juliana followed Jack and Robert into Helena's home, a small cottage just the right size to house a single woman of sixty-one. There was a living area with a couch, a small table, and two chairs knocked over. A fireplace mounted against the far wall, and on the mantel, canisters of herbs infused the cottage air with its pungent and wooded aromas. A bed nestled inside an alcove, and alongside, stood a small dresser with its drawers opened and clothes strewed on the floor. A candleholder rested tipped over on the table next to the bed. Some of the floor's wooden planks in the living area were lifted and personal items scattered onto the floor. Everything had been touched.

"Someone's been here," Robert said.

"What were they hoping to find?" Juliana asked.

Robert shook his head. "I cannot say. They lifted some wooden planks. They're aware these cottages have hiding places."

Jack surveyed the room. "King Edmund must have found out that Helena was connected with what happened to Prince James. He may have ordered his guards to look for her."

At that moment, a moan came from inside the cottage.

"Shh." They froze and listened for the direction of the sound.

Robert took slow steps toward the sleeping area, and following the sound, tapped the floor. He found loose boards by the wall of the alcove next to the bed and removed three boards. To everyone's surprise, an older woman lay beneath it. She was trembling.

Juliana gasped. "Is she all right?"

Jack rushed to help Robert lift the woman from underneath the floor. Juliana grabbed a chair.

"Helena, are you hurt?" Robert held on to the woman as he lowered her onto the chair.

"I am well. I managed to get in, but I could not get out." She was a spunky woman with a head full of gray hair and missing teeth. Her green eyes stared at the faces of the people surrounding her, and when she glanced at Juliana, she blinked several times with a look of confusion. "Lucinda?"

"Helena, this is Her Majesty, Queen Juliana of Yorkford," Robert said, "and this is Lord Jack, our new baron."

"Forgive me, Your Majesty. You bear a striking resemblance to a child I once knew. It's an honor to meet you." She bowed her head, then turned to Jack. "My lord."

"Helena, Lucinda was my mother, and my father was King Matthew."

Helena's eyes widened. "Lucinda was our queen, and you are her daughter?"

Juliana nodded, her face beaming.

"I never saw the queen. I wish I had," said Helena. "Lucinda was a lovely girl, very sweet."

"Helena, what were you doing under the floor?" Robert asked.

"Hiding, of course. The king's men were looking for me. I told the animals to alert me if they saw anyone suspicious coming toward my cottage. They saw the

133

knights coming, and they warned it could be trouble. My powers are weak, and I would have had a difficult time defending myself, so all I could do was hide. The animals distracted them before they searched below my sleeping area."

"Why do you think they were looking for you?" Jack asked.

"They wish to kill me. The king wants to finish what Prince James started twenty-two years ago, which is why they came for Robert, and now they are coming for me. They seek to kill all Majian people."

Robert picked up the jug of ale, poured the liquid into a cup, and handed it to Helena. Her hands trembled as she brought the cup to her lips and swallowed a mouthful. After a few minutes, her nerves steadied.

"Helena," Juliana said, "my mother died six years ago, but on her deathbed, she revealed that we come from magical people. I did not believe her."

"She spoke the truth, Your Majesty."

"I realize that now, but I have questions. What happened with Prince James and Beth twenty-two years ago, and why did he betray her?"

Helena remained still, and her eyes moistened. "It's a sorrowful story, Your Majesty."

"I must know what happened. This concerns my family."

Helena sighed. "Very well. Please sit, Your Majesty, and I shall tell you." She looked at Robert as he pulled out chairs for Juliana, Jack, and himself. "Robert, please add what you remember. My memory is not what it used to be."

Robert nodded.

"It began with my beautiful daughter, Beth. She was a happy, young woman full of life and love and very trusting. Some might say a bit naïve. She loved to go to Yorkford during the Festival of Flowers because it brought people together to feast, buy goods, and be entertained. That was where Beth met James. We didn't know at first that he was a prince."

***

Yorkford, twenty-two years ago

Helena watched the procession of knights on horseback through the streets of Yorkford with her nineteen-year-old daughter Beth. Beth held a red rose she had caught during the queen's carriage ride and was taking in the aroma when she eyed a tall, handsome man with honey brown eyes, dark brown hair, and a rugged appearance riding his brown destrier. In an instant, she was smitten. He met Beth's eyes. She was beautiful with long-flowing raven black hair, soft red lips, clear milky skin, and green eyes that sparkled. He smiled at her and kept moving forward as he led the knights of Westmore in a procession carrying their blue and yellow banners.

Helena, a petite woman in her forties, showing signs on her face of too much worry, squeezed through the mass of people as she and Beth made their way toward the tables where local merchants displayed their goods. They found themselves surrounded by the busy roar and fast-talking of sellers and buyers bargaining and fighting for a sale. Beth loved to shop and eyed the various merchandise on the tables. Her eyes brightened when she came across a merchant selling small statues and sculptures and marveled at a beautiful six-inch statue of a fairy sitting on a mushroom holding a small butterfly.

"My good man, how much for this statue?" Beth asked the merchant.

"Twenty pence," the old merchant said in a rush.

"I have only five." Beth held out her hand, five coins resting on her palm.

"The lowest I can go is fifteen, m'lady." He huffed as he tended to another patron.

"Surely, you can go lower, for I have no more." She smiled, hoping it would encourage him to lower the price.

He completed the transaction with the other patron and came back to her. "Twelve is my final offer, m'lady."

"I will give you ten," a deep masculine voice behind Beth spoke to the merchant.

"M'lord." He smiled, showing a few missing teeth. "You have a deal." The merchant handed the man the fairy statue and collected ten pence from him.

Red-faced, Beth fought to restrain her anger at the gentleman who outbid her for the statue. She turned to show her irritation, and her eyes widened when she saw the tall, handsome man that smiled at her from his horse.

"My lady, please accept this as my gift to you. The Festival of Flowers is about beauty, and you are very beautiful." He offered her the fairy statue and the most captivating smile she had ever seen.

"Th-thank you, kind sir." Beth took the statue and clutched it to her chest, a look of disbelief on her face.

"Permit me to introduce myself. I am James from Westmore. What is your name, lovely lady?"

"My name is Beth Porter, and this is my mother, Helena."

"My lord." Helena nodded.

"A pleasure to meet you both. Are you visiting Yorkford?"

"We are. We're from Maiden Hills."

"I have never been there. What's it like?"

"It is very peaceful and beautiful. There are mountains, streams, and many trees and wildlife." Beth twirled her long black hair, trying to restrain her giddiness.

"I would love to see it." James smiled.

"You are welcome anytime, my lord."

"Please, call me James." He reached for Beth's hand and gallantly kissed it. "I must go now, but I hope to see you again soon." James disappeared into the crowd.

Beth's face beamed as she squeezed the hand that met his lips, stunned that a handsome knight showed an interest in her, and gave her a gift.

"Beth, dear, please be careful," Helena said in a mother's tone.

Beth sighed and rolled her eyes. "Oh, Mother, always the worrier."

"What about Robert?"

Beth's mood changed when Helena mentioned Robert. Beth loved Robert, for he was a handsome young man with a generous and noble heart and the father of her son, Peter. She blinked, holding back tears. "Robert is obligated to someone else."

"But the baby—"

"Mother, there is nothing I can do. Robert must care for Olivia. Peter and I shall be fine without him."

"It's not only that. The knight is from Westmore, a foreign land, and they know nothing of our people."

"Mother, please do not worry. Let's see what happens." She hugged the fairy statue and the red rose close to her heart and spun around.

A week later, James visited Beth, and she gave him a tour of her quaint village. He visited her at least twice a week, and everyone in Maiden Hills wondered the identity of the handsome stranger courting Beth. He seemed familiar, some said, but no one remembered where they had seen him. He didn't dress like a knight, but rather as a villager. Beth's brother, Simon, did not trust the man from Westmore, and he and Robert warned Beth to beware. Beth accused Robert of being jealous and not wanting her to be happy with another man. Despite all the warnings, Beth was falling in love with James, for he was gentle, kind, and attentive.

One summer day, Beth held six-month-old Peter in her arms. Helena watched and listened as Beth sang him a song that brightened his face. "Fly little butterfly, fly up high, your wings will carry you to the sky, do not look back, but know I am here, mummy's love will always be near." He gurgled as she smiled at him, kicking his feet. Beth positioned him in his cradle. "I love you, Peter." She leaned down and kissed his forehead.

There was a knock on the door, and when Beth opened it, it was James. She gave him a wide smile as he presented her with a white carnation, a traditional symbol of love. She clutched it to her heart as he kissed her cheek and stroked her hair. He walked toward baby Peter, handed him a metal rattle, and watched his face light up as he shook it. James picked up Peter and held him over his head. Peter giggled at the exhilaration.

Helena smiled. She liked James, but something about him unsettled her. She had a heightened sense of intuition that all Majians had, and although her instincts were strong, they felt blocked, but she couldn't shake the odd feeling. He was a knight, yet he dressed in common clothes. Perhaps he did it to blend in or maybe to hide his true identity.

Helena excused herself and departed to her bedchamber, where she picked up a dress, threaded a needle, and began to stitch.

Beth set down a tray containing a jug of wine, two of her finest wineglasses, and cheese cut in squares and placed it on a table in front of the fireplace. As she placed the tray on the table, James noticed the jewelry around her neck.

"That's an unusual locket."

She wrapped her hand around the pendant. "My grandmother gave it to me who got it from her grandmother. It's been in the family for years."

"I noticed other people in this village have the same locket. Does it have a particular meaning?"

Beth hesitated, searching for the right words. "It's... worn for protection." She poured wine in the two glasses and handed one to James.

"I am not a believer that jewelry can protect the wearer." James took a sip of his drink.

"It's not the locket that protects, but what's inside." Beth opened the pendant and showed him two small glowing gemstones.

James stared at the stones. "I have never seen gemstones like that."

"They are rare and only found in Maiden Hills." She closed the locket. "Perhaps someday you shall be privy to the secret of the stones." She smiled playfully.

He sipped his wine. "There is a secret?"

"Yes, but only for those who are loyal and trustworthy."

"I am loyal and trustworthy. You can tell me."

She stared at him with eyes of love. "I know I can trust you, James." She grew serious. "But you must tell no one."

"I give you my sacred honor."

She leaned in closer to James and whispered, "The stones give me the ability to do magic."

Helena stopped her sewing and listened, unsure of what she heard.

James furrowed his eyebrows. "Magic? What kind of magic?"

"I can move objects with my mind, and I can communicate with animals."

James shook his head. "Beth, that's not possible." James' eyes widened when the fairy statue floated from across the room and landed on the table in front of him.

Beth giggled. "Do you wish for more wine?"

The jug of wine rose on its own and poured wine into James' glass. His face turned pale with shock. "H-how did you do that?"

"The stones give me the power once I recite the spells in *The Book of Secrets*." Beth scanned the room for the book and saw it on a table in the corner and levitated it toward James. His eyes were wide open.

140

"This book tells the history of how we came to be and the spells we must recite to empower the stones."

"How many people can do this?" James asked.

"Practically the entire town of Maiden Hills. We call ourselves Majians after the maiden that gave us the gift. Some Majians married non-Majians. Their spouses can't do magic, but their children can."

"Can you do magic without the stones?"

"No, I need the stones. There is a story about it in the book."

Helena stood at the doorway of her bedchamber with a stern look. "Beth, what are you doing?"

"It's all right, Mother."

James bolted from his seat. "Beth, I just remembered, I must go to Yorkford and attend to business." James seemed jarred at the scene that had played out before him.

"James, what I told you may be unusual to you, but I hope it changes nothing between us," she said, her voice jittery.

"Everything is fine, Beth," he reassured her. "I will see you again soon. I must leave now." He hurried toward the door.

Beth followed him. "Before you go, James, there will be a wedding in a week for a dear friend up on the Majian Mountain. I wish for you to accompany me."

"I shall if I'm able to." He opened the door and left without kissing Beth on the cheek. Beth leaned against the door, her face pained with worry. "Did I make a mistake?" she muttered to herself.

Helena stared at Beth, dread in her eyes. "Why did you tell him?"

"Don't worry, Mother, I trust him." Although Beth attempted to quell her mother's fears, the strained look on her face revealed the anxiety she felt inside.

***

At the local alehouse, Robert sat with Simon, Beth's brother, to enjoy a meal and beer. Simon shared the same green eyes and black hair with Beth, but their personalities contrasted, for she was sweet and trusting, and he was tough and suspicious. Simon, at eighteen years old with shoulder-length raven black hair and a clean-shaven face, loved eating and drinking, as evident by the thickness in his mid-section. Robert was nineteen years old with short dark brown hair and deep-set, smoky gray eyes, but maintained a lean form, not having a penchant for alcohol or food as much as Simon. They took notice when at the far end of the alehouse, sat James with another man in intense conversation. When James was in Maiden Hills, it was to see his older sister, but Simon had not seen him all day and found it unusual that he was in town without coming to see Beth.

"What's he doing here?" Robert asked with a scowl. He loved Beth, and although he accepted that she found love with another man, the jealousy would unwillingly seep out.

"I shall find out." Simon rose from his seat, and Robert followed him.

Simon loomed over James as he sat in his chair. "James! I'm surprised to see you here."

James turned his head and raised his eyes at Simon standing over him. "This is my favorite place for beer in this town. I'm here with Leopold. I told him many fine things of Maiden Hills, and he wished to see for himself."

"Maiden Hills *is* a fine place, and we want it to stay that way. We are hospitable to strangers, but we want no troubles."

"We are not here to cause trouble," James said.

"See to it you don't," said Simon as he glared at James.

James rose from his seat. "Have I offended you, Simon?" They stood within inches of each other.

"I don't want you near my sister, lest she gets hurt. I don't know what you're after, but I don't trust you."

"I would not harm Beth."

"I hope not, because if you do, I shall come after you."

James glared back at Simon. "Are you threatening me?"

"Take it however you wish." Their eyes locked.

"Look here, my good man." Leopold rose from his seat and faced Simon. "That is no way to speak to a prince, the heir to the throne of Westmore."

James gave Leopold a piercing stare.

Robert furrowed his brows. "You're a prince?"

Simon grabbed James' tunic. "What are you after? What do you want with my sister?"

With fury in his eyes, Leopold yanked his dagger from its sheath. James held up his hand at Leopold, waited for him to back down, then slowly removed Simon's hands from his tunic.

"I have nothing but respect and admiration for your sister," said James.

Simon's eyes narrowed into thin slits. "What does a prince want with a common villager?"

"Simon," Robert interrupted, "we shall leave these two fine men to enjoy their meal."

He stared at James. "Stay away from Beth. You are not to see her again."

"Or what?" James' nostrils flared.

"Let's just say, it will not end well for you, Your Highness." Simon and James locked eyes.

"Let's go, Simon." Robert pulled Simon's arm, well aware of his friend's fiery temper.

Robert and Simon walked out of the alehouse. Simon clenched his teeth. "He lied to Beth. He shall pay for that."

"We must be careful, Simon. A battle with Westmore would be very bloody."

Simon curled his fist. "Yes, for them."

***

Helena peeked from her bedchamber to see James at the doorway of their cottage. Beth's face beamed, but James was distant. He was not as affectionate as he had been with her.

"James, what's wrong? You look grim." She stared at his clothes made of fine silk and velvet—clothes typically worn by royalty. "Why are you wearing such fine clothes?"

James closed the door behind him. "Beth, I have come to warn you, for there will be an inspection. The kingdom forbids the practice of magic. The king of Yorkford found out about the magical people in Maiden Hills and gave his knights strict orders to arrest anyone found wearing the locket with the stones."

144

"How did he find out about our powers?" Her eyes widened as she stared at James. "You told him! You betrayed me!" She dug her fists into James' chest as tears streamed down her face.

He held her arms. "Beth, I did not tell him. Somehow, he found out, but when he questioned me, I said nothing. I did not betray you. You must believe me." He paused. "But I could not deny the threat. It was my duty."

"The threat? We are no threat to you." She shook her head in anguish. "I trusted you. I thought you... you loved me."

"You must understand. Someone from Maiden Hills threatened me in front of a king's knight from Yorkford. He reported it to King Matthew, and I could not deny it."

She had a shocked look on her face. "Who threatened you?"

"Your brother." James sighed. "It's against the law to threaten a prince."

The color drained from Beth's face. "You... you're a prince?"

"I am. The Kingdom of Yorkford protects my kingdom, and they will not sit idle and wait until I am attacked. My future as king is at stake."

Beth placed her hand over her mouth. "You lied to me! Why?"

James paused, then shook his head. "Forgive me, for I was not thinking straight. I wished to be with you, but the truth would have kept us apart." He gazed deep into her eyes. "I never realized it would become... complicated."

Beth looked away. "What did my brother say to you?"

"He told me to stay away from you, or there would be trouble. He fears I would hurt you."

She turned and stared into his eyes. Her lips quivered. "Would you, James? Would you hurt me?"

James looked down at her tear-filled eyes. "Not intentionally, Beth." He hesitated. "I am married."

Beth gasped, eyes wide.

"I'm sorry I hid it from you, but there is a signed agreement, and there is nothing I can do to change it, although I wish I could. I don't love her." James stared at Beth as if wanting to say something to take away her pain, but he just said, "I must go." He walked out and left Beth in tears.

Helena ran out of her room and held her daughter as she sobbed on her shoulder. She rubbed her daughter's back to comfort her, but then realized the seriousness of James' warning.

"Beth," Helena turned her face toward her, "I must warn Lord Gavin."

Beth wiped her eyes and sniffed. She nodded, dejected.

***

Lord Gavin called for an emergency town meeting in the courtyard. When all the villagers arrived and assembled, Gavin stood before them and said, "It has come to my attention that the knights from Yorkford are planning an inspection to search for our enchanted stones. We must not allow outsiders to be privy to our secret. I am asking all of you to give up your stones until the inspection is over. I shall safeguard them."

"Why don't we fight back?" asked a villager.

146

"This is not a battle, but an inspection. Once we pass inspection, they will be on their way," Gavin reassured them.

"What if they don't leave us alone?" another villager asked.

"We have lived in peace for over a century. There is no reason for them to clash with us," Gavin said.

"We should notify King Carlton of Etheland. We're under their rule, not Yorkford."

"One of our own threatened the Prince of Westmore. They have close ties with Yorkford. I spoke to King Carlton, and he has allowed the inspection. We want to avoid bloodshed as much as possible."

"If we give up our stones, when shall we get them back?" someone yelled out.

"My son's nuptials will be this evening at the sacred Majian Mountain. I will arrive with the stones and distribute them to you."

Many of the villagers agreed. Although some were reluctant, they had no choice but to yield to the decision of the majority. Gavin passed around a wooden box, and everyone dropped their stones and lockets.

On the day of the inspection, a group of two dozen Yorkford knights ordered the townspeople out of their homes and gathered them in town central. The knights searched everyone, then went inside their cottages, rummaging through drawers and hiding places. Once the inspection was over, King Matthew's men were satisfied that no one had the magical gems. They mounted their horses and rode back to Yorkford. The villagers cheered and thought the worst was over.

Helena and Beth lived in the wooded area of Maiden Hills and thus escaped the inspection held in town central, as did Simon, Robert, Robert's father Maxwell, and Robert's uncle and his wife.

That evening at the cottage, Beth sat in front of the mirror, patting her face with powder.

"Beth, I wish you would not go," Helena said.

"The inspection is over, Mother. James knows I will be at the wedding, and he will be there waiting for me."

"He betrayed you, Beth, he lied to you about being a prince, and he kept from you that he was married," Helena said. "What more proof do you need that you can't trust him?"

"He loves me, Mother. My intuition tells me so. Simon threatened him, and it was his duty as a prince to report it. I am certain it was a misunderstanding, and Simon did not mean to threaten him. I shall speak to James and Simon, resolve our differences, and come to an agreement. I don't care that he is married. I wish to be with him." Beth grabbed her cloak and headed toward the door.

"Beth, no!" Helena held Beth's arm. "I beg you, do not go. I have a sense of foreboding about this night."

"Mother, please, you imagine things. I must go." She looked at her mother and released herself from her grip. "Please watch Peter." She bent over Peter's cradle, kissed his forehead, then removed her locket and placed it around his neck. She walked out the door.

***

Cedarville, present day

148

"That was the last time I saw my beautiful daughter." Helena wiped the tears spilling down her face. "I had to feed the baby, so I went to the barn across the lake to fetch milk. I left him in his cradle. When I returned… the cottage was in flames." She paused. "I lost my daughter and my grandson that horrible day. I also had a younger brother and a young niece, and they died too."

Robert had his head down, and so did Jack.

"I am so sorry, Helena." Juliana dabbed the corner of her eyes with a kerchief. "I'm aware of how difficult this is for you." She put her hand over Helena's. "Do you know how many survived?"

"Six adults and twenty-four children survived. Three of the adults have died since then, leaving only Robert, my son Simon, and me. The children found homes throughout Cedarville, so I don't know how many live this day. Many of the children were too young to understand what happened, and they never had the magical gemstones and recalled nothing of Maiden Hills. The older ones remember the massacre and fear it would happen again. There is danger ahead."

"What do you mean?" Jack asked.

"It's the prophecy," said Helena.

"My mother said something about a prophecy," said Juliana.

"The prophecy states that two decades and two years after the massacre, there will be an uprising. The Majians will regain their power and destroy those who wish to destroy them. There could be more bloodshed," Helena said. "It's in *The Book of Secrets*."

"Does anyone have a copy?" Juliana asked.

"Alas, mine was in the cottage when it burned," Helena said.

"There were three books," said Robert. "My father gave me his, but it was in my home, and it too was destroyed."

"That leaves Lord Gavin's book. Without the book or the stones, the Majians can't do magic. If we are attacked again, we will not have a chance of surviving," Helena said.

"My mother gave me her stones and said she hid her book in the castle's dungeon. She told me to search for it."

"Your Majesty, if you have the gemstones, I can teach you the spell to communicate with the animals," Helena said. "Alas, I have forgotten the first spell."

Juliana hesitated. "I don't know if I should." All eyes were on her. "I am not convinced this practice does not go against the law of my land, or the teachings of the church." She turned to Jack for guidance. "There are prohibited practices when it comes to magic."

Jack leaned toward her. "Your Majesty, this power is not evil. You knew your mother, she was a sweet, loving lady and you can see the kind of people Robert and Helena are. They are not sorcerers or witches, and they don't cast spells on people. You can trust them."

Juliana stared at Jack, then looked at Robert and Helena. She sighed, yielding, although not convinced. "All right. What's the spell?"

Helena leaned closer to Juliana. "Your Majesty, take the green stone with black waves in your hand and hold it to your heart and recite this spell—Stone of power I ask of thee, to speak to creatures of land and sea, heed my commands in thought that be or words I say to assist me."

"I don't have the stones with me. I shall write it and recite it later. Do you have parchment and ink?"

"I may have some here." Helena combed through her ravaged cottage and found parchment, a quill pen, and ink. She handed it to Juliana and repeated the spell. Juliana wrote the spell, folded the parchment, and tucked it in the space between her bosom.

"Before she died, my mother told me to find Simon. Do you know why?"

Helena shook her head, confused. "I cannot say, Your Majesty."

"Where can I find him?"

"Apologies, he does not tell me where he lives."

Juliana sighed, frustrated at not having all the answers. "All right. She also mentioned a third stone. Where can I find it?"

"The third stone, a deep-red gemstone, appears to the leader who unselfishly protects the Majian people." Helena stared at Juliana, and her eyes widened as a wonderful revelation occurred to her. "You shall lead us, Your Majesty." Helena's green eyes sparkled.

The breath caught in Juliana's throat. "Me? No! I don't know this magical life." Juliana spoke with firmness.

"It's the prophecy coming true. Someone will lead the Majians, and we shall regain our power and triumph."

"Helena, you are mistaken. I am not a Majian—I am the queen." She glanced at everyone in the room. "I should not even be here."

"Your mother would have wanted it."

Juliana's eyes moistened. Her mother was dear to her, and this was a part of her mother's life, a life she had spared her daughter from knowing until her final hour. But this was not Juliana's life, and they could not expect her to embrace it. She looked at Helena. "I would not know what to do."

"You will know. Who better to lead us than the granddaughter of our leader and the daughter of a king? It's in your blood." Helena's face lit up. "Why do you suppose your mother told you before she died? She did not have to tell you, but she did because of the prophecy."

"I wish not to disappoint you, but I am not a leader. Besides, it's my husband who seeks to destroy your people. If I go against him, he will have my head. If the Majian people are to face him, they will surely lose, for he is too powerful." She paused, feeling pressured to find a solution. "I shall speak to him."

"No! Forgive me Your Majesty, but that's what Beth said, and it did not work. We *must* fight. It's the only way we can live as a people without persecution."

Juliana looked at Helena with regret. "Alas, I am not the one."

Jack was familiar with Juliana's stubbornness and not easily swayed. It was a trait she shared with her father. "Helena, if you don't know where the survivors are, how can anyone lead them?"

"There are ways, my lord, to find them and find them we will. But we need a leader."

"Don't worry, Helena, Robert, and I will do what we can," said Jack.

Robert nodded in agreement. "We shall inform Jeb. He will join our cause. He is, after all, Lord Gavin's son. I have my uncle's stones. I shall give it to him."

"Very well. You shall all handle it." A relieved Juliana turned to Jack. "Lord Jack, will you please take me to my castle through the tunnel? I shall search for the book so the Majians can learn the spells." She glanced at the faces in the room. "It's the least I can do."

Jack looked at Juliana and nodded. "Aye, your Majesty."

***

At the local tavern, boisterous laughter filled the atmosphere, and plenty of beer and ale poured into mugs and into the patrons guzzling them in a steady stream. Sir Paul was among the patrons mingling with the villagers. He dressed as a commoner to hide his identity as one of King Edmund's knights. As a newcomer to the tavern, Paul sought to gain the men's confidence, so he bought them beer, hoping to get them drunk enough to talk. Paul laughed at their jokes and told stories to distract the men while he nursed his drink. He was on a special assignment from King Edmund to find sorcerers, and he could not allow the alcohol to cloud his judgment. He befriended Kent, a man in his late twenties with brown hair to his shoulders and a scraggly beard and mustache. Kent had consumed more than his share of beer pints and was clearly inebriated, and to Paul's liking, overly chatty.

"Kent, this story about the magical people and the massacre is just a tale, is it not?" Paul asked.

"I will let you in on a secret." Kent glimpsed over his shoulder, his head bobbing and words slurring. "I am one of them."

"You can do magic?" Paul looked for a locket hanging from his neck, but he didn't have one.

"No, I can't, but I was there."

Paul drew his ear closer to decipher Kent's mumbling, taking in a whiff of alcohol on his breath. "I don't understand."

"They rescued me when I was a child. To do magic, one must have the enchanted stones, but I didn't have them because I was too young."

"Are there any adults who escaped and who have the stones?" Paul was eager to get a lead on who might have killed King Edmund's father.

"Doctor Robert has them. There's an old woman, a seamstress." He tilted his head to the ceiling. "I can't remember her name." He scratched his head. "Halley… Lana… oh! It's Helena, that's it. Two men drove the carriage when we were rescued, but they died long ago. There could be others, I think, but no one speaks of it."

"Does Doctor Robert or Helena use their magic?"

"Not much. Helena's too old, and Doctor Robert does not use it except for defending himself. I saw him use it on a man a few days ago in this very tavern," he said, pressing his finger on the wooden counter. "The man got so scared he ran out of here like he saw a bloody ghost." Kent let out a belly laugh. "You should have seen him floating in the air, screaming, 'Put me down, put me down.' Everybody laughed."

Paul laughed along with him, aware that the man floating in the air was Sir Quinn.

154

Sir Paul swallowed the rest of his beer and rushed out of the tavern.

***

Edmund sat hunched over his desk with his eyes fixed on the book he found in James' chamber. He sensed someone at the door.

"Pardon me, Your Majesty," said Ella. "Sir Paul is here to see you."

Without lifting his eyes from the book, he said, "Let him in." He then closed the book and placed it behind him on a table.

Sir Paul walked into the library and bowed. "Your Majesty, I have news for you."

"What do you have?"

"We found Helena's cabin, but she was not there. We searched the cabin for stones and lockets but found none. I then went to the tavern and met a man who told me he was a survivor of the massacre. He was a child at the time and told me many children were saved. He also said there are at least two adults who survived the massacre and still live. One of them is Helena, and the other one is a doctor. His name is Robert. Doctor Robert was the one that had the encounter with Sir Quinn at the tavern."

Edmund sat in the chair, contemplating his next move. Juliana was missing, no doubt she was hiding in Cedarville, and now Helena was missing. He needed answers. He finally had the name of the man who used sorcery on Sir Quinn in the tavern. It seemed this doctor was a critical piece to the puzzle. "Bring me the doctor."

Chapter 10

The soft galloping through the dark forest echoed for miles, breaking the stillness of the night. Not long after midnight, at the edge of the forest, Juliana and Jack reached the entrance to the tunnel that led to the dungeon of Yorkford Castle. The secret passageway was well hidden for a good reason, but Jack knew where to find it. Juliana dreaded having to walk through the long, damp tunnel again, but there was no other way to get inside the castle undetected. At this late hour, the guards had raised the drawbridge, and the castle was in lockdown.

After what seemed an eternity through the tunnel, they arrived at the dungeon. It was eerily quiet, for even the prisoners were asleep. Juliana and Jack examined the cement blocks one by one with the light of one candle.

They searched for hours, tapping each block, checking for a loose one. Drops of water echoed in the hollow halls as they labored. Juliana sighed. "It's no use. This area is too large."

"Did she offer any clues?" Jack asked.

Juliana strained to recall. "I remember she said it was at her eye level. She was about sixteen years old when she moved into the castle."

"So, we should look for the block that's a few inches below your eye level."

Juliana smiled. "Why didn't I think of that?"

They hunched down a few inches and examined the blocks. Juliana touched one, and it shifted. The block was slightly uneven with the others. She brought her eye up to it, and an 'x' was etched in the right corner. "Jack, this is it!"

With care, Jack lifted the block from its place, and Juliana inserted her hand. She tapped the bottom, sides, and back. Her face dropped. "It's empty." She examined the outside of the block. "The 'x' is clear. There can be no mistaking that this is the one. What happened to the book?"

"Someone must have taken it," Jack said.

"But who? Who knew there was a book in there?"

"They could have seen your mother hide it." Jack saw the look of disappointment on Juliana's face. "I'm sorry. I know you wanted to find it."

"We *must* find it. Without it, the Majian people will not have the spells. They do not stand a chance of defending themselves." A thought occurred to her. "Could it have been Edmund?"

"I don't think so, Edmund does not come down here. It surprised me that he came to see you when you were in the cell." He paused, sighing, at a loss for a solution. "What will you do?"

She pondered the next step. "There is nothing more to do here. I must return to the castle."

"Juliana, that could be dangerous. Edmund imprisoned you because he suspects you warned me about the attack. He is not very forgiving."

"I will be fine. There are many people in the castle. I shall make sure I am never alone. Besides, I need to search for the stones my mother gave me and recite the spell that will summon the help of the animals, and then I must keep searching for the book. It has to be somewhere in the castle." A lump formed in her throat, and with sad eyes looked at Jack. "I gave my mother my word."

Jack stared at her, then nodded. "It is not my will to leave you here, but I suppose there is no other option."

"There is not. I just remembered—tomorrow is the annual Festival of Flowers. There will be more people than usual around town and in the castle. We are hosting the banquet. If I am not present, the townspeople and visitors will suspect something's amiss. Edmund will dare not harm me."

"All right." Jack reached into his pouch, took out a candle, passed the flame from his onto it, and handed it to Juliana. "Please be careful."

"I will."

"Goodbye, Juliana." Jack turned toward the tunnel.

"Jack."

He stopped and turned around.

She stared at him for a moment. "Thank you for rescuing me. It was just like old times, me getting into trouble and you coming to my defense. I... I missed you." She gave him an awkward smile.

He grinned. "I missed you too."

She watched as he disappeared through the tunnel, and the candlelight faded.

Juliana climbed up the narrow stairs from the dungeon and into the main castle. She hid behind every column and alcove along the way and peeked before moving forward, not wanting to run into Edmund or his knights. When the path was clear, she scampered to the next area and searched again for signs of life. She made it to her private chamber on the second floor, relieved. Juliana glimpsed herself in the mirror. *Have I ever looked worse?* She placed the candle on a candlestick and removed her cloak and shoes. Her bed invited her to climb in, and when she did, she fell into a deep sleep.

Her eyes popped open, awakened by the sound of the metal hinge on the door. She sat up, squinting from the sun's glare as it came through an opening in the drapes. The door swung open, and her maidservant Liza walked in, holding a feather duster.

Liza, with wide eyes, put her hand to her chest. "Oh, Your Majesty, you frightened me. Forgive me for coming into your private chamber and waking you up, but you have not used this chamber since before you married." She stared at Juliana's ragged appearance. "Your Majesty, what happened to you?"

"It's nothing, Liza. I am well, but I require your assistance to get ready for the festival. Find an appropriate dress for me to wear, something that will cover my neck. Get my bathwater ready, and then you must wash and style my hair. I ask that you make great haste. We don't have much time."

"Aye, Your Majesty." The maid hurried into Juliana's wardrobe and chose an exquisite gold-colored satin dress with long sleeves, a high neck, and lace trim. Liza directed the servants to bring up warm water to fill the tub.

As the servant undressed Juliana, the parchment tucked in Juliana's bosom fell onto the floor. Juliana picked it up and scanned the room for a safe place to hide it. Her eyes came upon her jewelry box, and she placed the parchment inside. She then searched for the black bag her mother had given her with the locket, but

159

it was not among her jewels. *Where did I hide it six years ago?*

The servants brought up warm water, and when the tub was filled, Juliana climbed in. Liza tossed in rose petals, herbs, and spices. At once, the fragrance and warmness soothed her skin and relieved the aches in her muscles. The tepid rose water washed away, not just the dirt, but also the stress and turmoil of the last two days. She melted into a calmer state as her servants scrubbed her body and washed her hair. She breathed in deep and allowed her mind to focus on the Majian people. Life in the castle was predictable, and she knew her place and her duties, but this time was different, for there was much at stake. Although she didn't want to admit it, she had no choice but to accept that she had magical blood running through her veins. She had to protect her mother's legacy and what her grandparents risked their lives for.

She thought of her grandfather Gavin, trying in vain to save his people from those who sought to destroy them, and her grandmother Victoria, sending away her only daughter, Lucinda, so she would live on with the gemstones and *The Book of Secrets* to continue the story of the people from Maiden Hills. Juliana could not fail to carry on their legacy. Although they were long dead, she felt compelled to keep their memory alive. She didn't want her life to change, but she couldn't turn her back on them, for they were a part of her.

She closed her eyes, sinking into the warm pool, when all of a sudden, her eyes sprang wide open, and her face lit up—she remembered where she had hidden the stones.

As Juliana stepped out of the copper tub, Liza and the maids patted her skin with soft linen cloths, absorbing the moisture, and squeezing the excess water from her hair. Her undergarments and corset laid on her bed, and her gold dress hung on a standing hook.

Juliana reached for the bottom drawer of her dresser. There, tucked between old clothes, she found the small black bag that contained her mother's locket and gemstones. Her wonderment turned into melancholy as she remembered her mother's final day. She opened the bag, took out the locket, and examined the glowing stones. Her mother's words came back to her. "*Let no one see you with the stones.*" She closed the locket.

"Liza, please put this on me."

The young maid marveled at the gold locket, then fastened it around Juliana's neck. "It's beautiful, Your Majesty."

"It was a gift from my mother."

Liza wrapped the corset around Juliana's waist and tightened the laces. "It's too tight, Liza. I can't breathe."

"Apologies, Your Majesty." She loosened the corset, and Juliana exhaled. She then slipped the gold-colored gown over Juliana and draped it over her slim figure.

Juliana tucked the locket under her dress.

"Such a beautiful pendant should be worn over the dress, Your Majesty, so that others can admire its loveliness."

"Truly, but for now, I shall keep it hidden."

Juliana gazed out the window of her bedchamber overlooking the city and watched the crowd grow, anticipating the annual event. The morning of the Festival of Flowers was a spirited spring day with the sun

161

shining bright and hundreds of sparrows chirping with excitement as if they too were to join in the festivities. On this day, the kingdom celebrated beauty by adorning the town with flowers. Juliana recalled the story her father had told her that started the tradition. It began with her grandmother, King Matthew's mother, Queen Matilda. She was a fastidious queen, and everything in the castle had to be up to her standard of beauty. One day, she proclaimed a holiday where flowers would be scattered all over the kingdom. The gardeners planted flowers in the castle's garden, and throughout the country, to bloom in time for the festival. When the flowers were at their fullest, the gardeners gathered them for the queen to pass on to the young maidens. The queen rode a horse-drawn carriage filled with cut flowers and tossed the flowers to the maidens on the royal route. The legend was that whoever received a red flower from the queen would wed within the year.

To mark the start of the festival, the royal family lowered the drawbridge and allowed the townspeople to enter the garden area, where they would wait for the king and queen to appear. Every member of the king's guard would be at their post, keeping watch on the crowd and restricting the number of people allowed inside the garden. The local merchants would set up their tables along the castle route, eagerly awaiting visitors with bulky bags of coins to spend. It was indeed a festive day and produced a joyous atmosphere in the kingdom.

The hour of her anticipated entrance neared. Juliana stealthily descended the stairs and hurried through a passage inside the castle leading toward the garden. She peeked through a window and watched the crowd as they gathered below the balcony, waiting for the royal couple to appear. In an unexpected sight, the people saw King Edmund by himself on the balcony. Juliana chuckled.

Murmurs passed among the townspeople. "Where is the queen?"

"Good morning, good people of Yorkford," Edmund said in a booming voice. "You must all be wondering where your queen is."

The crowd hailed and waved purple and red banners, the colors of Yorkford.

"Your queen is—"

Cheers erupted when the guards opened the double doors leading to the garden, and Queen Juliana walked out dressed in her full majestic attire. Her dark auburn hair was tightly curled up adorned with her jeweled crown. She wore her long scarlet red cape with gold trim, and underneath, a gold satin dress with a high neck. Hidden under her gown, unbeknownst to anyone, was her mother's locket with the enchanted gemstones. She smiled at the crowd, taking in their love and admiration for her.

The crowd may have suspected Juliana planned this unanticipated and unconventional entrance to stir up excitement in the opening festivities. They applauded with enthusiasm, expressing their appreciation for the queen's ingenuity. Juliana glimpsed up at Edmund on the balcony as he glared at her with dagger eyes. She gave him a casual smirk and continued to greet the people lovingly.

Edmund strolled toward Juliana. She looked up at him, and they both knew they had a role to play. He took her hand, and she allowed him to kiss it, eyes locked. The crowd cheered.

Juliana put her arm inside his, and they strolled side by side toward the carriage. He spoke low so no one would hear. "How did you get out of the cell?"

"It's my castle. I can find my way around it," Juliana said while smiling and waving at the crowd.

"Your memory has returned?"

"It has, and I know what you did to me."

"You deserved it. We shall speak of it later."

They rode through the town in the carriage, greeted by thousands of townspeople and visitors, hoping to get a glimpse of the king and queen. Juliana tossed the flowers to the crowd, and the single ladies fought for the red flowers. Some ladies rejoiced while holding a red flower, while others expressed disappointment and even tears at the thought of having to wait another year to wed.

After the ride through town, prominent noblemen and noblewomen filled the rows of tables at the castle for the traditional banquet. Seated at the head table with Juliana and Edmund were the high-born guests from various towns and villages in the kingdom. Juliana sat with Edmund on ornate chairs under a canopy surrounded by dukes, barons, and the most esteemed of all the knights. Among those seated at the high table were Princess Katherine, Duke Richard of Westmore and his wife Duchess Isabel, and the king's knights, Sir Leopold and Sir Quinn. Distant family members and other lords and ladies filled the remaining chairs. Lord Jack, who would have sat at the king's table, was noticeably absent. Juliana did not expect he would attend.

Juliana and Edmund traded stares as the servants appeared with trays filled with the finest meats from peacock and venison, potatoes, soup, and bread. As the servants placed the food in front of them, Juliana and Edmund had a food tester taste the food and wine before they ate or drank. It was a long, exhausting day.

As the day came to a close, Juliana's chest tightened, and her heartbeat quickened. She dreaded being alone with Edmund, for he would continue to torment her for her actions.

After all the guests departed with full stomachs and many quite inebriated, Juliana rose from her seat and broke through her anxiety. She turned to Edmund. "I shall sleep in my private chamber this night with a guard at my door. Do not think of coming near me." Juliana turned away from Edmund.

Edmund grabbed her arm, pulling her toward him. He clenched his teeth. "What were you doing in the forest that night?"

"I went for a ride."

"Do you think I'm a fool? You went to see Jack, didn't you? Admit it—you're having an affair with him."

"Release me. Jack is my friend, not my lover, and unlike you, he would never hurt me."

He released her, eyes glaring. "Did you warn him we would attack Cedarville?"

She narrowed her eyes. "Why *did* you attack Cedarville?"

"If you must know, they broke the law."

"How did they break the law?"

"It's none of your concern. I will do what I must do to keep my kingdom safe from lawbreakers."

"The accused must stand trial. We must ensure peace and stability among all our people. In the absence of an actual threat, I suggest you work to resolve disputes instead of attacking them without good reason."

Edmund's eyes narrowed. "I have reasons for my actions, and you would do well to stay out of my affairs." He grasped her arm. "*I* am the ruler of this kingdom, not you."

She pulled her arm back and freed herself from his grip. "You are only the ruler because my father's dead." She studied him. "He put his trust in the wrong man." She glared at him, then marched out of the room.

"Stick to your duties, Juliana. You are to tend to the castle and give me an heir, not chase after a lowly peasant."

Juliana stopped, opened her mouth, but held her tongue. Edmund was provoking her, and she thought it best not to give him the satisfaction of a rebuttal. She gave no weight to his words filled with lies and hatred for Jack. She charged ahead, climbed up the stairs, and turned toward her private bedchamber. Edmund was to sleep by himself, and she took comfort in that it was at the far end of the hall. She could not imagine sleeping next to him, for she feared the night would be her last.

She summoned her maidservant, Liza. "Please fetch Sir Mark." Sir Mark was Jack's closest friend and someone she could trust to be loyal to her. When Mark arrived, Juliana asked him to keep watch over her chamber while she slept. Mark was happy to do her bidding and stood guard by her door. Liza followed

Juliana into her chamber and remove her gold-colored gown and corset and slipped a white satin nightdress on her.

"Will there be anything else, Your Majesty?"

"That will be all, Liza. I shall retire for the evening." Liza departed, and Juliana locked the door and hurried toward her bureau. She dug into her jewelry box and retrieved the parchment with the spell. From underneath her dress, she pulled out her locket, took out the green stone with black waves, and stared at it as it glowed with a faint pulse. Holding it to her heart, she let out an audible breath, then recited the spell written on the parchment.

The stone became warm, and the heat traveled throughout her body. She wasn't sure if the spell worked, but the warm sensation indicated that something magical happened. She had to test it. But how?

Uncertain of the next step and anxious to get off her feet after a long and exhausting day, Juliana proceeded to her canopied bed. When she pulled the blanket from the bed, she shrieked upon seeing a black spider crawling on her pillow. She opened her mouth to call Sir Mark but stopped before the words came out. She stared at the spider and spoke out loud. "Please get off my bed and leave my chamber."

"Aye, Your Majesty," the spider replied.

Juliana gasped.

The spider scurried off the bed and onto the floor. She watched it as it disappeared into a small crack in the wall.

Chapter 11

Juliana lay wide awake in her bed. The thought of a spider talking to her was unsettling, and finding her mother's book lay heavy on her mind. *It has to be somewhere in the dungeon.* She put on her blue robe, picked up the candleholder, and opened the door.

Mark was standing guard, and it surprised him to see Juliana awake after midnight. "Your Majesty, is everything all right?"

"I must search for something in the dungeon. Would you kindly accompany me?"

He furrowed his brow. "The dungeon?"

She nodded. "Please."

"As you wish, Your Majesty."

"No one must know where we're going," Juliana added in a whisper.

They stepped furtively through the grand hall and down the long winding staircase, then through the narrow stairs, two levels down to reach the dungeon. The castle was hauntingly silent until they arrived at the jail. Moans and cries of prisoners arrested during the festival echoed through the passages. Juliana shuddered, for only two days ago, she too occupied a cell.

"Sir Mark, please wait by the entrance and alert me if you see anyone."

"Aye, Your Majesty."

Juliana examined the cement blocks as she went deeper into the dungeon. Perhaps there could be another block with a small 'x' that she missed. She kept searching until she came upon the same block that she and Jack found. She removed the concrete with care, but the cavity was empty. "I wish I knew what happened to the book," she uttered to herself.

"It was the big guy."

The childlike voice startled Juliana. She jerked her head over her shoulder. "Who said that?"

"It was the big guy."

She scanned the dark hall, lifting the candlestick, her hand shaking, but no one was in sight. "I demand you show yourself."

"Down here."

Juliana lowered the candlestick to the floor where two small mice stood on their hind legs, big round black eyes looking up at her, twitching their noses. Her eyes widened.

"You wished to know what happened to the book. The big guy took it," a mouse said.

Juliana's eyes widened. "You saw who took the book?"

"Yes, it was the big guy," the other mouse repeated.

"What big guy?"

"I think they mean me."

Juliana flinched, when looming over her, stood a large hooded man. He looked familiar—a black beard, a mustache, and a round stomach—she had seen him before.

"Forgive me for startling you, Your Majesty," he said, his voice deep.

"Do I know you?" She searched her memory. "Wait. You're the dungeon guard who brought me supper when I was in the cell, are you not?"

"I am, I—"

Before he could finish, Juliana held up her hand. "Wait." She looked up at the guard, then down at the mice, then back at the guard. "Did… did you hear the mice speak?"

"I did. I am Simon."

Juliana gasped. "You're Helena's son! How long have you been in the castle?"

"I have been here for almost nineteen years. I came here after Queen Lucinda moved in to watch over her. After she died, I stayed to keep watch over you."

"You're the one my mother told me to find." Juliana recalled her conversation with Robert. She stepped back and cupped her hands over her mouth, eyes wide. "You killed King Edmund's father, Prince James."

His face tightened at the mention of Prince James. "Because of him, I lost my sister, her baby, and my kin. Our people were killed, and our village destroyed. Because of him, we live in hiding."

Juliana trembled to be face to face with a murderer, but then she thought of the grief this man had experienced at the hands of Prince James, and she understood. It was the same grief that continued to haunt Robert and Helena. "It's rather bold of you to reside in this castle all these years after what you have done. Nonetheless, I gave Robert my word that I would not bring you to justice."

Prisoners moaned in their cells, raising the hairs on Juliana's skin. She cringed. "We shall leave now. Do you have the book?"

"It's in my chamber."

"Why did you take it?"

"I did not wish for it to be in the wrong hands. I saw Her Majesty, your mother, hide it, and I feared someone might take hold of it. It's the only one left of its kind."

"You shall give it to me. It belongs to me."

Simon nodded. "Aye, Your Majesty."

At the entrance, Mark's eyes widened when he saw Juliana with the dungeon guard. He tightened the grip on his sword.

"It's all right, Sir Mark." She turned to Simon. "You shall lead us to your chamber."

Juliana and Mark followed Simon through the narrow halls of the dungeon. He opened a door and led them into a small room furnished with a bed, a chest, and a small table. He walked toward the table, opened a drawer, and pulled out a book. He handed it to Juliana.

Juliana's excitement grew as she held the book. The words *The Book of Secrets* stood out in gold lettering against the black cover, and in the center, three gold circles linked, just like on her locket. She opened the book and read the first-page inscription: *This book belongs to Lord Gavin Archer, a descendant of Sir Kolby.*

"I shall take this to my chamber." She looked at Simon and gave him a grateful half-smile. "Thank you."

Mark escorted Juliana to her chamber, and she locked the door. Once inside, she sat in her chair and held the candle over the book. She placed her hand over the cover and closed her eyes. Gratitude filled her having the book in her possession, fulfilling the promise she made to her mother. "Mother, I did it, I kept my word."

She turned the page to the first section entitled: *History of the Majian People.*

Long ago, three noblemen gave up their land and fortunes to travel to towns and villages and help those in need. Sometimes they were welcomed, but other times they were beaten and told never to return. They worked the land, fed hungry people, and helped build cottages. The only payment they requested was food and a warm place to sleep.

While sleeping outdoors in a meadow with beautiful flowers, hills surrounding them, and a large mountain behind them, a young maiden appeared. Her appearance startled them—not because she was frightful, for she was rather beautiful, but because she seemed to be floating. She wore a long white dress that flowed around her, although there was no breeze. Her complexion was luminesced, her eyes were sparkling violet, and her long hair was white as the brightest star. They thought they were in the presence of an angel. Her name was Majia. She told them not to fear, for she had chosen them to receive special gifts. The men sat up and listened. She told them that she had seen their acts of compassion, kindness, and bravery, and because of it, she would reward them with three magical gifts of their choosing.

The first young man, Sir Clayton, thought for a few minutes. "I wish to move objects without touching them. This will help me stop swords, arrows, or stones from coming at me, and when I am tired, I can build cabins faster." The maiden agreed and gave him a black gemstone with golden tones and said to him that the gem would help him magically move anything he desired.

The second man, Sir Drake, pondered for a moment. "I wish to communicate with animals and seek their assistance when needed to help guard and protect us."

The maiden agreed and gave him a green stone with black waves and said to him that the stone would help him communicate with wild animals and seek their help.

The third man, Sir Kolby, thought for a while and said, "I wish to protect my friends and all the good people who are threatened." The maiden agreed and gave him a deep-red stone and said that with the stone, he could create a shield around those he wished to protect, including himself. She said this stone was the rarest of all, and since his main concern was for the safety of others, it would make the wearer the leader and protector of the people.

Majia instructed them to carry the stones around their neck, so it was closest to the center of their energy. She said their powers would make them and their offspring defenders of the mortal realm. The stones would appear to their descendants when they had proven their kindness and courage, and any offspring of a magical parent would also have supernatural abilities when wearing the stones. Anyone who possesses the gemstones could pass it down to their descendants who they deemed worthy. A word of caution she provided—wearers of stones can become unworthy. Nonetheless, the magic will remain with them. They may use their power for evil instead of good.

The maiden told them they would need to recite spells to activate the power of the first two stones. The third stone did not require a spell. When it appeared to the leader, it would work upon their intention to protect others. The protection would last for a moment, giving them enough time to escape danger.

The three men thanked Majia for their magical gifts and lived long lives helping others. They were paid well for their services and accumulated a vast fortune in gold. The king who owned the land where the maiden appeared, granted the property to the three nobles to develop and care for it. The noblemen had built cottages in the area, cultivated the land, and raised farm animals. They had wives and children of their own, and they passed on the story of how they acquired their abilities. They named the area Maiden Hills, after the beautiful maiden who gave them their mystical gifts, and the magnificent sacred mountain was named the Majian Mountain. They called themselves Majians. With flowing streams, luscious green trees, and vibrant flowers, Maiden Hills was the most beautiful village anyone had ever seen. Hills and mountains surrounded the village, and to the north, there was a creek and to the south, a river.

Juliana turned the page. The next section was entitled: *Spells for Activation of Magic.*

To activate the power within the black and golden stone, hold the stone to your heart and recite the words:

Stone of magic and yellow light, move those objects within my sight, heed my command to protect or fight, in the bright of day or dark of night.

To activate the power within the green and black stone, hold the stone to your heart and recite the words:

Stone of power I ask of thee, to speak to creatures of land and sea, heed my commands in thought that be or words I say to assist me.

There is no spell to activate the deep-red stone. It will appear to the leader who unselfishly risks their life to protect others. The stone's energy shall activate upon the sincere request of the wearer.

Juliana moved on to the next section entitled: *To Summon Majian People*.

To summon the Majian people, proceed to the tallest mountain, light a fire, and add special herbs. All Majians will be called to it and will congregate around the fire.

She came across a section on healing with magical herbs. She skimmed through that one and other chapters then flipped to the last section entitled: *Prophecies*.

After one hundred years have passed, and all is prosperous, an army will rise to eliminate the Majian people. Most will perish in a bloody massacre, and the Majians will flee their land. Keep the secret of the magic and only share with those who are loyal and trustworthy.

Two decades and two years following the massacre, more violence will occur, but a new leader and protector will emerge, and the Majian people will regain their power. The Majians will triumph over their enemies and overthrow the king. Maiden Hills will once again belong to the Majian people. The Majians must continue to form a bond of unity with each other and stand with the three protectors and the three kings to triumph against evil forces that threaten our world.

Juliana flipped back to the first spell and took the black stone with golden tones out of the locket. She held it to her heart and recited the spell, "Stone of magic and yellow light, move those objects within my sight, heed my command to protect or fight, in the bright of day or dark of night."

Shivers swept through her body, a different feeling than the last spell, more intense, and it frightened her. She stared at the book, and her hands trembled. *What is happening? I must dispose of this book.* She glanced at the bottom drawer of her wardrobe, and to her surprise, the drawer slid open, and the book levitated from her hands, floating across the room until it descended inside the drawer and closed by itself. Her heart pounded, and her breathing quickened. *Did I just do that?* She sat back and crossed her arms in front of her, rubbing them, thawing the chills. *This can't be happening.* Her powers terrified her, and she feared for what lay ahead.

***

"Your Majesty."

Juliana opened her eyes, blinking away the fog. When her surroundings came into focus, her maidservant's face was in front of her.

"Pardon me, Your Majesty. I have come to wake you. It is morn, the hour of your rising." Liza opened the drapes, inviting the sunshine to brighten the room.

Juliana sat upright in her chair, squinting from the sun's glare. She tapped her chest, felt her locket, and recalled the floating book. *It wasn't a dream!*

"Would you care to break your fast, Your Majesty?"

"I'm not hungry. There is someplace I need to be." Juliana removed her white nightdress and, with Liza's help, changed into a maroon silk dress with lace embroidery. She tucked her locket underneath her dress and reached for her purple cloak. Outside her door, Mark remained on guard.

"Sir Mark, please accompany me to the stables."

"Of course, Your Majesty."

As they made their way downstairs, Juliana was careful not to chance upon Edmund. She looked around, relieved he was not in sight. The servants were tending to their morning duties and busily preparing breakfast for the residents of the castle. Juliana and Mark passed through the garden and headed for the stables. Juliana summoned a stable boy to saddle her horse and take her to the front of the castle. Mark hurried to the gatehouse to lower the drawbridge.

Once outside, Juliana scanned the area for Edmund's knights. A few people strolled the castle grounds in the early morning, but no one seemed to be watching her. She would not be surprised if Edmund had men surveilling her. She eyed the castle guards suspiciously, as they stood dutifully at their posts, subtly observing the people.

Juliana mounted Millie, sprinted over the drawbridge, and sped out of the castle grounds. She headed south toward the forest, galloping at a swift pace.

A short while after entering the forest, Juliana's ears perked at the thumping of hooves behind her. She turned and spotted two knights attempting to hide behind the trees. She rolled her eyes. *Wonderful!* She tugged on Millie's reins and spun around toward them.

"Good morning, sirs," she called.

"Good morning, Your Majesty." Their faces reddened at being caught.

"Are you following me?"

"We are making sure you are safe, Your Majesty."

"If I wanted a guard, I would have asked for one. Are you certain King Edmund did not order you to spy on me?" Juliana tried to keep the venom out of her voice.

The men glanced at each other, then one of them spoke. "The king wanted us to keep watch over you, Your Majesty. He is concerned for your safety."

"I'm sure he is, but that won't be necessary. You may tell the king that I went for a ride and wished to be unaccompanied. Please return to the castle at once and leave me to continue my ride without interruption."

"Aye, Your Majesty." The two men hesitated, then turned their horses around and headed for the castle. Juliana watched until they disappeared from sight.

She crossed the Cedarville bridge and trotted along the trail toward Jack's castle. When she arrived, a young squire grabbed her horse's reins and led Millie to the stables. The castle guard opened the door for Juliana, and Audrey, the maidservant, greeted her.

As she walked into the great hall, she observed the large framed paintings on the wall. Most of the subjects were familiar. There was a portrait of her uncle, Prince Marcus, standing behind Princess Katherine sitting on a chair—Jack's adoptive parents. With his dark hair, hazel eyes, and a prominent nose, Prince Marcus resembled her father, King Matthew, but without the beard or gray hair. Princess Katherine was lovely in a violet gown and golden-brown curls, but with sadness in her eyes. She had suffered many misfortunes.

Juliana did not recognize the young couple in the next painting, standing in front of a small wooden cabin. They wore common clothes but seemed content. The man had ash blond hair just like Jack, and the woman's hair was light brown and short, which she wore underneath a white head covering. Two young boys with ash blond hair and a young girl with light brown hair stood in front of the couple.

"Those are my natural parents."

Juliana turned her head when she heard Jack's voice.

"They did not pose for the painting. An artist sketched them from my memory." He turned to look at Juliana and smiled. "It's good to see you."

She embraced him and held on for a few seconds. Seeing Jack's face filled her with warm feelings, and her worries seem to disappear, at least for a moment. "It's good to see you too, Jack."

"I am about to break my fast. Would you care to join me?"

"I would."

He led her to a charming dining hall with a table that seated eight, and underneath it, an exquisitely woven red rug. A large chandelier suspended from the ceiling with twenty-four candles and shimmering crystals dangling from the rings. Vibrant tapestries adorned the walls.

The servants came in and placed a tray of warm bread and butter, a bowl of fruit, and a jug of wine.

Jack pulled a side chair for Juliana and waited for her to sit. "I worried about what Edmund might do to you."

Juliana reached for a piece of bread, and the servant poured wine in her glass. "I was fine. I slept in my private chamber. Sir Mark guarded my door all night." She scooped a small piece of butter and spread it on the bread.

Jack sat next to her, forgoing the head of the table. "Sir Mark is a good man, except he beat me in a mock tournament a few months ago, and I have yet to retaliate." He grinned. "What brings you here?"

"Much has happened in the last two days, and I don't know what to do. I find it overwhelming, and I fear I am unable to handle the consequences that might arise from it."

"What happened at the castle?"

Juliana sighed. "I found my mother's book."

Jack's eyes widened. "Where did you find it?"

"The dungeon guard had it. It turns out the dungeon guard is Simon, Helena's son. Apparently, he never told his mother or Robert he was living at the castle, but my mother knew. He said he moved in to watch over her."

"That explains why he helped you escape when Edmund put you in the dungeon. He's loyal to you, not to Edmund."

"Yes, but he's tempting fate. He killed Edmund's father, and he's living in the castle. Edmund will kill him if he finds out."

Jack sipped his wine, washing down the bread and butter. "He's very good at hiding out. He can go in and out of the castle undetected. Besides Mark and me, he's the only other person who knows about the secret passageway."

"Jack, it unnerves me to know there is a way to get into the castle without being seen. Who built them?"

"They were built when the castle was designed centuries ago. Mark and I stumbled onto an opening in the dungeon. We went through it and saw it led to the dark forest. It was a great way to sneak out at night and visit other villages. One night, the dungeon guard saw us and swore he would tell no one. I remembered he said his mother and daughter live in Cedarville, and it was a quick way to leave the castle to see them."

Juliana tilted her head. "You would sneak out? I thought I was the mischievous one."

Jack grinned. "I had a bit of a mischievous side too."

"You had everyone fooled, Lord Jack, including me." She smiled, then her expression changed. "I also learned the spells. I can do magic, and it frightens me. If Edmund seeks to cite the law and execute the Majian people, he will execute me too."

"Juliana, you must fight to protect yourself and the Majian people. Perhaps Helena is right. You may be the leader they have been waiting for."

Juliana shook her head. "I can't be responsible for their lives. It is not a burden I wish to undertake." She would not think of it. Juliana was the queen of her kingdom—not a maiden of the country who fought for others' rights and lives. That was not her station in life.

"They are your people."

"I have my kingdom to think about. They're my people, too. I must protect what my father built."

Jack sighed. "I understand. It's not just your mother's legacy you must protect, it's your father's as well."

181

"Yes, and at the moment, they are at odds. I can't side with one without losing the other."

He hesitated, then nodded. "Don't worry. My village will fight back, and we shall defend the Majians if necessary."

Juliana shook her head. "Jack, this is not your fight. Besides, you would go against your king."

"My code of chivalry is to be faithful to God, above all else, including the king, and to put others' lives before my own, especially the weak and defenseless. I will do what I must do to protect the Majian people. I must do what is right."

"You're risking everything."

"So be it." He looked at her. "I would do the same for you."

She gazed into his eyes and saw the resolve within him. She knew he meant it. It was the same eyes of the young boy who defended her when they were children—protecting the young damsel of the castle—now he was a man, a knight, faithful to his code of chivalry and determined to defend the people in his village at all costs. Warm feelings swept through her, and she breathed in deep. Jack leaned closer and gave her a soft kiss on her lips. Juliana froze, stunned by this unexpected move, the thumping quickening in her chest. They steadily gazed into each other. He kissed her again, but this time the kiss lingered. She immersed herself in the closeness and the sweet touch of his lips, but then backed away.

"Jack, I… I can't."

Jack pulled away. "I'm sorry."

"Why did you do that? Are we not just friends?"

182

He peered into her eyes. "Are we, Juliana, or is there something more?"

"If there is more, it is not to be. Alas, I am not free. I am bound to my husband."

"Are you bound by love?"

Juliana's heart gave a squeeze, never feeling for Edmund what she felt for Jack. "There is no love between Edmund and me, only an obligation, but it is one I must honor."

"Then, I shall no longer interfere with your obligation."

Juliana sensed frustration in him. "Jack, I do not wish for things to change between us."

Jack swallowed the rest of his wine. "They won't. I shall be here for you, Juliana, just as I have always been." Their eyes locked for a moment, then Jack broke the stare and refilled his wineglass. "What do you wish to do?"

Juliana pushed through the awkwardness. "I wish to see Robert. Will you take me to him?"

Jack nodded.

***

They galloped through the back route, and when Juliana and Jack approached Robert's cottage, he was standing by the doorway with a young woman. She was attractive, with long brown hair and a slim figure. Her arm was bent in a sling.

Juliana heard him say to her, "Come back in a few days, and I shall examine it. I want to make sure it is healing properly."

"I will." She gave him a sweet smile and walked to the village with a subtle sway in her hips.

Juliana and Jack came down from their horses and saw a well-rested man, unlike the tired, unkempt man from the other day.

"Your Majesty, my lord, I am surprised to see you both," Robert said with a broad smile.

"I hope we are not imposing," Juliana said.

"Not at all, Your Majesty. Would you like to come inside?"

"I would, thank you." Juliana stepped inside and lowered her hood. "She seems like a lovely lady."

"Geraldine is very sweet, but she is often ill. She comes to me at least once a week with a different ailment."

"I think she has a fondness for you." Juliana grinned.

Robert smiled, and his face blushed, presuming it might be true. Juliana had not seen Robert well-rested and noticed his strikingly handsome features. He had a firm chin and expressive smoky gray eyes.

"Please have a seat." They sat in front of the fireplace. "What brings you here?" Robert asked.

"I wish to see Maiden Hills," Juliana said.

Robert's cheerful expression disappeared. "I have not stepped foot on that land for twenty-two years." He paused. "It would be a rather depressing sight, Your Majesty."

"I need to put the pieces together, Robert. I found the book and learned the history of the Majian people, and I recited the spells. I need all of this to make sense." She observed Robert's disheartened expression and took note of his silence. "I understand your hesitation, but I assure you it is not a command. It is not my will to force this upon you."

Robert reflected. "I still have nightmares of that terrible day. Not for a moment did I ever consider going back." Robert took a deep breath. "All right, I will take you." He looked at Juliana and Jack. "Perhaps it will make sense to me too."

Chapter 12

Robert led Juliana and Jack past the wooded area and into the flatlands, a sign they were leaving Cedarville and entering Maiden Hills. His stomach jittered as he stared ahead. At a distance, he saw the mountains and hills that surrounded his former village. He wiped his brow with a trembling hand. Robert stopped his horse and pointed to the highest peak of a broad, flat mountain. "That's the Majian Mountain. On that mountain was where the nuptials were to take place." He took a deep breath. "It was where the massacre occurred."

"Can we go up?" Jack asked.

He paused, then nodded. "Follow me."

They continued through the open grassy lands until the wall of the mountain towered over them. They urged the horses up the trail, but midway up the path narrowed, and they walked the rest of the way. After an arduous trek in the sizzling heat, the summit was in sight. Robert braced for what he would find.

All eyes scanned the area where the Majian people had gathered for the nuptials and met their fate. The passage of twenty-two years had not wiped away the remains of over one hundred human skulls and bones. Robert treaded through the grounds with care and wondered which one belonged to Beth.

As Robert came upon the remains, he found himself reliving the surprise attack of the knights from Yorkford. His heart began to palpitate, and his breathing quickened. The cries of his people were deafening as they were mercilessly slaughtered, succumbing to the blades of the assailants as one by one they fell, blood spilling on their festive attire. Robert, Simon, and Robert's father Maxwell disarmed as many men as they could, but there were too many, and those with weapons skillfully executed everyone in their path, and they were swift in their slaughter. Robert, Simon, and Maxwell relentlessly defended their people, but as they continued to fight the king's knights, their friends and family members perished.

Robert heard a piercing scream—a scream he will never forget and continued to hear in his nightmares, waking him up in a cold sweat. He turned and saw Beth on the ground with a stab wound to her chest. He ran to her and cradled her in his arms as tears swelled in his eyes. Beth had murmured her last words to him, "Please... look after Peter." He stared at her lifeless body and realized there was nothing more they could do to help the people on the mountain; thus, Robert, Simon, and Maxwell rushed to save the people in the village—and to rescue Peter. Robert looked toward the homes, as the king's men lowered their torches, igniting the wooden structures, and slaying the people as they scurried out, avoiding the flames.

"Robert, are you all right?" Juliana asked.

Robert wiped the sweat from his brow with the back of his hand and took a deep breath to control the quivering nerves. "We must establish this as sacred ground."

"How do we do that?" Juliana asked.

"There's a ritual we must do. We must bring Helena here and gather a few Majians to pray with her, whoever's left."

187

The ride down the mountain was silent as Robert fixed his eyes ahead, dismayed, as he looked upon the remnants of the thriving village that was once his home. A place where people lived and worked, and where family and friends gathered for a meal, became a sea of blackened wood. It was a place full of life and energy, and in an instant, it was gone.

"Robert, where did the maiden appear to the noblemen?" Juliana asked.

"It was in town central. I shall take you there."

As they rode through the ruined town, the smell of burned wood drifted in the air. Some homes and merchant stores had burned to the ground, while others were stubborn and held up. The fire destroyed row after row of cottages. Robert recalled going inside the burning cabins and pulling out children huddled together in a corner, surrounded by flames, weeping with unimaginable terror in their eyes. "There are more children in here," Simon had yelled from the other room. The sweltering heat from the blaze and thick black smoke was suffocating.

Robert closed his eyes and prayed the images would leave his mind. He lay his hand on the side pocket of his horse's saddle and felt the wine flask. He took a deep breath and released his grip.

At town central, the benches, lampposts, and other structures escaped the fire. Robert searched for the statue of the maiden and, to his amazement, found it intact. He came down from his horse, as did Jack and Juliana, to inspect it. The beautiful maiden survived the fire, but the statue appeared downcast, reflecting the condition of her surroundings.

"It's amazing that the statue still stands," said Robert as he stared at the bronze face. "Interesting, I don't remember the statue having that expression."

"Robert, who owns the land?" asked Jack.

"It's owned by King Carlton of Etheland. King Carlton and his ancestors protected our land from invaders."

Juliana turned toward Robert. "Robert, the survivors must reclaim this land and rebuild."

"But, Your Majesty, there's nothing here. It's completely destroyed."

"The land is still here, and it can be cultivated, and homes can be rebuilt," said Juliana. "Robert, I read the prophecy, and it said that Maiden Hills will once again belong to the Majian people."

Robert wrinkled his brow. "I had forgotten that."

Jack walked around, surveying the land. "We can do this. It will take time, and we will require assistance, but it's worth pursuing. I can help supply labor and tools, but we must speak with King Carlton. It's in his best interest to help, as he stands to profit from it."

Robert sighed and looked at the surrounding destruction. "There are so many bad memories here."

"It was not always bad, was it?" Juliana asked.

"No. It was good for a long time." Robert's eyes hazed over as he recalled one night long ago of a gathering in town central with friends in front of an open fire. They were laughing and drinking, and for a moment, he looked up and laid eyes on the most beautiful woman he had ever seen. Beth walked toward him, and in an instant, he fell in love. They had a courtship, but it was not to be, for he could not abandon Olivia. Although he and Olivia were no longer bound to each other, she was incapacitated and could not care for herself. Beth had a way of washing away his troubles, and being with her felt right, and when she told him she was expecting his child, it was the most thrilling and the most frightening time in his life.

"Robert, all of this must be washed away." Juliana's words snapped Robert back to the present. "All the burned buildings and what's left of this town must be removed. What we have here is the product of hate and fear, and if this place is not rebuilt, if all this remains, then hate wins."

Robert looked at Juliana. "I never thought of it that way."

"The statue still standing signifies hope. She survived, and if she can show you that she can't be destroyed, then neither can you, nor this land."

Robert considered the possibility of returning to the place where he was born, where he played as a child with the other children, and where he fell in love. He had to fix his mind on the good memories. "Perhaps you're right." Robert looked at Juliana and Jack. "We need consensus to do this. The survivors must want it."

Juliana nodded. "Agreed. Shall we go?"

"There's something else I must see," Robert said.

The horses galloped with a quiet gait until they came upon a wooded area where homes were reduced to charred wood. Robert recalled the torrential rainstorm that fell after the knights left the village and had put out the fire; unfortunately, none of the homes were saved.

To Robert's amazement, massive flourishing trees replaced the burned trees. Rabbits, foxes, deer, and other forest animals frolicked and scurried the wooded area. They passed a pond with ducks and geese swimming and diving for food.

"I can't believe there's life here among the burned homes." This was an unexpected but welcome sight.

"Where are we?" Jack asked.

"We're in the woods where I once lived, but nothing had survived." Robert pointed to a cottage burned to the ground, a somber look on his face. "That was my home, where I lived with Olivia. She was in the cottage when it burned." They rode past it in silence.

Farther into the woods, to Robert's surprise, a charred cabin remained standing. It stood slanted to one side with a window shutter swinging from the breeze. He directed his horse toward it, and Juliana and Jack followed him. Robert stopped, came down from his horse, and slowly walked toward the cabin. With caution, he pushed the door open.

"Robert, whose cabin was this?" asked Juliana.

"This was where Helena and Beth lived with my son, Peter."

Robert scanned the room and could make out the remnants of the beds, tables, and fireplace. His face fell when he came across Peter's cradle, and his chest sank in as though punched in the heart. Tears stung his eyes, and the quivering in his hands returned. The cradle was charred but still recognizable as a baby's bed with the fragments of a metal rattle laying among the ashes. His mind drifted to the burning cottages with the children inside and realizing he had to get to Peter. He had told his father and the others to continue to rescue the children while he went to the woods to find his son, but the soldiers held him back. He had to fight his way through, and by the time he arrived at Beth's cottage, it was too late.

"Robert, are you all right?" Juliana asked.

He held back tears. "This is the most heart-wrenching sight my eyes have seen this day." Robert's mind shifted again to the wine flask nestled in his horse's saddlebag, hands trembling, but once more, he fought against retrieving it. His eyes remained fixed on the cradle. He curled his hands into a fist to stop the shaking. Visions of baby Peter's smile came to him, and the baby's laughter echoed in his mind as Peter kicked his small feet and stretched out his arms. Robert reached down to stroke him, and Peter grabbed his finger with his tiny hand and, with a firm grip, held on tight and would not release. "He's a strong one. He's going to be a fighter." He recalled telling Beth.

"We shall leave when you're ready," Jack said.

Overwhelmed with emotion, Robert did not hesitate. "I'm ready."

As Robert and Jack walked toward the door, Juliana called out, "Wait." Robert turned and saw her gazing at the cradle. "Something's missing." She had a puzzled look on her face. "Where is the burned locket with the stones? Helena said Beth placed her locket around Peter's neck before she left for the nuptials."

Robert gave thought to her words, edged over to the cradle, and examined it. "You're right. But what's more is that I don't see the human remains. We should see bone fragments." Robert, in his grief, had not noticed the missing remains.

Robert scanned the room. "Peter must have crawled out." They rummaged through the cottage but found nothing resembling human remains or the locket. It left them bewildered.

They rode toward town central, then passed the mountains and hills and through the wooded area, and finally to the village of Cedarville. No one spoke a word.

***

In the king's library, the two knights tasked to follow the queen stood, face pale, waiting to meet with the king's ire. Edmund slammed the door behind them. The men flinched, perspiration trickling down the side of their faces. Edmund's nostrils flared as he walked around his desk to face them.

He sat down with arms crossed, glaring at the men as they fixed their eyes straight ahead on the wall, avoiding his stare. He clenched his teeth. "Where did she go?"

One of the men bravely spoke, "Sh-she went into the dark forest and said she was going for a ride, Your Majesty."

He banged his fist on the table. "She has been gone since this morning. You were supposed to keep watch on her."

"Forgive us, Your Majesty, but the queen spotted us and waited for us to leave. We turned back, but lost sight of her," said the other knight.

"My wife is too clever even for the smartest knights. Leave now!"

The knights fumbled with the doorknob, yanked the door open, then rushed out.

Edmund knew where Juliana was. She was with Jack, and there was no doubt in his mind they were having an affair. They were both traitors to the Kingdom of Yorkford and the memory of King Matthew.

He rose from his seat and paced as he scanned the room. There were many memories buried in King Matthew's former library. This was where they planned battles and conquered lands to become the wealthiest country in the Sparian continent. This was where they organized the most feared and the most intimidating army ever assembled.

He strolled to the chess table where Matthew had exhibited his superb chess skills and taught Edmund how to win every time.

"Winning is all that matters," Matthew would tell him.

Edmund recalled Matthew often used a game of chess to educate him on matters of war. "Edmund," Matthew had said, "battles are a lot like playing chess. You have your defensive strategy, and you have your offensive strategy, but keep in mind, defense does not win battles—offense does, every time! Strike first and strike hard and take no prisoners. Never have the need for a defensive strategy."

"What's the best offensive strategy?" Edmund had asked him.

Matthew moved his bishop piece on the far end of the game board, took Edmund's rook, and said, "The best offensive strategy is the one they don't see coming." He grinned. "Checkmate!"

Edmund turned and walked toward his desk when something in Matthew's collection of books caught his eye. Edmund drew closer and pulled out a piece of parchment inserted between the pages of a large tome. His eyebrows arched when he read the document. He took his quill, dabbed it in ink, and wrote on the document, then rushed to his door and called for his steward to fetch Sir Leopold.

Within a few minutes, Leopold appeared at Edmund's door. "What can I do for you, Your Majesty?"

"Look at this parchment." He handed the document to Leopold.

Leopold read the document and looked at Edmund. "I shall go there and take a few men with me."

Edmund grinned. "He will not see it coming."

Leopold rolled the parchment, bowed, and departed. Edmund turned his attention to reports on his desk when a woman singing interrupted his concentration. It was a sweet tune, but he found it distracting. "Ella," he called.

Ella came rushing in. "Aye, Your Majesty."

"I heard a woman sing. Was it you?"

"No, Your Majesty. Would you like me to find out who it was and ask them to stop?"

"That won't be necessary. Close the door on the way out."

***

Juliana rode in silence, trotting through the dry dirt road, still recovering from the rattled nerves of touring a village where people were mercilessly slaughtered. The sights and smells were haunting. She thought of her grandmother Victoria, whose remains lay on top of the mountain, and her uncle Josef, his life coming to an end during what was to be a joyous occasion. She glanced at Robert, realizing the horror he had lived through and wondered what an experience like that does to a man. Scars on the outside can heal over time, but inner scars

195

sometimes never close, and the pain dwells inside continuously.

The sun blazed at its highest point in the flawless blue sky when Juliana entered Helena's cottage with Jack and Robert. All the furniture was back in its rightful place, with Helena's items neatly displayed. They sat in front of the fireplace, sipping warm ale, and relieving the tension from an emotionally exhaustive trip.

"What brings you to my home?" Helena asked as she sipped her ale.

"Helena," said Juliana, "you must gather the remaining Majians and reclaim the land of Maiden Hills."

"Your Majesty, Maiden Hills no longer exists. Yorkford destroyed it."

"The land is still there, and it belongs to the Majian people."

"You speak as is if you are not one of us. If there is land there, then it is yours too, Your Majesty."

"I have my land, and King Edmund's army will seek to destroy the Majian people. The Majians must organize and be ready to fight so they can leave Cedarville and reclaim what is rightfully theirs. I am the queen. I must return to my castle."

"Your Majesty, please don't deny who you are—you are a Majian! Your grandparents and mother sacrificed much. Do not turn your back on their memory."

Juliana's voice was firm but respectful. "I am not turning my back on them. I can't be a part of this and go against my father's land."

Robert, noticing Juliana's unease, deflected the conversation away from her. "Helena, we went to Maiden Hills."

Helena's brows furrowed. "You did what?"

Robert leaned into Helena. "We went to the sacred site of the nuptials and to town central. The statue of the maiden is unharmed, and the forest is alive with vibrant trees and animals dwelling in it. It is a sign that perhaps we should go back and rebuild."

Helena shook her head. "I can't." Tears filled her eyes. "It's too painful."

Robert met Helena's gaze. "I know how you feel, but Yorkford set out to destroy us. If we don't go back and rebuild, then they have won." Robert gave Juliana a brief glance and smiled. "The prophecy states that Maiden Hills will once again belong to the Majian people."

Helena pondered Robert's words. "If true, how are we to rebuild?"

"Lord Jack will help us organize and supply tools and labor." Robert looked at Jack, and he nodded. "We shall speak to King Carlton, who owns the land. He may be willing to help us and pay to rebuild since he stands to profit from it, just like in the past. It's a huge undertaking and will cost much, but we must try."

Helena remained in deep thought, then her face beamed. "We have gold!"

Robert's eyes widened. "There's gold?"

"There is. As the leader, Lord Gavin was entrusted with guarding it. In the past, whenever the nobles did good work, the kings of those kingdoms rewarded them with gold. It has been hidden ever since, probably buried in the manor."

"We shall search for it." Robert smiled.

"Helena, you must gather the survivors. Is there a way to identify them?" Jack asked.

197

Juliana interjected. "There is a way that I read in *The Book of Secrets*. We shall go to the highest mountain and light a fire, and the Majians will come toward it."

Helena's face lit up. "You found the book?"

Juliana smiled, then nodded.

"Then there is hope," Helena said. "The prophecy was right. It said that after twenty-two years, the Majians will organize and triumph." Helena rose from her seat and walked to the mantel where six canisters of herbs were arranged in a row. She opened the third canister and took in the aroma. "We will need these."

***

For the first time, Jack felt a sense of optimism rising for the people of Maiden Hills, but there was much to do. He mulled over how best to proceed and help them reclaim their land. As a knight, he learned to consider all possible actions and choose the one most likely to succeed. Edmund was clever and not happy with Jack and somehow would watch his every move. Jack had to be clever as well.

His eyes glimpsed Juliana looking at him, and she quickly averted her eyes. His impulsive action earlier was foolish. What was he thinking? She was married, and although no love existed between Juliana and Edmund, she was his wife. But he couldn't stop thinking of their kiss—the soft touch of her lips and the warmth of her breath on him. He yearned for her, but he had to push those thoughts out of his mind and accept that she will never belong to him. He had to remain focused on the task at hand.

Jack took a few steps out of the cottage, followed by Juliana, Robert, and Helena, and halted when he noticed

198

the increased activity and mutterings in the village square. Days ago, Sir Leopold appeared there to request, by order of King Edmund, to turn over the magical man, which the townspeople had refused. This day, the same scene played out before them except this time, the number of men on horseback had doubled. A dozen of Edmund's men led by Sir Leopold lined up in the square. The townspeople emerged out of their homes and businesses to observe.

Jack fumed, feeling the heat rise inside him. "What is it this time?" He charged toward them.

"Lord Jack, it's good to see you." Leopold came down from his horse looking smug.

"Sir Leopold, why is there a small army here?"

"King Edmund wishes to be informed of the progress in his territory and thought it best to send guards to keep watch."

Jack pursed his lips. His stomach churned as he suspected Edmund was plotting retaliation. Edmund was spiteful, and he would not allow Jack's defiance to continue without consequence.

Jeb and other villagers approached Jack. "Lord Jack, what does this mean?"

Leopold pulled out the parchment. "It's here in the accord that Lord Jack made with King Matthew to acquire Cedarville." Leopold unrolled the parchment and read the last words in the document. "This accord shall become subject to new terms upon the crowning of a new king." Leopold faced the crowd. "Per King Edmund, there shall be a curfew of sundown, longer workdays, less pay, and higher rents and taxes."

Gasps and grumblings arose among the townspeople.

"Sir Leopold," Jack said, trying to contain his anger. "Those words were not in the accord that King Matthew and I signed."

"Be that as it may, Lord Jack, they are there now, and I am under orders of the new king to enforce the law."

Jack eyed the man he had served for six years as his squire, whom he accompanied on numerous battles, and who trained him to become a knight. He thought to appeal to his sense of reason. "Sir Leopold, you served King Matthew and knew him well. You and I both know he would not have added that statement to the accord."

Leopold met Jack's stare. Jack worked harder than anyone and was determined to prove he deserved to be among the elite fighters. Leopold treated Jack harshly, but he could not break him. Jack had earned the respect of his mentor. Leopold leaned into Jack and whispered, "Sorry, Jack, alas, it is out of my hands. I am charged by my king and yours to instill order and stability in this village." They locked eyes.

"Lord Jack, I thought it would be different with you," Jeb said, breaking the stare between the two men.

Jack pulled Jeb aside, his voice low. "Jeb, it *is* different with me. King Edmund is doing this to get back at me for defying his order."

Leopold turned toward the knights. "Men, set up your posts." The army dispersed. Leopold faced the crowd. "The guards will enforce the curfew. Anyone found on the streets after sundown shall be arrested."

As Jeb tried to calm the villagers, Robert strode toward Jack and pulled him away. "Jack, I believe this was not part of the plan."

"No, it was not. The document was forged." Jack felt the heat burn his face. He looked at Robert and spoke low, "You must organize the remaining Majians and reclaim Maiden Hills. I shall speak to King Carlton and ask him if he is willing to help rebuild it. The time has come to fight King Edmund and his army and reclaim what belongs to you and your people." Rage filled Jack. He had just made a declaration of war against his adoptive brother, and there was no turning back. He was prepared to face him. The fury he felt all those years, putting up with Edmund's intimidation and cruelty, was bubbling to the surface, and he would now meet him head to head, not in a frivolous sword fight, but in a battle that would change the course of their lives forever. It had become personal.

Jeb charged toward Jack. "My lord, we put our trust in you. I thought you wished to help Cedarville properly?"

"You can trust me, Jeb. I will figure something out, but for now, we must obey their laws, and not give them a reason to clash with us."

Robert turned to Jeb. "He's right. Other things need our attention. You must come with me."

Jeb followed Robert with a puzzled look.

Juliana pulled Jack away, hiding her face underneath her cloak. She whispered, "Jack, you must explain what is happening."

"I will explain everything later. Right now, you must go to the mountain with Helena and Robert and gather the Majians."

She furrowed her brow and shook her head. "I will not leave without you."

"You said it before—it's not my fight. It's something you must do, not me. Besides, I must keep my eye on Sir Leopold and his men and try to distract them."

"The people will not trust me. They will recognize me as the wife of the king who seeks to impose harsh rules on them."

"When you tell them who you are, they will see you differently. You are one of them. Besides, you have Robert and Helena to defend you."

Juliana glanced back at the petite woman waiting by her door.

"Go, I shall meet with you later," Jack urged.

Juliana was torn. "Jack, I can't be dragged into this."

He put his hands on her arms and looked into her eyes. "You already are."

"But Jack… I—"

Jack interrupted. "It will be fine. Please go," he said, his voice firm.

She stared at Jack for a minute, then let out an irritated sigh. "All right… I wish I did not have to do this."

***

Juliana strode toward Helena and said, "We must go." She turned her head and met Jack's gaze, then watched him leave. The kiss they shared earlier came to mind, and it squeezed her heart. She wished it could go on forever, but it was wrong. Edmund was her husband, and she vowed to be faithful. She couldn't tell Jack how much he meant to her. Once this was over, she would go back to being Edmund's wife, and she would have to forget about Jack. *Oh, Jack, I wish things were different.*

Juliana saw Robert approaching with another man.

"Your Majesty, I would like to introduce you to Jeb Archer. Jeb, this is Her Majesty, Queen Juliana of Yorkford."

"Your Majesty, it is an honor to meet you." Jeb bowed to Juliana, then looked at Robert, confusion on his face. "Forgive me for my agitation at Lord Jack, but I had not expected this. We will, of course, obey King Edmund's laws."

"I understand. Are you Lucinda's brother?"

Jeb's eyebrows raised. "Yes, I had an older sister named Lucinda, but she died a long time ago." He furrowed his brow. "If I may, Your Majesty, why do you inquire?"

"Robert told me you survived the massacre twenty-two years ago. Lucinda also survived and married the king of Yorkford, King Matthew, and they had a daughter. That's me." She smiled. "Alas, my mother died six years ago."

Jeb's eyes widened with surprise. "You are my niece!" he exclaimed. "This is incredible. I saw Queen Lucinda on one of my visits to Yorkford, but I never knew she was my sister. I am saddened that she is gone, but it pleases me to know you're her daughter. I have three young children of my own—they are your cousins."

Juliana smiled. "I would love to meet them someday." Juliana turned to look at Robert and Helena. "Shall we go?"

Robert nodded. "Let's go."

Juliana, Robert, and Jeb climbed on their horses, and Helena followed in her horse-drawn carriage. When they arrived at the top of the mountain, everyone was concerned for Helena's reaction. How would she respond once she stepped foot on the site where her daughter and other family members and friends perished? She was older and could be overwhelmed with emotion. Helena stared at the remains, taking careful, deliberate steps as she observed the fragments of a once joyful occasion. She surprised everyone with her strength.

Helena turned to Robert and Jeb. "We must gather the remains and place them at the altar."

With great reverence, Robert and Jeb picked up the bones, one by one, and placed them at the foot of the altar where marriage vows were once exchanged. After the men gathered the remains and set them in a pile, Helena asked everyone to join hands as she recited a prayer. She instructed Jeb to light a fire, and they watched in silence as the flames turned the bones to ashes.

When the last flame extinguished, the men gathered the ashes and bone fragments and deposited them into a tin container and placed the box in a small cave by the site. Robert levitated a large rock and sealed the opening. They walked to the other side of the mountain where Robert and Jeb gathered wood and started a fire. Helena reached into her pouch, took a handful of herbs, and sprinkled them onto the logs.

"What are the herbs for?" Juliana asked.

"These are magic herbs. It makes the fire visible only to the descendants of Majians. If the fire were visible to non-Majians, they could capture us. The herbs also have the power to call to them so they will notice the fire on the mountain and come toward it, sometimes not aware of why they are doing it." Helena smiled. "We shall wait and see who comes."

The four of them sat on boulders in front of the fire, and Juliana listened as the Majians who once lived in Maiden Hills spoke of a beautiful and serene place. At six years old, Jeb did not remember much, so he sat back as Helena and Robert reminisced. They spoke of a time of great prosperity and peace among their people. They traveled to other lands, and since they descended from nobility, they were treated warmly. Lord Gavin was an exceptional leader and an honorable man and urged his people to work together for the common good. All Majians owned their land, and they became wealthy and paid their share of taxes. Unlike other villages, no lower classes existed in Maiden Hills. Everyone enjoyed living a good life.

"Why didn't Father fight the king's army?" Jeb asked.

"No one expected a battle. Lord Gavin trusted that they would leave after the inspection, but they did not," Robert said.

"But could Father have prevented it?"

"Your father confronted many men who tried to intrude onto our land. But he did it peacefully and prevailed every time. That makes what happened twenty-two years ago even more difficult to comprehend. It all went terribly wrong so quickly." Silence fell among them as Robert described the inner struggle that united them.

Juliana said, "I ask that all of you, please keep my secret. I am not ready for everyone to know that I am also of magical blood. I have my kingdom to think of."

Everyone nodded.

Juliana walked toward the west side of the mountain overlooking Cedarville. She saw people approaching, some on foot, some on horseback, and others in carriages. "I see them coming," she said excitedly.

Several hours later, forty-five people gathered on the mountain. Helena and Robert recognized many of them as townspeople from Cedarville, although unaware they were the surviving children of the massacre. They ranged in age from twenty-two to thirty-three. Others that came were offspring of the survivors between twelve and eighteen years of age. Simon's daughter, Alice, was among them, an energetic fourteen-year-old with long raven black hair and jade green eyes. A few of them came from Yorkford, including the dungeon guard Simon, a monk from the monastery, and a seamstress who worked on Juliana's wedding dress. A young man from the crowd looked familiar to Juliana, but she could not remember where she had seen him.

Helena looked at the people and smiled. "There are so many."

Robert stood up before the crowd and conversations ceased. "I am pleased all of you made this journey to meet here on the sacred mountain. Some of you may not know why you are here."

A few of them nodded their heads. They were the ones too young to remember the massacre or were children of Majians surprised to learn of their heritage. The surviving older children, now in their thirties, vividly recalled the slaughter and destruction.

Helena spoke to the crowd and told them the story of how the Majians came to be. She told them about the three courageous noblemen, and of Majia, the lovely maiden who gave them their gifts. She also told them about the prophecy that came true and the men who destroyed their land and slaughtered their people. "But we can't allow that to destroy us. We shall organize and rebuild."

"But we have no powers," a Majian said.

Robert spoke up. "We must find the gemstones. We can find some of them in the land or buried in the rubble. Maiden Hills is the only place where the enchanted gemstones can be found."

"But that can take weeks or months. We must protect ourselves now," another Majian said.

A burly man spoke up. "No! The practice of magic is illegal. The king's men will arrest us."

"The practice of *black* magic is illegal," Robert corrected him. "We were given a gift to defend ourselves and to protect the innocent, not harm anyone. We must honor who we are."

"How can we protect ourselves if we do not have the gemstones?" a young maiden asked.

Juliana kept her head covered, hoping no one would recognize her. "What if we found the box of stones taken from the leader Lord Gavin?" All eyes were on Juliana.

"How can we do that?" Robert asked.

"The knight who took them lives on the castle grounds. We shall search his home." As soon as Juliana said it, she realized she had said too much.

"Is she not the queen of Yorkford?" a Majian asked, staring at Juliana.

"She is!" someone else said.

"Why is she here?" asked another.

"Her Majesty wishes to help us," Robert said. "We can trust her."

Juliana was grateful Robert did not expose her secret.

"We can't trust anyone. She is the daughter of the king who ordered the killing twenty-two years ago."

"No! It was not my father," Juliana said vehemently. "It was one of his knights, Sir Leopold. He took it upon himself."

"It was Prince James from Westmore who ordered the killings, and Sir Leopold carried it out," Simon said. "Prince James betrayed our people."

Another Majian said, "Her husband, King Edmund, ordered an attack on Cedarville. He wants to destroy us."

"Everyone, please calm down," said Helena, trying to instill order. "We don't know who was responsible. Perhaps it was all of them, but blaming will not help us now."

"Helena's right. We need a plan, and we must make haste," Robert said. "The attack three days ago was not just an attack on Cedarville. They were looking for me because of my magic. King Edmund learned a Majian killed his father, Prince James, twenty-two years ago." Robert glanced at Simon. "He's coming after all of us, accusing anyone with magical abilities as practicing sorcery and calling us heretics. We can't turn on those who wish to help us, especially someone of royal blood." He turned toward Juliana. "What do you wish for us to do, Your Majesty?"

Juliana paused as she scanned the crowd of Majians waiting for a response. "Let us look for the stones within the rubble. In the meantime, I shall search the castle grounds for the stones taken from Lord Gavin." She cringed inside, wanting to take back those words, but it was too late. She had committed to helping the Majian people.

Robert smiled and nodded in appreciation.

When the meeting ended, Juliana watched as the Majians dispersed and headed toward the town of Maiden Hills to examine the rubble. From atop the mountain, Juliana saw them combing through the burned wood and twisted metal looking for the mystical stones. They would prove difficult to find, as the gems were small and easy to blend in with the dirt and rocks. She sighed. Finding the box with the gemstones would be the only way to empower the Majians. She felt the anxiety rise as she realized the survival of the magical people rested with her.

Chapter 13

The sun had dipped below the horizon when Juliana reached the entrance to the drawbridge. The guards stood in a rigid stance as they allowed her passage across the span. She rode with her head held high as if this was an ordinary end to an ordinary day. Fortunately, she arrived before the guards lowered the portcullis and raised the drawbridge. Although they would have lowered the bridge and re-opened the castle for her, she would not have wanted to bring attention to herself. Juliana had spent the entire day away from the castle and shuddered at the certainty of another confrontation with Edmund.

She dismounted, and a young squire rushed to take Millie to retire her to the stables. A chill swept through the air, and Juliana tightened her cloak. She raised her eyes. Thick, black rain clouds hovered above accompanied by flashes of light and soft rumbles. *It looks like a storm is brewing.*

Inside the castle's great hall, a young maidservant approached her. "Good evening, Your Majesty, supper is served in the dining hall."

Juliana's stomach grumbled, and she looked forward to enjoying a warm meal. She had not been eating well and was feeling the effects of a lack of solid food. She realized she had to keep up her strength to fulfill the task of finding the box with the gemstones. Her insides jittered at the thought of sneaking around the castle late at night, but she felt obligated to help the Majian people. *I will find the box, deliver it to Robert, and return to my role as queen of Yorkford.* She longed for a normal life again.

Juliana wondered who would attend supper as it was often a time for the residents of the castle and other invited noblemen and noblewomen to share a meal with the king and queen. She hoped to immerse herself in enjoyable conversations with them and avoid Edmund's glare as much as possible.

When Juliana arrived at the dining room, it was empty except for two maidservants setting the table. "Where are the guests?"

"His Majesty has requested a private dinner with his queen."

"Perfect," Juliana muttered under her breath. She composed herself and forced a smile. There would be no other guests to serve as buffers between her and Edmund. Her anxiety level rose at the thought of having to deal with him by herself. She sat at the far end of the long dining table.

Edmund appeared. His eyes pierced hers as he sat at the head of the table opposite Juliana. They were quite a distance from each other, but for Juliana, it was not far enough.

"Sit by me," he commanded.

"I am comfortable here," she said. One servant was serving her meal, and another servant filled her wineglass.

Edmund banged his fist on the table, rattling the maidservants. "I said, sit by me."

The servants hastened to move Juliana's soup, meal dish, and wineglass to the setting next to Edmund. Juliana had no choice but to follow her meal. This would be a long and unpleasant supper.

They ate in silence as Juliana sensed Edmund's eyes on her. After a few minutes, Edmund casually asked, "How are things in Cedarville?"

"Why don't you ask Sir Leopold? You sent him there." She realized her response came across snippier than she intended. She nonchalantly dipped her bread in her vegetable soup, bracing for Edmund's caustic retort.

He narrowed his eyes, eager to fire back, but controlled his ire. "I wish to hear it from you."

Juliana hesitated. "All right. Things are well. It's a thriving village."

"So, you admit you were there."

"You know I was there. You had me followed."

"The question is, what were you doing there all day?" Edmund took a bite of the venison and washed it down with a mouthful of wine.

"I was visiting Lord Jack and the residents of Cedarville to acquaint myself with them. They are part of our kingdom, and it is our duty." This was as good a reason as any.

"Why were you visiting Jack?"

"I told you, he's my friend."

Edmund leaned over the table and banged his fist. Juliana jumped, her bread falling into the broth, causing a splatter. "I will say this once—I forbid you from seeing Jack! That is no place for you. Do you understand me?"

As much as Juliana wanted to argue back, she thought against fighting a losing battle. "Fine, I shall visit Jack no more."

Edmund sat back with a skeptical look. "There are consequences if you go against me." He glared at her. "You are aware."

"I am." She took a bite of the meat, wiped her mouth with the napkin, sipped the soup, and wiped her mouth again. Her nerves were jittery. After a long silence, she spoke. "Can you leave the people of Cedarville to be?"

"Why would I do that? As you said, they are part of our kingdom." Edmund tore a piece of bread and dipped it in the soup.

"You need not send armed guards and set curfews."

"When I receive a report from Sir Leopold informing me that the peasants are following the rules of the kingdom, I will withdraw the men. For now, they shall remain."

"My father entrusted Jack with the land and gave him full authority to govern as he saw fit."

"Until the crowning of a new king, that was what they both agreed upon and signed."

"My father would not have written that into the accord. You forged the document."

"It does not matter, does it?" Edmund had a smug expression on his face.

Juliana's face tightened as she stared at him. "What do you hope to accomplish? What are you after?"

"As I told you yesterday, one of their people broke the law, and the villagers disobeyed my command to surrender him. Until the lawbreaker surrenders or the villagers deliver him, I shall keep a close watch on them." He narrowed his eyes suspiciously. "You were there. Were you not informed of the incident in the tavern?"

Juliana looked down at her plate. "I was not." Juliana sensed Edmund's eyes on her. She felt like a child lying to her father, keeping from him some mischief she had done. But, if she had told Edmund the truth, he would

213

have been furious with her for gracing a village with her presence, knowing they harbored lawbreakers, and not admonishing them for disobeying his command. He would have seen it as an act of disloyalty.

"I expect you are being truthful. I shall not discover that you have lied to me."

Juliana stared at her plate. She let out a heavy sigh, then wiped her mouth with a napkin. "I am finished. I shall retire to my private chamber with a guard at my door." She rose from her seat.

Edmund stood towering over her, blocking her path. "Very well, but I have already commanded a guard to stand by your door. You shall not leave your chamber until I call for you."

"Am I a prisoner in my own bedchamber?"

"You are my wife, and I can do whatever I want with you. Be grateful I am not sending you to the dungeon."

Juliana cringed. Spending a night locked in a dungeon cell remained imprinted in her mind. "Very well." They glared at each other. She then lowered her eyes, glided around him, and exited the dining hall.

When Juliana reached the second-floor landing, Sir William had assumed his post at her door. He avoided eye contact with her and did not utter a word. Juliana glanced at him as she entered her room, a scowl on her face. A knight guarding her door would hinder her plan of looking for the stones.

The night sky rumbled.

She paced the length of her chamber, and after a few minutes, thought of testing the guard. She grabbed the candlestick and opened the door.

The knight blocked her path. "Forgive me, Your Majesty, but I have strict orders not to allow you to leave your chamber."

"I must retrieve something I left downstairs. I won't be long." She pivoted around him, but he blocked her again.

"Alas, I cannot allow that, Your Majesty."

"I am your queen! You take orders from me," she declared.

"King Edmund commands me. Please retreat to your chamber, or I shall call for him."

Juliana sighed. "All right. I shall go back. You need not call him." Juliana stomped into her chamber and slammed the door just as a loud clap of thunder boomed. A chill swept through her as the rain fell in a steady stream, pounding against the stone walls, and bursts of lightning created eerie shadows in the room. She closed the shutters, fed logs to the fire, and climbed into her bed. She tossed, fluffed her pillow, but refused to sleep. *If only Jack were here to rescue me again.* She sighed—it was not likely to happen.

She stared at the ceiling when from the floor came soft squeaks. She picked up her head, lifted the candlestick, and tiptoed following the sound. "Hello, where are you?"

"We are here."

Juliana flinched when by her feet were two small mice.

"Forgive us, Your Majesty, for we wish not to frighten you."

"It's all right. I'm happy you're here. I have a request."

"How may we serve you, Your Majesty?"

"Go downstairs to the dungeon and look for the guard with the black beard and a big belly. Do you know the one?"

"You mean Simon?"

"Yes, that's the one. Tell him I must search for the stones, but I can't leave my chamber, and I wish for him to relieve the guard at my door."

"We shall do your bidding, Your Majesty." They scurried off.

"Thank you, and make haste!" Juliana sighed. *I hope this works.*

The downpour and thunder continued throughout the night as Juliana waited.

Two hours had gone by with no activity, and Juliana sat in her chair, legs fidgeting. Finally, voices muffled in the hall. She rushed, pressed her ear to the door, but could not make out the spoken words. Footsteps plodded toward her, then a soft rap on the door. She opened it, and Simon stood on the other side.

"What was the delay?" she whispered.

"I had to be certain the king was slumbering before I relieved the guard. The guard will not wake him and must wait until morn to confirm the order came from him. In the meantime, you can search for the box with the stones."

"But won't King Edmund know he was tricked?"

"Yes, but I hide very easily in this castle." Simon grinned.

That statement troubled Juliana, but she would address the security at the castle at a later time. "All right,

216

you stay here. Wish me well." Juliana wrapped her purple cloak and fastened it at the neck.

"Your Majesty, you should not go by yourself. I shall accompany you."

"Don't worry, Simon, I have my stones for protection. Besides, if King Edmund wakes and sees my door unguarded, he will suspect something's amiss. From a distance, he will not notice you are not the guard he sent."

With candlestick in hand, Juliana moved like a prowler through the halls, looking over her shoulder and hiding in nooks at the slightest sound. She stopped when she heard squeaks. "Mice, are you there?" she whispered.

"Do not worry, Your Majesty, we are right behind you."

Juliana smiled, grateful for the company. "Thank you. I could use extra protection. You will alert me if you see someone?"

"Aye, Your Majesty. We have great big ears."

Juliana went down the stairs and headed toward the opposite side of the castle, across the bailey where the residents' apartments were located. She passed by Princess Katherine's apartment, Sir Quinn's, Sir Mark's, and finally arrived at Sir Leopold's.

When Juliana reached Leopold's apartment, she bent down and whispered to the mice. "Please go inside and tell me if he's in there. He should be on guard at Cedarville, but I must be certain."

"Aye, Your Majesty." They scurried in through a small opening beneath the door.

Within a few minutes, they re-appeared. "No one is in there, Your Majesty."

"All right, I'm going in." Juliana opened the door to a space consisting of a large room with a living area and a private bedchamber. The living area had a couch, a table, two chairs, and a fireplace. There were few places to hide a box in there, so she moved to his sleeping chamber, where she saw a chest with drawers, a small table, and in the corner, a suit of armor. She opened the chest with drawers and looked for a box that could hold hundreds of small stones and lockets. She searched through every corner of the room, inside and under the furniture. Under his bed, she found two boxes—her heartbeat quickened. When she opened them, one of them contained parchment, the other contained spurs. She exhaled in frustration.

She left the room mystified. *What do I do now? Perhaps Sir Leopold had given the box with the gemstones to Prince James*, she thought.

Juliana headed toward Prince James' former private chamber, a separate dwelling he maintained from the apartment he lived in with Princess Katherine. James kept a separate residence to avoid distractions when preparing for military duties. It was located at the opposite end of the castle near Edmund's library.

The thunderous booms disrupted the eerie silence as she slinked through the halls with a candlestick in hand and two mice leading the way. Sporadic lightning illuminated the castle's gloomy interior for a few seconds, helping Juliana find her way quicker.

She arrived at Prince James' chamber, and once the mice assured her the room was empty, she opened the door and stepped inside. She pulled open the drawers and wardrobe and peered under furniture. The box was nowhere in the room.

Something on the table beside the bed caught Juliana's eye. She walked toward it to get a better look. It was a six-inch statue of a fairy sitting on a mushroom holding a butterfly. She held the figure, bewildered. *Why is this familiar?* Chills crept inside her when she remembered the story Helena told her about the time Beth met Prince James, and the statue James bought her at the festival. The statue's description matched the one in James' room. *Could this be the same statue? If so, what is it doing in Prince James' chamber?*

"Your Majesty, we hear someone," said a mouse in a high-pitched voice.

Juliana quickly put the statue back on the table and hid behind the door until the faint clatter faded. "Who was that?"

"We don't know. You must go back, Your Majesty."

She shook her head. "No, it must have been the wind. It's very stormy out there, and the castle is creakier than usual. I have one more room to check, and then I shall return to my chamber."

Juliana quickened her steps and arrived at Edmund's library, the room where her father had conducted business. James or Leopold could have given the box to her father, and if so, it might be in the library. She wasn't sure why they would give him the box since her father had nothing to do with the massacre of the Majian people, but something inside her directed her to the library. Juliana couldn't explain it, but she had a second sight she didn't have before she activated the gemstones. Random mental pictures and insights would come to her.

219

She recalled Helena saying that Majians have a heightened sense of intuition. She hoped her instincts would lead her to the exact spot of the box's location.

Inside the library, Juliana opened drawers, searched under furniture and inside crevices. She let out a heavy sigh as she surveyed the room. *Where could it be?* Her eyes stopped when resting on top of a table against the wall was her father's sword. She picked it up, breathed deeply, and closed her eyes, feeling her father's presence, and taking in the memory of his scent. Images of her running to see him in this room as a young child and sitting on his lap while he told her stories filled her thoughts. She recalled the warmth of his embrace and his prickly beard on her cheek when he kissed her. Her giggles echoed throughout the room. Vivid memories flooded her mind, and she blinked back tears. Her heart ached, for she missed seeing him and talking with him. She held his sword of exquisitely polished steel and ran her fingers across the coat of arms imprinted on it.

"Your Majesty, Your Majesty, we hear someone," said the mice, their voices panicked.

Juliana put the sword down and turned to face the door. She screamed.

"Are you looking for this?" Edmund held a wooden box in his hands. He opened the box, revealing hundreds of lockets and glowing gemstones—half of the stones were green with black waves, and the other half were black with golden tones.

"H-how did you know I was looking for that?" Her heart pounded viciously, on the verge of breaking out of her chest.

"Juliana, you underestimate me. I planted a spy in your little magical group." His arrogance was shining through.

Juliana gaped. "You will stop at nothing." She glimpsed at the box in his hands. "Why do you have it?"

"I found it, just a bunch of stones and lockets. Does it mean something to you?"

"I'm sure your spy told you, they were stolen."

"I asked you if you knew about the incident in the tavern, and you lied to me. Why are you helping them, Juliana?"

"They're good people, Edmund, people who wish to live in peace."

"In peace? They're wicked people who threatened my father. One of them snuck inside the castle and murdered him."

"Because of your father. He betrayed them. He ordered their killing."

"Is that what they told you? You need to know the truth. My father did not order the attack."

"Then who ordered it?"

"It was your father, Juliana—King Matthew!"

Juliana glared at Edmund. "That's a lie!"

"It's true. Your father hated those people for their evil black magic and what they can do to us. He told my father to kill them, but he was in love with one of them. Your father ordered the attack, and Sir Leopold had to carry it out because my father could not do it. Love made him weak."

"It's not true. My father was a good man. He would not have ordered the senseless killing of decent, law-abiding townspeople."

"It's time you knew the truth. Your father was a ruthless man. There was a side of him you did not see."

"I shall not believe it." Juliana's blood surged at the unfounded accusations against her sweet father.

"After my father died, Matthew was like a father to me. He made me who I am. He taught me to be fierce and relentless and win at any cost. Why do you think your father was undefeated? Winning was all that mattered to him. He taught me that if I wanted to be powerful, I had to be ruthless."

Edmund's words troubled Juliana. He was not describing the man who loved and cared for her.

"I never knew my natural father because of those people," he continued. "I will avenge my father's death, and they will all pay, including anyone who helps them." He glared at Juliana. "Do you still wish to help them?"

Juliana fell silent, thinking back to the Majian people, the danger they faced, and the reason she was there. "How did you come across the box?"

"I found it in the library. Sir Leopold brought it to King Matthew for gold. Your father paid him handsomely."

Juliana's face reddened hearing Edmund's lies, for her father would never pay for the blood of innocent people, but Edmund finding the box in the library troubled her. Her intuition had been right in guiding her there, although it made little sense.

She glared at Edmund. "Let them be, Edmund. They do not deserve to die because of the actions of one man."

"You're a fool."

"Give me the box."

222

"No, they need the stones to be powerful. I will not hand this over to you or anyone else. I would rather destroy it." Edmund bolted out of the library and rushed up the stairs.

Juliana followed him with shaky legs, picking up her dress as she climbed up. "Edmund, where are you going?"

He reached the second level and headed toward a window opening, rainwater gushing like a vicious waterfall. Juliana's heart quickened, hurrying to catch up to him. Edmund peered out the window, lifted the box over his head, and flung it downward. Far below, the box splashed in the moat.

"Nooo!" Juliana screamed and rushed down the stairs and out the side door.

Edmund followed her, and soon they were both drenched as they stood by the moat. "What are you to do, Juliana, dive into the water and grab the box? You can't swim," he shouted above the torrent.

The rain saturated Juliana's hair and clothes as her eyes darted from side to side, hoping to spot the box in the water. It was dark, a river of blackness before her, then a flash of lightning, and to her delight, a corner of the wooden box glided against the waves. She focused, and in an instant, the box emerged from the water and landed in her arms.

Edmund's eyes widened as he looked at her in disbelief. "You're one of them?" Edmund walked toward her, unsheathed his knife and pointed it at her. "Give me the box, Juliana."

Juliana held up her palm. "Stay away from me," she shouted, clutching the large wooden box.

Edmund inched closer. "What are you to do, use magic on me?" he asked, baiting her.

Juliana's hand began to tremble, and an energy force burst from her hand, sending Edmund flying backward several yards, landing on his back.

Edmund groaned as he got to his feet. He searched for the knife, tapping his hand on the wet slab, grabbed it, and aimed it at Juliana when suddenly Millie came cantering from the stable, knocking Edmund to the ground.

Surprised and grateful to see Millie saddled, Juliana moved quickly, inserted the box in the pocket of Millie's saddle, mounted up, and galloped toward the front of the castle.

Unsure of how to flee from Edmund, Juliana continued sprinting through the castle grounds when the loud screeching ahead roused her and, guided by her instincts, she charged toward the sound. To her surprise, the drawbridge was coming down. *Who's lowering the bridge?* As Millie galloped toward it, the bridge had not yet touched the ground. She rode Millie as fast as she could, up through the bridge, squeezed Millie's sides, and jumped over the gap, landing on solid ground inches from the moat. She exhaled, surprised they made it. Relieved, she followed the trail south toward the forest.

After riding for some time, Juliana sensed someone behind her. She turned her head, and at that moment, a flash of light brightened the forest, and in the distance, she saw Edmund's shadow on his destrier racing toward her. She applied more pressure on her horse. "Go faster, Millie. He's catching up to us!" Juliana's heart pounded, for her palfrey, Millie, was no match for Edmund's charger.

"I'm going as fast as I can, Your Majesty," Millie replied.

Juliana blinked, stunned that her horse spoke to her, then her surprise faded and turned to excitement knowing she could communicate with Millie. She tightened her grip on the reins as she sped through the forest.

She turned her head, gushing rain soaking her face, pushing back her hood, and weighing down her velvet cloak. Edmund continued to shorten the distance between them. *I must do something!* She focused her attention on a large tree behind her, it uprooted and came down with a loud *thump*, blocking Edmund's path.

Edmund yanked on his horse's reins seconds before the tree reached the ground. He screamed something incomprehensible as he came to a stop.

The rain continued to pour, but Millie weaved quickly through the forest, and Juliana sighed in relief, smiling, as they were far ahead of Edmund. Then her smile turned to worry as it was a long ride to Cedarville, and Juliana feared her palfrey would not be able to maintain her current speed and would soon tire, allowing Edmund time to catch up.

Juliana looked back. "I think we lost him."

Hours passed and they were coming upon the bridge, and Juliana was amazed at Millie's endurance, when suddenly Millie halted, rearing up on her hind legs.

"Millie, what's the matter?" asked Juliana.

"Your Majesty, the creek has risen. The bridge is underwater."

"Oh, no, we can't cross it." Juliana looked back. Edmund's charger was galloping toward them. "He found us!" Juliana focused on the rocks and hurled them toward Edmund, making him lose his momentum. "I don't know how much longer I can hold him back. What am I to do?"

"Use your magic."

"But I'm already using—" Juliana stopped, remembering the story that Jack told her of Robert levitating Sir Quinn in the tavern. "Millie, I can try using my powers to lift you over the creek."

Edmund's horse's hoofbeats were getting closer. "Run, Millie, run toward the bridge!"

Millie bolted toward the wooden bridge immersed in the creek. Juliana focused on her mount. She closed her eyes, envisioning the horse soaring through the air. She felt a sharp movement forward and up, and when she opened her eyes, Millie leaped over the creek and flew high above it, soaring as a large winged bird.

Juliana looked back to see a rain-soaked Edmund pulling on his horse's reins, staring openmouthed at the white horse flying over the creek.

Millie landed on a puddle on the other side, splashing, and continued galloping toward Cedarville.

"We did it, Millie!" Juliana let out a sigh of relief.

As they reached the village of Cedarville, Juliana spotted the guards. She slowed Millie and hid behind the trees. The rain-drenched guards blocked her path to Jack's castle. "I must distract them."

Juliana spun around, recalling Jack told her that the alligators had remained hidden below in the creek after the attack on Cedarville. She summoned them, and from the raging river, a dozen alligators emerged. When the alligators reached the guards, the guards pulled out their swords—but there were too many to fight off. Juliana exhaled as the guards retreated to safer areas. She had a clear path to Jack's castle.

Moments later, Juliana banged on Jack's door, shouting out his name. After a short while, Jack opened the door, surprised to see Juliana soaked.

"Juliana! Come in." He called out for his servant Audrey, who was walking toward him in her nightdress, shaking from the commotion. "Audrey, find some dry clothes for Her Majesty."

"Of course. Come with me, Your Majesty. We will get you out of those wet clothes."

A few minutes later, Juliana walked into the great room, trembling. She wore a white linen robe with a wool blanket wrapped around her. On her head, a linen cloth covered her hair. Jack fed logs to the fire and placed a soft blanket by the hearth. He led her in front of the warm flames and held her close, his body heat warming her.

"What happened?"

"Oh, Jack, it's terrible." Juliana sobbed on his chest. "I can never go back, for Edmund will surely kill me. He knows I have magical powers. He had the box with the gems and threw them in the moat. I retrieved them magically. You should have seen the look on his face."

"But you have the stones. That wonderful!"

"Don't you see? I lost my kingdom!" Tears streamed down Juliana's face. "I have lost everything. Edmund planted a spy in the group. I mentioned that I would search for the gemstones stolen from my grandfather Gavin. Edmund knew, and he was ready for me."

Jack held her close, his hand rubbing her arm. "Try to remain calm. Do you know who the spy could be?"

Juliana shook her head and buried it in her hands. "I don't." She then picked up her head. "How can we find out?"

"We shall find a way. We will meet with Robert and Helena in the morn." Jack hesitated. "How did you get past the guards just now?"

Juliana sniffed. "I had help from the alligators. I remembered you told me they were in the creek."

"That's it! You can get the animals to eavesdrop on Edmund and lead you to the spy. You can talk to the birds and have them fly to Yorkford."

Juliana grinned behind soaked eyes. "You're brilliant, Jack."

"Always at your service, Your Majesty." He smiled.

Her smile disappeared as her mind's eye replayed the events at the castle. She turned toward Jack. "Someone lowered the drawbridge, saddled Millie, and sent her to me so I could escape after getting the stones from the moat. I think it was Simon."

"He's a good man. He's been keeping watch over you."

"I am grateful for him. I shudder to think what would have happened if he had not been there to help me."

Juliana leaned on Jack, and he put his arm around her. Soon her nerves steadied, and the chill left her body. She slid the wool blanket off from her and began to unravel the linen cloth wrapped around her hair.

"Permit me," Jack said. He untwisted the cloth from around her head and allowed her long, damp, auburn hair to cascade down her back. He used the cloth to squeeze the moisture out of her hair, then ran his fingers through the strands.

Juliana closed her eyes and allowed his touch to calm her. She sighed and breathed in deep, and when she opened her eyes, she caught his gaze. He was inches from her, her heartbeat quickened, his breath on her.

"You look beautiful," he said.

She scoffed. "I look horrid."

"You always look beautiful to me."

He brought her face toward him, and he kissed the side of her forehead. He caressed her face with a light touch then, with his hand cupping the back of her head, he brought her lips toward his.

As their lips touched, she yearned for him, and she kissed him, slow at first, then her hunger for him grew, and she held him tighter.

Realizing what she was doing, Juliana stopped. "Jack, I—"

"Juliana, don't fight your feelings."

He pulled her in, and their passion intensified. Juliana felt she should stop, but the fire burning inside her heightened her yearning, and she could not pull away. She wrapped her arms around him, and they fell back onto the blanket.

Chapter 14

Juliana awoke in front of the gentle fire and turned to watch Jack as he slept. They spent the night together cuddled in each other's arms. Conflicting emotions struggled within her—happy to be with Jack, as he filled the void in her heart, but guilt at being with another man. Although Jack did not dishonor her, it was wrong to be with him. He was not her husband. *How can something wrong feel right?*

She thought of their kiss last night, filled with passion, and it stirred the fire deep inside her, and she wanted to give in, but Jack had pulled away. "I'm sorry, Juliana, but I can't help myself when I am with you."

Juliana sat up, tightening the robe around her waist. "I am to blame. I should not be here, but my life is in chaos, and I have come because you're the only one I can trust."

"And I don't want to take advantage of it. I have always lived my life to do the right thing, even when it's difficult."

Juliana smiled and lightly touched his face. "You're the strongest man I know, Jack."

He held her hand and brought it to his lips. "Then why do I feel weak when I am with you?"

Juliana gazed into his eyes. She had no words.

He took a deep breath. "Get some rest," he had said. "You have been through a lot." She lay next to him, and he covered her with the blanket and held her.

Now, she stared at him, asleep in front of the burning logs. His chest rose and fell in a quiet contentment, and his eyes moved behind his closed lids. *Is this love that I am feeling for him… that I have always felt?*

Juliana recalled when fourteen-year-old Jack had returned to the castle after being away for two years in knight training. There was something different about him. The days of playing childish games were over. He was confident and chivalrous and dedicated to serving the king's army. She noticed a change in the young boy who had followed her throughout the day. She would catch him staring at her at suppertime, and he frequently offered to do things for her. He taught her to hit a target in archery and to ride a horse, not like a dainty princess, but an expert rider. She looked forward to being with him. Her childhood friend had become a man, and she saw him with different eyes. It was no longer just friendship she felt for him. It was something more. Only she didn't know what it was.

The maidservant walked into the great hall. Jack stirred and opened his eyes.

"Forgive me for waking you, my lord," Audrey said. "I thought you might be asleep in the great chamber." She turned to Juliana. "Good morning, Your Majesty."

Juliana sat up on the wool blanket and wrapped her robe around her. "Good morning, Audrey."

"Don't worry, Audrey. Please prepare breakfast." Jack sat up and turned toward Juliana. "What's wrong?"

A lump lodged in her throat. "I am confused. Last night at the castle… Edmund's rage, and then with you…" She buried her head in her hands.

"Juliana, nothing happened between us."

"Jack, you're a man of honor—you always have been, but something happened. We shared a night together. It makes us more than friends. It complicates things."

"I don't believe things can be more complicated."

"You are mistaken. Edmund accused me of having an affair with you, and even though nothing physically happened, I betrayed my marriage by being here with you. I can't look him in the eye and tell him he was wrong."

"Juliana, you no longer have a marriage with Edmund. Do you think you are to walk into the royal castle and be his queen? You can't go back. It's over."

She stared at him, then her eyes watered and tears streamed down her face. He held her tight as she sobbed on his chest.

"I'm sorry," he said. "Please forgive me."

"No, you're right. The worst part is that I have failed my father. I was to protect his kingdom. It belongs to Edmund now."

He pulled her from him, looking deep into her eyes. "Listen to me. You must fight for what's yours. You can't give up on your kingdom. You can't allow Edmund to take what belongs to you."

She shook her head. "I can't go against him, for he will surely kill me. I don't see how I can win."

"Juliana, I will not give up on what's right. I will fight him to the end."

"It's too dangerous. It *will* be the end of you."

"It doesn't matter. I will not back down. I have always been there for you, and I will not leave you now."

She saw the resolve in his eyes. "You will not leave me?"

He shook his head. "No, we are in this together."

Perhaps this was what her father meant when he told her she would be tested, and she should stand firm and yield to no one. Jack understood that, but he was trained to be brave and draw from his inner strength. Where would she get her strength from? Juliana could only pray she had it in her, just like her father had told her. She put her head on his chest, and they lay back on the blanket with the soothing sound of the fire crackling behind them.

Juliana looked up and gazed steadily at the portrait of his natural parents standing in front of a small wooden cabin with their three young children, two boys and a girl. They wore clothes typical of the working class with plain colors and fabrics. She recalled Edmund referring to Jack as a peasant.

"Jack, if I may ask, how did Uncle Marcus come to adopt you? What happened to your natural parents?" Juliana had never brought up the subject of Jack's past. His origin was a mystery to most everyone except Edmund and his adoptive mother, Katherine.

Jack stared at the portrait. His eyes moistened. "My father worked for Uncle Matthew for many years as a blacksmith. One day our cottage went up in flames, and my father pulled me out, but when he went back for the others… he never came out. I had an older brother Cliff, named after my father, Heathcliff, and an older sister Winnie. They died along with my parents."

"Once King Matthew found out what happened, he asked his brother Prince Marcus to adopt me. Princess Katherine was thrilled because she could not have more children, and Edmund had gone off for military training.

They brought me up as one of their own with all the privileges their natural child would have been entitled to. I wished to prove to them that I deserved it, which is why I worked harder than anyone to be the best knight in the kingdom."

"You accomplished that, Jack. Is that why Edmund resents you?"

"He resents me for a lot of reasons, but that is one."

"I'm sorry you lost your family." She held his hand. "What do you remember about your mother?"

Jack's eyes shifted down. "I remember little. Her name was Daisy, and she was kind and God-fearing and wore her hair short, tucked under a linen cap." He stared at the portrait. "Just how she looks in the painting."

Her eyes lingered on Jack, finding it hard to imagine the deep sense of loss he must have felt losing his parents at a young age and not having a connection to blood family for most of his life. She was grateful that loving parents adopted him, but she could not help thinking a void existed in his heart, just like the hole that burned in hers since her mother and father died.

Jack sat up. "We must send a message to Robert and Helena to meet with us and come up with a plan."

"All right. I shall ask the birds for help." Juliana tied the sash around her waist and headed to the bailey where a multitude of sparrows filled the sunny square, fluttering their wings, hopping from branch to branch, and dipping their beaks into the overflowing birdbath. "Good morning, little sparrows," she said to them.

"Good morning, Your Majesty," they replied in unison.

"I have two requests. Can any of you help me?"

"At your service, Your Majesty," they all said.

"I would like for some of you to go to Helena's cottage, the seamstress, and others to go to Doctor Robert's cottage and ask them to come to Lord Jack's castle. Tell them to be mindful of the guards, and please tell them to make haste. I would also like for some of you to go to King Edmund's castle and find out who he has spying on the magical people and provide any other information that might be helpful."

"As you command, Your Majesty." A flock of sparrows flew toward Yorkford, and others flew toward the village and the woods.

Juliana walked inside the castle to find Jack at the dining table. She stopped for a moment to appreciate what he had become—a man born with little means had captured the heart of the most prestigious royal family in the land, was raised as a prince, became the youngest man ever knighted, and was now a wealthy landowner. If anyone deserved it, it was Jack. Unlike many princes who were arrogant and condescending, Jack was indeed a noble man with a benevolent heart.

She sat next to him and helped herself to fresh cheese and bread. "Jack, about the accord... I believe Edmund forged the document. I don't believe my father would have added that statement, nor would you have agreed to it."

"I did not agree to it, and I am certain Edmund forged it. Uncle Matthew would have protected me and not have allowed a future king to undo everything I have done, or undermine my authority."

Juliana recalled Edmund's words. "My father was a good man, was he not?"

Jack nodded. "He was." He cocked his head. "Do you doubt?"

"Edmund said my father was ruthless and ordered the killing of the people from Maiden Hills. I refused to believe it."

Jack sat back in his chair, seemingly searching for the right words. He gulped his wine. "Your father was a mighty ruler, Juliana. To maintain his dominance, he did what he had to do, even if it meant hurting people."

"But you said he was a good man."

"He was a good man to his family, and he cared for those he loved, but he fiercely defended his kingdom. He craved power, and being the most feared meant everything to him, just like it is to Edmund."

Juliana's eyes shifted down. "It hurts me to know my father was that way."

Jack put his hand on hers. "I'm sorry to tell you, Juliana, but you must remember he loved you more than anyone."

She nodded. "He did. After my mother died, he was everything to me." Tears welled up in her eyes. "I miss him so much."

"I miss him too."

She fought the tears and blinked them away. Not wanting to harbor sadness, she shifted her thoughts. "How did you come to learn of Cedarville?"

"I was at the tavern in Yorkford with Sir Mark when I overheard Sir Leopold tell one of his knights that Lord Godfrey, was killed by his own people. They were searching for a baron to replace him. They wanted someone young and with a vision, so I went to

Cedarville and saw that it had potential, and the people needed help."

"But why Cedarville? My father would have given you the best land in his kingdom. You were like a son to him."

Jack stared into Juliana's eyes. "I wished to be far away from the castle where Edmund was the king and you were his queen. My oath as a knight would not allow me to leave the Kingdom of Yorkford, but Cedarville was far enough."

"Why did you wish to leave?"

He gazed into her sweet hazel green eyes and leaned into her. "I love you, Juliana, and I have always loved you. I knew you would marry a true prince someday, and you could never be mine, but that did not stop me from loving you." He sighed and shrugged his shoulders. "The best thing for me to do was to leave."

Juliana closed her eyes, trying to fight back the tears. She wanted to do the right thing, but her feelings for Jack tormented her. It was sinful, and it engulfed her, and she wasn't strong enough to fight it, and a part of her didn't want to fight it. Jack dabbed her eyes with a kerchief, and Juliana put her hand on his and held it to her face.

"I love you too, Jack, with all my heart. I realize that I have always loved you, but I felt I should not, and I pushed those feelings aside."

Jack leaned over and kissed her lips. She kissed him back, then softly pulled away and stared into his eyes. "Jack, I would give up everything for you."

Jack smiled. "Looks like you don't have much, Your Majesty."

Jack's levity interrupted a tense moment, which Juliana welcomed. She smiled, although his words marked a sad reality for her.

Audrey walked into the dining hall. "Your Majesty, your clothes are dry. Would you like to change into them?"

"I would, thank you, Audrey." Juliana followed Audrey into a private changing room, and the maid helped her get into her corset and maroon silk dress. She tucked her locket underneath her dress as Audrey brushed her hair, then applied makeup to even out her complexion. Juliana glimpsed in the mirror, grateful that the anxiety she experienced at the castle last night had disappeared from her face, and once again, she had the appearance of a refined queen. Her role as queen was dubious, but she at least wanted to look the part.

Juliana entered the great room to find Jack waiting for her by the hearth. He had changed into a green belted tunic, beige leggings made of fine wool, and leather boots. He gazed at her, and it lingered. His warm sky blue eyes melted her heart. They shared a smile, and he took her hand and led her to the red velvet couch. Audrey brought a carafe filled with red wine and two wineglasses.

A short time later, the knock on the door startled them.

"My lord, you have two visitors, Doctor Robert and Helena. Will you receive them?" Audrey asked.

Jack rose from his seat. "Please send them in."

Robert and Helena entered the grand hall and sat opposite of Jack and Juliana, their faces confused, unaware of why they were called to the castle. It was the first time either of them had seen the inside of Lord Jack's castle, and soon Helena's confusion turned to awe.

"My lord, your castle is grand," said Helena.

Jack smiled. "I have the townspeople to thank. They labored for many days to repair it."

The servant brought two wineglasses for the guests and placed it on the small table by the hearth.

"We are most grateful to you, Lord Jack. The former baron did not care for his people. It surprised no one that his own men killed him," said Helena.

"Did anyone see what happened?" Juliana asked, sipping her wine.

"No, we received word from King Matthew's herald. At first, we all rejoiced, but then we realized there was no one to govern, and people lost their jobs. A meager wage was better than no wage at all, and soon the villagers were suffering the effects of poverty and starvation until Lord Jack came along. He saved our village."

Juliana glanced at Jack and smiled. "He is truly a hero."

Helena nodded. "Indeed!"

"Pardon me, Your Majesty, my lord, but why were we called here?" Robert asked.

Juliana looked at Robert and Helena and smiled. "I have good news. I have the box with the gemstones and lockets."

Their faces lit up.

"That's splendid!" Helena said.

"We shall call for a meeting up on the mountain and distribute the stones," Robert said.

"There is trouble there. King Edmund planted a spy in the group. We must be careful of what we say."

"Robert," Jack said, "we must form an army."

Juliana turned toward Jack with furrowed brows. *Did I hear correctly?*

Jack continued, "King Edmund will attack again, but this time he will send more men. I have one hundred soldiers, but we need more fighters. My knights and I can train the villagers to use a weapon and teach them fighting techniques. The Majian people can help, but King Edmund's army is large and strong. We need all the manpower available to us."

"I will ask Jeb to gather the best men in town. Shall they come here?"

"Yes, I have plenty of room in the courtyard. We shall begin training at sundown."

Jack turned to Helena. "Helena, you and Robert must gather the Majians and teach them the spells."

Helena said, "There is a problem, my lord—I don't remember the first spell."

"I have forgotten it as well," Robert said. "Your Majesty, didn't you find the book?"

Juliana paused, trying to grasp the direction of the conversation. "I—I did, but it's in a drawer in my chamber back at the castle."

"Helena, you can teach them the second spell to communicate with the animals. That will help us when we are attacked," Jack said.

"Aye, my lord, I shall do that."

"Robert," Juliana said, "the box is in my horse's saddlebag in the stable. Please help yourself to it."

Robert walked toward the rear of the castle, where Millie rested in the stable. Helena exited from the main entrance where her horse-drawn carriage stood. She didn't require a driver. She simply told the horses where to take her.

Juliana watched them leave, then turned toward Jack. "Have you gone mad? You're training an army?"

"What did you think I meant when I said I would fight him to the end?"

"I did not think you would declare war."

"What am I to do, sit back and watch him destroy us? Whether or not you want to accept it, we are at war with him. I'm not backing down."

Juliana shook her head in anguish. "Jack, this is treason. If he finds out you're training an army, he will be furious. He will destroy this village, and he will have your head."

"Juliana, I know you're afraid, but please do not doubt me."

"Forgive me, Jack, but you're no match for him. He's ruthless."

"I have no choice. I will do what I must do and accept my fate."

Juliana put her arms around him as she trembled inside. Jack held her tight before pulling away and met her eyes. "You must go with Robert and Helena. No doubt Edmund's men will come for you. This is the first place they will look."

"I do not wish to leave you."

"You will be safe with them. Robert will protect you. Please go."

"What are you to do?"

"I shall meet with King Carlton in Etheland. We could use his help."

Juliana hesitated, a wave of anxiety running through her. Her world was crumbling around her, and she could only pray that Jack knew what he was doing. She had no choice but to concede. "All right. Please be careful." She kissed Jack on the cheek, grabbed her purple cloak, and walked toward the rear of the manor to fetch Millie and meet with Robert.

Chapter 15

The king's guards arrived at dawn to accompany Edmund on his scheduled hunting trip. Edmund was a superior marksman, a skill he learned from King Matthew as a young boy. He had relished those moments with the man who was like a father to him. This day, he especially looked forward to the hunt. It was a way to relieve tension that came along with ruling a kingdom, and after last night with Juliana, the tension had swelled to unimaginable proportions.

Atop his black destrier, Edmund rode along with ten of his most trusted knights and arrived in the middle of a large wooded area in northern Yorkford to scout for large prey. He breathed in the fresh morning air cleansed by last night's heavy rain as he and his men waited for the animals to awaken. It was quiet. After a few minutes, a rustling in the bushes disturbed the silence. Edmund turned, the thumping of his racing heartbeat sharpened his senses, and his eyes darted in the direction of the sound. A deer grazed several yards away. He reached back, removed an arrow from his quiver, nocked the arrow on the bow, and kept his eye on the deer. He saw Jack's face superimposed on the deer's head. He aimed between the eyes, pulled back the arrow, and released it, *thwack!* Two of his men rode toward it and picked up the carcass.

He continued seeking and killing, and his men gathered the carcasses, all the while thinking of Juliana and her unforgivable actions. *How is it possible that Juliana has magical powers?* That question baffled Edmund, for she came from royal blood and from one of the finest noble families in Westmore. There had to be an explanation, and Edmund would find it. The next deer had Juliana's face on it, and he killed that one too.

Edmund took pride in living a life of discipline and order; however, the revelation of the truth of his father, James, three weeks ago, and Juliana's betrayal had shaken that order and created a disruption he found difficult to contain. He didn't think it could get worse until he met with Sir Paul the day prior, just before he had supper with Juliana.

"Your Majesty, I found Queen Juliana," Sir Paul had told him.

Edmund's eyes narrowed. "Where is she?"

"She was on a mountaintop on the edge of Cedarville with the doctor and a group of magical people called Majians, but alas if I had captured her or the doctor, it would have jeopardized my spy mission."

This puzzled Edmund. "What in heaven's name was she doing there?"

"She was observing them and offered to search for a box filled with lockets and gemstones in Sir Leopold's chamber."

Edmund recalled stumbling upon such a box weeks ago while searching for documents in King Matthew's library. He had questioned Leopold about it, and Leopold told him that King Matthew paid him in gold for the box. Not seeing any value in it, he had dismissed it. That is, until he met with Sir Paul. He retrieved the wooden box from the library and kept it hidden, suspecting that Juliana might search for it there.

Last night, unable to sleep, he left his room, peered from the upstairs landing, and spotted Juliana below with a candle walking toward James' chamber. He presumed Juliana had tricked the guard at her door into letting her out. Edmund, dressed in his tunic and tights, tied a belt with a knife in its sheath around his waist and grabbed the box filled with stones and lockets. With light feet, he walked down the stairs and hid behind an alcove. When he saw Juliana head toward the library, he followed her and chose that moment to confront her.

Edmund's thoughts switched to the drawbridge. Someone inside the castle had lowered the drawbridge and let her horse loose after midnight just when Juliana retrieved the box with the stones from the moat. In the morning, he discovered that another guard had relieved Sir William from his guarding post. *The same man may have lowered the drawbridge for Juliana and most likely helped her escape from the dungeon*, he concluded. There was a traitor in the castle—that was the only explanation—and Edmund would find him.

After a few hours of hunting, Edmund returned to the castle. He entered the library and sat behind his desk, fingers tapping. He had an appointment he was most anxiously looking forward to. As he waited, his mind drifted to Juliana, flying over the creek with her horse. His first instincts were to send his army to Cedarville to search Jack's castle and every home until they found her. However, foremost on his mind was finding his father's killer, and he had to restrain himself from doing anything rash. She couldn't hide forever. He would eventually find her, but for now, there were other questions he needed answered. He gave Sir Paul twenty-four hours to bring in the doctor from Cedarville. He suspected Doctor Robert was vital in exposing the mystery surrounding the death of his father.

He was absorbed in his internal chatter when Samuel walked in. "Pardon me, Your Majesty, but Duke Richard Maddeson of Westmore is here to see you."

"He's right on time. Send him in." At last, he would find out the truth about Juliana.

A few seconds later, Duke Richard appeared at the door. He bowed before Edmund. Usually, a jolly man with a round face and perceptive eyes, Richard had a bewildered expression.

"Duke Richard, please come in and have a seat." Edmund smiled, trying to hide his anxiety, hoping that the meeting would give him the answer to the question that had stumped him.

"Your Majesty, I must say it intrigued me when your guards came and told me you wished to speak to me. How may I serve you?"

Edmund sat back in his chair with his arms crossed. "Something has come to my attention that has left me quite perplexed, and I hope you can help add clarity."

"I would be happy to help if I can, Your Majesty."

Edmund leaned on the table, hands folded. "It's about your late sister, Queen Lucinda."

Richard tilted his head. "Lucinda? What about her?"

"I must know, was she adopted?"

Richard fidgeted in his chair, surprised at the unexpected inquiry. "No one was to know. But if you're inquiring, that means that somehow you discovered the truth. Yes, Your Majesty, Lucinda was adopted. My mother had four sons and wished for a daughter. When

Lucinda came to her as a young child after losing her family, my parents took her in."

Heat flushed through Edmund's body. "How very convenient. No doubt your parents wanted a daughter so they could marry her to a king. Your father was very shrewd." Edmund fought to compose himself, even as spite spewed out.

"That was not their intention when they adopted her. She was an orphan, and they gave her a home."

"But you can't deny that all of you profited from it. King Matthew granted you the town of Westmore to govern, and your brothers benefitted as well with land of their own."

"With all due respect, Your Majesty, I was a loyal servant to King Matthew."

"Of course, you were." Edmund's cynicism came through as he studied the duke. Richard came across as gentle and naïve, but underneath he was a clever man. His father, Duke John, was part of Edmund's grandfather King Thomas's inner circle, and Edmund felt Richard's loyalty aligned closer with his grandfather than with him. He wasn't sure he could trust him. "Where did she come from?"

"I don't know the answer as my parents never revealed it to me. I suspected she was of noble blood, for she had the proper mannerisms and speech expected of a noblewoman."

"She certainly did. Tell me, Duke Richard, do you remember when your parents took her in?"

Richard raised his eyes to the ceiling, seemingly performing mental calculations. "That was twenty-two years ago, Your Majesty."

247

Edmund's nostrils flared. His suspicions were confirmed. Lucinda had escaped the massacre at Maiden Hills twenty-two years ago and found her way into Westmore. "That will be all, Duke Richard. Please see your way out."

"Your Majesty, before I leave, I must inform you of your grandfather King Thomas."

"What has come upon him?"

"He has taken ill and may not be around much longer. He is weakening by the day."

Edmund leaned on his folded hands with eyes shifted downward. He had a great deal of respect for his grandfather Thomas, James' father, the sole survivor, besides himself, of the Wadham dynasty. He raised his eyes and met Richard's. "I shall visit with him soon."

"Very well. Good day, Your Majesty." Richard turned to leave.

Edmund's thoughts went back to Lucinda, and rage swept through him upon learning of the boldfaced deception that the duke and duchess of Westmore had orchestrated against King Matthew. To pass off as nobility a woman whose lineage was unknown and allow a stain in the royal blood was reprehensible. He would not fault Duke Richard because he was not much older than Lucinda at the time, but if his parents the duke and duchess were alive, he would have them executed.

***

Robert started the fire on the mountain, and Helena sprinkled the magic herbs. One by one, the Majians trekked up the broad mountain and sat around the fire, making light conversation. Simon arrived with his daughter, Alice, and a young lad accompanied Jeb.

Juliana studied the faces in the crowd, hoping to detect an uneasiness in one of them, shifty eyes, or other signs of a spy.

Jeb walked toward Juliana with the boy. "Your Majesty, I would like to present to you, my son Victor. He is your cousin," Jeb said with pride.

Victor bowed. "It's an honor to meet you, Your Majesty."

"A pleasure to meet you, cousin Victor." Juliana smiled then turned toward Jeb. "He's named after your mother, is he not?"

"He is, Your Majesty—your grandmother Lady Victoria. I have two other children, but they're younger and stayed at home with my wife, Mildred. She's not a Majian."

"I'm sure I will meet them soon."

Juliana pulled the purple hood over her head and sat to the side with a wide view of the faces in the crowd. The Majians sat on the ground in front of the fire, occasionally glancing at Juliana. Robert stood before them, and all eyes remained fixed on him with marked anticipation. Helena sat on a large boulder next to Robert.

"We have the box with the gemstones, and we will distribute them to all of you," Robert announced. Excitement grew within the crowd. "There will be enough for everyone. These stones once belonged to your natural parents."

Sorrow reflected on their faces, as many of them never knew their Majian parents, and those who knew them remembered that terrible day when they were taken from them. Helena gave each person a green stone with black waves, and Robert gave each one a black stone with golden tones. Simon distributed the lockets.

Helena instructed each person to hold the green stone with black waves to their heart and recite the animal spell.

Juliana watched for signs of a spy in the group. If there was such a spy, he played the part well and blended in. If the spy were a Majian, she would not be able to set him apart from the others.

Helena offered instruction on the use of the magic to talk to the animals. "This power will allow you to communicate with animals either out loud or in your mind, and they will heed your command. A non-Majian can't hear them talk, but a Majian will, and for as long as you wear the stones, a wild animal will never harm you. You could never instruct an animal to harm another Majian. Trained animals such as warhorses will be loyal to their masters, and you can't command them unless it is to benefit their master. Now, please, practice on the mountain with birds, spiders, and other small creatures."

The Majians dispersed. Juliana observed each person, attempting to identify the spy among them, but a non-Majian could do a convincing job of pretending to be talking and laughing with an animal.

When they finished, they gathered around the fire, waiting for the next instruction. Helena said, "Alas, I don't remember the first spell. We need *The Book of Secrets,* and we do not have it."

"I know the first spell," said Simon. "I had the book and memorized it."

A smile spread across Helena's face. "That's splendid!" She instructed the crowd to hold the black stone with gold tones to their heart as Simon recited the spell, and the group repeated it. They all experienced an intense reaction, and some of them had frightened looks on their faces.

Robert said, "This power will allow you to move objects within your sight, and it is extremely powerful. You must practice often to perfect it." He continued, "Unlike the animal power, this power can be used against you by another Majian. If that happens, you have the ability to defend yourself and move any movable object, even another person or animal. You must focus on the object you want to move, and in your mind, direct it where you want it to go. It will be slow at first, but after a lot of practice, you shall be able to focus your mind, direct the object, and move it in an instant. You will not be able to move something you can't see, so make sure you look at it, even for a second. The force that moves it will depend on the emotion that drives it. With strong emotions such as anger or fear, the object will strike hard. If someone hurls a knife at you, look at it, and direct it to turn around. You need to practice moving objects quickly because your life could depend on it. Please practice now on the mountain with rocks and other objects."

The Majians scattered to work on the power. Juliana surveyed the group as they playfully moved rocks, hitting their friends. She scouted for the spy, but with all the rocks flying around, she couldn't tell where they originated from. She was no closer to finding the spy than when they began.

When practice ended, Robert said, "Please remember to practice often in private and never in front of non-

Majians. You must keep your powers secret except in cases of self-defense. Also, keep your lockets hidden under your clothes since King Edmund's guards will be watching and will arrest anyone wearing them."

Robert strolled toward Juliana, sitting by the fire with Helena, Robert, Jeb, and Simon. "Were you able to detect the spy?"

"No. If he was here, he blended in well," Juliana said.

Simon narrowed his eyes. "Spy?"

"King Edmund planted a spy in the group. He mentioned it to me last night at the castle. Did you recognize anyone from Yorkford?"

"I thought I saw a familiar face, but I can't be certain. Was there anything said that might be used against us?"

"I think not, except King Edmund will find out how effective the magic is and will use whatever means possible to destroy the people," Juliana said. "He is to be feared."

Simon agreed, having witnessed Edmund's wrath first hand while working as the dungeon guard. "I must return to the castle. I shall keep my eyes open for anyone I recognize from the group." Simon turned to Helena. "Mother, shall I accompany you to your cabin?"

"I would like that, son."

Juliana asked, "What about the gold?"

Helena turned toward Jeb and Robert. "Jeb, find the gold buried in your father's manor. Robert, do you remember your way around it?"

"I do. Come, Jeb."

Juliana saw Robert walk over to Simon and overheard him say, "You must distract the guards to get into the village square. Escort Her Majesty to your mother's cottage and make sure she is safe. The king's men will be looking for her. I don't wish to leave her, but I must stay behind with Jeb and search for the gold. I will get to Helena's cottage as soon as I can to take her to Lord Jack's castle."

Simon nodded. "I shall make sure she is safe."

He then walked toward his mother and held her arm as they descended the mountain.

Juliana followed Simon, staring at the blackened ruins in the distance, trying to imagine the terror her family and all the Majians must have suffered that dreadful day. She hoped her actions last night would make up, at least in some small way, to the horror her kingdom had committed. Juliana did not want to believe her father had issued the order to massacre the people. She wanted to continue to remember him as a sweet and loving man.

When they reached the bottom of the mountain, Juliana and Simon mounted their horses and headed toward Cedarville. Helena followed in her carriage. They soon arrived in the village square just as the villagers scurried into the merchant shops for supplies before the shops closed for the evening. Juliana and Helena stayed out of sight, while Simon used his magic to distract the guards. When all was clear, he went inside Helena's cottage, inspected the room, then waved in his mother and Juliana. Simon threw wood in the fireplace and lit several candles throughout the cabin.

He turned to Juliana. "Your Majesty, please remain here until Robert returns for you. He won't be long. You are safe here; however, do not hesitate to use your powers to defend yourself if necessary."

253

"I shall." Juliana reflected for a moment. "Simon, you told me that you moved into the castle to watch over my mother, then you stayed to watch over me."

Simon nodded. "Yes, Your Majesty."

"Why?"

"Because of the prophecy."

"I don't understand."

"After the massacre, I had to go into hiding, for I knew the king's men would be on the hunt for me. I traveled to Westmore and stayed in the monastery. Four years later, a voice came to me telling me that young Lucinda Archer married the king of Yorkford and told me to watch over her but to tell no one. I snuck into the castle to see her, and she hired me as the dungeon guard. I grew a beard and mustache and wore a hood so no one would recognize me. The prophecy predicted a leader would emerge and help our people rise again. Queen Lucinda and I both believed it would be one of her heirs. Out of her three children, you were the only one that lived."

A chill ran up Juliana's spine. "That's why she told me the secret before she died, and that's why she wanted me to find you."

"Yes, if she had not told you, it would have been up to me. I had to wait until the right time. Fortunately, you found Robert through Lord Jack, and now the prophecy is unfolding."

"But why would you believe I would be the leader and not Robert or Jeb?"

"Majians have a gift of second sight, and sometimes it comes to us, and sometimes it doesn't. But when it does, you just know it's true."

Juliana sat in silence, trying to grasp this new revelation, recalling her mother's words, *"You must be prepared for what is to come. You must help save our people."*

"If you'll excuse me, Your Majesty, I must leave now."

"Of course." She recalled the narrow escape from the castle. Her fate would have been in Edmund's vengeful hand, and the stones would have been lost to the Majians forever had she not escaped. She shuddered at the thought, but then realized someone was looking after her. "Thank you for lowering the drawbridge last night, and for sending Millie," she added with a faint smile.

"You're welcome." He smiled, and his eyes naturally squinted. Simon had a temper, but he had a softer side that Juliana witnessed tending to his mother, and when she was in the dungeon and had brought her supper.

Simon fussed over Helena, making sure her needs were met. When Simon was satisfied that everything was in order, he turned to his mother and kissed her forehead. He jumped on his horse and headed north toward Yorkford.

"Would you care for a cup of wine, Your Majesty?" Helena asked.

Juliana's thoughts wandered, replaying the events of the day up at the mountain, last night with Jack, and at the castle with Edmund. *It's curious how unexpected circumstances can toss someone into an entirely unpredictable and chaotic direction in their life*, she mused. One minute she was the queen of a large and great kingdom living a life of luxury, and the next minute she was sitting on top of a mountain with people practicing magic. It was bizarre, and she longed for the familiar. *If all of this is leading to something greater, I cannot see it.*

"Your Majesty?"

Juliana found herself back in Helena's cottage. "My apologies, Helena. Yes, I would like wine, please."

Helena poured wine into two cups and handed one to Juliana. They sat by the fire, allowing their minds and bodies to relax after a long and exhausting day. Juliana studied the woman who appeared frail on the outside but had more strength than most people on the inside. She seemed content to have the Majian community that had been her way of life for so long return after it had been cruelly snatched from her.

As Juliana drank her wine and enjoyed the warmth of the fire, something nagged in her mind. "Helena, you had told me that when Beth met Prince James, he gave her a statue of a fairy sitting on a mushroom holding a butterfly. Is that not true?"

"It is true."

"Did Beth ever give that statue back to James?"

"No, Your Majesty. Why do you ask?"

"At the castle, when I was searching for the gemstones, I went into Prince James' former chamber and came upon a statue that matched that description."

"Might there be two statues, Your Majesty?" Helena asked.

"I suppose there could be."

"The one that Prince James gave Beth was in the cottage before it… burned." She took a deep breath and continued. "It was in Peter's cradle when I left to fetch milk for him. He loved to play with it."

"I see." Juliana recalled Peter's cradle was empty except for a burned rattle. "I guess you're right. There must have been two statues." Juliana was not convinced.

***

As Robert came down the mountain with Jeb, he observed the Majians, pleased to have his people united once more. He had lived a solitary existence since the massacre, not wanting to form intimate bonds with anyone. Healing and caring for others gave him a sense of purpose and a reason to live, and it eased his conscience to have survived where many others had perished. He never dreamed that the Majians would re-organize, and he hoped that maybe the sadness that lived in his heart would someday find a glimmer of happiness.

As they continued the trek down, Robert saw someone familiar. As the town's doctor, he knew most everyone in the village, but he could not attach a name to the face. He took a few steps closer to him. "Pardon me, young man."

The young man with gray eyes turned toward Robert.

"You look familiar. Have I treated you?" Robert asked.

"You treated my son, Max. My two-year-old boy had trouble breathing, and you gave him herbs to inhale, and it cured him." The handsome, dark-haired man gave Robert a smile of gratitude.

"I remember now, you're Randall, Geraldine's brother, but I don't see her here."

"My sister is not from Maiden Hills. Her parents adopted me after I was saved from the attack. I was not yet a year old when the massacre occurred, and I never knew my natural parents."

Robert's throat swelled, for this young man would have been the same age as Peter had he lived. He smiled at Randall and urged him to practice his magic. Robert stared at Randall as he continued down the mountain and watched him climb on his horse.

"Robert, is something wrong?" Jeb asked.

"I was thinking about my son." He suppressed tears and stared at his ruined village. "This fight... this land. I must do this... for him."

The baron's stone manor remained standing, but items inside were either burned or beneath a pile of rocks from the collapse of the upper floor. Robert and Jeb searched through the rubble, digging through hidden spaces underneath the manor and behind walls. They used their magic to lift the massive rocks, and after an exhaustive search, came up empty. There were many rooms and crevices to rummage through, and Robert thought it best to suspend the search and return with more men to assist.

When the sun hung low in the sky, Robert and Jeb headed to the village square through the woods. They were near Robert's cottage when two mounted knights wearing helmets and partial armor waited by the door. Robert and Jeb reined to a halt.

"Doctor Robert," the knight shouted.

"What can I do for you?" Robert called out.

"You are to come with us by order of His Majesty, King Edmund of Yorkford."

"What does the king want with me?"

"He wishes to speak to you."

Robert stood firm. "What if I refuse?"

The knights looked at each other, not expecting Robert to object to the king's request. "Then, we shall arrest you."

Robert challenged the men. "Then come and arrest me."

Jeb had a worried look on his face, but Robert gave him a reassuring nod.

The knights raised their swords and charged toward Robert. They expected to chase him, but Robert didn't move. Jeb began to fidget. Robert stretched his arm and motioned Jeb to stay. As the knights approached, their swords flew from their hands and into Robert and Jeb's grip. The knights pulled back their horses and were dumbfounded to see their own weapons pointed at them. Rocks and stones flew toward the knights. They lifted their shields, twisting their bodies to block the rocks flying from every direction.

Robert raised his eyes and spotted two hawks soaring above him. In his mind, he spoke to them, and soon, the hawks swooped down and encircled the knights, making screeching, threatening sounds. Jeb stood beside him in awe, as he had not yet seen the tremendous power of their magic—he had only heard of the incident in his tavern with Robert and Sir Quinn.

The knights pivoted, trying to dodge the birds of prey, but the sharp claws grabbed their helms and gashed their necks through the chainmail. The knights cried out. They yanked at the creatures, pulling them away and in fright, turned their horses, and fled toward the village.

Chapter 16

The tall, lanky manservant escorted Jack to the great hall of Etheland Castle. "Please wait here while I announce your arrival to the king."

Jack scanned the grand hall. King Carlton's castle resembled in many respects the royal castle of Yorkford, except the portraits on the wall had different faces. Four generations of King Carlton's ancestors beginning with King Carlton I to King Carlton IV graced the walls. The tapestries illustrated the rich heritage of the Goldwell's family rule over the southern part of the continent, their battles, and their celebrations. A map on the wall depicted Etheland's possessions, a considerable size but smaller than Yorkford's. Up to the north on the map was a small territory labeled Maiden Hills crossed out in thick black ink.

King Carlton and King Matthew had a friendly rivalry, but neither one dared to battle the other, for both armies were formidable. Still, Yorkford had a slight advantage over Etheland, which they demonstrated by their superior performance in the jousting events. They often invited each other to their banquets and festivals in their respective palaces to flaunt their wealth, and with each event, they tried to surpass the other. When Edmund became the ruler of the Kingdom of Yorkford, the relationship between the two kingdoms cooled. King Carlton attempted to establish relations with Edmund, but Edmund distrusted the king and preferred to keep his distance.

The manservant approached Jack. "His Majesty will see you now. Please follow me."

Jack followed the servant to the garden. King Carlton, a man in his fifties with white hair, a long white beard, and a round face, sat in a large ornate chair surrounded by flowering trees. His two lovely daughters, eighteen-year-old Alexandra and sixteen-year-old Amelia, both thin with long, flowing platinum blond hair, sat at an angle from him on a decorative bench. The majestic king had a cheerful disposition and greeted Jack with a wide smile.

"Lord Jack, it has been a long time. I believe the last time was at the ball King Matthew held in honor of his lovely daughter, Queen Juliana. You remember my daughters, Princess Alexandra and Princess Amelia."

Jack bowed to the king and kissed the princesses' hands. "Your Highnesses, it's a pleasure to see you again." The two young ladies blushed and gave Jack broad smiles.

Jack sat on the bench opposite Carlton's daughters. A servant placed a tray of fruit, bread, and cheese on the table and filled a glass of wine for Jack. "I remember that ball well," Jack said, thinking of the dance with Juliana and remembering Edmund's irritation over it.

"King Matthew certainly knew how to host a celebration. I invited your kingdom to take part in one of our festivals not long ago, but King Edmund refused."

"He's a different ruler than my uncle King Matthew was." Jack lifted his wineglass and took a sip.

"Indeed, he is." King Carlton eyed Jack, trying to determine where he fell on the trust scale. Jack expected Carlton to be wary since this was the first time the two had met outside of social gatherings. A typical business reason would not had brought them together, but for Jack, nothing had been typical as of late.

"What brings you here, young man?"

"I'm here on behalf of the people of Maiden Hills."

King Carlton raised his eyebrows. "Maiden Hills was destroyed years ago. There is nothing there but a bunch of burned cottages. I never quite forgave your uncle for destroying it, but a small piece of land was not worth a long and bloody battle with Yorkford."

Jack's insides tensed at the thought of Matthew ordering the attack on Maiden Hills. He had seen his uncle act ruthlessly, but he justified it to himself, accepting it as the duties of a powerful king. But Maiden Hills was different. It had become personal for Jack. He pushed his anger aside. "There are survivors living in Cedarville, who should reclaim their land and rebuild their homes. It will take a lot of work, and I have offered the Majian people my assistance, but they will require much more. Your kingdom had benefitted from their land and services in the past."

"Indeed, we have." Carlton leaned forward. "Tell me, son, are you planning on expanding your land of Cedarville to include Maiden Hills?"

"No, Your Majesty. It belongs to your kingdom and to the original people of Maiden Hills, whose town was destroyed. It is my will to help them reclaim what belongs to them. I have no intention of taking it over."

"What's in it for you, Lord Jack?" Carlton did not seem convinced that Jack's motives were purely altruistic.

"Aside from doing what is right, they would make great trading partners. Twenty-two years ago, Maiden Hills prospered with rich soil, livestock, and an abundance of crops. It would help Cedarville since they are their closest neighbors. Because of the rising creek in stormy weather, the bridge to Cedarville is sometimes impassable, and food and needed supplies can't get to the town. When I took over Cedarville, the people were impoverished. They suffered years ago when Maiden Hills was decimated and never fully recovered since they had more people to feed but less food. Cedarville is now thriving, and I wish to help restore Maiden Hills to the prosperity they enjoyed before the tragedy twenty-two years ago."

King Carlton stroked his beard as he stared at Jack. "You make a compelling case, Lord Jack. It would be noble to restore the village to the productive land it once was as there's a long history between the Majian people and my family. My great-grandfather gave them their land and protected them. The massacre caught us by surprise, or we would have aided them." He studied Jack, eyes narrowed. "I assume you are aware of why they were massacred."

Jack twisted his mouth. "I do." It was no longer a well-kept secret that the Majians had magical gifts. He recalled reading about the massacre in the library at Somerville.

"My ancestors kept their secret, but tragically twenty-two years ago, Yorkford discovered it, and the Majians paid the price for it."

"I was not yet born, but perhaps I can help make up for the injustice they suffered at the hands of the kingdom that I serve."

"And you're seeking my assistance?"

"Yes, Your Majesty."

King Carlton's eyes tightened, then turned to his daughters. "Please leave Lord Jack and me to speak in private."

"As you wish, Father," said Alexandra. His daughters giggled as they strolled out of the garden. Jack, having risen from his seat, stared at them as any man would in the presence of beautiful women. When they departed from sight, he sat and returned his full attention to the king.

"Lord Jack, you are a fine young man, brought up as the son of a prince. Are you betrothed to anyone?"

"No, Your Majesty."

"As you can see, I have two beautiful daughters that I wish to marry off. An arranged marriage with a nobleman from Yorkford could help relations between our two kingdoms."

Jack did not like where this was going. "Perhaps it could, Your Majesty."

"I would like to betroth you to my eldest daughter Alexandra. She is very gracious and will serve you well."

"Forgive me, Your Majesty, but if it's better relations you are seeking, I am afraid that will not result from a marriage between your daughter and me. King Edmund and I do not get along. In fact, he despises me."

"I shall speak with him, but perhaps you will find it in your best interest to repair your relationship with him." He leaned closer. "It would mean the difference between restoring Maiden Hills or keeping it abandoned." Carlton smiled behind his veiled threat.

Jack swallowed his wine. "I understand, Your Majesty." Jack found himself in a situation he could not win. Matthew had warned him about King Carlton, but

Jack expected the king to realize that it would be to his advantage to restore Maiden Hills. Jack did not expect Carlton to see the bigger prize of setting his foot on the soil of Yorkford. It was no wonder Matthew had warned him about Carlton. They were both shrewd and manipulative in their dealings. Maybe he had been overconfident in believing he could negotiate with a powerful ruler, but he soon realized he was naïve in such matters. Jack had much to learn. One thing was certain—he had to marry, and who better than with a princess? As the adopted son of Prince Marcus, Jack inherited his wealth, which made him one of the wealthiest men in the kingdom, fit to marry royalty, but the only royalty he desired was Juliana. What would she say if she found out he was betrothed to another woman?

The situation with Juliana was precarious. Edmund knew she was of magical descent and would kill her once she returned to Yorkford. Maiden Hills had to be restored, and if Jack agreed to the arranged marriage, King Carlton would help rebuild the village and provide Juliana a safe place to live outside of her kingdom, if necessary, with the protection of Etheland's army.

The right thing to do was obvious, although he would be playing into Carlton's manipulation.

**

Juliana peered through the small opening in the door, observing the calmness imbued in the village square. Evening fell, and King Edmund's guards watched the people as they closed their shops and headed home to meet the curfew. The orders from Lord Jack were not to give the guards reason to arrest them. They were to obey all laws and wait for further instructions from either Jack or Jeb. Jack trusted Jeb, but his fondness for him grew once he learned he was Juliana's uncle.

Juliana closed the small opening and paced inside the cottage. She waited anxiously for Robert, who had stayed behind to search for the gold after the Majians received their gemstones and recited the spells up on the mountain. It was taking him longer than expected.

She sat by the fireplace, and soon her eyelids grew heavy and began to come down. It had been a long day, and staring at the fire flickering in a rhythmic pattern was making her drowsy. She leaped at the knock on the door and peeked through the opening—it was Robert.

"Your Majesty is everything all right?" he asked when he entered.

"All is well." She pointed to Helena, sleeping in her bed. "The events of the day exhausted her, and as soon as she drank her wine, she fell asleep."

"She needs her rest."

"Did you and Jeb find the gold?"

Robert shook his head. "There's a lot of rubble to go through. We must continue to search and bring more men to assist."

Robert helped himself to a cup of wine. Juliana handed her cup to Robert, and he filled it. They pulled up two chairs and sat at a small table. Juliana felt comfortable with Robert. Although he wasn't a blood kin, something about him made him feel like family. Perhaps, she reasoned, it was because of the connection he had with her mother as a member of the same community.

"Is Jeb gathering the village men for training at Lord Jack's castle?" Juliana asked.

"He is. They should be there by nightfall."

"We need every man out there if we are to defeat King Edmund's army. They are formidable." Juliana paused. An image of her encounter with Edmund came to mind. "Robert, last night at the castle, I lifted my hand, and without touching my husband, he fell back. How did I do that?"

"There's an energy field around us, and when concentrated, it is powerful, and you can move it just like you can move any object. Your intention was clear. You wanted King Edmund away from you; thus, you focused the energy onto your hand and pushed it toward him." Robert furrowed his brow. "However, that does not come easily." He cocked his head, bewildered. "What else did you do?"

Juliana rehashed her encounter with Edmund and the use of her magical abilities to overpower him and escape, including flying Millie across the bridge.

"I have never known anyone to master their skills as quickly as you have without training. I'm beginning to think Helena is right. You may be the leader, and the first protector prophesied."

She stared at Robert, feeling the enormous responsibility upon her. "I don't know if I can do it."

"If you are the leader of the Majians, you will find the strength within yourself."

Juliana sipped her wine, reflecting on Robert's words. "There is much I need to learn."

"This magic is powerful, and as you work with it, you will discover what you can do. I must teach the Majians

267

how to use the energy field. It will be useful when faced with Yorkford's army."

"We must use whatever weapon at our disposal." She sighed. "They always win."

"We have more to lose, so we shall fight harder, and we must trust in the power of the stones and in Lord Jack as our commander. He knows what to do. We did not have that twenty-two years ago."

"Do you think my grandfather Gavin made a mistake?" Juliana had to ask but feared the answer, for deep down, she felt her grandfather could have done more to protect his people.

"We were not prepared. We lived in peace for many years and did not expect something like that to happen. I don't blame him." Robert poured himself another cup of wine.

Juliana noticed that Robert drank more than usual when talking about the past. "Robert, I know this is still very painful for you."

Robert put his cup down and looked at Juliana. "Your Majesty, I live with this every day. This is not something that happened twenty-two years ago. For me, it *just* happened. The alcohol helps me cope, and I can do my job and heal people, but this never leaves me. Being up in that mountain and in the burned village is more difficult than anyone will ever know, but I must continue. We must fight back, and I can't fail my people. I have failed too many in the past."

"Was Beth one of those people?"

He nodded and drank from his cup. "I loved her, but I had married Olivia when I was very young. She got pregnant but got sick during the pregnancy, the child died, and Olivia could never walk again. I met Beth one year later and fell in love with her. Olivia released me from the marriage vows, but I could not abandon her. Someone had to care for her, and she had no family. I fell in love with Beth, for she was a beautiful and sweet girl. When Beth got pregnant, I was both happy and scared. I feared the same thing that happened to Olivia would happen to her. But it did not. She had a healthy baby boy, and Beth was healthy too. She wished for us to be married and be a family, but I failed her." Robert looked at Juliana. "Do you understand now why this still haunts me? If not for me, Beth would be alive this day, and so would my son, and all the Majians would not have suffered the massacre, and the village would not have been destroyed. Beth met Prince James and fell for him because I could not be with her."

"Robert, you are placing a heavy burden on yourself for something you had no control over. You can't continue to blame yourself and drown your pain with beer and wine."

"It's the only way I can cope." He swallowed the rest of his drink.

Juliana studied him and found him to be a handsome man with strong features and a generous heart. "Robert, if I may be so bold, why have you not remarried?"

"Forgive me, Your Majesty, but is it not obvious? I have failed two women. I can't do that again."

"That is the only way you can let go of this pain. You need an heir, and you need someone to care for you. Your magic is too strong. You need to pass that down to your children."

269

He stared at the empty cup and shook his head. "It's not easy."

"You're one of the strongest men I know."

Robert fell silent, shifting his eyes downward, then looked at her. "I have no choice but to be strong." They sat in silence. After a few minutes, he rose from his chair. "Your Majesty, I must go to Lord Jack's castle and help train the Majian people. Allow me to escort you there."

***

Documents piled on Edmund's desk. His tasks were numerous, but he found it difficult to keep his mind focused on his work. His men stood stationed throughout Cedarville, and the reports he had received showed no unusual activity in the village. He had his best knights surveilling the town, yet it baffled him that Juliana continued to avoid capture. Jack may think he's clever, but he would be wise to watch his step. Eventually, Juliana will be found, and Jack will be held accountable for his actions.

His mind turned to his grandfather Thomas and hoped to see him soon. He wanted to spend a few moments with him before he passed. His grandfather was his only blood connection to his father, and he had many questions for him. He wanted to know who James was.

Edmund's ruminations were interrupted when Samuel walked in. "Pardon me, Your Majesty, you have a visitor, King Carlton from Etheland."

"Why is he here?" Edmund snapped, irritated at an unplanned visit from a man he did not care for.

"He did not say, Your Majesty. Shall I inquire?"

Edmund huffed. "Send him in." Edmund expected Carlton's visit would be a gesture of solidarity—with a hidden agenda. He did not trust Carlton. He would sit through it, try to be pleasant, and find an excuse to end the meeting quickly.

King Carlton sauntered into the library with a regal posture exhibited by older kings. King Matthew had such a stance. Edmund rose from his chair, and they bowed to each other. "Your Majesty, please have a seat. To what do I owe this surprise visit?" Edmund forced a smile.

The older king sat confident and stately. "Your Majesty, I realize that we have not spoken since you became king. I invited you to one of our festivals, and you declined; nevertheless, I wish to maintain the amicable relationship with you that King Matthew and I once had."

Edmund's blood simmered. This was Carlton's way of trying to soften him by beginning with pleasantries, and it annoyed him to have to endure it even for a few minutes. Soon enough, Carlton will reveal his true intention. "Forgive me for not attending the festival, Your Majesty, but I had urgent matters that required my attention."

"I understand, which leads me to the purpose of my visit. I wish to take a first step in bridging the gap that exists between us at present."

Edmund leaned back in his chair with his arms crossed, studying the white-haired man. "What do you have in mind?"

"I'd like to arrange a marriage between one of your barons and my eldest daughter."

He narrowed his eyes. "Would you not wish for your daughter to marry a prince?"

"There seems to be a shortage of eligible princes," he said with a smirk. "Besides, forming an alliance between our two kingdoms would benefit us both."

Thoughts of acquiring Etheland raced through Edmund's mind. He had not considered it, believing it was out of reach, but a way to acquire land was arranging marriages with royalty or high nobility between kingdoms. King Matthew had mastered that superbly, but no doubt, Carlton had amassed his empire in a similar way. Edmund had to be craftier than Carlton and beat him at his own game. "I'm sure we can arrange that." Edmund pondered which of his chess pieces to move. "Lord Bradford of Somerville is available. He would make a good suitor for your daughter. He is the son of a duke."

"I was thinking of Lord Jack of Cedarville."

Edmund's lips curled at the mere mention of Jack's name; however, he composed himself. "You are interested in Lord Jack?"

"I am. He's a fine man and would make a good husband for my daughter Alexandra. He was raised as a prince and came to a large inheritance. As baron of Cedarville, his land sits between our primary kingdoms and would create a physical bridge between the two nations."

The last thing Edmund wanted was to enter into an agreement involving Jack, for his days were not many, but he had to end the meeting and send Carlton on his way. However, he could not reject the betrothal without appearing insolent. If he opposed it, he would have to

272

come up with a suitable explanation, but Edmund had other pressing issues on his mind. If he agreed to the proposition, he could back out of it by not accepting its terms.

Edmund leaned forward and stared at King Carlton, his hands in a steeple. "Very well, Your Majesty, I agree to the arranged marriage. You may proceed with preparing the contract, and we shall set a date for the ceremony. I shall see to it that Lord Jack's mother, Princess Katherine, is present to sign it."

"Thank you, Your Majesty. I hope this is the beginning of many other arrangements that will be mutually beneficial."

"As do I." Edmund gave him a disingenuous smile seeing right through Carlton's scheme. If Carlton thought that Edmund's youth and inexperience would be to his advantage and allow Carlton to take over Yorkford, he would be in for a great disappointment.

***

Juliana and Robert arrived at Lord Jack's castle, and Jack directed Robert to the courtyard where the men from the village assembled, ignoring the curfew unbeknownst to the guards scattered throughout the town. Once Robert was out of sight, Jack escorted Juliana to a private seating area. Juliana saw the strain on his face.

"How was the meeting with King Carlton?"

Jack twisted his mouth. "It's complicated. We may have to come up with another plan."

"What do you mean?"

"I do not trust him, but I will explain at a later time. I have an army I must train, and I must do it in great

273

haste. We do not know the hour when Edmund will attack."

She nodded. "Do you have enough men?"

"Alas, I do not. I have three hundred men but lack an elite cavalry, and many are inexperienced. We will require the assistance of all the Majians if we stand a chance of defeating Edmund's army. They will outnumber us, but the Majian's power should help balance the battlefield. We also need chainmail. I have extras, but I would like for all the men to wear them."

Aside from the stress on Jack's young face, Juliana saw determination. Jack would not allow defeat before the battle began. He would train his men to fight fiercely until the end.

"Forgive me for doubting you earlier, Jack. I have faith in you."

She kissed his cheek. Jack gazed into her eyes, then turned away.

"Is something amiss?"

"I must set my mind on the task at hand. There are many lives at stake, and I can't allow myself to get distracted."

"I understand." Juliana smiled. "Please ask Audrey to show me to a guest chamber."

Juliana followed Audrey to a bedchamber on the second level, and once inside, the maidservant pulled the thick amber drapes over the large window. Juliana scanned the room, a lit fireplace, a small table with a candelabra, and a fine linen bed—a most welcome sight.

"I trust you will be most comfortable here, Your Majesty. If there is anything you require, please call on me."

As soon as Audrey shut the door, Juliana lay on the bed. Thoughts raced through her mind as she rested her head on the pillow. The turmoil and excitement of the last few days drained her energy, but much more lay ahead, and she needed to rest. She feared for the people of Cedarville and the Majians, but she could not allow fear to crush her spirit. Juliana thought of Robert and the pain and regret he lived with for twenty-two years. She didn't want to have any regrets. Her mind drifted to Jack, so young and brave, and single-handedly training an army to take on Edmund, a powerful ruler in his own right. Jack had a lot riding on him.

Then she pondered her marriage to Edmund and how he became a man she no longer knew—or did she ever really know him? Was the charm just an act to get her father to warm up to him and make him an heir to his kingdom? What would her father say if he knew what was happening? Would he side with her, his only true blood offspring, or with the man who was like a son to him?

The prophecy troubled her—a leader will emerge and lead the Majians to victory. Her mother believed she would be their leader, but she didn't feel like one. A leader should have courage and conviction for their cause, and she had neither. Her only objective was seeing another day.

***

Three hundred men crowded the courtyard, consisting of one hundred men from Jack's army and two hundred village men recruited to fight. They were young and strong from years of manual labor, and all had some training in warfare. Mixed emotions filled the

275

villagers. They exhibited a fierceness in protecting their land but also trepidation in facing a formidable army, but one thing was certain, and they all agreed, it was what they were called to do. They had no choice. Their village would be attacked, and they would defend it at all costs.

Among the trainees was Jeb. He had lived an ordinary life, tending to his tavern, and learned how to fight like all the other men. But now, he embraced the powers he inherited and prepared himself to use them against the king's army. He brought his young son Victor to train using his magical powers and also to train without them, like a true warrior. Jeb's pride showed when Victor defeated boys bigger than him during practice.

"He would make a great squire," Jack said of the young boy.

Victor gleamed. "I wish to be a knight, my lord."

"And you shall be. I shall train you." He smiled at Victor.

Although the Majians would help in the attack with their magic, they also had to learn to physically engage with Edmund's army in the event they would lose their locket and gemstones during a confrontation. Jack, along with his knights, instructed the villagers on the use of a sword, a knife, and other ways to defend themselves. The men who displayed marksmanship in archery were outfitted with a bow, a quiver, and dozens of arrows.

Jack spoke to the group. "If you have a horse, you will need it to block the foot soldiers from going into town. We will be outnumbered, but the Majians will disarm as many men as they can and summon the animals to attack King Edmund's army at the entrance of the bridge; however, many will get through. These battles are a fight to the death, so you must do whatever you can to stay alive. Be ready, observe, and act in haste. A delay of a second could be costly."

He continued, "Knights with full armor will be difficult to defeat, so avoid them and allow our knights in armor to face them. Go after the foot soldiers without armor and carry a shield to protect yourselves from flying arrows. The armored knights will get off their horses and fight on foot. If they engage you, look for gaps in the armor where you can thrust a sword or a knife, such as the armpits or the neck. Since their warhorses are trained to trample on people, you may have to use your weapons against them. Aim for their bellies or legs."

As the knights practiced with the village men, Jack walked around, offering guidance. "Use your feet! Move quickly when waving a sword." At times, Jack would step in to demonstrate moves he would use to overpower his attacker. They put blunt ends on the swords and knives to prevent accidents while they trained. The look of determination on the villagers' faces pleased Jack as they worked hard to perfect their fighting skills.

When practice neared its end, Robert walked up to Jack. "It has been a tiring day. I shall leave now but will wait to hear from you in the morrow."

"Thank you, Robert. I am forever in your debt." Jack put his hand on Robert's shoulder.

Robert smiled and said, "As I am in yours."

Jack turned toward the courtyard and took a few steps when Robert called out, "Jack, about Her Majesty…" He stopped and met Robert's eyes. "I hope you know what you're doing."

Jack sighed, aware that Robert sensed something between him and Juliana. "I don't. I know about fighting and training, but I know nothing about women."

Robert gave Jack a half-hearted smile. "No man does, but one thing is certain, it's difficult to love someone that one can't have." Robert spoke from experience, and Jack appreciated the older man's fatherly tone. He lost all the men that were fathers to him—his natural father Heathcliff, Prince Marcus, and King Matthew—and he felt alone at times, but he saw Robert as a friend and someone he could turn to when he needed guidance. Jack nodded, feeling the heaviness in his heart of not being with the woman he loved. He turned, and they walked in opposite directions.

After a long and exhausting night, the village men departed, but fifty stayed behind to continue to practice in the great room. These were the most competent fighters chosen by Jack to train as knights and strengthen his army.

They practiced for hours when a scream echoed at the far end of the room. Jack turned and saw his maidservant running, waving her arms frantically.

"Lord Jack, Lord Jack! They're in the castle! Intruders are in the castle!"

Behind Audrey, six of King Edmund's knights in full armor marched into the hall. The village men and Jack stepped back, hands on their weapons. Jack feared there would be a bloodbath in his castle. His men outnumbered Edmund's knights, but six knights in full armor could easily slaughter dozens of inexperienced men. His heart raced, and his senses sharpened as his body prepared to engage the threat. He thought of Juliana sleeping upstairs in the guest chamber.

The knights in armor stopped in front of the men and placed their hands on their swords.

Jack removed his sword from its sheath, staring at his adversaries. "I charge you to adhere to your sworn oath and make this a fair fight. Send forth your best man and remove his armor. I shall challenge him."

The knight leading the group took a few steps toward Jack, the clang of his armor echoing across the room. Jack tightened his grip. The knight stopped, lifted his visor, and said, "Come on, Lord Jack, you don't want a repeat of our last tournament, do you?" He grinned.

Jack beamed at the familiar face. He sheathed his sword. "You know, I was distracted."

"It was fortunate for me, for I could never beat you."

"What are you doing here, Mark?"

"We have come to help. We're on your side."

The other men lifted their headgear. They were the knights from Jack's training group, The Magnificent Seven Knights.

"These secret passageways come in very handy," Mark said with a smirk.

"Thank you, Mark." Jack put his hand on his friend's shoulder and looked at the other men. "I now have an elite cavalry." He smiled. "But Mark, why the armor?"

Sir Mark shrugged his shoulders. "We just wanted to bloody scare you." Mark and all the men roared with laughter.

Jack laughed too, delighted to have the men he considered his brothers fighting with him. Knight training was physically and mentally demanding, but these men got through it by supporting each other, and it was that kind of support Jack desperately needed. Jack wasn't alone anymore.

The knights-in-training practiced with Jack, Sir Mark, and The Magnificent Knights from Yorkford until dawn.

Chapter 17

Edmund lifted the wineglass to his lips, hoping it would calm his nerves, eager for his next appointment—meeting with the doctor from Cedarville known for his magical powers. He would soon find out if this man killed his father. It would be easy to identify the murderer, for he would be missing his right ear. But if the doctor wasn't the murderer, would he know who killed his father, and if he did, would he divulge the killer's name? He swallowed the wine, refilled his glass, and guzzled it. After some time, he began to pace. He had commanded Sir Paul to meet him at noon with the doctor, and he was late.

He stopped when his eyes met the portrait of King Matthew. He wondered what Matthew would have done if he had discovered that the duke of Westmore betrayed him and that his wife, Queen Lucinda, was one of the evil sorcerers he had sought to destroy. What would he have thought if he knew she passed that trait onto his daughter? It was that evil energy that made Juliana go against him. He had no choice—she practiced magic, and for that, she would be executed. Matthew entrusted him with her, but even he would have agreed that Juliana's powers went against the laws of the church, and her evil magic posed a threat to his kingdom. Edmund gazed at King Matthew's eyes and wondered if the former king had ever been tested the way he was being tested.

The sound of a woman softly singing interrupted his thoughts. He scanned the room and saw a few servants tending to their duties, but no one close enough to produce the sound he heard. For years he had heard stories of old castles being home to ghosts. He didn't believe such tales, but then he didn't believe people could do magic, and yet he witnessed Juliana's supernatural abilities. With all the strange occurrences happening, he feared his sanity was failing, and his imagination was taking control of his mind. He shook it off, poured himself another glass of wine, and sat by the hearth.

Sir Paul rushed into the great hall, panting. "Forgive me, Your Majesty, for my tardiness." He had one knee on the floor and his head down before Edmund.

Edmund stood up and placed his wineglass on the fireplace mantel. "You may rise. Where is the doctor?"

"Your Majesty, we could not capture him. He has strong powers."

Edmund's face reddened. "I ordered you to bring him to me. It was not an option."

"My apologies, Your Majesty, but the magic is real. My squire and I charged toward him, but he overpowered us." Paul grabbed his tunic by the neck and lowered it to expose deep, red claw marks. "He commanded hawks to attack us, but please, Your Majesty, I have other important news for you."

"What do you have? It better be good—for your sake."

"There was another meeting of the Majian people yesterday. They recited the spells and practiced their magic."

Edmund clenched his jaw. "So now we have more of these people to contend with?"

"They are preparing to fight us. The word is that Lord Jack is gathering the men from the village, and he is training an army himself."

"I have guards all over Cedarville! How is it that all this is happening right under their noses!?"

"They distract the men with their sorcery."

It's the prophecy in the book coming true—the Majian's will regain their power! Edmund's eyes narrowed, fiery blood coursing through his veins. He yanked a dagger from the display case over the fireplace and studied it in a slow, methodical manner, flipping it over, running his finger down the steel. He glanced at Paul, who had beads of sweat on his upper lip, eyes twitching.

"So, Jack thinks he can gather an army to defeat me?" In a quick move, he tossed the knife over Paul's shoulder and watched it hurl across the room until the blade struck the wall. "I have had all I can take of Jack and his treachery." He glared at Paul. "Leave now, but wait by the library for my next order."

A relieved Paul responded, "Aye, Your Majesty." He hurried out of the great room.

Sir Leopold and Sir Quinn had been tasked to find Juliana in Cedarville and bring her to Yorkford, but Edmund had not seen her since she flew her horse over the bridge. He understood why she had taken part in the meetings, as she was one of them and most probably using her magic to avoid capture. Heat burned his cheeks.

Edmund strolled to the other side of the room, where the dagger protruded from the wall. As he pulled the blade out, the corner of his eye caught sight of a man he was not expecting to see.

"Where have you been? You were supposed to guard my wife in the dungeon. How did you let her escape?"

The dungeon guard stood before him in a bold stance. His eyes flicked to the dagger in Edmund's hand. "Someone found their way into the castle and freed her."

"It was your job to keep her in the cell." He stared at him. "Wait a minute, was it you that lowered the drawbridge the other night and allowed her to flee?" He slowly approached him, a firm grip on the dagger.

The guard did not respond.

Edmund stood within inches of the guard. He pointed the dagger and lifted his bearded chin, pressing the point until a drop of blood appeared. "You shall pay for your betrayal."

The guard glared at Edmund, then in an instant, Edmund's body zoomed backward. The decorative knives on the opposite end hurled toward Edmund and pinned his clothes to the wall. The dagger slipped out of his hand and into the guard's hand. Edmund found himself several inches off the floor, stuck to the wall, unable to move. With eyes wide, he caught sight of the locket around the dungeon guard's neck. With fire in his veins and through clenched teeth, he growled, "You're one of them!"

The guard's face was up against Edmund's, glaring at him, his face tight. He lifted Edmund's chin with the dagger. "I know you have been spying on us, and I know about your vendetta against the Majian people. You would be wise to drop it, or it will not end well for you, Your Majesty."

Edmund narrowed his eyes. "Who are you?"

"I am someone who knows about revenge." He lifted his hood, exposing a burn mark on the right side of his head and an opening where his ear used to be.

Edmund's eyes widened as rage burned inside him. "It's you! You killed my father!"

"Your father killed everyone I loved. He destroyed my town and my people." The guard raised the dagger, the steel point facing Edmund, and in an instant, stabbed the wall an inch from Edmund's face. Edmund flinched. "If you do not stop this, you shall be next. You have been warned, Your Majesty." The guard stormed out of the great room.

Edmund exhaled, recovering from a moment of intense panic, fearing his life would end at the hands of his father's killer. He watched the man escape as fury swept through him, having learned his father's murderer had been brazenly living in the castle for years. He recalled the words he told Juliana when King Matthew had died. *"If your father was murdered, the killer is lurking somewhere inside the castle."* His insides flared. He yelled, "Guards!"

Six guards rushed toward him.

"Your Majesty, are you hurt?" They pulled the knives from his clothes and released him.

"It was the dungeon guard. Find him and make haste!"

The six guards ran with their swords in hand.

Edmund swallowed a glass of wine, his hands shaking. "Samuel, bring me more wine," he bellowed.

Leopold charged into the grand hall, gasping for breath. "Your Majesty, I saw the man who killed your father, James. He was running through the castle. The guards were chasing him, but I saw…" he stopped to catch his breath. "I saw the burn mark on the side of his head, and he was missing an ear."

"It was the dungeon guard! He has not been hiding. He has been living here in plain sight!"

The guards rushed in. "Your Majesty, we lost him inside the castle."

"Block the bridge and all entrances. I want everyone searching for this man. Bring him to me alive and remove his locket." Edmund had no plan to send this man to be executed—he would do it himself.

"Right away, Your Majesty." The men rushed out.

Sir Quinn strode into the great hall amid the commotion, taking notice of the men darting around him, confusion on his face. "Apologies, Your Majesty, but we have not been able to locate Queen Juliana."

Red-faced and crazed with anger, Edmund roared. "Bring Jack to me, and I want no failures, or I will have your head. Is that understood?"

Quinn trembled. "Aye, Your Majesty." He hurried out.

"Leopold!" Edmund shouted. "Leopold!"

Leopold hustled and stood before Edmund. "Your Majesty."

"Get the army ready. I want at least one thousand men. Notify all the barons to release two hundred knights and fighters, then wait for my command."

"Right away, Your Majesty." Leopold ran out of the room.

Edmund marched into his library, his teeth clenched and heart pounding. He swept his hand over his desk, sending scrolls and parchment swirling onto the floor.

He sat in his chair, placed his elbows on the table, and leaned his forehead on clasped hands. He had to gain an advantage over the magical people. Mere men he could conquer, but this magic was something he could not understand and did not know how to defeat. Edmund grabbed *The Book of Secrets* from the back table and flipped through the pages. *There must be a way.* A section of the book caught his eye, describing a way to summon Majian people. They were to light a fire on the highest mountain, and the Majians will come toward it and congregate around the fire.

"Paul!" he bellowed.

Paul, waiting for his next order, ran in and stood before Edmund. "Aye, Your Majesty."

"I have a task for you." He gave Paul orders.

"Right away, Your Majesty." Paul sped out of the room.

Drops fell on Edmund's desk. He lifted his eyes, and above his head, small birds hovered, flapping their wings. "Ella! Get rid of these birds and clean this up."

Ella ran in. "Of course, Your Majesty. Shoo, shoo." She waved her hands, and three small sparrows flew from Edmund's library.

***

The next morning, Robert picked herbs from the plants resting on the wooden shelf by the window. Geraldine sat on the high table. Her long brown hair draped in front of her in a braid, and she wore a simple mint green dress with a tight laced-midriff. Her arm hung in a sling.

"I don't know why I suffer so many ailments, Doctor."

Robert poured wine into a cup, added herbs, and stirred it with a small twig. He handed it to Geraldine. "This should relieve the headache."

"Thank you. You're a great doctor." She paused. "I'm curious, how did you become a doctor?"

"My father was a physician when we moved here twenty-two years ago. He taught me a few things, but then advised me to go to the big city up north and learn at the university. I spent two years there, but when he died, I returned since this town needed a doctor."

"You're a good man. I am puzzled why you don't have a wife." Geraldine's hand quickly covered her mouth at her imprudence and sought to correct it. "Oh, please forgive me, Doctor Robert. That was bold of me, but you would make someone a fine husband."

He gave her a half-hearted smile. "I was married a long time ago, but since then, I have dedicated my life to healing others."

"Don't you feel lonely?" She gazed into his eyes.

"I try not to think about it."

Geraldine stepped down from the table. "You have cared for so many. You need someone to care for you."

Robert leaned in closer to Geraldine, admiring her expressive honey-brown eyes. "Do you know of a woman who would be up for the task?"

Geraldine smiled, gazing into his eyes. "I would."

"I'm not perfect, Geraldine. There is much you don't know about me."

"I know you are a Majian, but to me, you are perfect, and you have a kind heart."

"I have struggled with a great deal of internal turmoil. My heart has been tested and beaten many times."

"Doctor, a kind heart is not corrupt by troubles, but it is made stronger."

Robert eyed Geraldine. She was lovely and had lived a simple existence for all of her twenty-four years. She had devoted the last two years to caring for her brother's child when his wife died at childbirth. Robert's days had been anything but simple, but perhaps he needed someone like Geraldine to bring balance into his life. He lifted her chin with his finger and leaned in until their lips met. She put her good hand on his arm and leaned in closer. As he snaked his arm around her waist, the heat between them intensified, and the kiss became more passionate.

A loud banging on the door shook them. Robert gently pulled away. "Excuse me."

When Robert opened the door, he saw Simon flushed and panting.

"What's wrong?" Robert asked.

Simon opened his mouth to speak but stopped when he saw Geraldine. "My apologies, I did not mean to intrude."

"It's all right. I must leave now," Geraldine said. "Thank you for the medicine, Doctor." She smiled at Robert and set the cup on the table.

"Come back in the morrow. I shall examine your arm, and if it's well, remove the sling." Robert gazed at her, reflecting on the tender moment they shared. She met his gaze and smiled sweetly as she headed out the door.

"I shall."

Robert stared at her shapely figure as she walked up the road toward the village.

As soon as Geraldine was at a safe distance, Robert closed the door, and Simon spoke. "Last night, King Edmund's guards chased me. I hid in the castle and escaped at dawn through the secret passageway. It's only a matter of time before he sends his army. We must prepare ourselves."

"Hundreds of men showed up last night at Lord Jack's castle for training. He's feeling optimistic."

"We must be certain the Majians are ready, for it is the only way we can win. The king's army will outnumber us four to one. Lord Jack is a brilliant commander, but they will destroy his army unless we help him."

Robert recalled the massacre twenty-two years ago and didn't want a repeat of the slaughter. He stared at Simon. "It's up to the Majians. This time, we must fight back—all of us."

"But we also need a plan," said Simon. "I have an idea, but we may have to convince Lord Jack that it is what we must do."

Chapter 18

Juliana splashed cold water on her face over a basin in the guest chamber. She grabbed a small linen cloth and patted her face dry, enjoying the refreshing tingling on her skin. It was late morning, and having slept many hours, she woke up renewed, erasing the tiredness in her eyes and the look of fatigue on her face from the events of the prior day. She brushed her hair in front of the mirror, and thoughts of Edmund came in. She took a shaky breath, realizing the danger she faced. He would kill her once he found her—of that she was certain. Her life as queen of the kingdom was over, and it brought tears to her eyes. She didn't know how much longer she could hide out in Jack's castle. Jack's life was in danger too. It was only a matter of time.

She dabbed her eyes and stared at her reflection, but something wasn't quite right. Her eyes appeared smaller, and her lips thinner. A light fog surrounded her. She touched a hand to her face, confused. From around her came a soft voice, "You are more powerful than you know."

Juliana gasped. How could she not see it? The woman before her in the mirror wasn't her reflection at all—it was her mother! She didn't appear sad or ill like when she last saw her six years ago, but rather happy and relaxed with sparkling hazel green eyes and glistening skin. The locket hanging from her neck emitted a blinding light, entrancing Juliana. Her eyes remained fixed on the glow.

"Mother?" Juliana laid a hand on the mirror.

"Trust in your power. Follow your intuition." The image faded.

The trance broke, and she stared at her own image. *What was that? Was it my imagination?* A sense of longing came over her as she deeply missed her mother and felt joy at seeing her. But there was something more to her appearance. Her second sight revealed that her mother's spirit had never left her, that she was with her, guiding her.

Juliana came down the stairs and looked toward the red velvet couch by the hearth, expecting to see Jack, but it was vacant. On the other side of the room, Audrey waved a feather duster over the furniture.

"Audrey, might you know where Lord Jack is?"

She scanned the room, leaned in closer, and whispered, "Lord Jack is in a secret meeting."

"Secret meeting? With whom?"

"I saw Sir Mark and Sir Ashton walk in and also Doctor Robert and a big man with a black beard wearing a hood, and Jeb, the owner of the tavern."

Juliana sat by the warm fire wondering what Sir Mark and Sir Ashton, two of the Yorkford's knights of The Magnificent Seven group, were doing in Jack's castle. Were they sent to bargain on behalf of Edmund? She shook her head—that seemed unlikely—Edmund doesn't bargain.

Moments later, Jack strolled into the great room and smiled at her behind tired eyes. From his expression, the meeting was intense and added to the weariness from the long night of training the villagers. It was a huge task, and the weight of it was coming down on him. He kissed her cheek and sat next to her on the couch.

"You look tired. Were you able to sleep?" Juliana asked.

"A few hours. Sir Mark showed up with the men from my knight training class last night to help us." He smiled. "I am confident we have a good chance."

"I am happy they're here for you." Juliana reached for Jack's hand, relieved that Sir Mark arrived with the knights to help support Jack. She was there for him, but not in the way men were there for each other. They fed off each other's strength, and they grew stronger together, especially when a bond of friendship existed between them.

Jack turned toward Juliana. "Juliana, about the other night, the night of the storm… I should have had more self-control. You were vulnerable, and I am sorry." He searched for the right words. "It's difficult for me to be around you and not show you how I feel."

"You *had* self-control, Jack, nothing happened. We just kissed."

"It was an intimate kiss. I should not have allowed it to go that far. I should have escorted you to a guest chamber and allowed you to sleep."

Juliana paused and took a deep breath. "My life has always been about rules and proper conduct, which I rebelled against in my youth. But as I matured, I adhered to those expectations; however, we lose the essence of who we are when we do not honor our true emotions or fail to express them. You alone are not to blame."

"But never was my intention for you to be confused or uncomfortable. You mean more to me than anyone I have ever known. There is nothing I would not do for you—you must believe that."

She leveled his gaze and squeezed his hand. "I do. I feel the same."

Jack put his arm around Juliana, and she rested her head on his shoulder, enjoying the closeness as they stared ahead, watching the dazzling flames release sparks. She had never felt so happy or so loved as she did at this time with Jack by her side.

A knock on the door interrupted their moment. They turned toward the door, and Prince Carsen from Etheland walk in with four guards. Audrey said to him, "I shall inform Lord Jack of your arrival."

"Why is Prince Carsen here?" Juliana asked.

"I shall find out." Jack rose and greeted the prince, the eldest of King Carlton's three children. He was twenty years old with platinum blond hair, handsome, and debonair. Jack invited Carsen to sit with him and Juliana by the great hearth.

Prince Carsen bowed to Juliana. "Your Majesty, I am pleasantly surprised to see you here."

Juliana smiled, aware this moment called for a contrived explanation for her presence in Jack's castle. "Your Highness, I'm here on a diplomatic mission. It's good to see you. How is your father?"

"He is well. We would be delighted to have you join us for supper at the castle sometime. My father is very fond of you."

Juliana continued with the pretense. "We shall plan on it."

Audrey brought out a tray with a jug of wine and three glasses and placed it on the table in front of them. Prince Carsen sat across from Jack and Juliana and said, "I have come on behalf of my father. He spoke to King

Edmund, and he has agreed to the arranged marriage between you and my sister Princess Alexandra."

Juliana froze with the wineglass just short of her lips. She wondered what events led to this unexpected announcement. She glanced at Jack, but his eyes remained fixed on Prince Carsen.

"I see," Jack said. He gave an awkward smile.

"As agreed, my father will help restore Maiden Hills. You have his support."

Juliana understood although it didn't help disentangle the knot in her stomach.

"I appreciate your coming here to inform me, Your Highness," Jack said.

"If I may inquire, Lord Jack, what is happening in the village? It appears to be heavily guarded."

"The Kingdom of Yorkford feels threatened by the people from Maiden Hills who now live in Cedarville, and they wish to destroy them. They are keeping watch over us, and we are expecting they will attack."

"But Cedarville is a territory of Yorkford. They will destroy their own land."

"King Edmund has a vendetta against the people of Cedarville and me. His pride is worth more than a small piece of land."

"My grandmother told me the story long ago of the three noblemen from Maiden Hills and how they helped restore my great-great-grandfather's kingdom. We are aware of their gifts, and we owe a debt to them. We shall provide weapons to assist you."

"The aid will be well received," said Jack.

"I shall speak to my father." Prince Carsen departed, followed by his guards.

An awkward, thick silence hovered in the air. Juliana waited for Jack to speak, but he drank his wine and stared at the fire. After a few minutes, she interrupted his quietude.

"What is this about, Jack? You asked King Carlton for help with Maiden Hills, and he gave you his daughter, and Edmund agreed?"

"I did not expect it from the meeting. King Carlton is shrewd. As for Edmund, I suspect he agreed to it to appease King Carlton. He intends not to fulfill the agreement, for I am certain he has other plans for me."

She closed her eyes and sighed. "This rebellion has caused much turmoil in our lives." She stared at Jack. "What will you do when it is over, and you have won? Leave the Kingdom of Yorkford and join Etheland? You can't defeat Edmund's army and continue to be part of his kingdom. And what shall become of me? I can't hide forever."

Jack stared at Juliana, and after a pause, said, "There is a plan, but it is best you do not know."

A worried look covered Juliana's face. "Is that what the secret meeting was about?" His silence answered her. "Jack, what will you do?"

"You must trust that I will do what is best for you, the Majian people, and the people of Cedarville."

Audrey came in and interrupted the tension. "Your Majesty, my lord, lunch is served in the dining hall."

They strolled to the dining hall without saying a word and sat at the table where Audrey had placed a spread of dark bread, butter, venison meat, tomato soup, and fruit. Juliana stared at the food on her plate and managed a few bites, but her mind floated elsewhere. *What will happen to me once this is over? If Jack wins, I lose my kingdom, for if I attempt to return, Edmund will kill me. If Jack loses, Edmund will kill me. Either way, I lose.*

After a lengthy pause, she turned to Jack. "What if Edmund attacks without warning?"

"Robert commanded the animals to be on the watch. They will block them for as long as they can, and the hawks will come and warn us."

"And the men will be ready for battle?"

"Yes, they will be ready."

Juliana stared at Jack. "Jack, why does Edmund despise you so much? It can't just be because Uncle Marcus favored you, or you're not of royal blood. There must be something else."

Jack sighed and wiped his mouth with the napkin. "There is. Four years ago, when I returned from knight training, I walked in the garden and found Edmund kissing Princess Catelyn Fuller from Somerville. Her father, King Aldred, betrothed her to another prince, which would have added to his kingdom. Edmund made me swear not to tell anyone. He planned to talk to her father and convince him to have her marry him instead. However, the next day, her father found out about them, and he was furious. He banished Princess Catelyn, and Edmund never saw her again. Her father tried to kill Edmund but failed. Edmund then attacked Somerville and won, killing King Aldred and his entire family in the battle. Edmund thought I told her father, but I had not. I suspected her sister told her father about the affair so she could marry Princess Catelyn's betrothed, but Edmund has always blamed me. He loved her and suspected I betrayed him."

297

"That's awful. Why would he think you would do such a thing?"

"He thought I envied him, but I had not." Jack averted his eyes and sighed. "I just wanted a brother."

Juliana put her hand on Jack's.

A sudden banging on the door shook Juliana and Jack. "They've come for me!" Juliana trembled. Jack grabbed Juliana's hand, and they bolted out of the dining hall toward the stairs leading to the dungeon.

"Juliana, hide in the dungeon and stay there until it is safe."

"Will you be all right?"

"I shall be fine. Go!"

Juliana rushed to the dungeon, ran into the hidden cell, and pushed the door closed. She pressed her ear onto the cold stone wall and trembled as heavy boots stomped hurriedly into the great hall.

She heard Sir Quinn say, "Bind him!"

"What's going on, Quinn?" Jack asked.

"Lord Jack, we are arresting you by order of His Majesty, King Edmund. You have betrayed your kingdom."

There was more bustling, a door slammed, and then silence.

Juliana ran up the stairs, grabbed her purple cloak, and hurried to the rear of the castle and through the concealed door where Millie and Dex remained hidden. She pulled on their reins and spoke to Dex. "Follow me, Dex, Jack is in danger, and you must help rescue him." Majians could not command trained animals unless it would benefit the owner, and since Dex followed her, she knew he understood.

Juliana quickly rode through the southern part of Cedarville, then through the woods. When she arrived at Robert's cottage, she banged on the door. "Robert!"

Robert opened the door with wide eyes. Simon appeared behind him.

"They took Jack. King Edmund's men arrested Jack, and I fear they will kill him."

"Don't worry, Your Majesty. We shall bring him back." Robert turned to Simon. "Let's go." They grabbed their cloaks and jumped on their horses.

"Take Dex with you."

"All right. Come on, Dex, follow us." Robert and Simon sped off, followed by Jack's destrier.

***

As the king, Edmund spent his days pacing, a stark difference from the exciting time involved in conquests for Matthew when he was a prince. Since he was ten, he trained with the other squires in Yorkford's Military School and took pride in being at the top of his class. He loved to battle for above all, Edmund was a warrior. However, as the king, he would fight in the larger battles—there weren't many of those, but he yearned to be on the front lines. As he paced in the great room, he stopped before a tapestry on the wall, depicting the Battle of Somerville, which Edmund brilliantly led and resulted in a new addition to Westmore and later to Matthew's kingdom. He stared at that one a bit longer. He remembered Catelyn, and his eyes grew misty. There were many memories imprinted on these walls.

His concentration broke when Sir Quinn brought Jack to him with his hands bound behind his back. Edmund glared at Jack, blood burning inside him.

Without taking his eyes off him, he said to Quinn, "Leave us." Quinn bowed and departed.

Edmund's heart pumped with the satisfaction of finally having Jack before him. His hands tightened into fists as he slowly walked toward him. "Jack, you have known me long enough to know I do not tolerate disloyalty."

Jack did not speak.

Edmund clenched his teeth. "You made a fool of me." His satisfaction turned to rage as he came within a few inches of Jack. He fought to control his tone. "Are you so arrogant to think you can go against me and win?"

Jack eyed Edmund.

Edmund circled Jack. "I suspect you have bedded my wife and are hiding her. You are helping the magical people and training an army in Cedarville to attack my army. You have committed treason against your own kingdom."

Edmund's eyes pierced Jack. "Do you wish to defend yourself?"

Jack glared back at Edmund.

"I think not. Tell me, Jack, did you seek vengeance on me because I married Juliana? Or was it because King Matthew favored me? He took pity on you, a scrawny little orphan peasant."

Jack's eyes narrowed.

Edmund smirked. "That's right. If not for my mother's kindness, you would be cleaning my horse's backside. And you think you can defeat me and take what's mine?" Edmund's eyes burned with rage. A vein throbbed on the side of his neck as he locked eyes with

Jack. "Do not think that I will send you to the dungeon. I warned you the last time you were here, that if you betray me again, I will have your head, and I meant it." He came within an inch of Jack, disdain in his eyes. "You have had this coming for a long time—brother."

Edmund stepped back. "Guards!" Two guards arrived. "Execute this man."

"What's the charge, Your Majesty?"

Edmund and Jack's eyes locked. "High treason."

***

The guards led Jack to the public square, where the townspeople gathered to witness an execution, and they gasped upon seeing Lord Jack, the adopted son of Prince Marcus.

In a booming voice, the herald spoke to the crowd of spectators. "Lord Jack has committed the crime of high treason against His Majesty, King Edmund of Yorkford. It is the highest crime in the land punishable by death." Cheers rose from the crowd to encourage the execution to begin.

The guards placed Jack on a boulder and bound him with ropes face down. The executioner lumbered toward him with a black mask covering his face with small holes exposing his eyes, nose, and mouth. He carried a broad ax. Four guards stood behind Jack. One of them held a large canvas bag to collect the remains.

"Lord Jack," the herald said, "for your crime, King Edmund has condemned you to death. Do you have any last words?" He waited a few minutes, but Jack did not speak.

I am resigned to my fate. Jack's thoughts turned to Juliana. *What will happen to her without me? Edmund will find her and kill her.* That was the worst punishment of all. *Please, God, keep her safe.*

The executioner got into position, and with a grunt, lifted the ax. Jack's muscles tightened. *I am ready to meet my maker.*

"Hey!" the executioner cried out. The ax flew from his hand and floated above his head, swiveling in a threatening manner.

Jack looked up, and a wide grin crossed his face.

The executioner ran from the ax, screaming as it continued to terrorize him. There were gasps among the people, and others laughed at the amusing sight, but then chaos erupted when the executioner ran into the crowd, his wide, frightened eyes peering through the mask.

The guards on the podium froze, dumbfounded, until rocks and stones assaulted them from all directions. They darted off the podium. Wolves ran into the crowd, biting the spectators and pulling on their cloaks. Screams erupted, and pandemonium ensued as the people fled in fright, avoiding the growling jaws.

Simon and Robert climbed up on the podium. Simon took out a knife, releasing Jack from the ropes.

"Simon, Robert, I am glad to see you."

"Let's go. We must make haste," Simon said.

Armored knights stormed onto the podium, and Robert and Simon magically removed their weapons. Jack caught a flying sword and thrust it into the knight charging toward him. Robert and Simon fought the knights and overpowered them.

Jack, Robert, and Simon finished the knights on the podium and jumped on their horses, breaking through the crowd, and headed toward the forest.

Behind them, the king's knights broke through the castle gates on their chargers and raced after them. At the entrance to the forest, the knights were met with large flying boulders, knocking them off their horses. The men cried out. One by one, they came down. Trees fell, blocking the knights' path, their horses stumbled, and the men were thrown to the ground. The attack against the knights continued, until halfway through the forest, there was no sign of Edmund's men.

Jack, Robert, and Simon galloped into Cedarville, hurling two large stones at the Yorkford guards standing by the bridge, knocking them unconscious.

**

Sitting in the great hall, Edmund swallowed his wine, then refilled his glass. A guard had informed him of the failed execution of his adoptive brother and the chaos that ensued. He told him of the floating ax, rocks flying in all directions, and the wolves attacking the people. In a rage, Edmund threw the glass of wine across the room, staining the wall a dark-red hue and shattering bits of glass over Juliana's new rug.

Katherine approached Edmund, holding on to a walking stick. Edmund took a deep breath, composed himself, and walked toward her. "Mother, allow me to help you."

Her hand met Edmund's face with a great force, leaving behind a stinging red handprint. "How dare you try to execute your own brother?" Edmund held back his innate impulse to strike. His mother was the only person who could touch him, and he would not retaliate.

Edmund restrained his anger and glared at her. "He's not my brother!"

"I raised him as my own!" she yelled. "What has gotten into you, Edmund?"

"He betrayed us, Mother," Edmund said. "High treason is punishable by death."

"What do you mean he betrayed us?"

"He's training an army to fight me, and he turned my wife against me."

Katherine shook her head in anguish. "No, it can't be. Jack would not do that."

Edmund clenched his teeth. "He did." He stared at Katherine. "It's time you realized your precious Jack is not the perfect son you thought he was."

Tears covered Katherine's face. The animosity between the two had lasted their entire lives together, and it tore at her. Her brow furrowed. "What is this rivalry you two have?"

Edmund's eyes narrowed. "Ask him. He'll tell you." He stormed out.

***

Juliana paced inside Robert's cottage, waiting for word on Jack. She feared Robert and Simon would not have arrived in time, and Edmund would have carried out his revenge. The thought crushed her, and she sat down and buried her head in her hands.

She jumped at the knock on the door. Juliana peeked through the small opening, and when she opened the door, Sir Mark had a surprised look on his face.

"Your Majesty, I'm looking for Lord Jack. I thought he might be here with Doctor Robert. Have you seen him?"

"Edmund's men arrested him at the castle earlier."

Mark's hand clenched into a fist, and his eyes tightened. "I shall bring him back." He turned to leave.

Juliana pulled his arm. "No, Sir Mark, Robert and Simon left some time ago to rescue him. It's in God's hands now. I need you here. I am worried and frightened."

At that moment, Juliana's eyes caught wisps of brown smoke against the pale sky rising in the distance. It billowed from the top of the sacred mountain.

Mark followed Juliana's eyes. "Your Majesty, why are you staring at the smoke?"

"It's a way to summon the Majians for a meeting. But it could only be Robert or Helena, but Robert is in Yorkford, and Helena would not call a meeting without Robert."

"Perhaps we should see what it's about."

They took a few steps forward, then Juliana halted and grabbed Mark's arm. "Wait. You can see the smoke?"

"I can, Your Majesty."

"But non-Majians can't see the smoke. Helena sprinkles special herbs to make the fire visible only to Majians." She felt the blood leave her face. "Sir Mark, someone is summoning the Majians to trap them."

Mark said, "We must stop them from going up the mountain."

They mounted their horses and rode through the grassland leading to the sacred mountain. There they saw Majians on foot and on horseback, obeying the call to assemble.

"Go back, go back!" Juliana and Mark yelled to the people on their way to the mountain. "It's a trap, go back!"

A young man on foot told Juliana that some people had already reached the top of the mountain. Chills spread in every part of her body. "Sir Mark, what are we to do?"

"Your Majesty, please return to Robert's cottage and wait there. I shall climb up the mountain and find out who's doing this." Juliana watched as Mark sped toward the mountain, alerting everyone on the path to turn back.

***

When Mark arrived at the summit, he hid behind a thick tree and saw one of Edmund's men guarding the entrance. Mark pulled out his knife, holding it with a white-knuckled hand, grabbed the man from behind, and pierced his side. He held the man as he fell to the ground.

Mark crept toward the area of the mountain where the fire burned. A knight stood over a dozen lifeless bodies with a smug look on his face.

The knight turned around, and when he saw Mark, he aimed his sword at him, then relaxed. "Hey, I know you. You're one of King Edmund's knights, are you not?" He sheathed his sword.

"I am," Mark said, standing tall. "Who are you?"

"I am his most trusted knight, Sir Paul. Look what I have done. He will reward me handsomely for this." The knight gleamed with pride at his conquest.

"Good job, Sir Paul. How did you know they would be here?"

"King Edmund told me to start a fire, and the wicked Majians would come, and he was right. They walked right into my trap. Clever, don't you agree?"

"Yes, quite clever."

"There should be more of them coming. I befriended one of them and followed him here for the last two meetings." He looked down at one of the bodies. "Sorry, Kent. There were about forty that showed up for the last meeting." He scanned the area, puzzled. "Where's Mike? I left him guarding and told him to lead them this way, but I don't see anyone."

Paul rushed to the entrance and found his squire lying on the ground, blood spilling from his side. He turned the body over. He was dead.

He stared at Mark and drew his weapon. "You're one of the traitors."

Mark slid his sword from its sheath, and their blades collided.

***

Edmund sat in his library for what seemed hours, still incensed over Jack's failed execution, the rescue by the magical people, and the failure of the guards to capture his father's murderer. *They will all pay for this!* He clutched his fist.

Sir Leopold walked in. "Pardon me, Your Majesty. I have gathered the men, and all the barons have agreed to send their men into battle, except we have six defectors."

"Who betrayed us?"

"The Magnificent Knights."

Edmund's insides seethed with rage.

"Your Majesty, when shall I order the men to be ready?"

307

"Attack at suppertime. Kill them all, and this time we will not fail. Burn Cedarville to the ground, but bring Queen Juliana and Lord Jack to me. I shall take care of them myself."

"Aye, Your Majesty."

As Leopold hurried out, Katherine entered the library, balancing herself on her walking stick. Edmund caught her staring at *The Book of Secrets* on his desk. She then met Edmund's eyes.

Edmund, harboring resentment toward his mother for laying a hand on him, averted his eyes.

"Edmund?"

He turned to face her as she stood by the door. She had a look of remorse, and for a moment, he considered forgiving her. His mother was important to him, and unlike Marcus, Katherine did not show favoritism. She treated each son as special, but Edmund felt she loved him more since he was the son of her true love, James. Still, there had to be retribution for her actions, for he was the king, and he could allow no one to question his ruling, not even his mother.

He rose from his seat and walked toward her. "You are to return to your chamber and remain there until I call for you," his tone firm. "Ella, come here right away."

"I wish to give you this." Edmund stared wide-eyed at the gold locket resting on the palm of her trembling hand.

***

Juliana sat by the hearth, staring at the fire dancing in front of her—exhausted from the pacing and worrying. She hoped Mark would return soon and tell her everything was fine except she had an ominous feeling she could not shake. Her mind drifted to Jack. *Had Robert and Simon arrived in time to rescue him?* She rubbed her hands and buried her head in them, her shoulders slumped. She felt powerless, and it tormented her. She clasped her hands together and closed her eyes. *Please, God, I don't ask for much, but Jack does not deserve this. He's a good man. Please, spare his life.*

Juliana rose to her feet and faced the mirror, yearning to see her mother's reflection, but she only saw her own, and it startled her, for she appeared pale with lines between her brows—not at all like the elegant queen of a mighty empire. But she didn't have her kingdom anymore, and she couldn't be a queen without a kingdom. Juliana was a fugitive, and in a matter of days, or maybe hours, she would meet her fate. She could arrive at no scenario in which Edmund would allow her to live, and they would continue as the king and queen of Yorkford. It was the end of the Allington dynasty. She remembered her father and her eyes watered. *I have failed him.*

"Your Majesty, Your Majesty."

Sweet child-like voices interrupted her thoughts, calling for her from the window. She brushed away the tears, opened the shutters, and saw three small sparrows perched on the windowsill. "Hello, little sparrows. Did you find out the name of the spy?"

"Yes, Your Majesty, his name is Sir Paul. We also heard the king is preparing his army to fight Cedarville."

"If he is preparing his army, then he will attack this day. Thank you, sparrows, you have been most helpful."

Juliana fixed her eyes toward the mountain, hoping to see Sir Mark. She sighed, relieved when in the distance, she saw Mark riding toward Robert's cottage. She ran to the door and waited for him.

When Mark arrived, he had a somber look.

"What happened?" Juliana asked, fearing the answer.

He dismounted and walked toward her. "Your Majesty, I regret to inform you that about a dozen Majians were killed on the mountain."

Juliana closed her eyes, and her legs trembled. Mark caught her before she fell.

"Your Majesty, come, I shall take you inside."

She found the strength to stand and allowed Mark to escort her inside the cottage. She sat by the table, her head in her hands, dismayed at the senseless killing of unsuspecting Majian people. Mark handed her a cup of ale.

"The spy was one of King Edmund's knights, Sir Paul. I fought him and killed him."

"He's dead? The sparrows just told me. They also said King Edmund is preparing his army."

"Then they will come soon. We must be ready," Mark said.

Juliana's hand shook as she took a sip of ale, trying to grasp the horrifying slaughter that took place up in the mountain. The situation was getting worse, and she felt the heaviness of doom looming over her. She put down the cup, remembering her mother's words in the mirror. "*You are more powerful than you know.*" Her breathing quickened. She had to find the power within herself.

"Sir Mark, the situation is dire, we are losing people, and we are losing this fight!" She rose from her chair. "We don't have a chance against King Edmund, for he is too clever and ruthless." She draped the purple cloak over her shoulders and rushed out the door.

Mark followed her. "Your Majesty, where are you going?"

Juliana climbed on her horse. "I must leave. I can't sit here and do nothing."

"Your Majesty, I can't let you go alone."

"Please, Sir Mark, do not worry. I have my gems for protection. I shall be fine."

Juliana spurred Millie and hurried east toward Maiden Hills.

***

King Carlton sipped his wine by the grand hearth. He had invited his son, Prince Carsen, to assist in preparing the contract for the arranged marriage between his daughter Princess Alexandra and Lord Jack to present to Princess Katherine and King Edmund. Carlton could not contain his delight, believing he would soon have his foot on Yorkford, and toppling Edmund's empire was within his reach. It was an exhilarating feeling. Edmund was a child playing a man's game, and Carlton was eager to show him real strength and dominance.

"Father, I'm surprised that King Edmund agreed to the arranged marriage. There seems to be a great deal of animosity between him and Lord Jack."

"Why do you say that?"

"When I went to visit Lord Jack, I noticed that King Edmund had Cedarville heavily guarded. Lord Jack said they were expecting Yorkford to attack them."

"That's odd. Could King Edmund have been trying to appease me?"

"Unless he had another motive," said Prince Carsen.

Princess Alexandra stormed into the hall, red-faced, taking shallow breaths. "Father, I heard terrible news."

"What is it, dear? Please sit down and calm yourself."

Alexandra sat down and took a deep breath. "I was just informed that King Edmund attempted to execute my betrothed, Lord Jack."

King Carlton's face darkened. "How is that possible? He agreed to the betrothal!" He rose from his seat. "I don't know what game King Edmund is playing, but this shall not go unpunished."

"What will you do, Father?" Prince Carsen asked.

King Carlton leaned against the fireplace. "If he is to attack Cedarville, we will help Lord Jack. We shall send our army to fight against Yorkford, and then we shall seize Cedarville. That will be just the beginning. For one by one, we shall take over his land until we destroy King Edmund's empire."

"But Father, Yorkford has the strongest army in the region."

"Yes, but Cedarville has the magical people," King Carlton said, clenching his fists. "Combined with our army, we stand a good chance of defeating them."

Chapter 19

An almighty force didn't want Jack to die. He was convinced of it. He had faced death from the ravenous wolves when he first arrived in Cedarville, and this day he faced death from Edmund's wrath. Twice Robert saved him, this time accompanied by Simon, who was also helpful in rescuing Juliana. It was no coincidence. There was a supernatural hand orchestrating these events. He was called to this mission, and now more than ever was determined to help the Majians regain their land and their right as a people to live without persecution.

They rode to Robert's cottage, certain that Juliana would be there waiting for them. When they arrived, they found Sir Mark standing by the doorway. The three men came down from their horses and walked toward him.

"I'm glad you made it back alive," Mark said with a smile.

"Me too, thanks to Robert and Simon." Jack peeked his head inside the cottage. "Where's Her Majesty?"

"She's gone," Mark said, "and she did not say where she was going, but she headed toward Maiden Hills."

Jack wrinkled his brow. "Why would she go there?"

Mark shook his head. "I cannot say."

Jack sighed. He hated not knowing where Juliana was, but he could not allow himself to get distracted. He had men to lead into battle, and although he feared for her safety, he took comfort in that she had her enchanted gemstones and would be able to protect herself. "All right, we have a lot of work to do. King Edmund's men will attack soon, probably before nightfall. We must assemble the army."

"Agreed," Mark said, "the sparrows told Queen Juliana they overhead King Edmund planning the attack."

"Did the sparrows learn the name of King Edmund's spy?" Jack asked.

"They did. It was Sir Paul, but I killed him." Mark paused. "I have grave news. Sir Paul tricked the Majians into going up to the mountain, and alas, about a dozen were killed."

The men were distraught. Simon's face reddened. "We must move on to the second part of the plan. The first one will surely fail."

Jack turned toward Simon. "You're right. King Edmund is beyond reason."

"He needs to be dealt with. I shall carry it out," said Simon.

"No, it shall be me," Jack said.

The men remained silent. Robert looked at Mark, a worried look on his face. "Was Jeb… one of the people killed on the mountain?"

"I'm sorry, I did not look at faces," Mark said.

"Let us pray that he is all right," Jack said. "If King Edmund is planning the attack by nightfall, we have but a few hours. We must prepare everyone for battle. Let's go."

The four men jumped on their horses and galloped toward Jack's castle, using the back route and the secret entrance. When they arrived, to their relief, they found Jeb in the courtyard with the remaining thirty Majians, practicing their magic. The Majians had received news of the slaughter up in the mountain earlier, and more than ever were fiercely driven to retaliate against King Edmund's army.

Jack observed the men and women training. Simon's daughter Alice, fearless and beautiful, practiced with the Majians. Her grandmother Helena had mentioned she resembled a young Beth, but with Simon's resilience and determination. Also practicing his magic was Randall, Geraldine's adoptive brother. He had taken command of his power and was hurling objects at top speed and hitting his target. Robert kept his eyes fixed on the young man who was the same age as his son Peter would have been, had he survived. "Randall's a fighter," Robert said to Jack with a look of pride.

Soon, one hundred knights and soldiers and two hundred men from the village filled the courtyard to continue to train under Jack's direction. Jack estimated that out of five thousand men in Edmund's army, he would send close to one thousand men across the bridge. He could send more, but he would not leave his land unguarded. However, one thousand men would be more than enough. The likelihood they would win was not in their favor, but the magical strength would give them an advantage. The animals from the forest and the creek, along with the birds of prey, would also aid them.

While the men practiced, Audrey entered the courtyard, searching until her eyes met Jack. She hurried toward him. "My lord, Prince Carsen is in the great room waiting to see you, and he brought a small army with him."

Mark looked at Jack. "Prince Carsen from Etheland? Why is he here?"

Jack sighed. "He offered to help. Let's find out what he has to say." The two men walked into the room and greeted the prince, accompanied by four guards.

"What brings you here, Your Highness?" Jack asked.

"My father sent me to assist in your battle against Yorkford. We have extra weapons for your army, and we brought two hundred men to help with the fight."

Jack was puzzled. The last time Prince Carsen came to see him, he mentioned helping Cedarville with weapons, not sending men. "Why would King Carlton risk his men for another kingdom?"

"My father intends to seize this territory from Yorkford. We are aware of the failed attempt on your life, and it should please you to know that my father plans on punishing King Edmund by siding with you."

Jack pursed his lips and had to end this before it went any further. "Cedarville is not to be part of King Carlton's kingdom. It is to remain with Yorkford."

Carsen cocked his head. "I don't understand. He ordered your execution. Why would you not wish to divest yourself from Yorkford?"

"I will deal with King Edmund, but I will not break up the empire that King Matthew built and which I fought to protect."

"But it's King Edmund's empire now, and he is looking to destroy you."

"It's my fight with King Edmund, and I will not back down. Please tell your father we don't require his assistance. We have loads of good men to fight with us."

"You're making a mistake, Lord Jack. There is nothing to stop my father from commanding his army to seize this land. It's obvious King Edmund wants nothing to do with it."

"This is my land, and if we must, we will fight you as well. We have the people of Maiden Hills, and they are a mighty force."

Carsen gave Jack a look of derision. "They were slaughtered twenty-two years ago, and there were more of them then. What makes you think they can help you conquer a powerful army?" He snickered, and his group of men laughed along with him.

"The difference between twenty-two years ago and now is that they will fight back. So please, take your army and weapons, and tell your father we do not require his assistance here, nor do we require it in rebuilding Maiden Hills. He abandoned it twenty-two years ago, and we shall take control of it. Also, please inform him that there will be no betrothal between his daughter and me."

Carsen's face reddened. "Very well, Lord Jack, but it is unlikely that you will win as you will be grossly outnumbered, and when you fail, we shall return." Prince Carsen stormed out of Jack's castle, followed by his guards.

Jack and Mark watched as Prince Carsen mounted his horse, and he and his army left the castle grounds.

"Do you think King Carlton will let this go?" Mark asked.

"I don't think so. But if we lose, he will then deal with King Edmund, and if we win, he will not attempt to challenge us."

Mark stared at Jack. "But we must win big!"

***

317

Juliana rode through the grassland between Cedarville and Maiden Hills and reached an area with scattered trees, large rocks, and tall grass. She surveyed the area. She recalled her mother had told her that on her way to Cedarville, she had witnessed her father killed and had hidden in a small cave when the men attacked him. Using her power of second sight, Juliana searched for a cave and was led to a small opening, just the right size for a young child.

She thought to explore the ground near the area where they attacked her grandfather and look for the third stone—the most powerful gem of all. According to her mother and *The Book of Secrets*, the third stone was a deep-red gemstone that carried with it the ability to create an impenetrable shield around the people the wearer wished to protect. With the third stone, Juliana could shield Cedarville's fighters and protect them from Edmund's army.

Sir Leopold had stabbed her grandfather and snatched his locket with the stones, but the red gem was not in the box that Edmund tossed in the moat. The locket must have opened, and the stones scattered on the ground. She hoped to find the third gemstone in the area where her grandfather fell. Juliana beseeched the assistance of the small animals to help look for the stones. The animals' ability to dig would uncover what the seasons and winds may have buried in the soil from twenty-two years ago.

Soon, the area swarmed with rabbits, raccoons, squirrels, and possums scurrying and digging. After some time had passed, they located the first and second stone. Juliana held the stones and squeezed her hand shut, letting out a heavy sigh, having in her hand a tangible remembrance of her grandfather Gavin. The animals kept digging, but the red gemstone was not found. Juliana was losing hope.

Discouraged, she rode into town central. At a distance, the bronze statue of the maiden stood, and she rode toward it. She came down from her horse, gazing up at the maiden's face as tears flowed down her cheeks. *None of this makes any sense*, she thought. "Why did you give the people magical powers and allow this to happen?" she asked aloud, not expecting an answer, but not knowing tore at her.

Suddenly, a strong gust of wind encircled Juliana, and it grew in intensity. As the wind became more forceful, she held onto the lamppost and grabbed Millie's reins. Through squinted eyes, she saw a wind funnel take shape. Then a bright light emerged from the sky and entered the funnel, becoming brighter and blinding, and in a moment, the funnel disappeared, the brilliant light took the shape of a young maiden, and the winds calmed.

The maiden stood on the ground, radiant and translucent with a young, exquisite face, sparkling violet eyes, long, shimmering white hair, and a white flowing dress that glowed. Juliana stared in awe at the young maiden.

"You asked me a question, and I have come to answer it." The maiden's sweet voice reverberated like soft music.

"Who are you?" Juliana asked.

"I am Majia from the magical realm of Akeron, a servant of the Creator of all things."

Juliana gaped, amazed to be in the presence of the maiden who appeared to the three noblemen over one hundred years ago described in *The Book of Secrets*.

The maiden continued, "I know you are troubled by what has happened. I gave the people magical gifts to defend themselves and combat the forces of evil. If they give in to fear, they will be in danger of being defeated. They must trust in the power of the stones."

"But there is reason to be fearful," Juliana said.

"If you have the stones and you trust in its power, there is no fear."

"If so, why did the massacre occur twenty-two years ago?"

"Evil found its way into the hearts of men, and without their stones, the result was death and destruction."

"But my grandfather did not wish for his people to fight or to reveal their secret. He wished for the Majians to live in peace."

"The secret was out, and the peace had been disrupted. There is much you do not know. The Majians were betrayed by one of their own, not from whom everyone believes."

"One of their own?" Juliana suddenly remembered her mother used those same words. She realized that perhaps Prince James had not betrayed Beth. Something must have happened that her mother and grandfather knew and that Robert and the others were unaware. "What if my grandfather had fought back?"

"If he had, future prophecies would not come to pass. He made a difficult decision, but it was the right decision."

Juliana struggled, trying to decipher the maiden's cryptic responses. "I don't understand. Why did it have to happen?"

"The truth of the past shall be revealed at the appropriate time. There is much at stake now."

Juliana understood that there was a reason for her grandfather's actions, and someday she will know, but for now, she had to remain focused on the current dilemma. "The next prophecy says the Majians will overthrow the ruling kingdom," Juliana said. "Will that happen?"

"If you trust in the power of the stones and fight, you shall win. If you give in to fear, evil shall win, and the prophecy will not come true."

"So, we stand a chance of losing?" That possibility disturbed Juliana.

"And of winning," said the maiden with a faint smile.

"To what end? What is our purpose?"

"The Majians are defenders of the mortal realm. There is evil lurking in this realm with forces that mortals cannot defeat. The Majians must learn to fight and protect themselves so they can face larger challenges."

Juliana recalled the trap set by Yorkford on the sacred mountain earlier, slaughtering the Majians. "But how could they have protected themselves against a mighty and cunning army?"

"When you trust in the power of the stones, you have the gift of second sight. Majians who wear the stones and practice magic are confident they cannot be harmed. They perceive danger and will be prepared to fight or flee The Majians this day blindly followed instead of asking the stones for answers. They had not yet become familiar with their abilities."

The maiden confirmed what Juliana had experienced and what Helena had told her, that her intuition strengthened once she activated the stones' energy. She had to learn to trust the power within, and the answers will come.

"Majia, I have searched for the third stone and have not found it. It will help our people if we have it."

"The third stone is the most powerful of all the stones. It appears to the leader of the people and protectors of the realm."

"Is Robert not the leader? He is the most masterful of the Majian people."

"It is not skill that makes a leader, but desire followed by action. It must come from the heart. You, Your Majesty, have the heart of a leader. It is why you are here now."

Juliana shook her head. "But I am not a leader. I have lived a privileged life where others did things for me, and I have only cared for myself. I have been... selfish." Juliana felt embarrassed at her admission. She was surrounded by people who displayed courage and put others before themselves, and she only cared about herself. But she was the queen, and she was to be served, not to serve others.

"You have strength and power within yourself, but you never had to use it—until now. You have not been selfish. The enchanted stones have revealed your bravery. It is that bravery that will lead the Majians to victory."

Juliana furrowed her brows. "How have I been brave?"

"You do not realize how brave you have been by the actions you have taken."

Juliana pondered the maiden's words. Facing Edmund in the castle, trying to get from him the box filled with the magical stones, although it terrified her, was something she felt compelled to do—and she prevailed. She didn't stop to think she was being heroic; in fact, she didn't think at all. She did what she had to do to help the Majians without regard for her safety. She thought of Jack, Mark, Robert, and Simon, who did what they did because it was right. They acted and led from the heart. She now understood that courage was not about being fearless, but rather doing what's right even when faced with fear. Jack embodied gallantry and integrity. He did the right thing, regardless of the consequences, and never compromised his convictions.

Juliana peered past the maiden. Majia's glow could not hide the burned village behind her and the sight of the crumbled baron's manor. "Robert and Jeb searched for the gold that my grandfather Gavin had hidden, but have not found it. Is there gold buried in Maiden Hills?"

"There is, but it is not in the manor where Robert and Jeb have been searching. Lord Gavin hid the gold, where only a Majian might find it if they asked the stones. Robert, in his grief, has forgotten to ask for help. I must leave now. You know everything you need to know."

"Will I see you again?"

The maiden began to fade. "When you need to summon me, gather a descendant from each of the three noblemen, and come before the statue. Touch the base of the statue, and I shall return."

The maiden vanished, and a peacefulness settled in the area. Leaves swirled from a light breeze where Majia stood. Juliana stared at the maiden's statue in front of her and clutched her locket. *Majia said I would know what to do if I trust in the stones' power and ask for help.* Juliana remembered seeing her mother's face in the mirror and the pendant's blinding glow. It showed the gemstones' enormous potential.

She put her hand on the pendant over her heart and said, "Please… help me find the gold." The locket glowed, growing warm to the touch. The statue of the maiden trembled and slowly slid back to reveal a large stone block.

Juliana bent down, touched the block, and it wobbled. She tried lifting it but could not grab the corner. She focused on the block, and it levitated and landed on the ground, exposing a cavity. Juliana peered in and found black cloths. She pulled one out, and when she unwrapped it, there were blocks of bright yellow gold. Juliana's eyes widened. She reached in again and pulled another cloth, and there were more blocks of gold. The cavity was filled with black wrappings. She left the rest inside and floated the block back in its place, the statue trembled, and slid forward, concealing the opening.

Juliana opened a pouch on Millie's saddle and placed the gold inside. She climbed on and kicked her horse into motion, galloping through the east side of Maiden Hills.

She crossed the northern strip and arrived in Westmore, a small region to the southeast of Yorkford, and the home of the people she had come to believe were her grandparents, the duke and duchess of Westmore. It was where her mother, Lucinda, had sought asylum after taking a carriage ride from Cedarville to escape the burning village of Maiden Hills.

Westmore was known for its hospitable people but less affluent lifestyle than Yorkford. They were a proud people devoted to the ruling dynasty, the Wadham royal family, Edmund's family, who had ruled for two centuries until Juliana's father took possession of it. According to King Matthew, the venerable King Thomas was happy to abdicate his throne, delighted that his grandson, Edmund, would someday rule a vast empire.

Juliana rode until she arrived at the castle of the duke of Westmore, Duke Richard, her mother's adoptive brother. Richard was thirteen years old when his parents took in twelve-year-old Lucinda. Because of their proximity in age, they were close as brother and sister, and Richard protected her. Lucinda's sudden demise six years ago devastated him, and he often invited Juliana to his castle to maintain the family connection. Through the years, he had grown fond of Juliana.

The steward escorted Juliana to the grand hall where her uncle Richard greeted her with a wide smile

"Juliana, what a pleasant surprise. What brings you to Westmore?"

"Uncle Richard, it's good to see you."

He held her hands and kissed her on the cheek. A surprised but worried look covered his face as he stared at her appearance. "Your hands are shaking, and you look so thin." He led her to the couch. "Please sit down, dear. Agatha, bring my niece a cup of wine, and some bread and a piece of chicken."

"Aye, my lord." Agatha walked toward the kitchen.

He yelled out, "Bring a glass of wine for me too." He turned to Juliana. "My dear, you look troubled and pale."

Juliana held on to her uncle's hand for comfort. "I have come into some difficulties, and I have nowhere else to turn. I am in need of your help."

"What is it, dear?"

Juliana looked into his eyes and exhaled. "I know my mother was adopted."

Richard's eyes widened. "You know?" He looked baffled. "That is the second time in a week that has come up."

"What do you mean?"

Agatha brought two glasses of wine, handing one to Richard and the other to Juliana. She gave Juliana a plate with dark bread and a leg of chicken. Juliana had forgotten to eat, and her stomach grumbled as the aroma of the roasted meat waft in the air. Juliana took a sip of the wine and a few bites of the chicken.

"His Majesty sent for me two days ago and asked me if Lucinda was adopted."

Juliana knew Edmund was cunning and would investigate until he uncovered the truth. She sighed. "He now knows why I am the way I am."

"I don't understand."

"Uncle Richard, before my mother died, she told me she had magical powers. I didn't believe her because she was ill, and I thought the illness made her mad. But alas, it's true, and… I also have magical powers."

Richard furrowed his brow. "Magical powers?"

"Yes. Twenty-two years ago, Yorkford destroyed the village of Maiden Hills and massacred the people because they could do magic, and they suspected the people were evil."

"I remember that incident. I was a young lad at the time in knight training. Something similar happened in Cromer decades earlier."

Juliana's brow wrinkled. "What happened there?"

"The Church of Somerville ordered to burn the people from Cromer at the stake because they practiced dark magic. They passed a law to prevent it from happening again. The kings of all the kingdoms signed it."

"But the people of Maiden Hills were not like the Cromers and did not deserve to be massacred. Someone from the village killed Edmund's father, Prince James, for his betrayal," Juliana paused, recalling the maiden's words, "Although I believe now he was innocent. But Edmund seeks to avenge his father's death by killing the remaining Majians, including me."

"My dear, this is shocking news."

"It sounds unbelievable, Uncle Richard, but truly it is."

"What do you wish for me to do?"

"Edmund's army will attack Cedarville where most of the remaining Majians live. We need help with weapons and chainmail for the villagers. They will fight back."

Richard stared at his niece, typically poised and calm and, above all else, rational. "The situation sounds grave. I can't refuse you, Juliana. Of course, I will help you."

"Thank you, but there's something else. The Majians must rebuild their village. We need help with supplies and labor."

"Who owns the land?"

"King Carlton of Etheland."

"Are you willing to fight him for it?"

"We shall do whatever is necessary." Juliana continued eating, her hands calmed, and her energy returned.

"A burned village will require a great deal of work. We don't have much money."

Juliana took the black cloth from her pouch and opened it, revealing the blocks of gold. "There are loads of it."

Richard's eyes widened. "Where did you get that?"

"It belongs to the Majian people." She leaned into her uncle. "Will you help us rebuild?"

Richard deliberated, then nodded. "Yes, I will help you." Juliana wrapped her arms around her uncle and squeezed him. "When do you need the weapons and chainmail?"

"We need them now. We were informed that Edmund is preparing to attack."

Richard did not hesitate. "Agatha!"

Agatha ran toward him. "Aye, my lord."

"Fetch Sir Francis and make haste."

"Right away, my lord." Agatha hurried out of the room.

Richard turned to Juliana. "I shall have Sir Francis get the supplies you need right away, and I shall send men to fight alongside Cedarville."

"You will send men?" Juliana felt a lump in her throat. She did not expect this kind gesture from her uncle.

"I will." He smiled. "Sir Leopold sent a herald earlier ordering me to send an army to Yorkford for an attack at suppertime. He did not mention where they would attack, but now I understand. Instead, I shall send my men to Cedarville to side with you."

"But Uncle Richard, Edmund will find out you disobeyed his orders."

"You let me worry about that. You are more important." He smiled, puffing his pink cheeks.

Juliana's eyes watered. "I am grateful, Uncle Richard."

"Whom shall I tell Sir Francis to see?"

"Please see Lord Jack, the baron of Cedarville," Juliana remembered Edmund's men arresting Jack, "or see Sir Mark. He is one of The Magnificent Seven Knights who came to help us."

Richard squeezed her hand. "Do not worry, my dear."

Juliana turned to see Duchess Isabel, the wife of Duke Richard, walk in with her daughter, seventeen-year-old Lady Lucy. Isabel was an elegant lady with golden blond hair and a beautiful broad smile. Her hair was rolled up and secured tightly around her head. She wore a lovely royal-blue gown strikingly similar to one Juliana remembered her mother had worn. Isabel reminded Juliana of her mother, and a sense of longing came over her. Isabel's daughter, Lucy, was a younger version of her mother and just as elegant.

Lucy had requested to speak to her father privately, and once Richard and Lucy departed, Isabel held Juliana's hand and sat with her. "What brings you here?"

329

"I'm in need of my uncle's help. Yorkford will attack Cedarville, and I have grown fond of the village and its people."

"Lord Jack is the baron there, is he not?"

At the mention of Jack's name, Juliana's heart warmed, followed by intense dread. "He is, but Edmund despises him and the people that live there. Edmund's men arrested Jack, and I fear Edmund might have… killed him." Her eyes moistened.

Isabel squeezed Juliana's hand and smiled. "Jack is fine. There was an attempt to execute him earlier this day, but it failed."

Juliana put her hand to her chest and felt an enormous sense of relief. "Thank God."

"Juliana…" Isabel leaned closer and, in a low voice, said, "there was talk in the town that he was saved by magic. Do you know anything about it?"

"I do. Jack and I know people who have magical abilities." She paused and sighed. "I am also one of them."

Isabel smiled, then nodded. "Your mother told me… and she showed me."

"You knew?"

"I did, but she swore me to secrecy. Your mother and I were friends, and she confided in me. How did you come to know?"

"She told me on her deathbed, but I did not believe it until a few days ago. I have wrestled with it once I discovered it to be true."

"Your mother wished to spare you the truth because of what her people had endured, but I am pleased she told you before the secret died with her." She studied Juliana. "You are rather fond of Lord Jack, are you not?"

Juliana let out a dispirited sigh. "I am. It is yet another thing I struggle with."

"Your mother felt that you and Jack belonged together. She knew how devoted Jack was to you, but she knew King Matthew was partial to Edmund, and it was certain that he would arrange for you to marry him."

"Edmund was devoted to me as well. He saved my life when I fell in the moat."

Isabel shook her head. "That was not Edmund—it was Jack. Jack saved your life."

"Forgive me, Aunt Isabel, but there were witnesses."

"Your mother saw what really happened. She watched from a window up in the castle. You fell in the moat and could not swim. Jack dove in to save you, and he pulled you out. Edmund must have been furious that it was not he who saved you. He looked around, saw people coming, then discreetly pushed Jack into the moat, and saved him. When people saw Edmund carrying Jack and laying him next to you, they assumed Edmund saved you both."

Juliana's eyes widened. All along, she thought Edmund had saved her, and she felt beholden to him. She could not comprehend how deceitful he had been, and cruel—Jack could have drowned. "Why didn't my mother tell my father?"

"Your mother was afraid to confront King Matthew. She was a strong woman, but with your father, she held her tongue. King Matthew had spread the news of Edmund's bravery, and quickness that he would have looked like a fool if she had told him the truth and he would have been forced to recant publicly."

Duke Richard walked in. "It's all set, my dear. Sir Francis is on his way to see Lord Jack. You shall stay here. A battleground is no place for a queen."

"I can help them with my magic."

"Then you shall have an escort."

Juliana smiled. "Uncle Richard, I love how you fuss over me, but I shall be fine."

Isabel said, "Juliana, there is someone you should speak with before you leave. He is ill, and I fear he may not be with us much longer."

Isabel escorted Juliana up the winding stairs of the castle and led her down a long corridor. Westmore Castle had a rich history illustrated on its wall tapestries. Juliana passed a portrait of Prince James, looking handsome and princely, and his father, King Thomas, in his younger years. Edmund didn't resemble either his father or grandfather. She supposed Edmund had blended features of both Prince James and Princess Katherine. As Juliana continued down the hall, she glimpsed the paintings of battle scenes showing lands conquered by King Thomas and his forefathers, the proud men of the Wadham dynasty.

At the end of the hallway, they reached a room where a thin elderly man lay confined to his bed, his head propped up with pillows. By his bedside, his maidservant fed him, wiped his mouth with a napkin, and took away his metal tray with an empty soup bowl.

Isabel said to the man, "Your Majesty, you have a visitor. Do you recognize her?"

The man stared at Juliana. "I do… come closer, my dear. It has been a long time. Forgive me for not attending your wedding. I was not well," he said, his voice low and weakened by age.

Juliana recognized the man as King Thomas, the former king of Westmore, Prince James' father, and Edmund's grandfather. He was old, but with a sharp mind. She remembered him as a once supreme and wise king who ruled justly. His subjects adored him, and her mother was devoted to him.

The maidservant dragged a chair from the corner of the room and placed it next to his bed. Juliana lowered herself onto it.

"Your Majesty, it's good to see you. How are you?" Juliana asked.

"For a man my age, I am not doing too badly, for I get lovely visitors like yourself."

Isabel said, "I will leave you two alone for a few minutes." She walked out of the room, and the maidservant followed.

"How is my grandson?" he asked.

Juliana could not answer in truth. What would she say to him? Your grandson has gone mad. He locked me in the dungeon, hit me, and knocked me to the floor. He tried to execute his adoptive brother. The words that came out were, "He is as he always is. Has he not come by to visit you?"

"He has. He came by a short time ago."

"Edmund was here?" Juliana felt the color drain from her face at the thought of almost bumping into him.

"Yes, but he did not stay long. He seemed distressed."

"What did he say to you?" *Did he tell his grandfather about me?*

"We mostly talked about James." His eyes gazed at Juliana with light brown eyes that had seen seven decades of battles, conquests, and triumphs, but also sadness at losing his wife at childbirth with their second child, who was stillborn, and losing his only son, James, at twenty-four. Juliana met his eyes and perceived unimaginable pain. "My dear, I hold no anger toward you for what your father did."

Her chest tightened, expecting to hear another unpleasant revelation about her father. "What did my father do?"

"He made me renounce my throne."

"But Father said you were happy to relinquish it."

"No, I was not!" King Thomas was fiery in his response. "He planned to take over my kingdom ever since the marriage of my son James to Princess Katherine was arranged. When James died, I wished for Princess Katherine and Edmund to stay here, in Westmore, as would have been proper. He was my only heir, but he wanted Edmund for himself, so he had his brother, Prince Marcus, marry Katherine to keep them in Yorkford, away from me."

Juliana lowered her eyes and sighed. "I have recently learned of many appalling acts by my father, which makes me believe I did not know him. I often wondered why Uncle Marcus would marry a woman unable to bear his children."

"Your father made him do it. He manipulated people like chess pieces, moving them around to suit his purpose."

"But you did not have to give up your throne. Did you?"

"When he arranged the marriage with you and Edmund, the purpose was to remove my only heir and give him to your father. I did not agree to the betrothal, but since his mother still lived, it was her decision, and she approved it. My choice was to give up my throne or fight. If I had fought your father, Edmund would have to choose a side. He wished not to go against the mighty King Matthew. It would have torn him apart, and I could not allow that to happen. Either way, I would have lost my kingdom, and my people would have endured a bloody battle for naught."

"Did Edmund know what my father was planning?"

"I do not know, but he is ambitious and may have been blinded by power. He admired your father, and he wished to be like him. Edmund desired to rule a large kingdom, and Westmore was too small for him."

Isabel walked in. "Your Majesty, are you ready to leave?"

"I am." She turned to King Thomas. "I must leave now, Your Majesty, but I shall pray for you." She gave his thin hand a light squeeze. "Be well."

He put his hand over hers. "You too, my dear. I hope to see you again soon."

She smiled. "As do I."

While Isabel and Juliana walked toward the great room, they spoke little. Myriad thoughts flooded Juliana's mind. King Thomas's words opened her eyes to a different side of her father. She was one of her father's pawns, just like her mother and Edmund, or did Edmund manipulate her father to make him the heir of his kingdom? Sometimes the student outsmarts the master. And what about Jack? Did Jack really wish to move to Cedarville, or was it her father's plan to keep Jack away from her and Edmund? Juliana felt her father had orchestrated everything and nothing happened by chance. Her power of sight made her see things clearly for the first time.

Juliana had allowed others to dictate her life. She rebelled in her younger years and later conformed to what was expected of her—to please her father. This day, she resolved to no longer allow herself to be manipulated by anyone, but rather to live by her own convictions of what was right and just, and no longer governed by outdated rules and conduct.

She pondered King Thomas's dilemma. He did not think solely of himself. He thought of his people and his grandson and sought to protect them, even if it meant losing everything. Juliana realized that her reign was not about her. It was about her people. She was their queen, and she would protect them at all costs.

Juliana stepped outside and gazed at the orange sun near the horizon. It was suppertime.

Chapter 20

Jack's men waited by the bridge, guarding the only entrance into Cedarville from Yorkford. Jack also stationed men on the border between Cedarville and Maiden Hills in the unlikely event Edmund's men took the long route from Yorkford to Westmore and through Maiden Hills. The Magnificent Knights, led by Sir Mark, stood mounted on the front lines in full armor with their lances ready. Behind them, the knights from Cedarville waited valiantly.

Jack sat atop his horse in the village square with an eye on the bridge when a squire from the east border galloped toward him. "Lord Jack," the young squire panted, "there's an army of men coming east from Maiden Hills."

Jack veered his destrier and sped toward the border. When he arrived, he looked in the distance and saw hundreds of men approaching them. The troop's weapons were not drawn and did not appear ready to engage. Soon, they were close enough for Jack to see the colors on their banners—blue and yellow—the colors of Westmore. As the men drew closer, Jack raised his sword, and they rode toward him. Jack's men stood vigilant, with their hands on their weapons. "Stay close, men," Jack commanded.

The knight leading the group stopped before Jack. "Are you Lord Jack?"

"I am."

"I am Sir Francis. We come at the request of Duke Richard Maddeson, duke of Westmore, to assist you in your conflict with Yorkford. His niece, Her Majesty,

Queen Juliana, has beseeched Duke Richard's assistance. We have two hundred men and extra chainmail and weapons."

Jack smiled, and in his mind, thanked Juliana. He thought it ironic that Westmore would help him in his fight against King Edmund, their once adored crown prince, but he was grateful Duke Richard chose to side with his niece Juliana over Edmund. Perhaps it was a way for Westmore to retaliate for being taken over by Yorkford and dethroning their beloved King Thomas.

"Thank you, Sir Francis, we can use your help. Our men are waiting alongside the bridge. We'll position some of your men by the bridge and others in the village."

"At your service, Lord Jack, please lead the way." Jack turned his horse around, and Sir Francis and his men followed him.

The elite knights of Westmore joined Sir Mark on the front lines by the bridge, others guarded the entrance to the village, and others secured the east border. The trained villagers on horseback and on foot positioned themselves behind the knights with their weapons and chainmail. Thirty-three Majian men and women were dispersed among the fighters to help with their magic. Jack wore a helmet and partial armor, allowing him the flexibility to move quickly to provide leadership and assistance where necessary. The alligators summoned by Robert waited below the water. Wolves hid behind the trees to surprise the attackers, and the birds of prey, hawks, and eagles, kept watch on the area perched on the rooftops. The non-fighting women, children, and elderly locked themselves inside their homes, and the villagers

338

who lived near the village square, including Helena, took refuge in Lord Jack's castle.

Jack rode along the entrance of the bridge and shouted to the soldiers, "Men, remember why you are here. We must protect our village from a king who has unjustly attacked our village and persecuted our people to satisfy a personal vendetta. We must protect the innocent!" There were cheers from the men. "We must fight harder than we have ever fought before. We shall not let them defeat us!" More cheers.

The thunder of galloping horses coming from the dark forest braced the fighters of Cedarville. Armored knights approached at high speed, and Jack was prepared to face a larger army as Edmund's intent was to lay waste to the village and its people. The knights lowered their visors.

"Get ready, men!" Sir Mark called out.

Within minutes, Edmund's army reached the bridge. Below the water, the alligators snapped their jaws. Horses tumbled. The men who made it past the alligators met with the snarling wolves and the raptors.

"Move forward! Cut them down!" came the call from Sir Leopold.

A few men escaped the animals' attack and made it across the bridge. Sir Mark and the elite knights raised their lances and charged toward them.

Horses galloped, and soon the sounds of lances cracking against the shields and the cries of injured men rang across the battlefield. As more soldiers made it past the bridge, the sound of metal swords clashing, men shouting, and the growling of the animals filled the air.

Yorkford's knights stormed into the village of Cedarville. The Majians disarmed them and levitated their swords to the village fighters, who grabbed them and used them against Edmund's men.

"They're taking our swords!" shouted a Yorkford soldier.

"Act quickly! Use your daggers!"

The wolves chased the horses and bit their legs, sending the equines running wildly. It was becoming a bloody scene with the blood of Yorkford spilling onto Cedarville.

Edmund's army far outnumbered Jack's men; however, Jack's army had a considerable advantage with the animals' help, and the Majians' ability to remove their weapons and push the men back with the energy force. When Edmund's men lost arms, they resorted to using their fists but were quickly defeated.

***

Juliana, having ridden from Westmore across Maiden Hills, arrived in the village square in the middle of the clash, setting her eyes for the first time on a deadly battle. Her heartbeat quickened. She mustered her resolve, focused on large boulders, and hurled them toward her own army attacking the small village. She used the energy force to push back fighters, sending them flying across the field.

Juliana glimpsed a toddler running out of his cottage, and she quickly dismounted and chased after him. A young maiden with a sling wrapped around her arm and fear in her eyes ran after the child. One of Edmund's men pointed a knife at the young woman. The woman looked at the man with horror and screamed. Juliana magically removed the blade from the man's hand and flipped it around. She turned away as the knife pierced him, splattering blood on his chainmail. She extended her hand, and the man's sword levitated toward her. She held the sword over her shoulder, picked up the child, and led the woman inside the cottage.

The woman recognized Juliana. "Your Majesty, you are a Majian! Thank you for saving us."

"Please stay inside. It's a dangerous battle out there."

"I am worried, for my brother is also a Majian and is fighting with the men. I am caring for his son. My brother was saved as a baby and just recently learned how to use his magical powers."

Juliana echoed her words curiously. "He was saved as a baby?"

"Yes, he was not yet a year old. He never knew his parents."

Robert's son, Peter, entered her mind. If only someone had rescued him like this woman's brother had been rescued—or was he? She remembered the missing locket and the missing human remains from Beth's cottage, for which they could find no explanation. *Is it possible that Peter had been saved? Is it possible he still lives?*

Juliana stared at the sling on the young woman's arm. "You are Geraldine, are you not?"

"I am. How did you know?"

"I saw you leave Doctor Robert's cottage."

"He's a good man. I am worried about him too. Is Doctor Robert all right?"

"I hope he is. I must go back." Juliana handed the sword to Geraldine. "Take this. Lock the door and hide."

341

Juliana peeked out of the cottage. When no one was in sight, she ran to Millie and jumped on. She stared ahead. The battle was raging. As Cedarville and Westmore's army fought and killed Yorkford's men, more men continued to pour into the village.

***

On the battleground, Jack rode Dex in a fury, piercing his sword into every attacker he encountered. Two men stormed toward Jack, roaring. He skillfully defeated the first one with his weapon, but before the other could strike, the sword bolted out of his hand. Jack turned to see Robert behind him. Robert then spun around the man's weapon toward him, and he fell from his horse and tumbled to the ground.

Jack surveyed the area. Sir Mark, The Magnificent Knights, and Westmore's elite soldiers were swiftly taking down Edmund's best fighters, thrusting them off their horses and leaving them vulnerable to animal attacks. Jeb took command of his magic, disarming men and fighting them off. Victor stood alongside his father, fighting the first battle of his young life. Jack looked in fright and raced toward Victor when one of Edmund's knights picked up the boy from behind and held him above his head, preparing to hurl him. In an instant, Jeb levitated Victor above the soldier's grasp and floated him to safety. Jack watched as in a rage, Jeb charged toward the knight, and using his powers, bolted the man's helmet off his head and detached his sword from his grip. Jeb took a boulder with his bare hands and crushed the soldier's skull. Sir Quinn was dead.

Jack continued to wave his sword. Amid the battle, he abruptly stopped when he saw a young man with long white hair, resembling the man from the Somerville library, standing on a rooftop with bow and arrow in hand, shooting at Edmund's men. Jack's gaze lingered, wondering who he was but was distracted when through the shouting and weapons clashing, he heard Sir Leopold call out, "Surrender Lord Jack!"

"I will never surrender!" Jack yelled, darting his eyes, searching.

Upon hearing Leopold's voice, Simon charged toward him. Simon turned to the wolves and ordered them to attack Leopold's horse. Leopold tumbled to the ground, and the wolves were upon him. A cry rang out, and Leopold dropped his sword when a wolf dug its teeth into his gloved hand.

Simon ran toward a fully armored Leopold and, with ferocity, removed his helmet. He was face to face with the man who carried out the massacre that killed his family and friends. He drew back his fist and let it fly, setting loose a torrent of bright red blood. Leopold tried to punch back, but lying on his back in his heavy armor, he could barely move and fell prey to Simon's fury. Simon grabbed Leopold's dagger that hung by his waist and stabbed Leopold in the neck.

Jack rode toward his mentor, lying on the ground. Sir Leopold was dead. He looked up, searching for the long-haired young man but he vanished.

***

Juliana stepped back to view the battle scene. Cedarville and Westmore's men were fighting aggressively and prevailing, but Yorkford's army was better trained—and there were many of them. She gazed into the distance and watched Edmund's men continuing to charge into the small village. She wondered how long Cedarville's fighters would endure before they wore themselves out and succumbed to the force of Edmund's army. She remembered her father's words, "*Stand firm and yield to no one.*"

"I will not yield, Father, but I will stop this!" Juliana headed toward the creek, away from the bridge and the battleground.

"Juliana! Juliana, stop!"

Juliana pulled back her horse's reins—it was Jack's voice. She spun around, and her heartbeat quickened as she searched for him. A knight on a dark brown destrier wearing partial armor rode toward her. He stopped and removed his helmet, ash blond hair mussed. She gazed upon his face, and for a moment, her breath stopped.

"Jack!" She jumped off Millie and ran toward him. They wrapped their arms around each other in a full embrace. Tears streamed down her face, releasing the tension lodged in her since Jack had been arrested. "Oh, Jack, I can't believe you're here. I was so worried. I feared Edmund had killed you."

"He tried, but Robert and Simon arrived in time. Thank you for sending them."

"Thank God." She caressed his face then remembered what her Aunt Isabel told her. "Why didn't you tell me?"

"Tell you what?"

"That it was you, not Edmund, who rescued me from the moat six years ago."

"How did you find out?"

"My mother saw what happened from her window, and she told my Aunt Isabel, but my mother feared my father and said nothing."

"That was a long time ago, Juliana."

"But Edmund took credit for it."

"It would not have made a difference. Besides, if I had not jumped in, Edmund would have. I was just quicker."

"It would have made a difference to me." She gazed into his sweet eyes. "It was you all along. You were always my hero." She drew him close to her and kissed him.

Jack pulled her away. "Where were you going?"

"I'm going to the castle to see Edmund and put a stop to this."

"Juliana, no! He will kill you."

"Jack, I know what I'm doing. I'm done hiding. Edmund has no control over me. I must stand up for the people of Maiden Hills and for all of my people, and I must stand up for myself. I will no longer hide the truth of who I am because of fear, the way my mother did. I must confront him."

"How will you get to Yorkford? Edmund's men have the bridge blocked."

"With my magic, I can lift Millie over the creek. I've done it before. It's how Simon goes back and forth to Yorkford quickly without being seen." She kissed him and mounted Millie. "I must go, Jack."

"Juliana, wait."

"I'm sorry, but I must do this." She rode off toward the creek.

***

345

Jack jumped on his horse and scanned the crowd. He found him. "Robert!"

Robert turned his head, looking for Jack amid the clash, then rode toward him. "Jack, what is it?"

"Can you lift my horse over the creek?"

He gave a casual nod. "Why do you ask?"

"Juliana left to confront King Edmund, and I must go after her, but I can't do it without magic."

"I shall go with you," Robert said.

"No, I need you here."

"We are doing well. Even though we're outnumbered, the Majians have disarmed most of them and killed them with their own weapons, and the animals are keeping a lot of their men at bay. Besides, you may need magical protection or medical help."

Jack didn't have time to waste and conceded. "All right. Let's go."

Jack and Robert galloped fiercely toward the creek, and when they reached it, their horses levitated above the water. They landed on the other side of the creek in the dark forest and sped toward the castle.

They hurried through the castle's secret passageway. Robert carried his pouch with special herbs and powders. They arrived at the dungeon area and ran up the stairs, but slowed when they reached the central part of the castle. The house servants tended to their chores as Jack and Robert crept through the halls, keeping an ear out for either Juliana or Edmund.

Jack turned to Robert and whispered, "Robert, when we find them, please stay out of sight. This is my fight with King Edmund—to win or lose."

Robert nodded. "I understand."

***

Juliana entered through the massive castle doors and marched toward the great hall.

Ella greeted her. "Your Majesty, it's good to see you."

"Where's my husband, Ella?"

"His Majesty is in the great chamber. Would you care for a glass of wine?"

"No, I must speak with him." Juliana rushed up the stairs. When she opened the door to his chamber, she found him sitting in a chair, staring at the ceiling with a book in his hand. She hesitated—the sight disturbed her—but she mustered her strength and stormed in.

"Call it off, Edmund. You can't win. Your men are dying."

Edmund glared at her with eyes of fury. He rose from his chair and dropped the book on the seat. Juliana's heart palpitated. She had to be brave and not give in to fear, and she had to trust in the power of the stones.

He stared into her eyes. "No, Cedarville is dying, for they are greatly outnumbered. We will win, and afterward, my men will burn the town."

"What has gotten into you? This vendetta is destroying you. You have gone mad."

"I see things very clearly now." He became disturbingly calm, deliberate with each footstep, as he approached her.

Juliana retreated a step. "I don't understand. Your father, Prince James, was a good man. He showed honor by not carrying out the massacre. Didn't you inherit his honor and character?"

"There is much you don't know about me, Juliana—James was not my father!" He lifted his hand, and the sword resting in the far corner of the room flew toward him, and he grabbed it.

"Good God!" Juliana's heart thumped erratically. "What just happened?"

The book on the chair floated toward Juliana, and with a stunned look, it landed in her hands. She looked at the title—*The Book of Secrets*. She stared at Edmund in disbelief. "You're a Majian?" Her eyes zoomed in on the locket around his neck.

"I am, my beloved queen. I am just like you."

"H-how is it possible?"

"Twenty-two years ago, James brought a child to Katherine to raise as their own. That child wore a locket around his neck that belonged to his mother, Beth. Katherine saved the locket with the stones, and this day she gave them to me. I had the book which I found in James' chamber, I recited the spells, and they worked."

Juliana's eyes grew wide. "It can't be!" She looked at the book in her hand and flipped to the inside cover: *This book belongs to Helena Porter, a descendant of Sir Drake.* Juliana's hands trembled. "It's true! You're Peter, Beth and Robert's son! Prince James saved you from the fire. Why are you trying to destroy your people?"

"It's about power, Juliana. That's what your father taught me. You can't rule if people do not fear you, and if there are others more powerful than you, you can't win. With this ability, I shall conquer many lands. But if I am to rule, everyone else with the magic must die, including you." He walked toward her.

She backed away, but not quick enough. Edmund reached for her neck and yanked the chain with a vicious force, knocking her to the floor. The locket slid across

348

the room. Juliana crawled toward the pendant, but it moved farther away from her.

Edmund raised his sword above her as she lay on the floor, her eyes wide, staring at the point of the blade. But before the steel came down, Jack stormed into the room and charged toward Edmund, pointing his sword.

"Edmund!" he yelled.

Edmund turned to face him and blocked Jack's swing. A knife floated toward Jack, but Jack quickly stepped back and blocked it with his sword, a shocked look on his face. His eyes darted between the locket around Edmund's neck and Juliana on the floor.

"Be a man, Edmund, and fight me without magic," Jack demanded. "If you're going to kill me, do it the honorable way."

"I am a far better fighter than you, for everything you learned, you learned from me." Edmund removed his locket and placed it on the mantel. "I don't need magic to kill you."

Edmund and Jack's swords collided with a force filled with rage well beyond anything they had ever encountered, grunting with every swing, and clenching their teeth. Edmund pierced Jack's arm, and Jack grimaced from the pain.

Juliana crawled to the far end of the room, searching for the locket. Edmund cried out. Juliana looked up and saw Jack had stabbed Edmund's shoulder. She turned away and continued her search. She spotted a glimmer of gold against the candlelight and rushed toward it. The chain was broken. Edmund pierced Jack's leg, and Jack stumbled to the floor.

Juliana held the locket to her heart, closed her eyes, and said, "Please help us." The locket glowed and grew warm, and a powerful force entered Juliana.

Edmund raised his sword and aimed for Jack's neck.

His sword came down, but he could not pierce him. Juliana had unknowingly created an invisible shield around Jack, preventing Edmund's sword from penetrating him.

Juliana's eyes clouded with a vision of the battle in Cedarville and saw the shield had extended to protect the fighters. Edmund's army could not penetrate the fighters, but the animals and the villagers continued to attack them. When Edmund's army realized they were vulnerable and unable to fight back, they retreated.

Edmund, with stunned eyes, turned to Juliana on the floor, clutching her stones to her chest. Their eyes met. "It can't be. It's the third stone!" In a fierce rage, he charged toward her and raised his sword.

She lifted her hand, gathering the energy force to push him back. Jack mustered his strength and rose to his feet, hobbling. "Get away from her." He lunged toward Edmund and dug his sword deep into his side.

Edmund cried out, arching his back. He veered toward Jack and collapsed. Jack's leg gave in, and he fell.

Robert rushed in. "Jack, are you all right?"

"Robert, I will care for Jack, please look after Edmund. Tell me what to do."

"Grab a cloth and put pressure on the leg and arm to stop the bleeding."

Juliana nodded, and Robert hurried toward Edmund. Juliana searched for cloth in Edmund's chest of drawers. She found a linen tunic, ripped it and placed it on Jack's wound, and quickly wrapped it around his leg and another around his arm.

Jack placed his hand on the red markings on Juliana's neck. His face pale. "Are you hurt?"

"I'm fine." She stared at Jack. "Edmund's army retreated. The shield protected the people of Cedarville. I saw it."

"How did you do that?" Jack asked.

Juliana opened her locket. Inside were three glowing stones, including a deep-red gemstone. "It's the third stone." She smiled. "It creates a shield over those we wish to protect. For the stones to work, they must be at the center of our energy. That center is the heart."

Juliana turned and crawled toward Robert. "How is he?"

Robert had torn Edmund's tunic and applied pressure on the stomach wound with a cloth, preventing more blood from spilling. "He's breathing, but it's labored." Robert looked upon Edmund's face and said, "Your Majesty, can you hear me? I am a doctor."

Edmund grimaced and gave a faint nod.

Juliana kneeled beside him. "Edmund, this is Robert." Juliana paused, hoping he would recognize the name.

Edmund stared at Robert. His eyes conveyed that he understood.

"Robert," Juliana's lips quivered, "this is Peter." She stopped, waiting for her words to reach him. His eyebrows wrinkled, confused. She continued, "Prince James saved your baby and brought him to the castle to raise as his own… and named him Edmund."

Robert fixed his eyes on Juliana, then gazed down at Edmund. His power of second sight would prove what

351

his heart knew to be true. He let out an audible breath, blinking back tears. "He has my eyes and Beth's raven black hair."

Juliana stared at Edmund, his face growing pallid.

"I fear he's lost too much blood," Robert whispered to Juliana.

Edmund struggled to let the words out, "You... you are my father?"

"Try not to speak," Robert said, "but, yes, I am your father. Beth was your mother."

"T-tell me about her."

As Robert continued to tend to his wound, applying magical healing herbs, and sealing his side, he spoke to his son. "Beth was beautiful with black hair and sparkling green eyes. She brightened a room with her smile." Robert's eyes watered. "She was kind, and she loved to laugh and sing."

"She sang me a song... about a butterfly."

Robert raised his eyebrows. "She did! Do you remember that? She loved butterflies."

"I would hear her sing it... when no one was around." Edmund's breathing slowed.

Robert looked at Juliana, and with sadness and tears swelling in his eyes, shook his head lightly.

Juliana held Edmund's hand. Despite everything, tears streamed down her face. "Hold on, Edmund." It was a strange feeling for Juliana. Edmund tried to kill her and had mistreated her, but before her was a different man, a lost man, a man who never knew his true self.

Edmund stared ahead. "I... I see her... my mother... she's calling me." Edmund turned to face Juliana. Juliana wasn't sure, but she thought his eyes conveyed a flicker of remorse. His eyelids came down. He breathed a few more shallow breaths, then breathed no more, and his hand went limp.

Robert placed his fingers on Edmund's neck, pressed his lips together, and looked at Juliana. "He's gone."

"I am so sorry, Robert." Juliana embraced Robert, and tears flowed. She felt the pain that Robert must have felt learning his son had lived only to see him die.

Jack put his hand on Robert's shoulder. "I'm sorry, Robert."

"He brought it upon himself with his need for vengeance and hate." Robert looked at Edmund's lifeless body. "But, I am grateful to have laid eyes upon my son one last time." He wiped his tears.

Juliana turned toward Jack. "We must tell the others."

Jack nodded. "But first, I must tell my mother."

Chapter 21

Maiden Hills, twenty-two years ago

Prince James arrived at the top of the mountain, but he was too late. Dozens of lifeless bodies lay scattered of what was to be a wedding. Blood covered the ground. A sight he had seen many times as a warrior, but this scene was different, for these were innocent people.

He trudged through the grounds, carefully turning them over, studying their faces, until his eyes came upon her. There among the lifeless bodies lay the woman he loved. He bent down and looked into her green eyes staring back at him, but the sparkle was no longer there. He caressed her beautiful face, and when he did, he could almost hear her voice, see her smile, and hear her laughter. She was full of life, and in an instant, she was gone. He recalled the last time he saw Beth and the pain in her eyes believing he had betrayed her, but he hadn't. He had kept his word. He wanted to comfort her and tell her how much he loved her, but it would have accomplished nothing.

James placed his hand over her eyes and gently closed them. "I'm sorry, Beth." Tears streamed down his face.

The fire in the village raged. He had to act fast. James spurred his horse, and riding at a swift pace, hurried toward the wooded area, passing King Matthew's men as they burned the cottages and slaughtered the townspeople trying to escape. James had to hurry before they discovered the cabins in the woods.

He arrived at Beth's home, where a faint light shone through a window. James knocked on the door, but no one answered. He pushed the door slowly and scanned the room with his sword drawn—a calmness permeated the cottage. In the small cradle, next to the gentle fire burning, lay Peter sound asleep. He believed everyone else was dead—Helena, Simon, and Robert. He sheathed his sword at his waist and picked up Peter, not yet one-year-old and an orphan. Peter let out an audible breath and continued sleeping.

Around Peter's neck hung Beth's locket with the magical stones. He stared at it, then pulled the wool blanket and wrapped the baby in it. In the cradle lay the rattle he had given him and the statue of the fairy sitting on a mushroom holding a butterfly. He picked up the figure and wrapped it in the blanket with the baby. He turned toward the door, and his eyes caught sight of *The Book of Secrets* on a small table. He lifted it and placed it under his arm. He looked back at the cabin, remembering the times he spent with Beth. A lump lodged in his throat. Those were the happiest days of his life, for it was then that he fell in love.

James inserted the book in a pocket in his horse's saddle, and mounted his destrier, holding Peter with the locket around his neck, and the statue snuggled inside the blanket. He turned his head at the sound of fire roaring behind him. In the distance, cottages burned, and knights on horseback were approaching with torches. Leading the men was Sir Leopold. James met Leopold's eyes. His blood seethed at the betrayal of his confidant. James spurred his horse and galloped toward Yorkford.

***

Simon rode alongside Robert, trotting hard through the woods. The fire raged all around them, devouring cottages and trees. Simon feared the knights had reached his home and killed his mother and nephew. The burning pain on the right side of his head was unbearable, but he pushed through the intense heat and the throbbing. Blood pumped through his veins viciously as he rode faster.

Moments later, Simon arrived with Robert to see his mother's cottage burning and Helena outside crying.

"Peter's inside," she said with a look of anguish.

"I'm going in!" shouted Robert. When he opened the door, the fire had consumed the inside of the cottage. Sparks jumped onto Robert, igniting his clothes. He threw himself on the ground and rolled, extinguishing the flames. He lay on the ground, his hands on his face, screaming at the agony of losing his child.

Simon fumed. With his head spinning from the excruciating pain on the right side of his head, and from the anguish of losing his family and friends, he let out a roar and clenched his fists. He jumped on his horse and sped toward Yorkford.

***

James arrived at the castle as darkness blanketed the kingdom. He strode through the halls, passing the servants tending to their evening duties. He gently pushed the door to his bedchamber and found Katherine asleep, surrounded by the faint glow and the soft crackling of the fire. James sat on the edge of the bed beside her, with Peter in his arms as he made sucking sounds.

"Katherine," he whispered, gently rousing her.

She stirred, and her eyes sprang open in a sudden movement, blinking, as she focused her eyes on the

356

infant wrapped in a blanket with his eyes wide open, scanning the room. She sat up. "James, why do you have a baby?"

James handed her the baby, and Katherine held him, ogling him. "He was abandoned. I know how much you prayed for a child. We can raise him as our own."

"Where was he abandoned?"

"It does not matter. He will be our child."

"Truly?" She smiled behind watery eyes. "He's beautiful." Peter yawned and stretched his tiny arms, then placed his thumb in his mouth and began sucking on it. "I think he's hungry."

"I shall have a maidservant fetch milk for him."

"What shall we name him?"

"How about Edmund?" He pinched his lips. "It was to be my brother's name."

Katherine reached for James' hand. "I love it." She smiled. "Thank you. You have made me very happy." She brushed the baby's face lightly and noticed the chain around his neck. "What is this pendant?"

James stared at it. "It's a unique locket. Put it in a safe place, and when he is older, we can give it to him. It's the only thing he has of his past life."

She opened the locket, and her eyes gazed upon two small stones emitting a faint pulsating glow. "It's lovely. I shall put it in my jewelry box."

James left Katherine and baby Edmund in their bedchamber and walked toward the opposite end of the castle to his private room. He placed *The Book of Secrets* on a table beside his bed, then took out the statue from his pocket and set it next to the book. He stared at the fairy, recalling that beautiful spring day at the merchant stand, and watching Beth's face light up when he gave her the statue. *Some day he will know who he is. I promise you, Beth!* He wiped his eyes. He left the room to search for a maidservant, and when he found her, he asked her to find milk and a horn to feed Katherine's baby.

***

Meanwhile, Simon's sense of intuition led him to a secret passageway near the entrance of the dark forest. He went through a long, winding tunnel and found himself in the halls of the dungeon where prisoners moaned, begging for mercy. He climbed up the stairs to the main part of the castle. A young squire carrying a pail of water walked by him.

"Pardon me, young squire, where might I find Prince James?"

The young squire stared at Simon, frightened at the sight of his burned head and missing ear, then pointed in the direction opposite Simon. "His chamber is on the east side of the castle."

Simon turned and marched with determination. He heard James' voice and hid behind a stone wall. James was talking to a servant in the great hall, instructing her to make sure his wife had enough blankets and was comfortable. The servant obliged and left the room. When James was alone, Simon followed him through a corridor leading to the bailey. He was soon within a few feet from James. He took a few more stealthy steps, stretching a rope, tightening it around his rotating fists. When he was close behind James, he swung his arms over his head and pulled on the rope.

"I warned you, Your Highness. I warned you to stay away from my sister," Simon growled. "This is for Beth."

James fought, tugging at the rope, unable to free himself from Simon's grasp. Simon tightened his grip. James fought for a breath until he could breathe no more. His hands came down limp. Simon released him, and James fell, his body motionless.

***

Sir Leopold, walking through the hall after an exhaustive battle, caught sight of a man standing over James' body. He recognized him as the same man who had threatened James at an alehouse in Maiden Hills, except the right side of his face was charred, and he was missing an ear. Their eyes met, then the man bolted out of the castle through the front entrance, shoving people, and pushing them out of his way. Leopold ran toward James, turned his body over, and saw he was dead. Leopold yelled, "Halt. Murderer!"

The night guards mobilized and chased the man with blades drawn.

The murderer pushed through the castle doors like a crazed beast. His horse galloped toward him, and he quickly mounted, dashed across the drawbridge, and headed toward the forest.

Leopold and six guards fetched their horses and chased after him. The Majian had a considerable lead, but Leopold owned one of the fastest chargers in Yorkville and would soon close the gap between them. His horse was a prized black stallion from a family of horses known for their expertise in battle and speed and recognized everywhere for its distinctive white lines on its hind legs.

Leopold was shortening the distance between him and the killer until a large tree uprooted and fell in front

359

of Leopold with a loud *thump,* causing his horse to dodge the tree and lose its momentum. Large rocks flew toward the guards behind Leopold and knocked them off their horses. Leopold recovered and regained his speed until another tree fell in front of him, and he pulled on his horse's reins. Then from behind the trees, a pack of wolves appeared before him, blocking his path, growling, baring their pointed fangs. Leopold stared ahead into the distance and watched as James' killer disappeared into the darkness.

***

Yorkford, present, earlier in the day

Twenty-two years after James' death, Princess Katherine stumbled upon the story about the people from Maiden Hills. She found *The Book of Secrets* on James' table a few weeks ago and read about the power of the stones, the same stones that Edmund wore when James brought him to her as an infant. She left the book in the chamber, but when she returned for it, it was gone. She feared Edmund had taken it.

In recent days, she learned that Edmund had vowed to destroy the Majian people to avenge James' death. But, if he were also a Majian, he would have to know his true identity. Only one person alive knew of Edmund's origin. She asked her servant to send Sir Leopold to her apartment. Katherine recalled that after James died, Leopold saw her with the baby and whispered to her, "I know you did not birth the child you hold, but do not fear, I shall keep your secret and protect him. It's what Prince James would have wanted." They never spoke about it again.

There was a knock on the door. "Come in," Katherine said. The door opened, and Katherine turned to see Sir Leopold walk in. Her heart began to beat faster.

"You wish to see me, Your Highness?"

"I do, Sir Leopold. Please have a seat." When Leopold sat down, Katherine clasped her shaky hands and looked into his eyes. "You were my husband's closest confidant and the only other person who knows that Edmund is not my natural child. I must know where he came from." She asked the question she had feared the answer. "Is he James' natural son?"

Sir Leopold wiped his forehead, hands trembling, then shook his head. "I swore never to reveal the truth."

"You must tell me," Katherine insisted. "Please."

Leopold swallowed, and after a lengthy pause, said, "Your Highness, King Edmund is not Prince James' natural son. He..." he took a deep breath. "He was the son of Beth, the young lady from Maiden Hills and another man. They died when we attacked their village twenty-two years ago."

Upon hearing those words, Katherine froze. After reading *The Book of Secrets*, she suspected he came from Maiden Hills, but Leopold's confirmation felt like an explosion in her chest, to finally know the origin of the child she fell in love with twenty-two years ago. Selfishly, a part of her, was relieved that another woman had not carried James' baby. Having an heir was crucial to James, and she feared he would look for another woman to bear his child. It pained her to think someone else had, and she lived with that pain even as she grew to love Edmund and care for him as if she had given him life.

361

Edmund was like James in many ways that, over the years, she accepted that he was his natural child. "Was Beth a Majian?"

Leopold nodded. "She was. The blood that runs through King Edmund is not that of royalty but of Majian people. The same people he seeks to destroy."

Anxiety swept through Katherine. The time had come for Edmund to learn of his true origin. She could not hide it from him any longer. She poured herself a glass of wine to help calm her shaky nerves before talking with her son. Leopold excused himself to meet with Edmund and receive his next order.

Katherine limped into the library, holding on to her walking stick. Her eyes zoomed to *The Book of Secrets* on Edmund's desk. She suspected he had taken the book to learn about the people so he could destroy them. She met Edmund's eyes, then he looked away, still angry with her for slapping him.

"Edmund?"

He walked toward her. "You are to return to your chamber and remain there until I call for you. Ella, come here right away."

"I wish to give you this." Katherine opened her hand, trying in vain to keep it steady, revealing an opened golden locket, with two glowing stones.

Edmund's eyes widened. Katherine suspected he recognized the locket and the stones from reading about them in *The Book of Secrets*. The book described them as the stones responsible for the Majians' power. He looked baffled at seeing Katherine with them.

When Ella walked in, Katherine said, "Ella, please leave us to speak in private."

Ella turned toward Edmund, and he gave her a nod. "Very well," she said and exited.

Edmund held her arm as Katherine lowered herself onto the chair. "Mother, where did you get that?"

Katherine swallowed the lump in her throat. "It belongs to you."

Edmund tilted his head, brows furrowed.

"You were wearing the locket when James brought you to me."

"What do you mean when Father brought me to you?" He controlled his voice, although he could not hide the tightening in his eyes.

Katherine's heartbeat quickened, sensing Edmund's anxiety begin to rise, but the truth had to be told regardless of what he might do to her. She pressed her lips, then allowed the words to pour out and reach his ears. "You are not my natural child... or James'," her lips quivered. "You were the child of Beth and another man... from Maiden Hills. James brought you here when your natural parents died in the massacre twenty-two years ago."

Edmund's face darkened, and his nostrils flared. Rage overcame the composure he had exhibited. He glared at Katherine, tears streaming down her face.

With a white-knuckled grip, he pulled a knife from the side of his tunic, holding the steel point toward Katherine. She braced herself, prepared for death.

Edmund gripped the blade with both hands and raised it over his head. He clenched his teeth as the blade came down, aimed at Katherine, and with the full force of his wrath, he let out a roar born out of fury and pain from living a life filled with deceptions and lies. In an instant, he turned away from Katherine and released his anger on the wooden table inches from her. His breathing heavy as he leaned over the table with burning eyes. Edmund slowly straightened his body, took a deep breath, and glared at Katherine. He yanked the knife from the table, inserted it into its sheath, and stormed out of the library. Katherine's body violently shook as she sobbed.

Chapter 22

Still numb from the tragic events of the day, Juliana walked down the long corridor leading to the residents' apartments. The look on Edmund's face when he died remained imprinted on her mind. He had been obsessed with vengeance for his father's death only to learn when it was too late that his natural father still lived.

She looked at Jack as he hobbled toward Katherine's door with his arm and leg bandaged and with the color back on his face; however, his expression was one of dread, not looking forward to telling his adoptive mother that her eldest son was dead.

When they entered the room, they found Katherine sitting by the fireplace, an empty wineglass in her hand, eyes red. A relieved smile crossed her face when she saw Jack.

"Jack, I am happy to see you. I was worried." Katherine remained in her chair and embraced Jack. Tears filled her eyes.

Jack had one knee on the floor to meet her eyes. "Mother, I am sorry to have worried you." He took a deep breath. "I have grave news."

"What is it?" Katherine's face was somber, fearing the worst.

Jack held on to her hands. "I am sorry to tell you that… Edmund is dead."

Katherine blinked as the news sank in. Then her expression crumpled, and she buried her face in Jack's chest. He held her tight as she sobbed.

Katherine wiped her eyes and lifted her head. "What happened?" her voice brittle.

Jack searched for the right words. "He was crazed with power and vengeance, and it controlled him. There was no reasoning with him. He tried to kill Juliana and me…" He paused and swallowed. "I stabbed him with my sword."

Katherine buried her face in her hands. She looked up at Jack. "I don't know what happened to him. I did not raise him in that manner."

"I know, Mother," Jack said, squeezing her hands. "You have the kindest soul of anyone I have ever known."

"It was King Matthew. He wished for a son but lost both of his." Juliana lowered her head. Katherine grasped her hand. "Oh, but dear, he loved you so very much, more than any father could love a daughter. You were his adored princess."

Juliana smiled, wiping her tears.

"King Matthew taught Edmund to be just like him. He taught him to seek power and control above all else," Katherine said.

"I never knew my father to be that way," Juliana said.

"He was a different man with you, dear. When you were not around, he was crazed with power too."

"Princess Katherine." Juliana dragged a chair and placed it next to Katherine. "Were you aware that Edmund was a Majian, able to do magic?"

Katherine took a deep breath. "Edmund was not my natural son or James'. I could never have children, and one day James brought me an infant and told me he was abandoned. The baby wore a locket around his neck with two stones inside. I did not understand what it was. I knew nothing about the Majian people until a few weeks ago when I found the book on a table next to James' bed. I brushed it off as a fable, but then it mentioned the stones—the same stones that Edmund wore around his neck. I gave Edmund the locket earlier this day because he had to know the truth of who he was."

"Princess Katherine," said Juliana, "I have something to tell you. I am also a Majian. My mother escaped the massacre at Maiden Hills and was adopted by the duke and duchess of Westmore."

Katherine gaped. "That is shocking. Did you always know?"

"No, my mother told me on her deathbed, but I didn't believe her until recently the truth came out—for me as well as for Edmund." She showed Katherine the gold locket with the broken chain.

"It's the same locket that Edmund wore," Katherine said.

"This one belonged to my mother." Juliana turned to meet Jack's eyes, then back at Katherine. "Princess Katherine, we want you to meet someone." Juliana gave Jack a nod. Jack hobbled toward the door, and Robert walked in.

"This is Doctor Robert Latham from Maiden Hills… Edmund's natural father," Juliana said.

Robert came closer and stood before Katherine. "A pleasure to meet you, Your Highness."

Katherine stared up at him with wide eyes. "Oh my, there is a resemblance. Forgive my surprise, but this is shocking news," her lips trembled. "Doctor Robert, I am so very sorry. My late husband James told me the baby was abandoned."

"He may not have known I survived. He saved my son seconds before the king's men burned the cottage."

Jack bent down in front of his mother and held her hand. "Mother, I wish to bring you to my castle so you can stay with me for a time. You should not be alone in your grief."

Katherine placed her hand over Jack's. "My dear, I would like that very much."

"I shall have a carriage ready to take you in the morrow after the wake."

***

Juliana instructed Samuel to notify Bishop Dalton of the king's death and to communicate with the public. She asked Ella and the maidservants to clean him up and for Ella to pick out an outfit for him for the wake. Juliana prepared herself for the townspeople's grief. They loved and respected Edmund, and she feared losing two kings within a month would cause instability in her kingdom. She exhibited strength and leadership to quell the people's fears and assure them that she was in control and would protect them.

The next day after the wake, Juliana crossed the Cedarville Bridge with Jack and Robert. As they approached the village square, the entire population waited for them, applauding and cheering. The townspeople worked for hours, cleaning up the carnage from the battle. Juliana looked for familiar faces and hoped they all survived the attack. Leading the cheers were Sir Mark, Sir Ashton, and the men that made up The Magnificent Knights. In the crowd, she saw Helena,

Simon, and Simon's daughter Alice. Next to them was Jeb, his wife, and their three children. She saw Geraldine carrying her two-year-old nephew, and her brother Randall stood beside her.

Jack came down from his horse, limping from his injury, and helped Juliana down from hers. Juliana walked toward Helena and embraced her. "We must go to Maiden Hills. We need a descendant from each of the three noblemen to touch the maiden's statue for her to appear."

Helena said, "I am a descendant of the second nobleman, Sir Drake, who asked for the power to speak to animals. Robert is a descendant of the first nobleman, Sir Clayton, who asked for the power to move objects, and you, Your Majesty, are a descendant of the third nobleman, Sir Kolby, who asked for the protection for all."

Juliana smiled. "Then, we are ready. We shall go."

Juliana, Robert, and Helena rode toward Maiden Hills, followed by Jack, Jeb, and Simon. They reached the statue of the maiden.

Helena looked at the surrounding devastation. "I remember a town full of people and children running, laughing, and playing. All that remains is destruction, a product of the evil that can fill a person's heart." Tears flooded her eyes. "It will take years to remove all the burned cottages, build new homes, and have the life we once had."

"But we must start," Juliana said.

"I only hope I live long enough to see it," Helena said.

Juliana, Robert, and Helena stood before the statue. Together, they placed their hands on the base, and suddenly the winds picked up, and just like before, the wind produced a howling sound, and a wind funnel took shape, and the gust grew in intensity. They stepped back and held onto the lamppost. Before them, a ray of light came from above, and the funnel turned into the beautiful maiden.

The Majians were in awe to be in the presence of Majia, the maiden that gave their ancestors their magical gifts—the same maiden in the story passed down for four generations.

"Greetings." She smiled. "You have done well. You have trusted in the power of the stones and have defeated your enemy. You shall now reclaim your land."

"But, Majia, there is much to do. There is a great deal of destruction that must be removed," Juliana said.

"This great land was destroyed by hate and fear, and only by faith and love will it be restored to its original beauty."

"Have we not demonstrated faith and love?" asked Juliana.

Majia smiled. "You have." She lifted her arms, and the wind began to gust, stronger than before, and Juliana held onto the lamppost and grabbed her horse's rope. A blinding bright light covered the area of Maiden Hills, and Juliana felt a powerful force descend upon them.

She shielded her eyes from the intense glare and the swirling wind, then the winds calmed, and the light dimmed, and when she opened her eyes, a most spectacular sight greeted them—beautiful luscious trees, flowing streams, wild deer, rabbits, and foxes scurrying through the meadow. There were no burned buildings or destruction, but open land where they could build and cultivate. At a distance, rolling hills and majestic mountains stood tall.

"This is breathtaking!" said Juliana.

"This, Your Majesty, is Maiden Hills," Robert said as he looked around and smiled.

The maiden disappeared, and Juliana smiled through tears.

The remnants of that horrible day twenty-two years ago were gone, and in its place, a new land emerged. And just like four generations ago, when the three noblemen stood before the maiden, the Majian people were given a beautiful land to cultivate, build homes, and raise families.

***

The servants in Jack's castle labored all day to prepare for the celebratory feast to honor the fighters and their families. The day also coincided with Jack's nineteenth birthday. The great hall and courtyard were set up with rows of tables to feed the entire village of Cedarville. Seated at the baron's table along with Jack and Juliana were Robert, Helena, Simon, Jeb, Jeb's family, Sir Mark, and The Magnificent Knights. Princess Katherine chose to forego the dinner and remained in a guest chamber to mourn the loss of her son.

The guests drank and enjoyed an abundance of food, but out of respect for the death of King Edmund, Jack prohibited dancing. The villagers had never experienced a feast of this magnitude.

Juliana sat on the dais and stared into the crowd. Two hundred people crowded the hall, and another three hundred sat shoulder-to-shoulder in the courtyard. As she looked upon the scene in front of her, mixed emotions filled her. A feast was warranted for the bravery and resilience of the villagers, but thoughts of the events leading up to the celebration had her feeling sorrowful.

She reflected on her kingdom and their pain, having buried their king, her former husband. It was odd for her at the wake to mourn the man who tried to kill her. As Juliana stared at him, she recalled the way he looked at her before he died. *I can only hope that at the final moment, he repented.* She observed his lifeless body, and for a moment, his hand moved, an involuntary postmortem twitch, and it spooked her. Unnerved, she shook it off and stepped aside. Helena approached the casket. She recited a prayer and bade farewell to her grandson, as Simon and Alice looked upon the body of their blood kin. Robert came to terms with his son's fate and was a source of great comfort to Princess Katherine, not once reaching for a glass of wine or beer.

"Are you all right?" Jack interrupted her retrospection.

"I am just overwhelmed with sadness, and I can't shake it. Since my father died, so much has happened, and I only wish he was here to make it better, just like he always had. I still love him and miss him very much, although I have learned he was not perfect."

"He was to you."

"Was he, Jack? He manipulated people, even those he loved, including me. He made me marry a man to strengthen his kingdom without regard for what I desired. He knew there was something special between us, yet he manipulated you to move to Cedarville to keep us apart."

"If he did, then the plan failed. Cedarville brought me great things, for I met good friends, and it brought us closer together."

"But the cost was high. Many lives were lost."

"We did the right thing. I had to protect the Majians, and I could not let you lose your kingdom. I would have done anything, even given my life to prevent that from happening."

Juliana stared at Jack, and when she did, her power of intuition spoke to her. With eyes wide open, she said, "You were going to kill him, were you not? Was that the secret plan, Jack, to kill Edmund?"

Jack paused. "Once we defeated his army, we planned to appeal to his good sense and if it failed… we would have sieged the royal castle…" His eyes turned down. "Yes, we would have killed him." He took a deep breath and met her eyes. "There was no other way. He would have murdered us all."

Juliana closed her eyes. "Oh, Jack."

Jack held her hand under the table. "Juliana, it's over. Do not think about it. You have been through a harrowing time, and you must look forward and find happiness."

She blinked back tears and forced a smiled. "You're right. Besides, it's your birthday. We have cause to celebrate."

Jack smiled, then rose from his seat. "My apologies, but I must leave for a moment. I won't be gone long. Will you be all right?"

She nodded. "I shall be fine."

Juliana watched Jack leave then took a bite of the peacock meat. Suddenly, chills swept through her, and she rubbed her arms for warmth. She felt the blood drain from her face, and she leaned back, fearing she would faint. *What's happening to me?*

Through the haze, she heard Helena's voice. "Robert, you must tend to Her Majesty. She looks pale."

Robert and Helena rushed to Juliana. Robert placed his hand on her neck, her pulse quickening "Helena, give her something to help calm her."

Helena gave her a glass of warm ale. "Here, Your Majesty, drink this."

Juliana drank the ale, and Helena waved a fan in front of her. She felt the warmth return to her face. "I don't know what came over me. I feared I would faint."

"What brought this on?" Robert asked.

Juliana shrugged. "Perhaps the weight of all that has happened has finally come down on me. I have not been the same since my father died."

Robert tilted his head. "Have you been emotional and fatigued with no appetite?"

Juliana furrowed her brows. "I have."

Robert and Helena exchanged glances and smiled.

"What is it?" Juliana asked.

Helena took Juliana's hand. "Your Majesty, you are with child."

Juliana put her hand to her chest. "I am?" Robert and Helena both nodded. Juliana's eyes opened wide. "I am! I should have realized it. It has been two months since the wedding, and I have not been regular." She looked at Robert. "It's Edmund's child, Robert, your grandchild.

You will have an heir after all." She smiled at Helena. "You both will."

Robert's face beamed, and Helena's eyes flooded with tears.

"You should rest, Your Majesty. If you feel well, you may sit here, but if you need to lie down, I shall escort you to a guest chamber," Robert said.

"I am much better. I shall stay."

Robert and Helena left when Jack approached to take his seat.

"You look a little happier. Did Robert and Helena cheer you up?" Jack asked.

Juliana reached for Jack's hand under the table. "They told me why I have been feeling this way." She took a deep breath and stared into his eyes. "I am with child."

Jack looked away for a moment, then looked at Juliana. "Edmund's child." By the look in his eyes, it was a fact he was struggling to accept. Juliana nodded. Jack fell silent, still holding onto Juliana's hand under the table. He then lifted his head and gazed into her eyes. "Juliana, I wish to marry you."

Juliana's eyes widened, not expecting this reaction from Jack. The weepiness returned, and tears clouded her vision. She stifled the urge to cry.

"I know it's sudden, and maybe the timing is wrong, but I had to say it. You know royal blood does not flow through me, and I don't deserve someone like you, but I love you, and I wish to care for you and make you happy. When Edmund's men bound me and were about to kill me, I thought of nothing but you. I do not fear death, but I feared never seeing your face again." He

375

paused, sighing. "If you deem me unfit to rule your kingdom, I would understand."

Juliana smiled, for before her was the man she loved more than anyone. She could not imagine her life without him. She stared into his sweet sky blue eyes and said, "Jack," tears streaming down her face, lips trembling, "I will be honored to be your bride, and I am confident that you will make a great ruler for my kingdom. You have proven to be a fearless and brilliant leader."

Jack smiled, moisture glistening in his eyes. "If there were not five hundred people here, I would kiss you."

They both laughed through tears.

"Wait we must, but it shall be much sweeter."

***

A few days later, Juliana held a knighting ceremony in her castle to elevate to knighthood the deserving men who fought with great valor and demonstrated loyalty to the queen. The first one knighted was Robert. Since Juliana needed a knight, she selected Jack to hold the sword while the dubbing was being done. Robert kneeled before Jack with Juliana's hand on Jack's shoulder. Jack took his sword and lightly tapped Robert's right shoulder, then his left and said, "By right of arms, the queen of Yorkford dubs you with our sword, lightning, and by all that you hold sacred, true, and holy. Arise, Sir Robert."

The next one to kneel in front of Jack was Simon, followed by Jeb and six more fighters from Cedarville, including Randall. Afterward, the royal castle held a celebratory feast for the new knights and their families.

At the feast, Juliana walked over to Robert. He was with Geraldine, and Juliana thought he never looked happier. Geraldine excused herself.

"Congratulations, Sir Robert," said Juliana.

"Thank you, Your Majesty. I am forever in your debt."

"As I am in yours, but please call me Juliana, at least in private, we are kin." She smiled. "I have something for you." She handed Robert a black leather tome with the words *The Book of Secrets* in gold lettering.

"Is this your book?" he asked.

"Open it."

Robert opened the book and read the inside cover: *This book belongs to Sir Robert Latham, a descendant of Sir Clayton.* He looked at Juliana with moist eyes. "I am at a loss for words."

"I had my scribes make a copy for you. You told me your father's book was destroyed in the fire."

"Thank you, your—I mean, Juliana. This means a lot to me."

"I have something else for you." Juliana opened her hand and showed him a locket. "This was Beth's, the one Edmund wore."

As Robert stared at it, he swallowed. "Please hold on to it. It belongs to Edmund's child... Beth's grandchild."

Juliana smiled behind teary eyes. "I believe..." She dabbed her eye. "I believe Edmund was remorseful when he died. I feel he's in the Afterlife."

The corners of his mouth came down. "I do too. When he said he saw Beth, I knew he crossed over."

"Robert, one of the prohibited practices, is summoning dead spirits. My mother appeared in the mirror, and she sent me a message."

"It was not your mother, Juliana. Dead spirits can't communicate with us. What you saw was the part of her that lives in you. That's why you saw her in your reflection. You have the answers inside of you. In my grief, I have forgotten to look inside myself and seek those answers."

Juliana nodded. "So, what's next for us?"

Robert took a deep breath. "We shall wait and see."

***

A month later, Juliana exchange marriage vows with Jack in a private ceremony at the church officiated by Bishop Dalton. Juliana sparkled with her jeweled crown and sequins sewn in her dress, but the real glow came from within. The warmth she felt in her heart made her realize that she belonged to Jack, and he belonged to her, and they will always be together. Whatever would come their way, their love will get them through it.

After the ceremony, the crowd waited for the bride and groom to appear on the balcony, and when they did, thunderous roars and enthusiastic applause filled the air. Juliana and Jack stood on the balcony holding hands, waving to the people below. Juliana met Jack's gaze. He leaned in, and they shared their first public kiss as husband and wife.

"Long live King Jack! Long live Queen Juliana!" the crowd chanted.

The usual feast followed the ceremony with food, wine, dancing, family, and distinguished guests from all the land. At the banquet, Robert delighted Juliana and

Jack when he informed them that he and Geraldine would marry.

Five months later, Juliana surveyed the village of Maiden Hills. With the heaviness of her belly weighing her down, she occasionally stopped to rest and catch her breath. Feeling the baby's arms and legs pushing against her womb, she rubbed her belly, and the baby relaxed. She smiled, then gazed at the scene before her. Maiden Hills had been restored to an incredible beauty, unlike any village she had ever seen. The Majians built cottages of stone, opened merchant shops, cultivated their land, and raised farm animals. She appointed her uncle Jeb, lord of Maiden Hills, and he proudly led in the spirit of his late father, Lord Gavin Archer.

On a chilly morning, after hours of intense labor, Juliana gave birth to a baby boy, and she and Jack welcomed their crown prince. She walked to the balcony with Jack holding her arm for support, and below, the crowd cheered as Juliana held the baby swaddled in a soft blue wool blanket.

She named him Peter, Prince of Yorkford.

The saga has just begun. It continues in *The Battle at Maiden Hills*.

Available in 2021.

N.L. Estrada is based in the suburbs of New York where she spends most of her time creating the world of Maiden Hills. When she's not doing that, she loves gardening and traveling.

You can stay up to date with regular updates on www.NLEstrada.com

Made in the USA
Middletown, DE
03 November 2020

23173861R10231